A CLOCKWORK MELODY

J.P. DUBHSHLÁINE

Book cover and illustrations by J.P. Dubhshláine, featuring assets by Amy "Bel" Maxhimer.

First edition 2024

https://dubhshlaine.com/

ISBN (ebook) 978-1-0689846–00

ISBN (hardcover) 978-1-0689846-1-7

ISBN (paperback) 978-1-0689846-2-4, 978-1-0689846-4-8

DEDICATION

For the readers who struggled in school;
You're smarter than you think.

DISCLAIMER
CONTENT WARNINGS

A Clockwork Melody contains dark themes and subject matter that may be unsuitable or uncomfortable for certain readers.

Throughout the story, there are explicit depictions of body horror and violence, including amputation, gore, mutilation, torture, and death.

There are implicit mentions and explicit depictions of sexual assault and sexual violence, one of which occurs from the perspective of a narrating character.

This story also contains implicit mentions of child abuse, emotional abuse, psychological abuse, and substance abuse, as well as explicit depictions of alcohol consumption.

The characters deal with grief and guilt in a variety of unhealthy ways, including consumption of alcohol, internalized ableism, shame, and suicidal ideation.

DISCLAIMER

Readers can find a detailed, chapter-specific list of applicable trigger warnings at https://dubhshlaine.com/

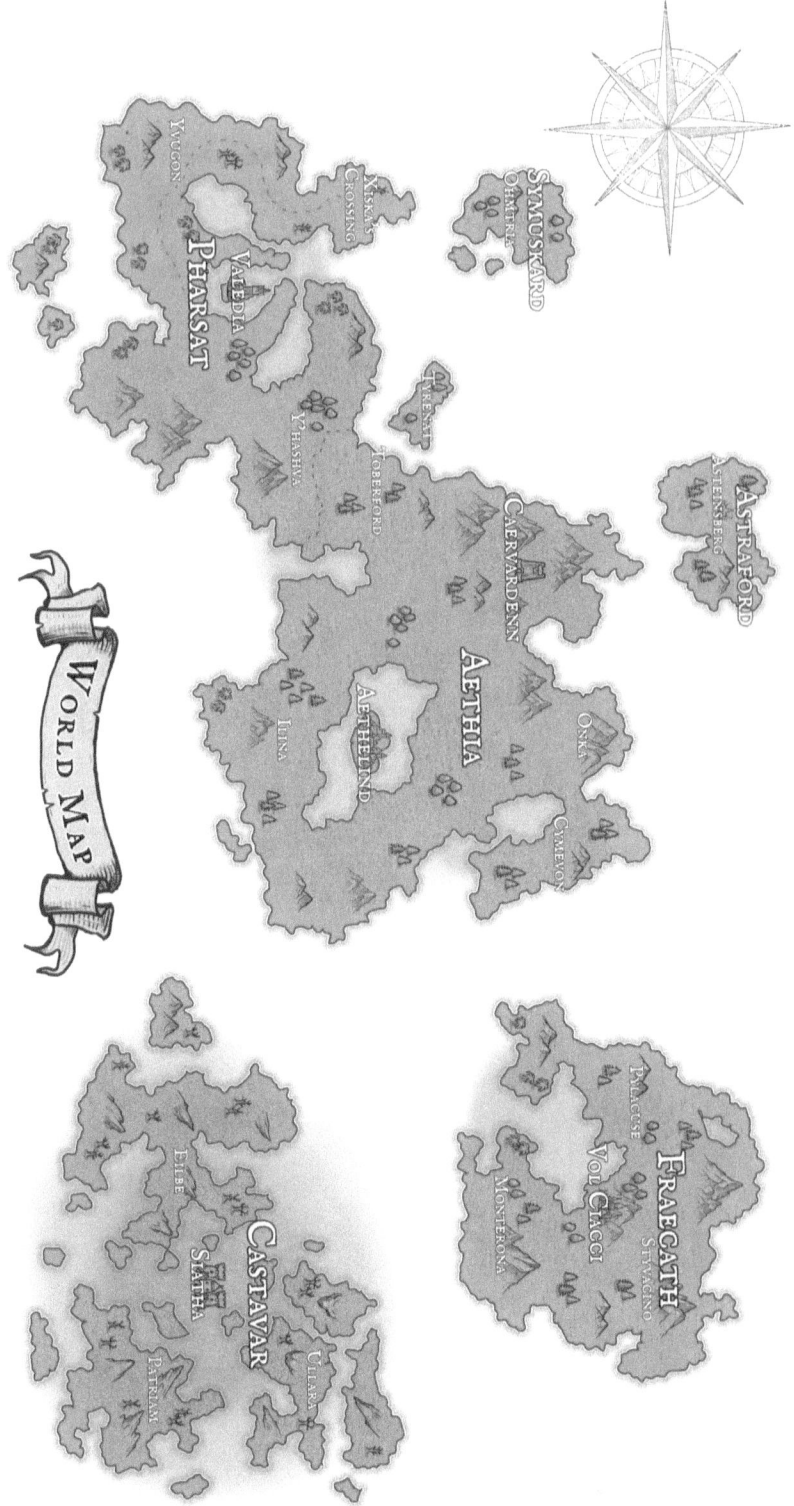

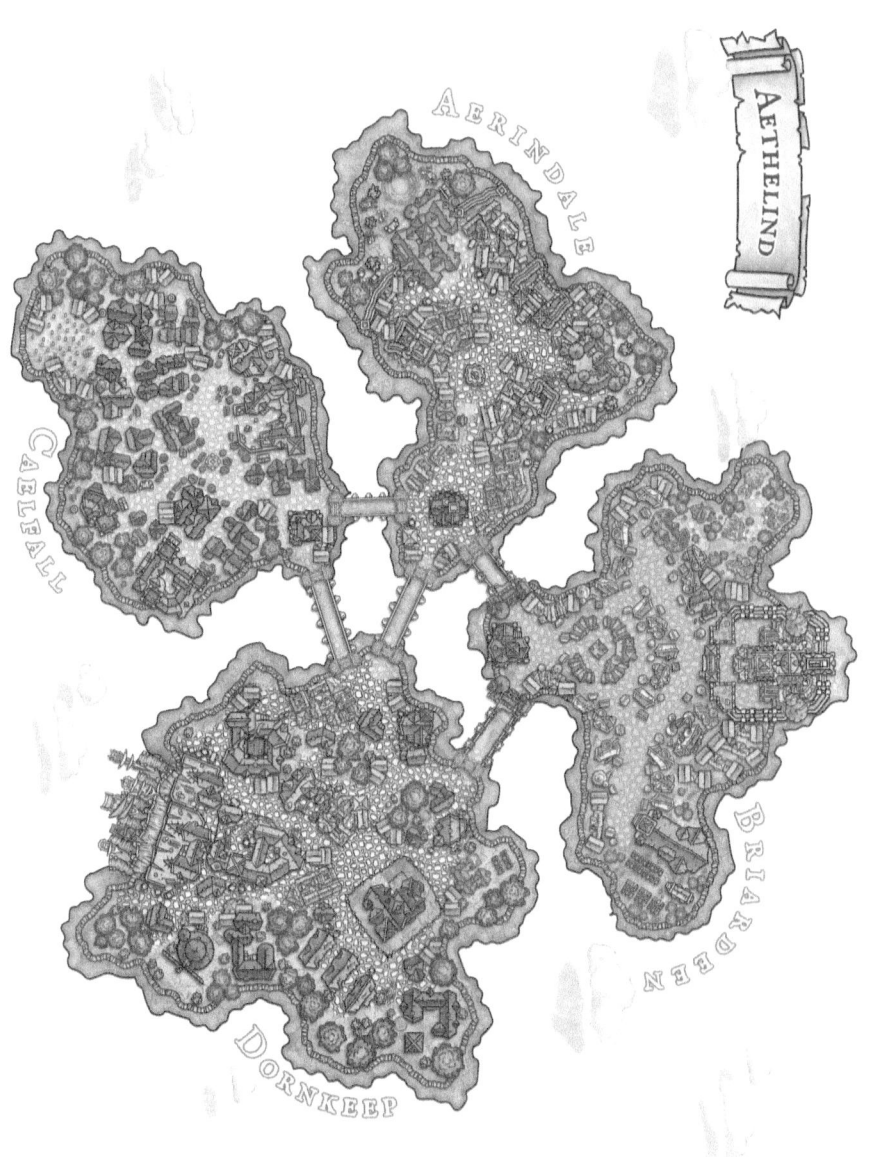

AETHELIND

AERINDALE

CAELFALL

DORNKEEP

BRIARDELN

ACT I

SPRING

AMENDMENT TO THE MAGE LAWS ACT
As per His Majesty King Gustaf Edmund Davenport III:

A mage shall not use their abilities for the purpose of bargaining for goods and services, to commit harm towards themselves or others, or to damage or destroy property.

A mage shall not conjure or cast in public spaces, except where strictly necessary due to risk of bodily injury, property damage, or death, or where necessitated by the operation of magically-powered devices and machinery.

All forms of magic are to be regarded equally in terms of legality, including those defined as "lesser magics" – comprising the use of glamours, telepathy, illusions, teleportation, enchantment of objects, and the creation of wards.

CHAPTER

ONE

JASPER

THE STREETS OF CAELFALL CLEARED IN A SUDDEN RUSH AS A
thundercloud shuddered overhead, the previously gloomy
day erupting into a vicious spring storm. The typical stench
of smoke, piss, and ale was washed away in the rain as
merchants and patrons alike scattered, the marketplace
temporarily deserted until the unpleasant weather passed.

Stamping through the heavy rain, Jasper made no effort
to tighten the collar of his trench coat around his neck as he
made his way towards the tavern at the north of town.
Raven's Haunt was a miserable little establishment to most,
but by Caelfall's standards it was warm and welcoming.
The inn's resident cat Roger made a beeline for Jasper's
boots as he entered, the doorbell cheerfully announcing his
arrival. The sound of the little bell and the fluffy black cat
nuzzling his ankles were seemingly at odds with the rest of
the inn; it was perpetually dreary inside no matter the time

of day, and the tavern clientele had a tendency to look at new arrivals with some measure of disdain.

Comparatively, the barkeep greeted him with a wave and a bright smile. Nadine, an enchanting and wicked woman, hailed from Siatha, the hot and arid kingdom in the far southeast. Much of her little tavern and her general outward appearance suggested this, dressed in light linen clothing that most would deem inappropriate for both the weather and propriety. Smelling of spiced rum and honeyed wine, Nadine's inn felt like Jasper had fallen into a pocket universe hidden within Caelfall.

"All right there, Jasper?" she greeted him warmly, leaving the bar momentarily unattended to say hello. Nadine wrapped her arms around him before he could protest, seemingly oblivious to both his rain-soaked attire and his visible discomfort. "What can I get you, love?"

As Nadine stepped back from the embrace, the cat at Jasper's feet began nuzzling him more urgently, peeved at being ignored for so long. Grateful for the excuse to break eye contact, Jasper bent down to pet the jealous cat. "My usual, please."

He glanced up briefly to see Nadine nod in response, her eye crinkling in a barely discernible wink as she turned back to her bar. Sighing, Jasper straightened as he stood up, much to Roger's chagrin, making his way towards a lonely table in the back of the room, furthest away from the tavern folk and the bar. To most of the people in the room, the table beside the staircase leading to the cellar was unoccu-pied. Jasper knew better.

As he approached the chair directly beneath the nearest window, a familiar voice greeted him. "You don't half look like a drowned rat, lad."

He didn't even flinch at the sudden sound. Jasper stared

into the seemingly empty space beside him, draped in shadow. With some practice, Jasper had developed a knack for spotting the infamous Varus Emery through the glamours he utilized to conceal himself. Glamours, despite being classified as lesser magic, were just as illegal when practiced by any but registered mages... if you were caught using them. As it happened, unlawful magic was the least of his employer's sins.

In an effort not to look like a drowned rat, Jasper attempted to smooth down his hair, careful to ensure it safely covered his ears. "It started raining," Jasper offered simply, settling into the chair beside the man. "'Tis the season." Slightly too long and resembling an ill omen's sunrise, his hair needed little encouragement to imitate a plume of flames.

"Damned Aethian climate," Varus agreed in his thick accent, shaking his head. "My bones don't much care for it."

Lounging in the aged chair positioned in the corner of the room, a man became visible as Jasper squinted in the dim light. His dark, chin-length hair had been scraped back in a knot, some of it coming loose to hang across his face. His posture was rather casual considering the nature of his work, though he still wore some of his signature boiled leather armour beneath a similarly damp coat, a brace supporting his right knee. He was visibly foreign with his hooked nose and russet skin, but hardly anyone in Caelfall was indigenous to Aethelind. He had the look of being perpetually tired or displeased or both, and all at once could have passed for twenty-five or forty-five.

Nadine arrived at the table then, carrying Jasper's drink and a plate of warm, steaming bread. As she drew close to Jasper, he could smell cloves and citrus clinging to her hair when she stooped to place the dishes on the table.

"Your pint, hon," she offered, tucking a wayward lock of brown hair behind her ear as she smiled down at Jasper. Since Jasper rarely drank anything stronger than cider, she had given him an opaque glass of spiced milk tea for appearances.

Varus, on the other hand, seemed to be halfway through something likely strong enough to take the varnish off the table. He drank spirits as if they were water, and he reached over the table now to clunk the dark bottle of liquor in his hand against Jasper's glass. "Cheers, lad."

Jasper mumbled a reply under his breath, taking a swig of his tea. "You wanted to see me, sir?"

As if remembering why they were there, Varus grunted. "Aye, I did," he replied. "I've a job I need you for tonight, and you're not going to like it."

"Well, that certainly doesn't bode well." Jasper reached for the loaf of bread, parting it where Nadine had divided it into quarters. The Siathan loaf was one of his favourites, and she always seemed to have one ready the moment he arrived at the inn. He gestured with the bread towards Varus, but the man shook his head. To this day, Jasper had never seen him eat.

"Cary has a buyer lined up for tonight at the brothel," Varus began, his voice so low Jasper had to stare at his mouth to be sure he'd heard what his employer had said. "Problem is the girl I'd initially assigned as back-up has had to bow out for personal reasons."

Jasper frowned. "Should I even ask?"

Varus' expression was unreadable. "She worked as a servant in the castle kitchens when she wasn't moonlighting for us. The king called upon her personally one day. She hasn't been able to tell me what happened, and I don't want to traumatize her further with an interrogation."

Jasper couldn't resist the shudder that came over him. Shoving a piece of bread in his mouth, Jasper struggled not to imagine what horrors the king might have inflicted upon this nameless girl.

"I need someone I can trust," Varus continued in a low voice, his dark eyes heavy on Jasper's face.

Jasper felt suddenly very ill at ease. "Mr. Emery—sir, I've only ever done dead drops before."

"Well, now you can try your hand at a live drop."

"*Sir.*"

"I'm serious," Varus insisted, leaning forward in his chair. The scent of alcohol was apparent on his breath – rum, Jasper determined – and yet Varus seemed to be sober as a judge. "You won't be alone, Cary knows what she's doing. You only need to be there to hand over the merchandise."

"And beat the shit out of the customer if he decides not to pay, you mean," Jasper noted glumly through a mouthful of bread. "I thought you didn't want me on jobs like this. You yourself said I wasn't cut out for it."

Jasper couldn't be certain, but the man did seem to be genuinely conflicted. "I don't like the idea of sending someone without much experience into situations like these," Varus agreed hesitantly. He leaned forward, glancing across the tavern as if he suspected someone might have seen through his glamour. "That said... I've seen you in a scrap, lad. I know you can look after yourself."

Jasper shifted uncomfortably in his seat. He vividly recalled the scene Varus was referring to, when a couple of ne'er-do-wells had attempted to mug him on his way home from the market. Jasper had handled the scenario in the only manner he knew how – fighting for his life, unaware his now employer had been watching from afar. He wasn't terribly fond of fighting, but he couldn't deny that his height and his weight gave him an advantage over most, despite his relatively limited training. It was part of the reason Varus had been willing to employ him.

"Do I have a choice?" Jasper asked, reaching for his pint.

Varus' gaze was heavy, his dark eyes reminding Jasper of archaic depictions of hellfire. "Yes," he said after a moment's pause.

It wasn't entirely true. Even if his employer wouldn't force him to partake, Jasper knew the mechanisms of this job meant his lack of participation didn't invite another alternative. If Varus couldn't find another party he trusted, Cary would simply have to smuggle the merchandise into the brothel on her own. Certainly, she was capable of defending herself… but what if something went wrong, and Cary was hurt? Perhaps Jasper *did* have a choice, but it wasn't one he was willing to make.

Sighing, he leaned back in his chair, the aged wood creaking under his weight. "I'll do it," Jasper agreed. "Is the rest of the job relatively the same as my usual work?"

Varus made a low noise in his throat as one of the tavern patrons seemed to stumble drunkenly close to their table. The man blinked, clearly having thought the seat was empty. Shaking his head, the stranger stumbled back in the direction he'd come, allowing Varus to turn his attention back towards Jasper.

"You'll still be dropping off the first shipment at the clinic," Varus confirmed, gesturing vaguely with the rum bottle. "Give Haeyin my love. After that, instead of the usual dead drop, you'll be heading to *The Raw Diamond* tonight. Cary will lead the way from there."

Nodding, Jasper quietly finished off the last of the bread. Varus stared at him for a long moment before stating, "You've never been in a brothel, have you."

He could feel his ears turning molten beneath his equally red hair. "No."

To his immense embarrassment, Varus laughed. It wasn't a sound he heard often, and though hardly unpleasant it was jarring in its rarity. "I forget how young you are, sometimes."

His comment served only to mortify Jasper further. "I'm not *that* young," he insisted glumly.

"No, you're all grown up, aren't you?" Varus agreed, his tone oddly pointed. "You could've told me it was your birthday, lad. Why didn't you ask for the night off?"

The inn cat seemed to have found Jasper once more, startling him as the overly fluffy animal leapt into his lap suddenly. "I—I didn't think—it didn't seem worth mentioning," Jasper stammered, petting Roger absentmindedly.

Varus sighed, rubbing the bridge of his long nose as he closed his eyes. "Don't be ridiculous. Haeyin would never let us ignore a birthday, especially not yours. He'll probably insist you come back to the clinic after this job to celebrate."

"That's really not—" Jasper began to protest, but Varus was already standing up, tossing a few coins onto the table for their drinks. He was an unusually tall man, taller even than Jasper, a trait that did little to lessen how intimidating he was visually. Jasper found himself standing in unison, sensing the conversation was ending. Roger landed on his feet, meowing reproachfully.

"It's not an optional assignment, Jasper," Varus said

sternly, but there was a hint of what might have been mirth in his dark eyes. He smiled crookedly, leaving his now-empty rum bottle on the table. "Consider it a mandatory debrief. I'll see you later."

Jasper could only watch with his mouth agape as his employer turned to leave, his gait marked by his signature limp as he pulled the hood of his coat over his head. Sighing, Jasper raked his fingers through his hair. Though the man was intimidating at best, he didn't dislike Varus' company, and he knew Haeyin and Cary meant well. The truth of the matter was that he didn't particularly enjoy celebrating his birthday, and it wasn't something he looked forward to revelling. Regardless of his feelings, however, he knew he would have little success attempting to convince them not to throw a party on his behalf.

Jasper offered Nadine a sullen wave before re-entering the gloomy Caelfall weather outside, shoving his hands deep into his pockets as he made his way towards the communal stables nearby. He fell into his practiced routine easily, and the stable employees were familiar enough with Jasper by now that his presence raised no concern. They either waved or nodded casually in his direction as Jasper passed by, leading a pleasant enough stallion towing crates of opium powders and poppy seed pods.

Positioned on the outermost perimeter of Caelfall, the stables were busy today with the newest shipments of goods from the Dornkeep shipyards, with the stable workers loading various carts with Valedian gold, Siathan silks, and finely glittering jewels. All of these carts were bound for the county of Briardeen in the north; Caelfall's own spoils were far less glamourous. Crates of meat, cheese, and produce were ready to be delivered to the markets, and Varus' shipment blended in seamlessly with the rest of the mundane cargo. It certainly paid for the kingpin to have a contract with Eodan Melicus, the man who owned nearly the entirety of Dornkeep.

Caelfall was by no means pretty, but it was home; Jasper had lived here all his life, and by now he was accustomed to each bend and curve of the weary streets. Home to all the kingdom's most unfortunate, the district saw the consequences of a monarch's negligence firsthand as it fell into disrepair. Now that the rain had subsided, the locals were free to resume wandering through the market streets, practiced steps dodging the misshapen cobblestones and uneven curbs. They parted quickly in the wake of the stallion carving his way through the crowds, carrying Varus' shipment towards the clinic.

Many of Caelfall's residents were far too poor to visit the more polished hospital establishment in Aerindale, where Jasper had heard horror stories of a mere check-up costing a fortune. He himself had required urgent care numerous times, and certainly couldn't afford stitches of that calibre on a blacksmith's salary, even with the income that moonlighting as a kingpin's errand boy provided. The old ammunitions factory served as a fine shelter for a makeshift hospital, with only a few holes in the ceiling and a mostly friendly feral cat population. Naturally, an apostate clinic needed the illegal drug trade to supply them with analgesics and sedatives for their patients, and that was where Varus' merchandise came in.

He could feel the ripple of the wards as the oily sheen in the air enveloped him, his presence here permitted by the powerful protective magic. Wards were equally illegal as glamours, but significantly more difficult to identify – their very nature prevented unwanted parties from detecting or traversing through them, making them invaluable for protecting Caelfall's clinic. Jasper left his horse secured in the crude atrium inside before he began unloading crate after crate into the main storage closet.

This was the easy part. He tried not to think about what would follow later that evening.

When the cart was finally empty and the storage closet was standing room only, Jasper shoved the wooden doors shut with his entire body weight, checking to make sure they were closed before making his way towards the main examination room. Despite its outward appearances, the clinic was clean and well-kept by its one-man-band of a medical team, Haeyin. The kind-hearted and quick-witted doctor was constantly at work, whether disinfecting surfaces or actively stitching up a patient. Thankfully, Jasper caught him today in the middle of the former, sleeves rolled to his elbows while he scrubbed a suspiciously dark stain from the floor.

"Good... afternoon," said Jasper with some trepidation, peering around Haeyin's shock of auburn hair to see what the stain was. "Have I come at a bad time?"

Haeyin looked up from his task of mopping up what was – Jasper was now convinced – likely blood. "Not at all," he insisted, pausing in his efforts to smile up at Jasper. "What can I do for you, son?"

At that moment, Jasper was startled by another person entering the room from another, more distant storage closet used as a laundry facility. Strolling into the room with all the grace of a lioness on the prowl, a familiar woman clothed in a high-necked, long-sleeved gown of midnight blue joined them. Jasper couldn't help but smile as he recognized Cary.

"Haeyin, darling, all the sheets are in the back soaking, they'll need a while," she began in her light, airy voice.

When she saw their latest arrival, Cary's face mirrored his smile. "Jasper, what a nice surprise! Usual errands, today?"

"Usual delivery, of course... and I was hoping to pick up Charlotte's order, while I'm here," he stammered, rubbing the back of his neck. With a meaningful nod, he added, "Did... did Mr. Emery tell you I'm joining you this evening?"

If Cary and Haeyin had adverse opinions on this, they kindly elected not to share them. However, there was no missing the way Haeyin's lips thinned at the question, while Cary was seemingly elated. "He did, and I'll certainly be glad to have such a strong lad at my side," she said with a wink, hands on her hips. "Don't you worry about a thing, it'll all go swimmingly."

"Yes," Haeyin said somewhat stiffly. "Well, let me see about getting you Charlotte's prescription..."

Abandoning his efforts cleaning the floor, Haeyin rose to his feet with some difficulty, many of his joints cracking in protest. Pushing his hair out of his weary eyes, a few strands of white were visible as the man adjusted his suspenders, busying himself with rummaging through the clinic cabinets.

Cary watched with pursed lips. "I think you had it in the far-left cupboard, Hae."

"I looked there, Cary."

"No, behind the salts, darling."

"Oh, yes, here it is..."

Haeyin retrieved two small paper bags before presenting them to Jasper, startlingly heavy for their size. "Same as always – one cup in the morning, one at night. And this one as needed."

Jasper wrinkled his nose as the stench of the dried herbs

reached him, turning his stomach. "Thank you, Haeyin. I know she appreciates it."

He smiled, his amber eyes crinkling at the corners. "Is she ill again today?"

"No, thankfully," Jasper explained quickly. "Just busy working the bakery."

"Good, good… well, give her my love," Haeyin replied, bending down to resume scrubbing the floor.

"Oh, Mr. Emery said to say the same to you," Jasper blurted out, the turn of phrase jogging his memory. To his horror, Haeyin looked positively murderous at the statement.

"Some bloody cheek, he has," he muttered darkly, shaking his head. "Not brave enough to come here himself after I've upbraided him about his nonsensical ideas…"

"Come on, Jasper, I'll walk you out," Cary interrupted, as if sensing Haeyin's brewing temper. She crossed the room gingerly, stepping around the stain on the floor, before ushering Jasper towards the exit.

"Have I upset him?" Jasper asked once they were back in the deserted waiting room, proceeding to untie the horse from one of the support beams.

Cary shook her head, moving to adjust the canvas attached to the cart. "You haven't upset him," she clarified, haphazardly folding the stiff fabric. "He didn't agree with Varus' decision to send you with me tonight. Haeyin very specifically told him not to involve you in this."

Jasper felt some of the colour drain from his face. "He doesn't think I'm cut out for it, then?" he offered, gently leading the stallion outside. "Even Varus—Mr. Emery said he didn't want me to do it." It was a bit risky to badmouth his employer with Cary, a colleague who held Varus in high regard, but Jasper was overwhelmed and Cary was easy to talk to.

Cary kept stride with him, sighing as she idly rubbed at a necklace he knew she wore beneath the fabric of her dress. "Jasper... Haeyin doesn't doubt you," Cary insisted, reaching as if to touch his shoulder before thinking better of it. She flexed her hand as she retracted it, visibly searching for the right words. "None of us do, I assure you. The only reason Varus hesitated to give you this assignment is because he and Haeyin worry about you getting hurt."

Chewing his lip, Jasper looked back at Cary. "What about you?" he asked, his voice softening. "What happens if you get hurt? Varus told me what happened to the girl you were supposed to be doing this with."

"Yes, well... Varus learned a long time ago that he can't make my decisions for me," Cary offered with a dark chuckle. "The difference is that I am twice your age, and while Varus and Haeyin obviously worry for my safety as well, they would feel personally responsible if anything were to happen to you."

Jasper found his cheeks darkening once more. "I'm not a child," he muttered.

Shaking her head, Cary smiled sadly. "No, I suppose you're not. Don't think I'm not cross with you for not mentioning your birthday," she teased, effectively steering the conversation into a different direction entirely. She crossed her arms over her chest, a suspicious grin on her face. "Nineteen today? You've grown up so fast."

He could feel his ears burning beneath his hair. "I don't usually celebrate it," Jasper admitted in a quiet mumble, and it was mostly true. Charlotte and her father would always insist on giving him extra cakes and biscuits, but they understood it wasn't an occasion he particularly enjoyed.

"Please, I insist – it won't be a huge, glamourous party, mind you," Cary noted. "Just... after we finish up tonight, we head back to the clinic for some birthday cake and a bit of fun." Noting the apparent apprehension on his face, she smiled apologetically, folding her hands behind her. "I promise you'll be allowed to leave as early as you like."

Jasper exhaled a lungful of emotions he couldn't name. Cary always seemed to innately know where his anxieties came from, and though he remained on edge at the thought of celebrating his birthday, Jasper was somewhat relaxed with the promise of a quick exit. "I suppose there's no way to talk the three of you out of doing this," he said finally, managing a small smile.

"Absolutely not," Cary sang cheerily, beaming. "Now run along then, I'm sure you've lots to do before we meet up again tonight. Our client is meeting us at the brothel at eleven o'clock, so try to be there before he turns up." Her grin turned positively mischievous, turning on her heel before she called over her shoulder, "This is going to be fun."

Jasper arrived at the brothel at half past ten, having only had time to do two things when he had arrived back at home – panic for several hours, and then wash up for the evening. He had kept his usual trench coat on over his attire, though he figured he may as well make the effort to look smart for the occasion. Blacksmithing and refined clothing hardly went hand in hand, but Jasper had donned his cleanest, least damaged white shirt and a simple pair of black trousers that managed to hide most of his silhouette. He had even attempted to polish his boots for about twenty minutes before giving up, accepting the worn and beaten leather would never quite shine like new.

Charlotte had been occupied when he'd stopped by, so Jasper had settled for a hastily written note. He left it in the loft above the bakery with her medication, detailing the circumstances and promising he'd stop by in the morning to help with the food drive they volunteered for. She hated the work he did for Varus, and she certainly wouldn't be pleased by what he was about to attempt tonight, but maybe she could at least understand his reasoning.

After dark, Caelfall took on a sinister atmosphere. The aged, crooked buildings seemed to lean into the streets, towering over Jasper as he waded through the crowds of residents making their way back home. Many of them had come from Briardeen, leaving the gilded county to return to Caelfall after a long day spent serving the more fortunate blue bloods in the north. Careful not to trip over the cobblestones, Jasper stalked towards the brothel in the distance.

Elsewhere in Aethelind, few establishments remained open this late. In comparison, Caelfall stuck out like a sore thumb on account of being the only district still awake and active at this hour. *The Raw Diamond* practically glowed in the darkness, the otherwise unremarkable building managing to draw attention to itself with the bright lights spilling out from the doorway. A woman in dark, subtly armoured clothing stood in the threshold, a harsh expression on her unlined face as she stepped in front of Jasper, preventing him from entering.

"You're aware of the curfew imposed by His Majesty this evening?" she asked in a husky voice.

Jasper nodded swiftly. There was often a curfew imposed after some tragic, violent event, and so Caelfall saw a midnight curfew roughly three nights a week. It seemed harsh to impose a curfew on the night of the spring equinox, but there was no refuting the royal decree.

The woman dipped her chin as she stepped aside, gesturing indoors. "Off you go, then."

He muttered his thanks as he entered the hallway, removing his coat and draping it over his arm as he made his way down the corridor towards another set of doors. These were opened for him by two more armoured women, their faces concealed beneath thick hoods, and suddenly Jasper was accosted by more sensations than he had been prepared for.

The brothel was lit with flickering oil lamps, smelling so strongly of incense and massage oil that Jasper's eyes watered. There must have been nearly a hundred people crammed into the vast manor, courtesans draped across patrons' laps, carrying trays of refreshments, dancing and singing on an elevated platform that could pass for a stage. The main performer this evening was a strawberry blonde woman wearing nothing but a corset, her bare skin glistening in the light as she danced.

He found himself at a loss for where to look. There was more skin on display than Jasper had ever seen, swathed in coloured silks and drenched in sweet smelling lotions and oils. Bodies undulated around him, beautiful men and women everywhere he looked. The lights, sounds, and smells were all so overwhelming that Jasper was about thirty seconds from losing his mind entirely.

There was a distinct sensation of hornets fluttering under his skin, beneath the collar of his shirt. His breath caught in his throat as a dancer edged past him, giggling as he brushed against Jasper's bare forearm before darting away. A sudden ringing in his ears began that threatened to drown out the sound and song—

"There you are," called a familiar voice. A veiled and bejeweled Cary appeared seemingly from nowhere, her attire drastically different from what he had seen her in previously. She wore a voluminous silk skirt of blood red, split along either side to reveal her bare thighs, and a beaded garment concealing her chest but leaving much of her abdomen uncovered. The only familiar article on her person was her mother's necklace, the heavy rubies settled beneath her collarbones.

"Jasper?" Cary said suddenly, and Jasper felt his head spin as he whirled back to face her, unaware she'd continued speaking to him.

"I'm—I'm sorry," he stammered, clearing his throat.

She seemed to understand, even though he could barely speak. "Come with me," Cary urged, tugging him along. He flinched at the contact on his oversensitive skin, but Cary was already adjusting her hold on him, taking him by the hand and linking his little finger in her own.

She began to lead him away from the stage, through the crowds of courtesans and inebriated patrons. Jasper could only follow numbly as he was led through the masses of brothel patrons, his head swimming as vertigo threatened to land him squarely on his arse somewhere amongst the brocade cushions and satin lounge chairs.

His companion tugged him into a semi-private room, a booth sheltered by thick, velvet curtains. There was a small, squat table with a single oil lamp close to the ground, surrounded by several plush seat cushions. She sat him down somewhat forcefully on one of the cushions, making quick work of the ties on the drapes. As the heavy fabric fell, Jasper could feel the pressure lifting off his mind as the light and noise of the brothel faded.

"Gods," he choked, burying his face in his hands as he breathed. The air was somewhat stuffy in here, likely owing to the curtains, but it was better than the oil.

"Are you all right?" she asked softly. She sat beside him, the silken skirts of her costume pooling around her. Her brown hair fell in heavy waves to her shoulders, the sparse grey glamoured well enough that Jasper barely noticed the enchantment. The kohl lining her pink eyes amplified her intense stare, and Jasper found himself unable to even attempt eye contact.

He closed his eyes, pressed his palms against his temples. "Yes," he assured her, though he was distinctly aware that he likely did not look or sound the part. "I don't think I'm an ideal brothel patron."

"Haeyin did warn me this might happen," Cary admitted hesitantly, which caused his eyes to snap open. At Jasper's perplexed expression, she smiled apologetically. "Don't take it personally. I always look into partners before a job."

Jasper shook his head, managing to chuckle at his own expense. "Probably good that you did." He surveyed their surroundings, the drapes that concealed them from the rest of the brothel. "Is this the meeting place?"

Cary nodded, her hands occupied with fixing her hair and adjusting the lacing of her skirts. "The client is expecting to meet us in here, yes," she confirmed. "The Madame knows we will be in here, but you will be a surprise to the client. We don't usually keep the protection inside the room, but... this individual has caused problems for us, before."

Her costume adjustments complete, she leaned over to straighten the collar of his shirt, mussing his hair up slightly. Jasper almost flinched, but she was careful not to touch his ears; if she'd investigated him, perhaps Cary already knew he didn't care for them to be exposed.

"Let me handle the talking," Cary instructed. "You do your best work without even thinking about it, you've got a good mean stare when you're irritated."

"Maybe so, but I can't just flip the switch and *be* irritated," Jasper protested.

Cary gave him a grim look. "Trust me, our client will do that for you."

They sat in near silence for several minutes. Jasper practiced twirling a loaned dagger between his fingers, an engraving of a magpie etched into the hilt. His hands were scarred and calloused from years of blacksmithing, permitting him to make repeated mistakes without injuring himself too significantly. Meanwhile, Cary shuffled and reshuffled a worn deck of cards, her nimble fingers cutting the deck three times before she finally spread them upon the table in a cross. Her expression sobered ever so slightly as she turned them over one by one, and after a while Jasper could contain his curiosity no longer.

"What's the matter?" he asked Cary, picking a bit of dirt clinging to the hilt of the knife. "That doesn't strike me as solitaire."

Cary raised an eyebrow in a mock expression of irritation, though he guessed by her tone that she was at least somewhat amused. "No, not solitaire," she agreed. She picked up the card she had turned over last, holding it closer so he might see what it was. A skeletal figure shrouded in curling black smoke was depicted on the card, boney hands crossing a scythe across their chest in a grisly sort of salute atop a similarly gaunt horse. At the bottom of the card, "Death" was printed in delicate letters.

"How charming," Jasper decided, frowning.

She smirked, replacing the card within the cross formation. "It's not as grim as you might assume," Cary insisted. "Death, in many ways, is only the inevitability of change."

He thumbed the dagger he held, the intricate metalwork of the pommel. "I hate change."

Though her eyes remained on her cards, turning them over one by one, she nodded slowly. "I've noticed. Change, loud noises, and any sort of touch. I'm slowly compiling a list of things so as not to upset you."

Jasper felt his face grow hot as he dropped his knife. "Well, I—I suppose that's thoughtful of you." He glanced at the collection of cards, similarly dark visuals depicted on their now exposed faces. A few of them seemed to be upside down. "Why do you use those?"

The silence lingered for so long that he thought perhaps Cary hadn't heard him. As he was about to repeat himself, she responded at last, "I read the cards for clarity where I can otherwise find none. Oftentimes, it's like having a little voice in the back of my mind that tells me exactly what I need to hear, even if it's not necessarily what I *want* to hear."

She paused for a moment, picking up one of the cards and examining it closely. "I suppose it's out of habit, too," Cary mused. "My mother read them daily when I was a girl, often under the guise of a fortune teller for travellers. She was far more gifted than I am, to be fair – but I still remember most of their meanings by heart."

Blinking, Jasper found himself staring openly at her shuttered expression. Cary rarely ever spoke of her family, or anything pertaining to her past; the most detail Jasper had ever been given was the origin of Cary's necklace, and that explanation had been delivered tersely and without room for follow-up questions. He found himself immensely curious, at war with himself over whether or not to press for details.

The decision was taken from him, however, when the curtains rustled with the arrival of a third person. Jasper tensed instinctively, but it was merely another of the brothel employees. "He's on his way," the young woman advised, leaving without another word. Her warning gave Cary enough time to collect her cards, hastily tucking them away. Jasper retrieved his knife from the floor, adjusting on his cushion until he was comfortable. Fidgeting would likely not intimidate their client.

The curtains parted briefly as their infamous client of the evening ducked inside. Eric Gibson's dark hair was distinctly oily in a way that suggested it was purposeful, or perhaps that he feared washing it too frequently. He seemed quite pale even by Aethian standards, but perhaps his pallor was in part nerves, for the man took one look at Jasper and seemed greatly discomforted by his presence.

"I—I'm—the Madame assured me this was a *private* reservation…" Eric stammered, tugging at the collar of his coat.

"It is," Cary replied sweetly, her pink eyes dazzling. She leaned casually on her elbow, her gaze stripping the man bare. "For the Madame's clientele. But you aren't here for the merchandise *she's* selling, are you?"

The man scoffed, shifting on his cushion. "Well, I might

have been... I have deep pockets, I'll pay you extra if your little voyeur sits out on this one."

Cary had been right about the irritation part. Jasper found the willpower to hold the man's gaze while he cut in, "Lay a hand on her and see how far it gets you, Mr. Gibson."

Infuriated, Eric opened his mouth to retort – and his response promptly ended in a startled cough as he caught sight of the dagger Jasper twirled in his hand.

"There's no need to be rude," Cary sang, clasping her hands together. "Why, my friend here is only trying to keep me safe. Besides, as I said... you aren't here for the merchandise the Madame is selling. You're here for what *we're* selling."

Jasper shifted where he sat, withdrawing the tightly wrapped bundle he'd transported in his coat. He placed it on the table firmly, keeping his hand over top of it. He watched with some satisfaction as Eric's gaze lingered on the stark contrast of the scars he knew were visible on his hands and arms, let him come to his own conclusions as to how he'd acquired them.

The client's eyes didn't linger on Jasper's scarred knuckles long. After a moment's pause his gaze trickled down towards the package beneath Jasper's palm, and he did not miss the way the man's entire disposition shifted slightly. His pupils dilated, a fresh wave of sweat beaded on his pallid skin, and Jasper had a fairly good sense Eric wasn't just selling for them. He knew Varus wasn't particularly bothered by *how* the product was consumed, only that they collected its worth. Nevertheless, the sight of the man's apparent addiction unsettled him.

The man withdrew a battered leather wallet from his vest, his hands trembling as he placed bill after crumpled bill on the low table. Jasper followed his count, knowing from experience not to trust a client's word on the sum of their payment. Cary leaned her head on her elbow, smiling sweetly as she watched and waited until at last the man made to put away his wallet.

"You're short, Mr. Gibson," Jasper said quickly. "By a few hundred."

Scoffing, the man shook his head. "You must have miscounted."

"Or you did," Cary replied. "Deep pockets, indeed. My darling, I don't think you can afford this shipment, let alone *me*."

"If you can't pay up, you can get out," Jasper agreed.

The man's eyes darted back and forth between Cary's sanguine smile and Jasper's cold stare, the knife he still held. In weighing his odds, their client made a fatal mistake. Thinking he stood more of a chance with Cary, Eric raised a hand to strike her, likely hoping to catch her unaware and flee with the goods. Everyone underestimated Cary.

Cary moved faster than Jasper could blink. She opened her hand, a hidden knife looped around her little finger spinning out to connect with the man's open palm. He cried out, retracting his wounded hand to his chest. In one swift movement, Jasper had Eric's other arm in his grasp, restraining their client as he forced the man's head into the table with a heavy thud and a crack. A dark puddle began to bloom from where Eric's face had collided with the wooden surface. Cary met Jasper's gaze, giving him a conspiratorial smile of approval.

"Did you forget our price?" Jasper asked calmly. "Seven hundred and fifty, no less. You're a bold man, trying to cheat Mr. Emery."

"Please, let me count it again, I must have—I must have misplaced some of it…"

Jasper could feel his eyes glazing over, releasing his hold on their client with no small measure of irritation. Cary appeared to be resisting the urge to laugh at whatever his expression must have looked like. Eric's hands were shaking so badly Jasper thought he might pass out, but the man managed to pull the last few bills he'd concealed within his pockets, careful not to sully them with his blood.

"You should've had them all on the table from the start," Jasper admonished as Eric straightened up. "We could have avoided all of this violence."

Their client just about spat at him, but Jasper's reflexes were unfortunately not to flinch when this occurred, but to grab the man by his face. He appeared about as startled as Jasper was by this turn of events. "You people are heartless," Eric whimpered, his voice strained by the manner in which his cheeks and lips were contorted. "My wife is ill, and what money I have goes towards her care and food for our children. Have you no compassion?"

His words caused Jasper's heart to constrict painfully, but he would not balk. "You live and sell in Briardeen," he replied in a low voice, holding the man's gaze. "We know you're selling this for double, triple the amount you've paid us now. If you're in such dire straits Mr. Gibson, perhaps you shouldn't be propositioning my friend over here."

With a sigh, Cary stooped to collect the bills inside one of the pockets of her voluminous skirts. "If that's all, you'd best be leaving," she instructed their client, taking a seat on her cushion once more. "The Madame won't entertain your continued attendance if you aren't going to be purchasing *her* goods and services."

As Jasper released him, Eric scrambled for the package

on the table, with Cary's watchful stare tracking the man's unadorned hands as he stuffed the parcel into the pocket of his jacket. The man left the curtained booth in a hurry, and Cary's gaze slid towards Jasper.

"He has no wife," she clarified with a sad smile on her face. "And even if he did... what a horrid, unfaithful husband a man like him would make."

TWO

JASPER

As THE BROTHEL BEGAN TO SETTLE FOR THE EVENING, preparing to close down entirely for curfew in thirty minutes, Jasper met Cary at the entrance after she had stuffed her silken costume in the Madame's changing rooms. She looked quite different without her previous attire on; Cary tended to favour a much more neutral, almost boyish expression when she was off the job. Her dark hair was braided cleanly back from her face, peppered with silver as normal, and a large grey trench coat concealed most of her body. She was so slight in comparison to him, she seemed dwarfed by the oversized coat.

"Not bad at all, Jasper," Cary sang approvingly, folding back her enormous sleeves to expose her hands. "For your first real job, you proved rather capable."

Jasper wasn't certain it was entirely complimentary to be good at what he did. "You were right, he made it easy to be irritated with him," Jasper offered in agreement, shrugging into his coat. "Even so… seeing Mr. Gibson, I almost feel bad for him."

Cary slowed in her efforts of rolling her sleeves, and he could feel her eyes on him. "You can't help people who aren't ready to seek help for themselves," she returned, as if sensing the dark direction of Jasper's thoughts. "When someone is in pain for a long time, it's unimaginably difficult to deprive yourself of something that seems to help. As unpleasant as it is to deal with a client like Mr. Gibson… it's not your job to save him, Jasper."

Even if there was some truth in Cary's words, it wouldn't serve him to think too long on the subject. "I know, I know," Jasper replied dismissively, clearing his throat.

Cary seemed to have more to say, but suddenly her eyes widened. "I've left one of my knives in the booth," she gasped, clapping a hand over her forehead. "Rosaline will kill me if someone found it, we're not supposed to carry bloody weapons—"

"Go, I'll wait out here," Jasper offered. Cary nodded and dashed back inside, her massive trench coat only barely revealing her thick, heavy boots as she ran.

Jasper turned to face the street ahead of them, the cramped alleyway mostly deserted. The only people here aside from Jasper were the steady trickle of brothel and tavern customers, drunkenly finding their way home after a long night of debauchery. *Raven's Haunt* was likely closing up shop at this hour as well. Caelfall was generally lax on what royal decrees they followed, but a curfew was one they couldn't ignore.

After a few minutes standing out in the cold, Jasper began to grow concerned. Cary should have been back by now. For a few moments, he stood motionless in the alleyway, his heart pounding in his throat as he imagined all sorts of reasons why Cary was delayed – some logical, some less so. How likely was it she'd just stopped to chat with a colleague? Chewing on his lip, Jasper clenched his fists and eased his way back inside the brothel between the exiting customers, weaving his way back towards the booth he and Cary had met their client in.

The Raw Diamond had a different atmosphere after hours, and Jasper was grateful for the reprieve from the earlier over-stimulating environment. The courtesans were now beginning to tidy up after their elaborate festivities, in what passed as a state of undress for them; partly in their lavish costumes, with their warm winter coats and scarves thrown over them. They looked up at Jasper curiously as he passed, but he kept his eyes fixed on the ground.

When he reached the private booth at last, there was no sign of Cary; the thick, velvet curtains had been pulled back into their golden rope ties, and Jasper could see there was no trace of their exchange earlier that evening. Not even a glimmer of a forgotten steel dagger remained, so where was Cary?

Jasper heard her before he saw her. "For the last time, I —am—*off*," Cary spat, stomping towards his general direction quite angrily. She was being tailed by two of the brothel's customers, lingering even as the establishment was visibly closing their doors for the evening. "Come back tomorrow when the curfew's lifted if you want to stay all night."

Oblivious to Jasper's presence, the two men continued their pursuit. The shorter of the two seemed nervous here, his blonde curls giving him an appearance of naiveté ill-suited for the environment of a brothel. The taller man, a dark-haired brute in a mostly unbuttoned blue dress shirt, caught up to Cary faster than his companion. He grasped her wrist, yanking her back towards him. Cary opened her mouth to retort but was silenced as the man backhanded her with a sharp crack. She sagged against his grip on her, clutching her face with her free hand as the dark-haired patron reached into her coat, the other drawing in close to join in.

As he witnessed the assault on his friend, Jasper saw red. From the quality of their finely crafted albeit rumpled clothing, Jasper guessed these men were nobility, making his subsequent reaction quite foolish. His feet moved of their own volition, closing the distance between himself and the altercation in a few quick strides. He shoved the blonde man aside with the full force of his weight, the nobleman yelping as he crashed to the floor. Grasping the taller man's hand where the fool had hold of Cary's wrist, Jasper clamped down on the soft joints with an iron grip until the patron released her with a shout. As the nobleman yanked his hand back from his offender's hold, Jasper took the opportunity to pull his friend behind him, positioning himself protectively between Cary and the affronting patrons.

"What's the matter with you?" Jasper interjected, hoping his expression was still as intimidating as it had been earlier. "She's asked you nicely, now get out of here."

The nobleman he had wounded shot him a bitter look, as if disgusted that Jasper would deign to touch him. His vile expression shifted into an unkind smile as he looked back and forth between Jasper and Cary. "What are you, her knight in shining armour? What are you going to do about it?"

The phrase shouldn't have been as painful a jab as it was, but it pressed down on a very sore spot in Jasper's mind. "I won't ask again," was all he could manage without growling, his fist clenched so tightly he could hear his knuckles cracking.

Whether the two men were ignorant to his barely contained rage or simply didn't care, the outcome was the same. The taller, bolder nobleman laughed, a low and bitter sound deep in his chest, before reaching forward in an attempt to shove Jasper. Instinctively, Jasper deflected the dark-haired man's drunken lurch and shoved him back, sending him tumbling to the floor.

While the enraged patron struggled to stand, the smaller of the two recovered enough to launch himself at Cary. Jasper batted the blonde man's reach away before driving his fist into his face, sending the nobleman to the ground as well. Cary seemed to be in a state of shock, one hand clutching her coat closed as she watched the brawl unfold before her.

He hoped to either incapacitate the men long enough to flee or until help arrived, the noblemen's assault tiring against Jasper's sober defensive strategy. He took a fair few blows to the face, his cheek throbbing as he retaliated. As he managed to deflect a strike from the taller man, Jasper was greeted by the blonde patron landing a sharp punch to his abdomen. It knocked the wind from him, and white-hot pain pierced through him – and as blood began to seep into the white fabric of his shirt, Jasper realized he had been stabbed with a smuggled dagger.

The impact of the blade in his gut shocked him out of his momentum, and it was all Jasper could do to grab the arm of his attacker, preventing him from ripping the knife away with equal fervour. The other patron was trapped in his grip, and Jasper managed to meet the young man's startled grey eyes. He was barely a man, in all fairness, perhaps within Jasper's age by a year or two. He seemed as out of place in *The Raw Diamond* as Jasper was.

Taking advantage of the man's shock, Jasper head-butted him with the last ounce of his strength, his grip tightening on the hilt of the knife as the young man stumbled backwards with the impact. His muscles seized in agony as Jasper sank to his knees, even as his every instinct urged him to get up, to keep moving. The sensation of a slender pair of arms around his waist startled Jasper, but it was only Cary trying in vain to haul him to his feet as his strength began to fail him.

"I didn't—I'm sorry—it was—" the blonde nobleman stammered, but whatever he wanted to say was drowned out by a booming voice.

"*How dare you!*" a voice thundered through the hall. From where he had fallen, Jasper struggled to look up to find the source of the voice, still holding the knife in his stomach.

A giant of a woman strode down the staircase to enter the main hall, a dark emerald gown hugging each curve of her. Her chestnut hair was coiffed and coiled up in braids, her face expertly polished and painted. And by the gods – if looks could kill, every man in the room would be dead.

"How dare you," she repeated, her voice low and dangerous. "You come into *my* house, you flirt and fawn with *my* girls, and you break our most precious rule – you bring *weapons* into my domain? Have you no decency? Have you no shame?"

The Madame strolled forward, and from her palms a bolt of scarlet electricity arced between her fingers. Jasper stared at the terrifying elemental attunement, at the distinct absence of silver cuffs on the Madame's wrists that would signal her as a registered mage — but what credibility would any of them have if they claimed that a Madame in Caelfall was a renegade?

"Go," Cary instructed Jasper, tugging on his arm. "Go now." She pulled with all her might, and Jasper somehow found the strength to stand as blood gushed from the wound in his stomach. The edge of the dagger inside of him was agony, and with each subtle movement Jasper's vision was pricked with stars – but still he held it by the hilt, keeping the blade steady.

The Madame turned on them, but her gaze was surprisingly gentle as she looked at Cary. "Get home safely, sweetheart," she said in a comparatively soft voice before turning towards the two noblemen, who certainly seemed quite aware of how terrible a mistake they had made. The last thing Jasper could hear of them as he and Cary fled the brothel was a series of desperate, panicked pleas for forgiveness.

Wake up, Jasper…

The scent of the rain mixed with the iron tang of the blood pooling in his mouth. Jasper spat as he sagged against the woman dragging his half-dead form through the deluge. His body ached for sleep, for release from the sharp, throbbing pain in his abdomen, his face, his very bones—

"Stay with me, Jasper," Cary's voice urged, sounding distant. "Just a little bit further, we're nearly there." Her arm around his waist tightened painfully, his own hold on Cary growing slack. Jasper only vaguely remembered who she was in this moment, the pain muddling his synapses into a tired cacophony of sound and light that he could no longer decipher. All he could remember was that he trusted her with his life, whatever that meant now.

Jasper had never given as much thought into how he would die as he had in the last five minutes. Or was it fifteen? It could have been hours, days spent bleeding out in these sullied streets, and Jasper would have been none the wiser. He wondered if he might see his uncle Zeke again, might finally meet his parents wherever it was that souls went after people died.

As he took another heavily assisted step, Jasper's knees buckled. Even with the support of his friend holding his waist, he felt himself falling, slipping from her rain-slicked grip on his side.

"No—no, Jasper!" Cary cried out as he collapsed against the cobblestones, the shock of the impact earning a grunt from him as his injured gut protested. He became dimly aware of the fact that his hand was still clenched around the hilt of the dagger embedded within him. Jasper coughed again, the blood in his mouth overwhelming him. The cobblestones were unpleasantly hard against his skin beneath the thin fabric of his soiled shirt, but the chill eased the pounding in his head despite his discomfort.

The woman pulled fruitlessly at his collar, his shoulders, her voice breaking. "Jasper, please… you have to get up, we're so close now—"

Jasper opened his eyes, staring aimlessly at the sky above him as he struggled to re-orient himself. The rain splattered his face in cold, heavy droplets, and the ache in his stomach seemed to dull at the temperature. When Cary reached for him once more, he could barely feel her grip on his hands.

"Cary!" a new voice called, pricking the last remnants of Jasper's attention span. "Cary, what's happened? Oh, by the gods…" A distant rumble of footsteps resonated through the cobblestones, through Jasper's bones as the stranger approached.

"Haeyin, help me lift him, I can't—"

A third voice spoke up, deeper and sounding quite cross. "I'll take him. Cary, help Haeyin clear the table." Jasper felt himself shudder against his will. Even inches from death he could recognize the cadence of his employer. Part of him prayed for oblivion; better that than whatever wrath Varus Emery would unleash for failing his first critical mission.

Even as his imagination ran away with him, the strong arms that lifted him easily from the pavement were exceedingly gentle. He groaned as the knife in his gut was jostled with the movement, but his employer seemed to be carefully avoiding putting pressure on his abdomen. They moved through the soaked streets with ease, as if Jasper weighed nothing at all.

He didn't realize they were indoors until Jasper felt the absence of rain on his bruised face, the solid surface of a table beneath him as he was set down gently. A pair of hands smoothed his hair back from his face, and he could see a woman's kind pink eyes staring down at him. Of course, it had been *Cary*. How could he have forgotten her, however briefly?

"Not good," said Varus overhead in his unique accent. "I'd wager he's lost a lot of blood by the colour of him."

"Anesthetic?" Cary suggested, her gaze turning away.

The doctor grunted from nearby in response. "No, no time. Not with his tolerance, anyway." Haeyin appeared a moment later with a metal tray that presumably contained medical supplies. "This won't be easy."

"Do what you can," Varus insisted, his voice thick.

"Do me a favour then and hold him down, he's not going to like this part."

Jasper was not lucid enough to process the conversation around him, oblivious to Haeyin's ominous instruction. As it was, it took all his focus to even keep his eyes open, his entire body feeling heavier by the second. Cary gently pried Jasper's hand away from the knife in his gut, Varus replacing it with his own. He barely noticed when the doctor's long-fingered hands hovered over his abdomen.

"Three... two... one... *Now!*"

Several things happened in quick succession. Varus removed the dagger with lethal efficiency, yanking it from Jasper's abdomen in the exact angle it had entered. Cary's grip clamped down hard on Jasper's arms, preventing him from doing what his body wanted to do in that moment — recoil and howl like a wounded dog with the last ounce of his energy. At last, Haeyin's outstretched hands pressed down on the wound in his stomach, his hands aglow with the golden light of his magic. For a brief second, a crackle of energy sparked into a pleasant warmth that flushed the sensation of pain from Jasper's mind. He sagged against the table as the warmth bloomed within him. Warmth, and then heat. Heat, and then blisteringly hot pain.

Jasper screamed, writhing away from the sensation. There was another set of hands pressing down on his shoulders – his employer's – preventing him from bolting up from the table, and he struggled against the iron grip of his companions. He wailed as he burned, as every inch of him seemed shocked back into life from the brink of death. The taste of blood began anew in his mouth, coating his teeth as Jasper recoiled from the pain. His bones burned within him, his muscles boiled, his nerves were electrocuted—

After what seemed like an eternity spent aflame, the

pain subsided. Jasper sank back against the table, sucking in lungful after lungful of blissfully cool air. He wasn't entirely convinced he didn't bear a striking resemblance to a pile of charcoal, but for the first time that evening Jasper was comforted by the distinct awareness that he was *alive*.

As his consciousness returned to him, Jasper recalled the events that had led him to sustaining his injuries, the man and his friend who had stabbed him, threatened Cary...

"Cary?" he breathed, struggling briefly to sit upright. His new wound protested and he winced audibly with the exertion, his hand reflexively moving to his abdomen as if he might physically hold himself together. There was a hand on his shoulder, and as he managed to open his eyes he saw Cary standing beside him. She smiled in a way that didn't reach her eyes, a cut on her cheek and a large bruise blossoming down to her jaw. Though he knew the noblemen had intended to inflict far worse harm upon her, Jasper's heart still stuttered with guilt at the fact that Cary had been injured despite his best efforts.

"What happened?" Varus spoke, his voice dangerously flat. Jasper's heart sank at the sound, and what blood he still had in his veins flooded his cheeks. "What were you thinking?"

Cary cut in before Jasper could stammer out a response. "Varus, please... He was only trying to help me," she replied, her hand still on his shoulder. "He's had a rough night, you can lecture him about this later."

"*You* can lecture him later, I can lecture him now," Haeyin interjected, jabbing a bloodied finger in Jasper's direction. "You arrived very nearly too late for me to save you, you daft fool. I hope you know you're not invincible."

"I know," Jasper insisted with a groan, painfully aware

of his mortality. "That's why I didn't pull the knife out this time."

The doctor's expression softened after a moment as he wiped the blood off his hands on a soiled kitchen towel. "I am quite relieved you clearly employed my advice," Haeyin conceded. "Keeping that dagger inside you, painful as I'm sure it was, is almost certainly what saved you."

Varus dragged a hand down his face. "Yes, by all means, congratulate him on *that*," he remarked bitterly, leaning against a countertop filled with surgical tools and supplies. "Please, do not encourage him. This is not the outcome this assignment was supposed to have."

"Respectfully, the assignment was completed by the time this incident occurred," Cary replied in a low voice.

Sensing the life-threatening injuries had been dealt with, the doctor moved on to the wounds on Jasper's face. Caelfall was blessed to have Haeyin, a skilled surgeon who doubled as a renegade mage. His irises heated with a golden aura, the veins in his face illuminated with power as Haeyin worked. The more minor injuries offered a much less painful experience for Jasper, permitting him to partake in the conversation that transpired around him.

"Sir, please — it wasn't our client, it was two other patrons I hardly expected to be armed," he explained, hoping he might spare his job. "They were going to... they could barely stand, let alone swing a knife, I thought."

Cary eyed him with a heavy, unnamed emotion in her countenance. For a moment, it looked as if she wanted to say something, but her reply was interrupted by Haeyin recoiling from Jasper's face with a hiss. Shaking out his fingers, the doctor stepped away to shove his hand into the sink in the clinic operating theatre, flooding his palm with cool water. Varus' eyes shuttered as he watched the doctor with a knowing stare.

"Are you all right?" Jasper asked tentatively.

To this, Haeyin merely scoffed. Barely turning around, he said, "You're carried into my clinic, you nearly bleed out on my table, and then you ask me if *I'm* okay…"

Cary narrowed her eyes. "Don't even think about trying to heal my face in your condition," she scolded. "One burnt palm is enough for this evening."

Sighing, the doctor glanced up from the sink, his expression visibly conflicted. Magical overuse could have devastating side effects for the caster, and Haeyin often burnt his hands exhausting himself on the unfortunate patients in his clinic. As much as the doctor wanted to protest, his body would allow no further argument. Varus seemed inclined to agree, gathering fresh bandages from one of the cabinets as Haeyin shut off the faucet. The kingpin began to bind his partner's blistered palm with the practiced, tender hand of someone well acquainted with Haeyin's self-sacrificing nature.

Growing uncomfortable witnessing what seemed to be a private moment, Jasper took this as an opportunity to leave. However, he had sorely overestimated his physical ability following his near-death experience, and his vision flickered the moment he attempted to stand upright. Gratefully, his employer had finished wrapping Haeyin's hands quickly enough to catch Jasper before he crashed headlong into the floor.

"Steady on," Varus said gruffly, assisting Jasper into a chair nearby. "Where do you think you're going? You may not be bleeding out anymore, but that doesn't mean you're in the clear."

Jasper began to stammer in protest, to explain that he

needed to go home, but it was in that moment he finally had the chance to properly take in his surroundings. The operating theatre was small and cramped, more of a multi-purpose room where Haeyin saw and treated many patients. It was typically not remarkably decorated, cold and bare to keep things tidy. Today, however, Jasper saw it had been brightly adorned with garlands and streamers in blue and green. A small chocolate cake sat on a side table nearby, with delicate pink icing that read **HAPPY BIRTHDAY JASPER.**

His heart did something strange in his chest. "Is this… is this for me?"

Cary rolled her eyes even as her mouth split into a grin. "You're the only Jasper we know," she reminded him teasingly, hands on her hips.

"I don't blame you if you aren't up for much in the way of festivities," Haeyin noted sagely, retrieving one of the recently sanitized knives from beside the sink. "That said, it will help with the dizziness if you're able to have a bite to eat. Besides, it *is* for you."

Finding himself in no condition to leave, Jasper was compelled to attend the strangest, most intimate birthday party ever held for him. The four of them sat in the mismatched clinic chairs with cake and sweet apple cider, laughing and singing and celebrating *him*. Jasper managed to eat a portion of cake amidst what cider Haeyin would permit him to consume, and true to the doctor's word it did seem to help a bit. For a moment, Jasper allowed himself to enjoy the occasion – briefly forgetting his bitterness towards his birthday.

As the miniature party came to a close, with Haeyin's magical exertion resulting in incessant yawning, the three of them began to quietly clean up the decorations around

Jasper. Cary bundled all of the streamers and garlands into her ridiculously oversized coat, the remnants of the cake being shoved into the fridge alongside whatever science projects Haeyin was keeping in there.

Despite the cake helping him feel somewhat better, Jasper was still worse for wear. Though he managed to rise from his chair, he quickly felt his balance suffer with his depleted energy. Stumbling into the archway leading towards the waiting area, Jasper struggled to regain his composure. Owing to the intimate nature of the small room, his distress did not go unnoticed.

"I hope you don't think you're walking home tonight," said Varus.

Leaning against the archway, Jasper pinched the bridge of his nose. He would force himself if he had to, no matter how long it would take. "I need to go home," he insisted, to himself or to his companions. Distantly, he remembered the need to be home for something in the morning, though he couldn't recall exactly why.

He had misunderstood his employer's words. "There's a curfew in place, and I don't need you fainting in the streets," Varus pointed out, a hand on Jasper's shoulder steadying him. "I'll take you home."

The thought of Varus taking him home was nearly as horrifying as the thought of not making it home at all. He turned to his employer, hoping to insist that he would make the journey on his own, but Varus' stone-faced expression could not be reasoned with. "All right," Jasper agreed at last.

Behind Varus, Haeyin and Cary bid them farewell with a sleepy wave and a smile. Varus proceeded to hoist him to his feet, securing Jasper's arm over his shoulders much the way Cary had done on their way to the clinic. Jasper couldn't deny the relief his bones seemed to feel as they were no longer required to carry his weight, Varus' strength keeping him upright.

"You know the drill," said Varus gruffly, adjusting his stance to better stabilize the pair of them. "Close your eyes, close your mouth, and do not let go, you hear?"

"I know, I know," Jasper sighed.

Varus cast one final glance back towards Haeyin and Cary, his mouth pursed in a tense line. "Be back in a few," he said, and then they were falling.

The clinic faded away as they melted into the shadows, folding sideways and upside down as the shapes of reality began to blur. Jasper squeezed his eyes shut quickly as a wave of nausea threatened to overwhelm him, focusing on the iron grip of his employer's arm around his waist as they tumbled through nothingness. This was the space between planes of reality, the unnamed and unknowable void through which Varus could traverse impossible distances in moments. Though there was nothing and no one that existed here, Jasper swore he could hear voices whispering in the unfathomable darkness, voices that would haunt him long into the night.

They landed roughly, though his employer barely stumbled as their feet hit the still-slick cobblestones. The man had a surprisingly strong sense of balance for someone with a bad leg. Comparatively, Jasper tripped as they came to a halt on the familiar cobblestones of one of Caelfall's alleyways. Were it not for Varus' arm still supporting him, he would have surely fallen to his knees in the gutter. The air out here was colder than it had been in the clinic, and the sensation of his still-damp shirt on his skin quickly became uncomfortable.

Varus hauled him roughly to his feet, dusting him off

briefly before he resumed his previous position, assisting him in a steady walk towards his uncle Zeke's smithy. Despite the brief merriment of the birthday party, his employer's mood seemed to have soured. After a few moments of deathly silence, Jasper cleared his throat awkwardly, wondering what to say – if there was anything he *could* say to alleviate the situation.

"Save it," Varus dismissed him suddenly, leading him out of the alleyway and towards the main road. The damp streets were deserted this time of night due to the curfew, and there was something eerie and unsettling about the quietness, the way even the patrolling city guard did not look towards the shadows that obscured them. More of Varus' favoured glamours, perhaps.

Jasper gaped. "I didn't say anything."

"You were about to," his employer growled, though the irritation in his voice did not extend to the firm hold he had on Jasper's waist, still supportive and mostly gentle. "Cary filled me in on what happened. We can have a proper discussion about your complete disregard for the integrity of the operation this evening *after* you've rested."

He resisted the urge to flinch at the man's words. He knew better than to protest, but something broiled within him – whether it was the irritating texture of his shirt or the way Varus had spoken to him.

"Disregard? Mr. Emery, sir, I… I can't help but disagree with that term."

"Damn it, Jasper," Varus hissed, coming to a stop so abruptly that Jasper nearly toppled over a second time. The kingpin glowered down at him, and it took everything within him to hold the man's gaze. "You risked our entire operation, getting yourself stabbed in a brothel. Are we really going to argue over my diction when I tell you that you've erred?'"

Jasper bristled. "I know that, that's not what I—I'm sorry, but I—"

"Sorry?" Varus repeated incredulously. "Perhaps I wasn't clear enough. You're damned lucky to be *alive*. Do you think that, had you been caught, you would have been brought before a court at all? You assaulted noblemen, and you could have been found in possession of opiates. That's if you even survived being stabbed, mind you. What were you thinking?"

Before Jasper could answer, to protest or plead his case, Varus continued in a hushed whisper. "Have you any idea how royally screwed you would have been if word got out? You wouldn't even get a trial, lad. Thugs, common thieves – I can protect you from those. I can't protect you from the wrath of the justice system, Jasper."

He saw now why Varus was nearly shaking with anger. There was panic in his voice, harsh as his words were. It was somehow more difficult to accept than the rage Jasper had anticipated from his employer.

The distant sensation of hornets fluttered in his skin as a chill caused him to shudder. Balling his fists and screwing his courage, Jasper ignored the sensation of his stomach dropping. "They attacked Cary, sir," he said finally. "Did she tell you that part? Mr. Emery, they were trying to... they wanted to..."

But he could not bring himself to say the words, to name the nobleman's horrid intentions. His thoughts drifted towards the nameless woman Varus had mentioned earlier in the day, the colleague who was supposed to be on this assignment. The unspeakable acts that men like that had wanted to inflict upon Cary... the thought was too heavy for Jasper to put into words, and they turned to bile on his tongue.

Gratefully, Varus seemed to understand. His expression remained as stony as ever, but the harshness in his tone had lessened. "She's a big girl, Jasper. She can take care of herself. Trust me, it's not the first time she's had a drunken patron attempt something foolish."

"Pardon my bluntness, sir, but ... that makes it worse," Jasper insisted. His thoughts drifted towards his uncle, and the stern lectures he would receive in his childhood on his treatment of others. "I wasn't raised to see someone in distress and do nothing, there's no honour in that."

He wondered to himself what Zeke would think of Jasper's honour now, moonlighting as an errand boy for a kingpin.

Varus eyed Jasper carefully, the corner of his mouth twitching into a smile. "You're correct," he affirmed finally. "But Cary's had more experience in fighting than you have. It's a rare occasion indeed that she's ever needed more than a stitch, whereas you seem to have a nasty habit of knocking on death's door." Sighing, he looked away, continuing to lead Jasper in a slow walk towards the smithy.

"I'm sorry, sir, truly. It won't happen again."

Varus shook his head. "I'm almost certain it will." His gaze slid back over to Jasper's face, and something about it caused him to frown. "Are you all right, lad?"

Blinking, Jasper nodded in response quickly, though he admittedly felt like hell. Even with Haeyin's magic, his abdomen ached from the fresh wound and there was an exhaustion in his muscles that seemed to weigh him down. The doctor could mend broken bones and stitch wounded flesh back together, but there were some natural healing processes that no mage could expedite. He could see the squat shape of the forge in the distance, his flat above it. He was itching to open the door and crawl into his bed...

"Jasper."

He craned his neck to look up at Varus, finding his employer's stern demeanour had settled back into place. "Yes, sir?"

"I don't think it's a good idea for you to be alone tonight," Varus explained simply.

Jasper knew better than to argue. He glanced towards the bakery that neighboured his shop, at the faint glow of the lamp in the upstairs window.

"Charlotte's still up," he offered quietly. "I'm sure she'd... well, she'll be mighty cross at first. But she'd let me stay."

Varus barked a short laugh, readjusting his grip on Jasper's waist before leading him towards the bakery. He rapped gently on the front door, a soft, quick knock. Jasper could picture Charlotte inside, rushing down the stairs before the noise could rouse her father from sleep.

The hallway light flickered to life as the silhouette of a woman appeared through the frosted glass of the front door, the lock clicking as a dressing gown-clad Charlotte opened the door for them, her dark curls haphazardly pulled back in a plait with a silk tie.

Charlotte, whom he had known for nearly all his life. Charlotte, whom he'd come so very close to never seeing again. Charlotte, the woman Jasper was going to marry someday, maybe.

The woman he was going to marry someday took one look at Varus and slapped him across the face. Jasper could only stare in shock as the other man barely recoiled, blinking more in surprise at Charlotte's audacity than any pain he might have felt. He was grateful his employer hadn't dropped him.

"Lovely to see you too, dear," he said evenly.

"Don't you *dare* act coy with me," Charlotte hissed, her hazel eyes dangerously bright as she jabbed a finger into Varus' sternum. She was the only woman Jasper knew who was brave enough to go toe-to-toe with arguably the most notorious kingpin in the Aethian underworld. "What in the name of the goddesses happened to him?"

"Charlie, I'm fine—" Jasper began, but Charlotte was having none of it.

"*You are not fine!*" Charlotte said in a choked whisper, her voice shrill and strained as she threw up her hands in exasperation. She seemed to be struggling to balance screeching at him with desperately trying not to wake her father. "You're drenched in blood, you're as white as a sheet, and you can barely stand, *do not* make excuses for him. What happened!?"

"We had a close call," Varus explained calmly, as if Charlotte's irate reaction had no effect on him in the slightest. "A couple of drunken men attacked Cary, and Jasper was gravely injured in his attempts to save her. He will need to rest, he lost quite a lot of blood this evening."

Jasper winced involuntarily; neither Charlotte nor Varus had said anything he didn't already know, but the verbal confirmation of his mortality made the ordeal seem far too real for his liking. He felt drained, sagging where he stood against Varus as the hateful texture of his wet clothing irked him further. Charlotte deflated as she took in what must have been visible exhaustion in his face, her features softening.

"Well, come inside," she said eventually, stepping back to let Varus inside as he half-dragged Jasper over the threshold. The bakery was an eerie place at night, but still smelled of the comforting vanilla cakes and spiced buns Jasper had come to associate it with. Locking the shop door behind them, Charlotte led Varus towards the staircase at the back of the shop, tiptoeing quietly past her father's living quarters on the ground floor.

Varus said nothing as he helped Jasper up the stairs, and even with the assistance of a knee brace it seemed to be a struggle for him. The loft was just as comforting in the dark as Jasper knew it to be in the daylight, cluttered and cozy. Jasper's hurried note to Charlotte sat on the desk beneath the window, illuminated by the lamp he'd seen from outside. His employer didn't let go of Jasper until Charlotte showed him to the bedroom in the loft, depositing Jasper onto the plush surface of the mattress. When Jasper managed to look up at the man, there was that curious, unreadable emotion lingering in his gaze once more.

"As I said before, Jasper... I'm grateful," Varus said quietly, his voice low enough that Charlotte would not hear him. "But please, try not to risk your life too often."

Whatever Jasper might have said in response, the conversation was abruptly cut short by Charlotte attempting to physically shove Varus out of the room. "That's quite enough from you," she cut in, her voice a low hiss. "Leave, now."

Her efforts were not exactly effective; Varus towered over her, and he seemed more amused than anything by her attempts to remove him. The kingpin didn't argue, smiling somewhat as he dusted off his hands before vanishing entirely. Charlotte didn't so much as blink as the man evaporated in a cloud of darkness, heaving a sigh of relief as she and Jasper were left alone.

Despite his exhaustion, Jasper forced himself to remain

upright. Now, sitting here in the silence, there was nothing to distract his mind from the sensation of his soiled shirt. The damp and blood-stained fabric stuck to his body unpleasantly, and the texture made his head pound. The sensation of writhing insects burrowed under his skin, and Jasper trembled as his breath caught in his throat, struggling to wriggle out of his trench coat. His pulse quickened to a thunderous drone in his ears as his weak fingers tried and failed to unbutton his shirt...

As if she were capable of reading his mind, Charlotte grasped at the sleeves of his shirt, assisting him as he wriggled free of the damp fabric. Jasper murmured a shaky "thank you" as he exhaled a shuddering breath, his hands moving to unbuckle his belt. Seemingly on the same wavelength, Charlotte knelt down at his feet, tugging his trousers down by the ankles. With her assistance, Jasper finally managed to free himself from the rain and blood-soaked garments, left shivering on the bed in only his underclothes. Propriety mattered little when Jasper was in danger of losing his mind at an offensive texture or sensation. Had he been in a room with anyone else, Jasper might have been embarrassed, or at least uncomfortable with being nearly naked. As it was, Charlotte had seen him in such a state so many times before, it almost didn't bother him anymore.

Almost.

Charlotte picked his ruined clothes up off the floor, draping them over the old radiator in the corner. Gratefully, Charlotte and her father were well-accustomed to the presence of bloodied clothes. "Feeling a bit better?" she asked gently. Her voice was neutral, but her expression betrayed her concern as her gaze drifted towards his abdomen.

Jasper hadn't seen the injury since the fight, when he'd looked down and seen the dagger buried in his stomach. As he looked himself over now, he saw what remained of that near-fatal wound. Amidst the expanse of stretch marks along his abdomen, the fresh scar dimpled the belly fat beside his navel. Absentmindedly, Jasper found himself running his fingers over the still-warm, knotted scar tissue, as if traces of Haeyin's magic still lingered in his skin.

"Are you all right?" she prompted.

His mind was drained, his body exhausted. Even Charlotte's lovely face was painful for him to look up at, and Jasper was unable to meet her gaze when he responded. "I'm fine," he insisted, his voice hoarse.

Charlotte was more perceptive than most, and Jasper was a notoriously poor liar. Sighing, she discarded her dressing gown over the nearby desk chair, crossing the room to take a seat beside him on the edge of the bed. Jasper shivered as her arm grazed against his own, shocked by the warmth radiating from her brown and freckled skin against his death pallor. Every inch of his body threatened to burst into flames at the proximity, hyper-aware of how little fabric there was between them.

"Why don't I believe you?" Charlotte said softly. "You're trembling, Jazzy-boy."

Her nickname for him made his ears burn beneath his hair. Still finding himself unable to meet her eyes, his hand idly traced that new scar on his abdomen, his thoughts a scattered mess of emotions he couldn't name. Eyeing his shaking fingers, Charlotte reached for his hand, tugging it gently away from the wound. Her fingers were warm, but as they brushed over that new scar Jasper shivered with a sudden chill.

"You're safe now," Charlotte whispered, and the gentleness of her voice did something strange to his heart. "Will you tell me what's on your mind?"

Despite the anxious tangle of his thoughts, the over-stimulated energy that seemed rampant inside of him, Jasper forced himself to meet her gaze. Even in the dim light, he could make out the vibrant hazel of her eyes, the constellation of freckles scattered across her skin. He wanted to say a thousand things, half-formed thoughts that had run through his mind as he had brushed so closely with death that Jasper feared he would never see her again. He wanted to tell her all the things he had been terrified of taking to his grave, secrets not yet shared and promises he'd yet to keep. He had come so close to oblivion, and Charlotte would have had no idea.

Instead, he said nothing. Charlotte didn't protest at his silence, for she had always possessed that peculiar ability of understanding Jasper better than he understood himself, better than anyone could. In a world that reminded him how different and alien he could be, she always made him feel as if he belonged somewhere.

After a few moments more in the quiet darkness, Charlotte tugged her hand from his grasp as she stood to cross the room. Jasper rose to pull the covers back from the bed, positioning himself as close to the wall as the mattress would allow. As she extinguished the lone lamp on the desk, Charlotte crawled into the bed beside him. Even with the space between them, he could still feel the warmth of her nearby, but it was the first sensation that night that did not overwhelm his weary mind. The stresses of the day caught up to him, every inch of his body settling into the stillness, and sleep came for him quickly.

In what might have been the beginning of a dream, he thought he felt Charlotte's hands brushing his hair back from his face before he fell soundly asleep.

CHAPTER

THREE

CHARLOTTE

When Charlotte awoke that morning, she found herself shivering despite the unusually warm spring weather. The damp air wreaked havoc on her joints, her bones aching as she sat upright. Careful not to wake the sleeping form occupying most of her bed, Charlotte crawled out from the covers. She padded softly across the loft towards the kitchenette on the far side of the room, aching for a bit of hot water to warm her up before she began the morning's food drive.

Filling a battered old pot with water and waiting for it to warm up on the stove, she glanced back towards the bed beneath the window and the comatose young man within it. It was entirely inappropriate to share a bed with a man she wasn't married to, but Charlotte and Jasper had been this close since they were children. Her father Samuel and Jasper's uncle Zeke had been neighbours for years, friends for many more. When Zeke had passed, it seemed natural that her father take Jasper under his wing, the boy only a year younger than his own daughter. Charlotte was more than happy to let him stay the night on occasion, especially after the incident he'd suffered yesterday.

She had stayed awake at the window, watching and waiting for a red-headed young man to return home after Charlotte had read the letter he'd left for her beside her delivered medication. *He said Cary would do the job alone, and I couldn't have that on my conscience.* Her brave, foolish blacksmith. The events of last night were still fresh in Charlotte's mind, and she shuddered at the memory of Jasper being dragged into the bakery – by Varus bloody Emery, no less.

It was hard to believe he'd nearly died. He looked serene, his large form stretched across the bedcovers in an unassuming way, hair mussed by a night of tossing and turning. The newest scar on his abdomen was exposed by the tangled sheets, joining an array of old wounds scattered across his skin. He had so many scars, so many new marks that he tried so very hard to hide from her. She knew them all, and in her mind's eye had memorized them, stretched maps across them. Who knew when the time came that the ambitious doctor of Caelfall could not heal her beloved friend?

Tearing her gaze away from Jasper, Charlotte took the now heated water with her to the bathroom, shutting the stove off as she went. The old-fashioned wooden panelling of the room offered a slightly warmer atmosphere than porcelain, but Charlotte had neither the time nor the energy for a full bath for herself – a sponge bath would have to do, and hopefully it would be enough. Dumping the pot of water into the smaller, lighter tub dedicated for this exact purpose, Charlotte shimmied out of her nightgown and began the arduous process of scrubbing at as many areas of herself as she could while the water was still hot, grateful for the soothing warmth against the pockets of pain in her skin.

Jasper slept the entire time. Appreciating the solitude, Charlotte bundled herself as warmly as possible. One of her heavier woollen shawls offered moderate protection from the chill, combined with the layers of her skirts. She coiled her dark curls into as tame a braid as she could manage, the ache in her hands somewhat reduced by the warm water. Careful not to rouse her friend, Charlotte quietly snuck through the loft before closing the door behind her. Jasper would likely complain that she'd taken on the food drive alone, but she couldn't bring herself to wake him up.

As she made her way down the stairs into the bakery, she trembled with a sudden drop in temperature. Her father was already up and about, the front door left ajar as he carried crate after crate to deposit onto their borrowed delivery cart, piling the boxes of bread neatly within.

"You're up early," her father noted chidingly, his blue eyes twinkling with amusement. "Did I overhear a certain young man arriving late last night?"

Charlotte felt her cheeks flush as she busied herself with carrying some of the remaining boxes to the cart. "Yes, Jasper had a rough night. It didn't seem like a good idea to leave him to his own devices while he was recovering."

Her father chuckled, shaking his head. "I'm only teasing," he insisted, bending down with a groan to pick up the last crate. "You both know he's welcome here any time. Do you know what happened?"

Charlotte swallowed a wave of anxiety. She had no interest in divulging Jasper's part-time occupation to her father. "Oh, I didn't want to ask, he was so exhausted," she lied, dusting off her hands as she set down the box of bread loaves in the cart.

"Well, I hope you're all right to manage the food drive by yourself, then," her father replied, his tone becoming more serious. "Are you sure you don't want me to go with you?"

She shook her head, fidgeting with a loose ringlet at the nape of her neck as her father loaded the last of the food supplies into the cart. "I'll be fine," she insisted. They couldn't afford to both do the food drive, else the bakery be closed all day.

He didn't appear to be fully comfortable with her leaving by herself, but eventually her father seemed to come to the same conclusion. "You be careful out there," he warned, pulling her into a tight embrace. "Don't push yourself too hard, and you be back home before sunset."

"Yes, father," said Charlotte, her voice muffled within his vast chest as he crushed her against it. He drew back to look at her fondly, his blue eyes searching her face. There was very little resemblance between Charlotte and her father, she thought; where her father was tall, fair, and broad, Charlotte was smaller and looked much more like her Valedian mother.

Clearing his throat, he pulled away at last. "All right, I'd best be getting back to work," her father said gruffly, clearly having met his emotional quota for the morning. "Take care, sweetheart."

Charlotte gave him a little wave and a mumbled "Bye, father," before turning her attention to the cart and the horse strapped to it. The communal stables had a good relationship with Samuel, regularly dropping off horses for the weekly food drive. Charlotte had become well-acquainted with the animals the stables would provide, and she was grateful to recognize today's companion. Rose was a well-mannered old palomino, though she certainly liked Jasper more than she liked Charlotte. She seemed somewhat disgruntled by his absence, but permitted Charlotte to pat her neck encouragingly before she stepped onto the makeshift seat at the front of the cart, reins in hand.

The weekend route was a ritual now, and every week Charlotte ventured out for the church's food drive. She and her father always contributed a fair portion of their own baked goods, with occasional volunteers signing up to supply donations all throughout the kingdom. Today, only their most significant regular donor would be contributing. The royal family – or more specifically, the palace kitchens – were always responsible for the majority of the food drive.

The sun was barely peeking out over the horizon as the carriage rumbled along the rough cobblestone streets of Caelfall, with Charlotte huddled in her shawl. By the time she made her way over the first bridge connecting Caelfall to the western district of Aerindale, the sun was fully in her eyes no matter how much she tried to shield them with her fingers. When she crossed the second bridge leading to the gleaming roads of Briardeen, Charlotte finally felt warm enough to shed her shawl. Her mind far away, she let Rose continue at a leisurely pace as she guided the mare towards the castle, in the northernmost region of Briardeen. The emerald banners caught the breeze as Charlotte approached, the crest of the dragon seemingly taking flight in the wind.

The gates to the castle premises were heavily guarded, as was to be expected. Charlotte was accustomed to spending a good five or ten minutes arguing her case with the knights stationed at the courtyard gates, insisting she was a member of the church orchestrating the food drive.

The war between Aethia and Pharsat had ended decades ago, but the distrust the locals held for anyone of seemingly Valedian origin had lingered.

This morning, however, she was in luck – a handsome, familiar face greeted her, waving as Rose came to a stop in front of him. Gideon had been a beloved friend of Charlotte for as long as Jasper had; five years older than her, he was something of an unlikely big brother to the pair of them. The three had grown up together sneaking across the kingdom to play hide-and-seek, often in the shipyards of Dornkeep and other areas where small children were prohibited. The day Gideon had turned eighteen, his lord father had sent him to the combat academy, and neither Jasper nor Charlotte had seen much of their friend as often as they once had.

Gideon was a charismatic young man with great skill and greater ambition. In only a few short years he had ascended the ranks to become captain of the royal guard, one of the most prestigious roles a knight could attain. He could have been a templar with his skill, but he swore his vocation was to serve the king. Charlotte alone knew that the truth was more complicated, that his faith had been irrevocably shaken with the passing of his mother when he was a boy.

Gideon's fine, polished armour was practically glowing in the sunlight as he approached, stroking Rose's mane as he smiled at Charlotte, blue eyes piercing in the morning light. "Morning, Charlie," he greeted her warmly.

"Good morning," she replied, unable to stop herself from smiling in Gideon's presence. "You certainly are a sight for sore eyes. I didn't particularly feel like debating with a guard this morning."

He gave her a wry smile, his chin dimpling with the

expression. "I was hoping I'd see you today. No Jasper this morning?" he noted neutrally, but she knew him too well to be deceived by his apparent nonchalance.

Charlotte shook her head. "He had a long night," she said by way of explanation. Gideon was another person who didn't know about Jasper's secondary occupation, and he *couldn't* know. As a member of the royal guard, Gideon had a responsibility to apprehend criminals, and Charlotte would not put him in the position to choose between Jasper or the king.

Sometimes, she wasn't certain who Gideon would choose.

Gideon nodded, sighing. "It's a damned shame he's not guarding these gates with me," he said, gesturing behind him. "We could have used a man like him among our ranks."

This wasn't a topic Charlotte felt like discussing today, not after seeing the state Jasper had been in last night. For the first time that day, she was grateful he wasn't there. "Well, sometimes things just… don't work out that way," she offered in a similarly neutral tone. She managed a cheeky grin as she added, "Are you going to let me in, then?"

Gideon laughed heartily, taking a step back. "You don't waste any time, do you?" he mused. With a wave to his counterpart opposite, a series of clanging and creaking pulleys yanked the gates aside. She knew the other man wouldn't refute the captain's word, but that didn't stop him from glaring daggers in Charlotte's direction.

She nudged Rose forward, giving Gideon a cheerful wave. "Maybe I'll come and say hello a bit later," Charlotte suggested as she turned back towards the path, following the manicured castle gardens towards her destination.

The servant's quarters exited directly into the courtyard where Charlotte pulled up, tugging lightly on the reins to bring Rose to a stop. The supplies were already packed into crates, stacked neatly outside the entrance to the living and kitchen areas. Charlotte managed to step down from the cart with little grace, her knees and her hips protesting with the action.

Movement in the corner of her eye caused her to start, a servant emerging from within the castle kitchens to assist her. Charlotte instinctively fixed her gaze on the floor, as if she might draw attention away from herself. As the individual spoke, however, Charlotte was both relieved and immediately disappointed that she knew this person.

"Good morning, Charlotte," said Cary as she approached. The Reinnairlei woman was dressed in typical servants' attire, clothed in a form fitting navy dress with a collar that reached her throat and sleeves that extended to her knuckles. Her dark hair was pulled back in a regulatory chignon, leaving the entirety of her face exposed for scrutiny.

Charlotte narrowed her eyes as she regarded the woman, whatever scathing remark she might have offered quickly forgotten when she caught sight of the flesh-toned paint and powder Cary wore on her face. She was not friendly with the woman, but Charlotte had seen her on the food drive often enough to know the woman never wore cosmetics, blessed with an even complexion.

"What happened to you?" Charlotte eventually spoke. "I've never seen you wear so much as rouge while you're working here."

Cary's hand rose halfway to her face before halting abruptly. It was all the confirmation that Charlotte needed. "I—I suppose you heard it from Jasper?" she asked politely.

"I heard it from *Varus Emery* when he dragged Jasper to my doorstep," Charlotte clarified in a low voice, taking another step towards the woman. "I'll give him credit where it's due, since I suppose his story holds up. He did say Jasper almost died trying to defend you."

She almost felt bad when Cary visibly flinched. "Yes," she admitted after a moment's pause. She chewed her lip, visibly at war with herself before she added, "Charlotte, I hope you know I would never have let anything happen to him, I swear—"

"But you *did* let something happen to him," Charlotte cut in. She was angry, but more than anything she was tired. She was tired of these people pretending that what happened to Jasper was merely an unfortunate accident, and not a scenario any of them had any hand in manufacturing. "Something happened, and he got hurt, and he nearly died. Is that so difficult for you to admit?"

Cary's gaze fell to the floor, her pink eyes shuttered. "It's my fault," she agreed. "I'm sorry."

Charlotte closed her eyes, her energy and her frustrations leaving her in an exhaled lungful of tension. "As much as I would love to continue berating you for nearly killing my best friend, I have a job to do," she said finally, gesturing to the stack of food crates.

Cary's eyes narrowed, but she said nothing as she set to work loading the crates into the cart with Charlotte. To her credit, she was stronger than she looked; Cary was taller and thinner in comparison to Charlotte, but her willowy form seemed to make quick work of the crates, whereas Charlotte felt her back beginning to ache after carrying three of the heavy boxes. The two of them moved in silence until at last the final crate was loaded. Charlotte was eager to leave but Cary slipped in close, halting her movements with a gentle but urgent hand on her wrist.

"I know you care for him," Cary said quietly, her voice brimming with a barely contained frustration. "I know it hurts, but he's not a child, Charlotte. You're going to have to come to terms with the fact that I am not some charlatan luring him into a trap he doesn't understand. He's a smart lad, he knows what he's getting himself into, and you do him no favours coddling him."

Her words reignited Charlotte's rage, and her gaze snapped up to meet Cary's steely expression. "Coddling him?" she repeated, snatching her hand away. "I know Jasper. I know he agrees to things he doesn't want to do out of this—this *instinct* to protect the people he loves, even at the cost of his own safety, and I am sick of the lot of you taking advantage of that!"

"He knew the risks!" Cary retorted, her voice rising. "We all did! None of us go into any of these places without knowing what might happen, and none of us have the privilege of knowing with certainty we will make it out alive. I know it, Varus knows it, and Shadows be damned, Jasper knows it too. What part of that is confusing to you?"

Charlotte couldn't help but chuckle darkly. "You don't get it," she laughed bitterly. "You're all so willing to lay down your lives for Varus. The moment he told Jasper that you were doing that assignment alone, he'd all but twisted his arm. And look where that's got him, a knife in the gut and all you've got to show for it are bruises you're hiding rather well."

The expression on Cary's face grew positively blistering. "Do you think," she said slowly, taking a step closer to Charlotte, "that these bruises are the worst of the injuries

I've ever sustained? Do you have any idea what Jasper was trying to spare me from?"

Her words stopped Charlotte in her tracks. Varus had said Jasper was trying to defend Cary, but she had no idea what had happened to warrant it. She hated to admit defeat, but she was at a loss. "No," she replied honestly, albeit with stubborn defiance.

The was a terse silence while Cary regarded her, an unnamed emotion warring in her rosy gaze. "I hope you never do," she said finally, and something in her voice told Charlotte she was sincere. "I don't wish to fight with you, Charlotte. I am sorry, truly. But sooner or later, you will have to accept that Jasper is an adult, and you have to let him make his own decisions."

Somewhere amidst her indignation, she knew there was a kernel of truth to Cary's words, but this knowledge only frustrated her further. Charlotte didn't want to live with the knowledge that ultimately, she couldn't protect Jasper forever. It was a more heartbreaking truth than the fact that she'd nearly lost him so suddenly.

Neither of them seemed to want to argue any further, but their conversation would have been cut short regardless. A woman in plain, rigid cotton garments had joined them in the courtyard. At first Charlotte had paid her no mind, having been too engrossed in her argument with Cary. As she approached, however, Charlotte was startled to realize the princess herself had joined them outside.

"Your Highness," Cary greeted her, curtsying gracefully. Charlotte struggled to follow suit. The princess Aurelia was dressed rather oddly this morning, wearing what might have passed for training gear or even light armour. If Charlotte had to guess, Aurelia had been sparring in secret with her handmaiden somewhere in the gardens.

Aurelia dismissed the honorific with a wave of her hand. "There's no need for that, Cary," she said chidingly. "You and Charlotte know me too intimately for stiff mannerisms." Despite the warmth that had finally started to seep into the morning, Aurelia was almost fully covered by her training gear, complete with a pair of darkly tinted spectacles. The princess was the palest person Charlotte had ever met, with hair and skin as white as snow. Her only colouring was her pale red eyes, sensitive as ever to any amount of light.

The princess' handmaiden followed her into the courtyard, another Reinnairlei woman – and a notorious one at that. Fortia was a legendary warrior in her time, long before being delegated as guardian of the princess following the passing of the queen. Her muscular form seemed to be cut from iron, her grey hair braided back tightly from her tattooed face, the underside shorn close to her scalp. Her gaze fell to Cary first and then to Charlotte, relaxing only when she seemed to have established that both of them were permitted to see the princess in such a casual setting.

"Charlotte, would you join me for tea?" the princess asked sweetly, a smile on her pretty face. Their friendship seemed an unlikely one, and Charlotte wasn't sure what business a princess could possibly have being so close with a baker's daughter. Despite their vastly differing circumstances, however, Aurelia hadn't yet tired of Charlotte's company after all these years.

"I would love to, but I should really be taking these back to the church," Charlotte replied, gesturing to the carriage.

"Oh, I insist," Aurelia returned, linking her arm with Charlotte. "And afterwards, we can help you with the food drive. Don't think I haven't noticed your charming blacksmith isn't here with you today."

Charlotte found herself blushing, either through embarrassment or remembered anger. Out of the corner of her eye, she saw Cary turn away, an action Fortia seemed to have picked up on as well.

"My lady, I don't think that would be wise, given your father's poor mood," Fortia noted calmly. Even with a neutral expression, the faded black line inked across the bridge of her nose from ear to ear gave her a daunting presence, a clan marking that Charlotte had never been brave enough to ask about.

Aurelia didn't seem particularly concerned. "Fortia, I have yet to witness my father in anything but a poor mood," she returned with a sigh. "Please, Charlotte, just while I change into something more suitable. We'll be on our way shortly."

Sensing this wasn't a battle she could win, Charlotte found herself at an impasse. There really was no refusing the princess, and Charlotte was in no hurry to continue with the food drive, already exhausted by the work she'd completed so far. "As her highness commands," she conceded, unable to stop herself smiling.

"Oh, please—there's no need for that," Aurelia scolded her playfully. "Come now, let's head inside. Your horse will be safe out here for the time being."

As it was, Cary had led Rose over towards the nearby stables, where the mare was happily munching on an apple. Charlotte wanted to thank the woman, but the way Cary had turned her back suggested she had no interest in a continued conversation. With a pang of guilt, Charlotte followed Fortia and the princess into the castle, grateful to be inside if only for a few minutes.

The princess' chambers were perhaps the most surprising thing about her – despite the servants' best efforts, Charlotte had yet to see Aurelia's room tidy. It was amusing to her that the most brilliant people she knew had the messiest living areas, for Jasper suffered a similar affliction. The princess had a knack for clockwork and mechanics, and her favourite pastimes tended to be deconstructing all manner of devices in an attempt to repair or modify them. As someone who generally spent a lot of her time alone, Aurelia had become skilled in keeping herself entertained. The most recent project seemed to be a decorative pocket watch, laying in several pieces beneath the lamp on the work desk in the princess' study.

As if noticing Charlotte's gaze had wandered to her project, Aurelia called from within the nearby dressing area, "What do you think? It's been sitting over my fireplace for ages, I hadn't been brave enough to attempt to repair it until now."

Charlotte pressed the switch at the base of the lamp, illuminating the project beneath it. She hadn't much of a mind for clockwork, but she thought she could see what Aurelia had been attempting to fix. "I think you're doing well, so far," she replied, not daring to touch the little watch. "Not that I would know, admittedly."

Fortia craned her neck around an ornate screen concealing the princess from the main chambers. "I do hope I'm mistaken, but that looks to be the pocket watch that Lord Jacobson gave you as a token of his affections," Fortia pointed out, gesturing to the mess. "Rather, what's left of it."

From behind the screen, Aurelia laughed. "Not what's left of it, it's all there," she corrected, emerging in her undergarments, having peeled off the training gear she had been wearing earlier. Thankfully, Charlotte and Fortia were both accustomed to the princess wandering her chambers in about as much clothing as she currently had on, no longer shocking to either of them.

As Fortia began to adjust the lacing on the princess' corset, Aurelia added, "I wonder sometimes if he had used it in previous engagement attempts."

"And why is that?"

"I feel that... being repeatedly tossed down a large flight of steps in anger is a likely hypothesis for why this clock never worked properly," Aurelia mused.

Charlotte was unable to stifle her laughter. Fortia raised an eyebrow, but a twitch in the corner of her mouth betrayed her amusement. "Or perhaps he was being honest in his explanation that it was his great-grandfather's pocket watch from the Valedian war. A relic of a bygone era."

The princess shook her head. "I think my theory is much more plausible," she insisted, stepping into the mauve gown that Fortia had set aside for her. Owing to the princess' sensitive complexion, the dress had longer sleeves and a higher neckline than what was typically considered fashionable for upper-class women in Briardeen.

Knowing a lost cause when she saw one, Fortia dropped the subject as she fastened the buttons of Aurelia's gown. "Charlotte, would you mind pouring the tea for Aurelia?" the woman instructed, nodding in the direction of the teapot nearby. "It should be steeped by now."

Charlotte nodded, making her way from the study over to a table by the fireplace. A fine old tea set was already prepared, the scent of the sweet herbs filling her nose as Charlotte poured a generous amount into the princess' favourite teacup.

Aurelia had not always been Aurelia in the time Charlotte had been friends with her. There was a time when the princess had been known by a different name, one Charlotte sometimes had to remind herself not to use. Two years younger than her, Aurelia had confided in her about four years ago now. Having found the words to describe the agony she had been living with, Aurelia had detailed the constant sense of unease and discomfort that had grown while living in a body that did not comply with her sense of self. There had been a brief period of confusion, but with time the kingdom had come to embrace their now beloved princess.

Ever since, her daily routine consisted of herbs and magic to nudge her physical form into one that suited her more comfortably. A small price to pay, Charlotte thought, for a far less painful existence for the princess. In a way, Charlotte could empathize, though her own situation was slightly different; the medication she took daily was tailored to prevent her body's insistence on betraying her.

With a sudden pang of anxiety, Charlotte realized she had neglected to take her own tea that morning.

As she offered the cup to Aurelia, the work lamp Charlotte had left on flickered irritably, leaving the pocket watch on the desk in darkness. Fortia sighed, shaking her head as she crossed the room to rap her knuckles against the base of the lamp. She didn't possess the skill Aurelia had developed for technology, and more often than not found that beating the devices into submission usually worked just as well. The lamp shuddered back to life with an erratic spark.

"If the damned castle can't sustain its own lighting, we're in a right mess," she muttered under her breath, returning to Aurelia's side as she began to brush and braid her hair. Charlotte leaned over to turn the lamp off, no longer trusting it to stay on.

"I wouldn't expect the castle to have issues with electrical power," she wondered aloud. It was fairly common to have meagre, inconsistent electricity in Caelfall, owing to the aged and poorly maintained power lines that had fallen into disrepair. The unreliable power supply left most of the city to rely on oil lamps even with more modern advancements available. With all the wealth and status Briardeen held, Charlotte assumed their situation wouldn't be so similar, especially not for the royal family of all people.

"Better here than the flight craft," Aurelia noted, sipping her tea thoughtfully as Fortia finished with the fastenings of her dress. "Or the academy. Or even the hospital."

Fortia shook her head once more, her hands on her hips as she glanced idly out the window. "I wouldn't doubt that your father would sooner cut the power to the hospital before going without," she said softly. "But I should like to think not."

Aurelia and Charlotte seemed to be at a shared loss for words. Charlotte knew the energy crisis in Aethelind was a deep-rooted concern for the princess, but her father didn't seem to share her worries. She had asked Aurelia about it in the past, but it seemed that King Gustaf was insistent on keeping his daughter in the dark when it came to matters of the kingdom.

Noting their silence, Fortia turned to face them with an uncharacteristic smile on her face. "Come now, there's nothing to be worried about just yet. I'm sure Aethelind isn't in any immediate danger of dropping out of the sky."

The thought of the kingdom dropping out of the sky made Charlotte weak in the knees. "On that note, I feel I really must be going," she piped up. "Are you sure you want to come with me, your—Aurelia? You really don't have to."

Aurelia set her empty teacup down beside her, taking Charlotte's hands and squeezing them. "Don't be silly, I would love to," she assured her. Fortia had braided the princess' hair back from her round, pale face, rose-flushed and wreathed in starlight. For a moment, Charlotte was taken aback by how effortlessly magical the young woman was. In some ways, she was just a little bit jealous of Aurelia.

Fortia seemed keen to hurry them along as well, and Charlotte's observation was interrupted. "Let's get moving then, before it's too late in the day," she agreed, gesturing for the door. "If you seem so keen on invoking your father's wrath, I would at least like to avoid meeting him in the corridors."

They succeeded in evading the king's notice as the three women snuck back through the castle towards the stables. Before long, Charlotte was back to traversing the streets of Briardeen towards the church, Fortia and Aurelia following along. Sneaking out of the palace meant the princess would forego her usual entourage, but Fortia's presence was easily worth half a dozen guards. Beneath a gauzy parasol, Aurelia chatted animatedly on all manner of subjects to Charlotte. She began with the history of the kingdom's enormous network of engines and flight craft keeping it aloft in the sky, deviating towards her theories on what the energy crisis stemmed from, eventually leading towards her research in ancient linguistics.

Charlotte was content to let Aurelia do all the talking; in truth, she was beginning to feel quite dizzy and unwell, likely owing to the absence of her morning dose of medicine. The beginnings of cramps low in her abdomen were making her nauseous, an ache blooming deep inside of her. The sun on her face was pleasant but the heat seemed to be contributing to her malaise, and she wished she had something lighter to wear.

As they approached, the cathedral bells were ringing in a symphony of iron, announcing the hour. The sounds reverberated through the expansive structure, between stone parapets and across stained glass windows. Charlotte led her party towards the side entrance where part of the cathedral housed the church's volunteer soup kitchen. Securing Rose and the wagon nearby, Fortia and Aurelia assisted Charlotte in carrying the crates of donated food into the church, with the princess surprisingly strong and agile.

The kitchen was stiflingly warm, with two women already hard at work inside. Charlotte had become close friends with Eleni and Maya from their shared participation in the church's choir. Eleni was about a decade older than Charlotte and had become something of a maternal figure towards her, while Maya was the closest Charlotte had to a little sister. When Charlotte entered the room, Eleni looked up immediately from her attempts to chop onions. The moment she saw the new batch of food being brought in, she threw down her knife and promptly gave up on the sad, soft vegetables before her.

"Oh, thank the goddesses," she exclaimed breathlessly, brushing flyaway blonde hair out of her eyes. The folded sleeves of her blouse exposed the mage's cuffs on her wrists, the heavy silver catching the light. "Fresh onions, please – these are awful."

As her gaze focused on the princess and her handmaiden, Eleni let out a startled sort of gasp, curtsying quickly. "Goodness, what a surprise! Good afternoon, Your Highness." Beside her, Maya dipped her head politely towards the princess.

Charlotte made a beeline towards the young woman, reaching forward to greet her with a quick kiss on her cheek. "Happy belated birthday, Maya."

The smile that spread across Maya's face halted at whatever she saw on Charlotte's countenance. "Charlotte, are you feeling all right?" she asked, tilting her head back to look up at her. "You look awfully pale."

Truthfully, Charlotte wasn't sure she'd looked pale a day in her life. "I'm fine, thank you, Maya," she lied as she leaned back against the nearby countertop for support. "How are you doing?"

Maya merely shrugged casually. "I'm fine," she echoed with a knowing smile, which Charlotte knew was probably also a lie. Though their conditions were very different, Maya and Charlotte had a shared sort of kinship that came from living with a body that often failed them. She was uncertain of what exactly had happened to Maya, the sickness that had taken her legs had also left little scars all over her, some of them framing her face. Charlotte sometimes felt discomforted complaining about pain to someone who had obviously lived through so much herself, but Maya always insisted she was happy to listen.

Fortia seemed to have single-handedly loaded the church's pantry with the majority of the food crates from Charlotte's cart. Aurelia had begun chopping onions with Eleni without a word, rolling up the sleeves of her gown as if this were the most normal thing in the world, and she wasn't the heir to the throne. Charlotte had set a pot of water on the stove to boil while Maya was in the process of drafting a new inventory with all the donations, documenting it all with perfect handwriting. The five of them chattered amongst themselves as they worked, preparing what Charlotte gathered to be a butternut squash soup.

"I shouldn't be telling you this," the princess began with a mischievous smirk, glancing around the room as if to see if anyone was eavesdropping. "But just between us… we have some very important visitors arriving in the kingdom tomorrow."

Fortia said nothing, but her eyes shuttered in a dull stare as she peeled potatoes, the skins falling away from the vegetables in complete spirals. Aurelia took no notice, dumping the onions she'd finished in a freshly washed and greased pan.

After a few beats of silence, Charlotte piped up to ask, "Well, don't leave us in suspense, who's visiting?"

The princess' eyes gleamed as she met Charlotte's gaze. "The Valedian council!" she finished excitedly. "They're staying in the embassy – the renovations just finished last week, I'm so excited. I've heard so much about the Valedian king, I wonder if he'd be willing to discuss modern methods of energy conservation with me…"

While Aurelia seemed thrilled at the prospect of meeting the king, Fortia had a vein throbbing in her temple. The potato skins fell away in chunks, rather than the perfect singular peels she had discarded before. Charlotte stifled a laugh as the handmaiden cut in sternly, "Aurelia, this is not something to be discussed outside the castle…"

"If the Valedian council is visiting, does that mean we're due for the accords to be revisited already?" Eleni interjected, her brow furrowing. Her outward appearance was not one that most would associate with a bookworm; with long blonde hair, deep blue eyes, and a tendency towards fine dresses and elaborate jewelry, Eleni fit in seamlessly with the upper-class ladies of Briardeen.

"It's hard to believe ten years have passed already," Charlotte agreed, leaning against the countertop behind her. The rising heat in the kitchens was contributing to her deteriorating state, and she regretted wearing so many layers. "But I think the official anniversary should be later this year, should it not? The war didn't conclude until next month, and the accords weren't finalized until... Goddesses, mid-summer, wasn't it?"

Eleni nodded in agreement. When she glanced towards the princess for further information, Fortia finally snapped. "*No*," she said sternly. "This is not something we are at liberty to discuss."

Aurelia sighed dramatically but did not argue her case. "I can't say," she relented at last, stirring the onions as they cooked. "You are correct, the timing is suspicious, and I must admit I don't know all the details myself. It will certainly be an interesting year."

Her attempts at inventory forgotten, Maya wheeled herself over to join the conversation, her dark eyes wide with curiosity. "I had the most curious dream last night," she noted in an airy tone, fiddling with her long brown hair in the braids Eleni had presumably woven for her. "It's so odd you mention this, because I dreamt that a stranger was arriving at the church."

If she had been about to say more, Fortia interrupted her. "It's bad luck to share dreams," she offered, though Charlotte would not have taken her to be the superstitious type. "Dreams are missives from higher powers."

"You haven't heard the half of it," Eleni teased, glancing over at Maya fondly. "Some of the nightmares

Maya's relayed to me, you'd be starting on the brandy before noon."

Maya flushed darkly, her golden skin taking on a rosy hue. "It wasn't a nightmare, just... just a dream," she insisted quietly, but Charlotte knew the bar for what qualified as a "nightmare" was concerningly high.

The water behind Charlotte had begun to boil, and she had half a mind to interrupt the conversation to ask Maya more about her dream, but at that moment the uncomfortable sensation in her abdomen could be ignored no longer. Her grip on the countertop tightened in vain as she stumbled, her mind shedding all threads of the conversation as it fell into what Charlotte could only describe as survival mode. Her vision was darkening already, an aura of a golden light blocking out much of the kitchen scene. There was a gnawing ache deep inside of her, an acidic pain clawing at her from within...

Her turmoil had not gone unnoticed. "Charlotte?" Maya called to her. Eleni's head snapped up in an instant, and Charlotte could hear her hurried footsteps as the woman rushed over to her.

"Honestly, I... I'm fine," was all Charlotte managed to wheeze out as she felt her legs give out beneath her, her head catching the edge of the countertop as she fell. The last sensation she was aware of was a pair of strong arms cradling her before she slipped away entirely.

CHAPTER

FOUR

DANTE

THE HARBOUR HAD BEEN BROUGHT TO LIFE IN THE TENDER
hours of the morning, before the sun had risen and before
Dante was coherent enough to make out the influx of noise
he was subjected to. He remained curled up in his hiding
place, tucked away amongst the rafters of one of the abandoned cargo ships in the Aethian fleet, discarded
temporarily while it waited for a mechanic team skilled
enough to repair Siathan engines. While entirely unsafe to
fly anywhere, it provided a warm and relatively comfortable
place to sleep in Aethelind's uncomfortable climate.

The Dornkeep port was a feat of engineering motivated
by commerce; the invention of airships had revolutionized
the shipping industry, now capable of exporting goods in
days rather than weeks. Though the technology that made
it possible had been invented in Siatha, it was also something that had been necessitated by Aethelind's unusually
similar circumstances – much to Dante's horror, the

rumours of the kingdom being entirely suspended in the sky were not exaggerated. Ancient mythos spoke of the kingdom being built upon the bones of an old god, but the intricate web of airship machinery built into the underbelly of the floating islands suggested otherwise. Whether through divine blessing or manmade blasphemy, Aethelind existed upon four connected islands floating in the sky, the vast Aethian sea visible far below.

Dante had never been so high above the surface in his life. The adjustment in altitude had been a slow one, and he had felt quite ill for the first week he'd resided here. He had been born and raised in Fraecath, and while Dante was accustomed to the mountains of Vol Ciacci and Monterona, he was ill-prepared for whatever this stone monstrosity was. Aethelind was grim and cold in comparison, and foolishly high up. It seemed like tempting fate, if not the Keepers themselves.

After several long hours, the morning start-up quieted down, and the docks were as close to silent as they could be. The last few ships of the morning had since departed, with the next arrivals not being anticipated for a few hours yet. The dock workers were taking their lunch breaks and the city guard were momentarily relaxed, and Dante looked forward to finally being able to get a few hours extra sleep in before he got up to search for food. He had been sleeping in this grounded ship for a few weeks now, growing smaller and smaller inside an increasingly threadbare coat. Through sheer dumb luck – or perhaps some godly being's idea of a joke – Dante had survived, but he wasn't sure how much longer he could keep going.

He was distracted from his attempts to sleep once more by a sudden commotion on the docks. Somewhere between disgruntled and curious, Dante shifted where he lay amongst the rafters, opening just one eye. He could hear distant shouts from the dock workers, something about an unscheduled arrival… Curiosity got the better of him and, against his usual judgment, Dante was crawling out of the rafters to get a closer look.

As he approached the cargo hold exit, Dante peered around the ship to make sure no one would see him. While it wasn't officially illegal to stowaway on a ship that wasn't going anywhere, he doubted he would be spared on a technicality. Finding the ship blissfully empty, he crept towards the bow to peek over the edge at the docks below, finding a strange confrontation before him.

A great ship had docked nearby, distinctly non-Aethian in its make; Dante possessed limited knowledge of airships, but he thought the construction hinted at Valedian design. *The Veiled Siren* was delicately crafted of polished wood and steel, gleaming in the sunlight. His suspicions were proven correct when the passengers disembarked, the depth of their complexions and elaborate coiled hairstyles confirming their origin.

To his immense surprise, Dante realized this was no mere passenger vessel as the king of Valedia himself exited the airship along with his council. King Fenyang was a giant of a man, towering over many of the dock staff and even his own council members as he made his way from the ship to the harbour, cloaked in furs and ceremonial armour. His council was composed of a group of women, one whom he led on his arm.

Their presence was not appreciated, whether due to their weapons or their country of origin. The dock workers seemed to be forming a blockade amongst a few stray city guards, refusing to let them pass. The king loomed over the lead worker in front of the group, his stance calm but commanding.

"Is something the matter?" King Fenyang asked politely, glancing between them.

The dock worker puffed out his chest, presumably the lead on their shift. "We have no record of your arrival, sir," he said gruffly, gesturing towards the ship. "This is an unregistered aircraft, we weren't expecting you. I'm afraid I can't let you into the city."

Dante frowned. Who would refuse the king? The council seemed to have similar thoughts, as one of the women stepped forward, armed with a spear. While the left side of her head was shaved, the remaining half of her hair was woven into several thick braids secured with metal beads.

"You speak to the King of Valedia, He Who Rises," she snapped, slamming the base of her spear against the pavement beneath them. "You dare to refuse entry? If the king is not permitted into Aethia, his absence alone will violate the accords. You wish to go to war, boy?"

There were several aggravated shouts from the dock worker and the guards, clearly distressed at her words. "Rules is rules, ma'am!" the lead retorted. "The king'll have my head if I let you in without your papers – the Aethian king, that is. Now, return to your ship, or there'll be trouble for you."

The council members were outraged, but the king seemed remarkably calm, merely raising a hand to silence his companions. "Be that as it may, we must enter the city for our peace to continue," King Fenyang offered simply. "You have representatives at your embassy who are aware of our arrival. I have no qualms with waiting here while you fetch one of them."

"That won't be necessary," a new voice called, and Dante searched the crowd in a vain attempt to find the source. After a moment, the dock workers parted to allow a stranger through, his cane tapping rhythmically on the stone as he strolled forward with some difficulty. Almost as tall as the Valedian king himself, the man was finely dressed in a suit of deep emerald brocade, the brim of his hat shielding his face from Dante's view.

"Mr. Melicus," the king greeted him, his tone pleasant. "You're a sight for sore eyes."

The man dipped his head, leaning on his cane. "I apologize for the delay, Your Majesty," said Mr. Melicus, his voice accented in a way that Dante struggled to place. "There was a mix up with our office and your papers were not forwarded to the docks. I hope you'll find everything in order here, lad." He handed a thick wad of paperwork towards the dock worker, who seemed to grapple not to drop the unexpected bundle.

"Of—of course, Mr. Melicus, sir," the man stammered, clearing his throat with a raspy cough. "Apologies, sir. Welcome to Aethelind, Your Majesty." His mannerisms struck Dante as being quite odd. Who was this man that the dock worker treated him with more respect than the Valedian king? He knew Aethia and Pharsat had been at war decades ago, but he hadn't expected tensions to run so high some eighty years later.

Mr. Melicus forced the crowd to disperse, dismissing the dock staff and the city guard. "I do apologize, Your Majesty," he repeated, bowing his head once more. "I'm afraid you've arrived at a perilous time in Aethelind. Please, allow me to escort you to the embassy, we will be able to discuss these matters at our leisure."

"Oi, you there! What do you think you're doing?"

Dante just about jumped out of his skin at the sound, his head spinning around to find the source of the voice. One of the dock workers had returned early from lunch, his face bright red with anger as he pointed towards Dante.

Well, this certainly wasn't what Dante had planned for his morning.

Without a second thought, Dante gripped the railing of the ship and launched himself over the edge, free-falling for a moment before he landed in a rough roll on the dock below. With a chorus of shouts, the dock workers broke into a run to chase him as Dante scampered across the harbour, ducking and diving around crates and barrels stacked haphazardly around him, losing one of his shoes in the process. If he could just get into Caelfall, he might be able to shake them amidst the crowd of civilians.

It had been several weeks since Dante had attempted any sort of movement beyond stalking through the city streets, skulking around after dark, and crawling through cargo ship rafters. At his current pace, he was quickly becoming fatigued; his withered muscles were burning with the exertion as he ran, partially barefoot, through the ship-yards, darting between buildings plastered with advertise-ments for the Aethian military.

HAVE FAITH IN YOUR KING, HAVE FAITH IN YOUR COUNTRY

His lungs heaved as Dante cleared the last of the ware-houses and rainwater reservoirs, the bridge to Caelfall visible ahead of him. "Stowaway! We've got a stowaway!" the dock worker roared as Dante bolted for the bridge to the neighbouring district. He pointed frantically at one of the guards stationed beside the bridge, and Dante didn't have time to panic as the guard broke into a run after him. Trained in the combat academy, the city guard were a formidable foe that Dante could not best in his current condition. The sight of the rifle strapped across the guard's back struck fear into his heart, and he quickened his pace. Running purely off of adrenaline, Dante pounded down the bridge, his feet growing disturbingly numb as he tried not to think about how little ground was beneath him and the body of water miles below.

The echo of a gunshot reverberated through his bones as a sharp pain cracked through his left shoulder. Dante cried out as he faltered, stumbling as he continued to run to the best of his ability. Something warm and wet was quickly dampening the ruined fabric of his shirt, but he didn't have time to investigate as he continued along the bridge, darting in between confused and frightened bystanders. So much for the safety of being surrounded by civilians. Dante would have to rethink his tactics.

With the time it would take to reload the rifle for a second shot, Dante knew he had a limited amount of time to lose his pursuer. The guard's armour clacked together loudly as he chased him into the district of Caelfall, but Dante had snuck across the bridge many times before. While not a local by any means, he had learned enough of the layout here to know that there was an alleyway nearby he could sneak into. He feinted to the left before ducking into the dark, narrow corridor, running as quickly as he could through the tight space. His lungs were burning as Dante launched himself into the street on the other side, pausing for a moment as he decided where best to attempt to hide.

There was a smithy nearby, with a pile of equipment and empty barrels positioned by the entryway. Dante forced his exhausted, aching body forward once more, darting towards the shop and sliding to a halt on the other side of the container. Crouching behind the barrel, he gasped for air as quietly as he could manage, his insides aflame with exhaustion as his entire body seemed to be trembling.

"What the hell are you doing back here?" a voice asked, and Dante almost fainted with shock. His head spun around to the source of the voice, and to his immense horror he saw the blacksmith was home; a red-haired man with soot smeared on his face was frowning at him, a half-finished sword in his scarred hand.

Dante tried to stand, but his body had finally given up; without the spike of adrenaline, his shoulder ached so badly that he was on the verge of losing consciousness, and he knew he was done for. "Please," he begged in a choked whisper, his chest rising and falling in frantic, shallow gasps. "Please, they're—they're looking for me—I need to hide, please, I ... I can pay you."

It was a white lie. Dante hadn't a penny on him, but there were other ways of repaying debts. He prayed to every god he could name while the stranger pondered his offer, eyes narrowed on what Dante could only assume was a fairly pathetic visual. The guard would probably circle back to find him soon, he had mere seconds...

The man gave a long-suffering sigh, as if this were a common occurrence in Caelfall. Maybe it was. "Who is 'they'?" he asked in a low voice, pinching the bridge of his nose.

Dante's heart thudded in his throat. "The guards, they... the dock workers, they caught me on one of the cargo ships," he stammered, knowing how damning his words were. "Please, I can explain everything—"

It seemed the man had heard enough. To Dante's

surprise, the smith lowered the incomplete sword, rummaging through his work apron with his free hand. "Keep your voice down and get upstairs, then," he said gruffly, withdrawing a key from his pocket as he unlocked the door. "Hiding behind a bloody barrel won't do you any good."

Half convinced he'd misheard the man, Dante hesitated for a second before he shot to his feet awkwardly. Pain lanced through him as he limped towards the open door, the smith promptly locking it behind him the moment Dante was safely inside.

The flat opened into a small landing at the foot of a staircase leading up to the main level. Dante collapsed against the stairs as he attempted to make his way up them, struggling with each step. He became aware of the fact that in addition to his shoulder, his bare foot was also bleeding profusely. Hemorrhaging all over his entryway seemed a poor way to repay the stranger for hiding him, Dante thought. As he clambered up each individual step, he became aware of the distant sound of a horse galloping outside.

Curiosity seemed to be determined to get Dante killed today. He glanced back towards the door, a sheer curtained window set into the aged wood giving him a small window into the scene outside. Against his better judgment, Dante leaned back against the wall of the narrow stairwell, watching as the horse slowed to a trot outside the smithy. Much to Dante's horror, he recognized the newcomer as a knight of the royal guard, distinguished by the polished insignia of the majestic dragon upon his armour.

The red-haired blacksmith came into view, leaning casually on the mop he carried. Dante flushed as he realized he had likely left a literal trail of blood, his heart sinking. The knight must have known he would be hiding in here. Was the blacksmith going to turn him in?

"Morning," the smith greeted the knight neutrally as the man dismounted his horse. "You seem a bit rushed."

The knight paused, staring at the smith for a few moments before responding. "Jasper," the knight replied a moment later, nodding his head. "I... have you seen anyone unusual run past?"

The blacksmith, Jasper, snorted in response. "That's a bit vague."

The knight shot him a pleading stare. "Jasper."

"You mean aside from the usual level of unusual folk seen in Caelfall?" the smith asked dryly.

"*Jasper.*"

"Yes, Gideon?"

From inside the stairwell, Dante frowned as the scene unfolded outside. Who was this blacksmith that he was on a first name basis with a knight? Neither seemed to be particularly pleased by this conversation, from what Dante could surmise from their interaction.

The knight called Gideon gave a huff of exasperation. "I'm serious," he sighed, gesturing towards the street. "The Dornkeep guards caught a stowaway amongst one of the cargo ships. They can't be certain, but they advised he was seen running this way."

"Well, they must be mistaken," Jasper insisted. "No one's been around this way. Besides, what does the captain of the royal guard care for stowaways in Caelfall?"

The two of them stood for some time, staring one another down beneath the awning of the blacksmith shop. Dante hadn't breathed for what felt like several minutes. The knight had a piercing blue stare, and for a moment he feared the man might see through the sheer curtain to find Dante hiding within.

"I heard Charlotte was unwell," Gideon replied at last, his voice so quiet that Dante could scarcely hear him. "Heard she'd had a fall in the soup kitchen. I thought I'd come to see if she was all right."

His words seem to unsettle the smith, the man bristling as his grip tightened on the mop in his hands. "She's all right," Jasper confirmed with a slow nod. "I'm afraid you're out of luck if you were hoping for a visit, she's been asleep all morning. I'll tell her you stopped by." He turned back towards the forge, resuming the task of mopping the cobblestones.

"Jasper," Gideon interjected, taking a step forward. "Are you going to avoid me forever?"

The blacksmith paused for a moment. "Yes."

"Jasper—"

"If that's all, Gideon," Jasper interrupted him, turning to face the man once more. "I was preoccupied attending to Charlotte yesterday. I have a backlog of arms requisitions to complete."

Dante couldn't be certain, but it seemed Jasper's words had struck a nerve. Hurt flashed across the knight's expression at the repeated mention of Charlotte, whoever she was. "Very well," he replied stiffly, shaking his head. "Good day, Jasper." He turned on his heel, mounting his horse and leaving without another word on the subject.

Sensing the immediate danger had passed, Dante struggled to drag himself up the remainder of the stairs, but his joints had locked painfully with exhaustion. He wasn't sure how much blood he'd lost, but he was beginning to feel dizzy and weak. This would be an unfortunate way to die, after so much effort spent on staying alive.

There was a scuffling noise from outside as the black-smith wiggled the key in the lock, opening the door once more. Reaching to lock the door again behind him, the smith looked up to find Dante sprawled across the top of the stairs. Dante flinched as he made his way up the steps towards him, but Jasper merely offered his hand.

"You can relax, I've not turned you in," he explained, unaware that Dante knew this from the conversation he had eavesdropped on. "But if you're planning to hide up here, I'd like to at least know your name."

He was taken aback by the kindness in the man's tone, the warmth in those eyes. Several beats passed before he took the blacksmith's hand. "Dante," he said finally. "My name is Dante."

"Pleasure to meet you. I'm Jasper."

The blacksmith hauled Dante to his feet with little effort, startlingly strong as he helped him up the rest of the stairs. The flat was small and cozy, with a shared kitchen and dining area that Dante found himself being led to. Jasper sat him down at one of the worn, mismatched dining chairs as gently as he could manage, but Dante still flinched with pain as his shoulder was aggravated by the movement.

"Thank you," he managed to croak, leaning back against the chair.

Jasper shook his head. "Don't thank me yet," he warned. "We're not out of the woods. The guards have passed by for now, but you're in bad shape, mate. How'd you get so roughed up, anyhow?"

In close proximity, Dante could see the faint freckles on the blacksmith's youthful face, the faded scar on his chin. Eyes the colour of the Aethian Sea were carefully avoiding Dante's gaze as the smith assessed his injuries. There was a peculiarity to his countenance, and Dante found himself at a loss as he struggled to place the blacksmith's origins, his rust-coloured hair at odds with the angular shape of his eyes.

At his silence, the smith's gaze met Dante's for a brief second, as if prompting him to respond. The urge to fabricate some sort of cover story was strong, but fruitless; he had already divulged too much to try and attempt to lie his way out of this now.

"I was... sleeping in one of the cargo ships when I heard some commotion on the docks. I shouldn't have gone to look, it was foolish of me, but I... I was curious. It's not every day you see the Valedian king and his council." He chuckled in spite of himself, cursing every ignored instinct that should have kept him hidden safely. "I've been to Caelfall before, so I tried to flee over the bridge... I was able to get away, but not without the guard on the bridge managing to hit me."

"I can see that," Jasper agreed, raising an eyebrow. "I'd wager you've lost a lot of blood." There was a dip in his voice when he spoke, an accent afflicting his words that wasn't present before.

Dante narrowed his eyes, pressing his hand against the wound in his shoulder as much as possible. "I'll be fine," he insisted stubbornly.

The blacksmith rolled his eyes. "Sure, you're only bleeding. And shivering, even though it's a scorching spring morning. Are you aware you've only got one shoe on?"

Dante resisted the urge to cross his legs to hide his bare foot beneath the chair, as if Jasper had not already seen it. "Look, I appreciate your hospitality..." he began, but the smith was having none of it.

"And my hospitality includes trying to keep you *alive*," Jasper interjected, gesturing towards him. "From both a practical and a compassionate standpoint, it does neither of us any good for you to bleed out in my kitchen. Will you please let me talk you into getting that looked at?"

Pursing his lips, Dante glanced down at the wound in his shoulder. He was at a loss; he knew Jasper was right, and admittedly he was feeling horridly drained. "What would you have me do?" he asked, his voice sounding thin to his ears. "Are there no guards stationed between here and the nearest hospital?"

The man's expression softened at his words. "Not a hospital," he elaborated. "There's a clinic in Caelfall. I'm close with the owner, they get… *stowaways* and the like all the time. They won't turn you in, either."

The prospect of an apostate clinic seemed too good to be true, frankly. It appeared to be the best chance Dante had, but there was another complication. "I believe you," Dante replied, sagging against the chair. "But truthfully, I don't … I don't know if I could make it there, not without bleeding out all over your kitchen floor, as you say. And I may not be so inconspicuous limping through the streets in my condition."

In spite of the situation, Jasper's mouth curved into a smile, his chin dimpling with the expression. "It's a good thing I've got a doctor who makes house calls, then."

In the mere five minutes it took for the doctor to arrive, Dante's condition had deteriorated. Jasper had ended up dragging him over to a dilapidated old sofa, likely for fear of him passing out at the table. He struggled to remain awake in solitude, waiting for Jasper to return. The sound of the front door opening jolted Dante, but it was only the blacksmith – and the promised physician.

"I have to say, I'm mystified that you claim it isn't *you* in need of my services," the doctor remarked dryly from the front door, his words oddly muffled. "Despite your repeated insistence that you are 'fine', whatever that word means to you."

"You're hilarious," Jasper remarked as he led the doctor up into the flat, shaking his head as he re-emerged at the top of the stairwell. "Aside from being tired, I *am* fine."

"For once, I actually believe you," the doctor agreed, stepping into the flat. His auburn hair and his curious golden-brown eyes were all Dante could see of the man; despite the warm weather, the doctor's words had been muffled due to the scarf that had been wrapped multiple times around his face, the tips of his ears just visible over the layers of fabric.

As he began to unwind the ridiculous scarf, he continued, "If you are fine, as you say, I wonder why it is you insisted I come by so urgently. Did you need company?"

Jasper laughed dryly at the remark, shaking his head. "It's a bit of a long story," Jasper began, gesturing towards the sitting area. "I had something of an unexpected visitor, and… well, he was in no condition to walk over to your clinic."

The doctor finally seemed to notice Dante's motionless form where he had been propped up on the loveseat, seemingly with every pillow and cushion Jasper owned. Dante blinked and the doctor was suddenly kneeling beside him, causing him to flinch in alarm. He couldn't stop shivering, even with the blankets draped over him and the towels Jasper had wadded over his still bleeding shoulder.

"It's okay," the doctor insisted, his amber stare intense

in Dante's feverish state. "My name is Haeyin, I'm a medic here in the city. Will you let me see to your wounds?"

Dante's eyes flickered over to Jasper where he stood beside him. The man seemed to sense his apprehension. "Haeyin's saved my life on… multiple occasions," he offered, kneeling at the foot of the couch. "He's a good man."

His reassurance helped. With what little strength he possessed, Dante shifted as much as the layers of blankets would allow, shrugging the towels off of him to reveal the wound on his left shoulder. His foot was already exposed, hanging off the edge of the couch for fear of tracking more blood and dirt into the furniture.

Haeyin didn't so much as flinch at the injury, his eyes scanning the torn flesh with calculating calm. His gaze betrayed him as a seasoned physician, and it was as if his mental process were written plainly on his face. Dante could almost see the way the man visualized the veins and tendons damaged by the bullet wound, assessing the depth of the cuts on the sole of his foot while Jasper began to gently clean the gravel and dirt from the wound.

He took Dante's hand in his own, calloused fingers gently supporting his arm. "Can you move your hand for me, lad?" he asked. Dante wiggled his fingers obediently, which was somewhat painful for him but seemed to please Haeyin greatly. "Good, good… shouldn't be too difficult, then."

The doctor shuffled where he knelt before the couch, settling more comfortably on his knees as he raised a hand above Dante's shoulder. Most alarmingly, his angular eyes began to glow a vibrant yellow, facial veins illuminated with the same light that flooded the man's outstretched palm. Dante jerked away instinctively as much as his current position would allow. "Doctor" was the word Jasper had used, not mage – and there was no trace of the mage's cuffs that Dante had come to associate with Aethian mages. Haeyin was a renegade.

"It's okay," said Jasper nearby, misinterpreting his panic. "He's just trying to help you."

Dante looked at the golden light that emanated from Haeyin's fingertips as if they were poison-tipped arrows. For all the good it did him, they may as well have been. He didn't think Haeyin intended to harm him – no, he *knew* Haeyin didn't intend to harm him, because that magic spoke to him, spoke to the deepest part of his soul that Dante was consciously aware existed.

The doctor's hand glowed brighter still, and his energy connected with Dante. It was as if his shoulder had been exposed to the warm rays of the sun, the waves of energy lapping over his flesh with a steady, rhythmic pulse. Dante was unable to resist, helpless as the warmth permeated deeper into his shoulder, knitting his ruined skin back together.

As the energy coursed deeper and deeper through him, the warmth slowly becoming unbearable, he saw Haeyin's gaze flit away from his wound to meet Dante's eyes, something akin to suspicion colouring his expression. The doctor's face glowed with the magic in his veins, pulsing in time with his heartbeat as his illuminated eyes shuttered. Just as Dante was about to recoil from the all-consuming heat, Haeyin retracted his hand, now blistered along his palm. Wordlessly, he redirected his energy towards Dante's bloodied foot, the familiar waves of warmth brushing over the broken skin.

"Your hand…" he managed to croak out, finding his throat dry.

"Has he burned it again?" Jasper asked, implying this was a normal occurrence. A dutiful doctor indeed to frequently work himself into magical exhaustion, knowing the cost.

"I'm almost finished," said Haeyin, not looking up. Dante wasn't certain who the doctor was trying to reassure with his comment. Just as his foot began to feel more like a brick of charcoal than a foot, Haeyin retracted his magic once more, standing up with a groan. He shook out his hand as if he were merely attempting to stretch out a cramped muscle, and to Dante's horror he saw the burnt skin of the man's palm was in far worse condition than before.

Dante's blatant staring did not go unnoticed. Haeyin offered him a small smile. "It's fine," he assured him.

"It's fine," Jasper repeated with a dull stare at the back of Haeyin's head. Dante had the feeling he was missing out on some sort of private joke, for the doctor had turned to look at Jasper only to laugh quietly when he saw the look on the smith's face.

"I do see how easy it is to resort to that as a response…" he mused. Clearing his throat, he turned his attention back towards Dante. His expression suggested he was at war with himself over what to say, and his golden eyes seemed to pierce Dante's very soul. "You've been patched up, but you still lost a lot of blood. You need rest."

Dante's heart sank. He was in poor condition to return to the way of life he'd adapted to; bed rest and a life dodging guards and dock workers did not go hand in hand.

"He can stay here with me, for now," said Jasper, much to Dante's simultaneous relief and despair. Gesturing towards Haeyin's injured hand, the blacksmith added, "As for you, let me bandage that before you go, please. I owe you that much, for all the times you've patched me up." He offered these gestures as if they meant nothing to him, as if it were merely in his nature to do such things.

Haeyin scoffed. "Don't be ridiculous, Jasper. You don't owe me a thing." Despite his commentary, however, Haeyin did indeed follow Jasper into the kitchen to hold his burned palm beneath the waterspout.

The events of the day had left Dante in shock, partly from wildly running for his life through the shipyard, and partly due to the unexpected hospitality of these two strangers. It was almost uncomfortable in its purity, and Dante had no idea how to repay them for their efforts. Sagging against the pile of cushions and pillows beneath him, Dante was too emotionally and physically drained to remove his clothes, still partially soaked in blood. Would the blacksmith still be so willing to take him under his wing if Dante ruined his furniture?

Though he struggled to remain awake, the exhaustion finally overpowered his anxiety. When at last his eyes closed, heavy with fatigue, it was not that the Soul Keeper had finally come to collect him in death. Instead, it was the blissfully thoughtless way most people fell asleep, safe and warm with a roof above their heads, a luxury Dante had almost forgotten the feeling of.

He was asleep long before Jasper came to check on him, tucking the pile of blankets around him with a gentle nudge.

CHAPTER

FIVE

JASPER

It had been a strange few days, to say the least. Jasper was beginning to think some deity was playing a very elaborate practical joke on him, springing surprise after surprise to see how much he could take.

After he had brought her home, Charlotte had slept for the rest of the day and the following day after. Her medications were a potent concoction that Haeyin tailored for her pain, but the resulting toll on her body was extensive. Jasper's attention was diverted between helping Samuel look after Charlotte in the loft above the bakery and attending to the curious young man named Dante in his own dwelling. He wasn't entirely comfortable leaving a stranger unattended in his apartment alone, but Dante seemed to be too physically weak to run off with his second-hand silverware.

Jasper handled change poorly, and his life had been filled with it as of late. He was noticing himself growing more and more easily irritated, as if his mind was nearing its breaking point by seemingly benign events. Something as simple as shrugging out of his clothes at the end of a long day was nearly enough to drive Jasper into oblivion if he wasn't careful, and he was disturbed by how mindful he had to be with himself not to succumb. Samuel told him he needed more sleep, but even sleep was more difficult for him nowadays. His dreams were plagued with visions of monsters, draconian beasts startling him awake drenched in sweat.

His work kept his mind off his fretting, bending and shaping iron and steel into tools and weapons. Zeke had trained Jasper from a young age in the art of metal-smithing, his large hands seemingly forging weaponry from nothing. His uncle had been a prolific blacksmith in his time; it was said he was a mage of metal, though Jasper knew he and his uncle hadn't possessed a drop of magical blood. Despite Zeke's insistence on living and working in Caelfall – the most forgotten and under-loved of the four districts – he had accumulated a wide variety of contracts for various clients, including the royal militia. Jasper was grateful for the training Zeke had given him, for he had been able to maintain most of those working relationships to keep a roof over his head.

Given that he hadn't received any notice of work from Varus since the night at the brothel, he was especially grateful to still have the smithy.

One afternoon, as Jasper's arms were beginning to grow heavy and his brow was slick with sweat, an unannounced visitor distracted him from his work. Much to his chagrin, a dressed-down Gideon had arrived at his smithy, and Jasper was running out of excuses to avoid the man.

"I come in peace," Gideon began, holding up his arms

in a gesture of surrender. His attire gave no hint to his rank or his lineage; though the captain was Lord Elroy McClelland's only son, he wore a comparatively plain coat over his pristine shirt and dark trousers, his blonde hair tucked back behind his ears.

Sighing, Jasper set aside his almost finished sword atop the dozen he'd already completed. "Afternoon," he said stiffly.

Gideon's expression fell, his arms dropping to his sides. "Jas, you can't avoid me forever," he pleaded. "It's been months and you've barely spoken to me."

Wiping his hands on his trousers, Jasper tried in vain to push his hair back from his face. It was too long, but if he cut it any shorter it would only draw attention to his ears. "I'm hardly avoiding you, Gideon," he fibbed, crossing his arms over his chest. "It's not my fault you rarely visit us down here."

Seeming genuinely hurt by the comment, Gideon mirrored Jasper's stance. "You know the castle doesn't permit much time off for the guards," he protested. "And I... hell, what am I supposed to say? You practically disappeared. You wouldn't even say hello – for weeks, I thought... I thought, maybe you didn't *want* to see me."

Gideon trailed off, and Jasper made no effort to pick up the pieces of the conversation as his gaze drifted towards the dilapidated cobblestones. It wasn't entirely fair for him to continue to avoid the man, but things had become increasingly awkward in the last few months, mainly following Jasper's brief attempts to become a knight.

Once upon a time, it had been all Jasper could dream about. It had been his uncle Zeke's aspiration, before he was crippled in his boyhood and unable to complete the required training. Growing up, Jasper had spent hours play-fighting with Charlotte and Gideon in the city streets, daydreaming and make-believing a world where the three of them went off on gallant expeditions. When Gideon, six years his senior, had successfully been knighted, Jasper had all the more reason to follow in his footsteps, to join him among the ranks and make his late uncle proud…

Things were so very different now; it was hard to reconcile the dreams of their youth and the reality of their adult lives.

"How is Charlotte?" Gideon asked finally, causing Jasper's eyes to snap back up – and therein lay the other aspect of his animosity towards the man, childish as it was. It was impossible not to look at a man like Gideon and not feel an ounce of jealousy. Courageous, chiseled, and handsome, Sir Gideon McClelland was everything that Jasper was not. It seemed fruitless to compete for Charlotte's affections against someone like him.

"She's better," Jasper replied eventually, burying his insecurities with a huff. "Samuel expects she'll be fit to leave the house by tomorrow morning."

Gideon tried to nod casually, but his concern was thinly veiled. Jasper wasn't normally one for subtle facial cues, but Gideon had the very specific tell of frowning so deeply his eyes nearly disappeared beneath his brows. "Well, give her my best."

"You can do that yourself if you visit more often, you know," Jasper pointed out.

His expression softened somewhat. "I miss both of you," he said quietly, and Jasper knew Gideon's words were genuine. Though their allegiances differed somewhat, with Gideon loyal to a crown that Jasper grew increasingly resentful towards, Gideon was a good man. He had never given Jasper a reason to distrust or dislike him, and yet…

"*We* miss you," Jasper replied at last, giving in to the naïve, boyish instinct that missed the other man's companionship. He was tired and irritable, and he couldn't pretend there hadn't been a Gideon-shaped absence in his life those last few months.

Gideon smiled a sort of strange half-smile, the edges of his mouth just barely twitching up at the corners. His gaze drifted towards the freshly finished swords on Jasper's workstation, picking one up from the batch to regard his handiwork. "Zeke would be impressed," he said approvingly. "Fancy sparring? I'm free for the rest of the day."

Jasper's throat tightened at the mention of Zeke, and he cleared his throat. "Sure, but not with these," he said quickly. "Bridge garrison supplies, no doubt they'll dock me if they arrive scratched up."

"Never one to bend the rules," Gideon sighed, placing the sword back on the pile as he went to retrieve one of the older, blunt practice swords that Jasper kept towards the back of the shop. Jasper cringed internally at the statement; Gideon had no idea of the amount of rule-bending Jasper practiced working for Varus Emery, and he didn't plan to tell him any time soon.

Feeling content enough with his progress on the garrison shipment to retire for the day, Jasper closed the smithy for the evening as he and Gideon headed towards one of their old haunts. There was a small clearing south of the smithy and the bakery, a graveyard that lay beneath the watchful stare of an ancient statue. Many of the graves here were so old that the names had been entirely worn away, but the feeling of being observed by the gaze of the undead remained. They were close to the border of Caelfall here, the stone wall separating them from a sheer drop towards the Aethian Sea below.

They started slowly for Jasper's benefit, as it was the first time he had raised a sword in months. The weight of it felt almost familiar to him as he sparred, a half-remembered dream or a memory of another life. His movements were clumsy at first, but even in his prime he could not have bested Gideon. Their shirts discarded as the sun beat down on their backs, Gideon could have passed for a statue hewn from marble, every inch of him muscular and trained to kill. Jasper had raw strength and instincts on his side, but Gideon's fighting style was as smooth and polished as he was.

With the last rays of the sun bathing the untended grass in amber light, Gideon raised his hand to stop. Jasper leaned forward heavily on his knees, his lungs burning with the exertion. He'd thought working for Varus had kept him fairly active, but the months spent without a spot of training had clearly affected more than just his physique. He would have to prioritize building up his endurance again.

"Are you all right, there?" Gideon asked wryly, his concern thinly veiled. Wiping his brow on the back of his hand, he gestured towards Jasper's abdomen, the knotted scar now exposed in his state of undress. "That's new."

Unsure whether Gideon was referring to his gut or the newest scar adorning it, Jasper resisted the urge to look down at himself. "New to you," he insisted. "I've gotten used to it." It was partly true. Had he managed to recover physically from the exercise, Jasper might have had a more alarmed response. As it was, he was still panting. "I could say the same of you."

Gideon's expression grew sombre. "I suppose it's been longer than I thought," he admitted. His own myriad of scars had faded to pale silver, an occupational hazard of being captain of the guard. Retrieving their shirts from the fence, Gideon continued as he tossed Jasper's clothing towards him. "You would have made a fantastic knight, you know."

Whatever good mood Jasper had been in soured at Gideon's platitude. Unable to find the words to respond, he tugged his undershirt over his head, cringing at the unpleasant way the fabric clung to his sweat-soaked skin. Once his head was free, he saw Gideon waited patiently for a reply still, and he could only sigh in exasperation.

"Gideon, please," he returned finally, hating how desperate he sounded. "Please just... just let it go."

"How can I let it go, Jasper?" Gideon demanded, his tone strained. "You're a fine blacksmith, but you could be a master swordsman if you wanted to be! We *need* good men like you, hell – *I* need you. There's—"

He cut off suddenly, his eyes scanning their surroundings in a fearful manner very atypical for Gideon. He leaned in closer, and his eyes were a brighter blue than ever before as he hissed, "I could use someone I trust in the castle. There is—there are darker things afoot than you can imagine, Jas... I have little trust in those around me at present."

His words unsettled Jasper deeply, especially when he was painfully aware he was being dishonest with Gideon. "I thought that was why you became a knight," he said coldly, against his better nature. "Because of your faith in your king."

Gideon sighed, shaking his head. "I—I know," he stammered. "I was... I was wrong, Jasper. I was so wrong, about so much, I—"

A sudden crunching of gravel cut Gideon's words short, and he and Jasper instinctively fell silent as they watched and waited. An old woman approached, hunched with age beneath a worn travelling cloak, guiding herself along with the aid of a gnarled wooden staff. A black cat followed closely at her heels, sniffing curiously as it darted ahead of her. The pair of them wandered past, following the same trail Jasper and Gideon had taken here but continuing along into the graveyard at a snail's pace. Jasper watched and waited for them to be out of earshot, but when he turned back towards Gideon, the other man merely shook his head.

"I shouldn't have said that," he muttered under his breath, so quietly Jasper wasn't certain he'd heard him correctly. "I shouldn't have... I'm sorry, Jasper. There are things I want to say, but this isn't the place for it."

Jasper was thoroughly unsettled. He stared openly at Gideon, the man who – up until very recently – had been the poster child for unwavering faith to the kingdom. Even when Jasper had grown up spouting repeated pessimisms he'd learned from Zeke, Gideon had assured him of his confidence in the king, in the iron fist he ruled Aethelind with. To see his faith so shaken... it was disturbing, albeit comforting.

Naturally, Jasper was immensely curious.

"You could come inside, we could talk there," Jasper suggested quickly, mentally kicking himself when he remembered that Dante was still cooped up in his flat.

Gratefully, Gideon was already shaking his head. "No, I've stayed away too long," he said remorsefully. "I really should be heading back to Briardeen, my father... well, it doesn't matter. Perhaps I will take you up on your offer another time, when Charlotte is feeling better. This is some-thing I'd rather discuss with both of you."

The seriousness of his tone sent a wave of gooseflesh down Jasper's arms. He could only nod weakly as Gideon handed his battered old practice sword back to him, the twilight illuminating the knight's practiced smile.

"Another time, then," Jasper agreed.

By the time Jasper made his way back towards the smithy, the sun had set completely over the horizon, leaving Caelfall cloaked in shadows. On an evening devoid of curfew restrictions, the city was coming to life in the late hour. The bars and brothels left their doorways open wide to illuminate the city streets, echoes of laughter and music bleeding out into the alleyways.

Depositing the practice swords in a container off to the side of the smithy, Jasper felt ill at ease without his routine dead drops. He had caught himself panicking twice this evening that he was late delivering product before remembering the truth. With a sigh and a shake of his head, Jasper let himself into his flat, eager for something to eat after the exhausting sparring session.

To his immense surprise, his guest was awake and wide-eyed at his dining room table. "Jasper—I'm sorry," he stammered, practically swimming in a loaned sweater that was three sizes too large for him. "I thought it was you at the door and—and he wouldn't take no for an answer, he said…"

Jasper's attention drifted towards the silhouette of the man in the sitting room, recognizable by the familiar armour and the brace on his right knee. A rarely unglamoured Varus Emery stared out of the back window overlooking the graveyard beyond, and Jasper knew that the clearing he had been sparring in with Gideon would be visible from that vantage point. How long had his employer been waiting here?

"Sir," Jasper said blankly, his voice betraying his shock. "What are you doing here? I mean... is there something I can do for you?"

Varus turned where he stood, and to Jasper's immense relief he did not seem to be furious with him. No, if anything the man looked to be deeply amused, and Jasper found his face heating in response. Dante looked flustered as well, his mouth opening and closing as if he kept second-guessing what he wanted to say.

"I didn't know you had visitors," Varus mused, crossing his arms over his broad chest. It was the first time Jasper had ever seen him without a coat, and he immediately understood why; beneath Varus' sleeveless black tunic, his brown skin was inked with an intricate map of dark lines and spirals, stretching up along his arms from his elbows to just beneath his shirt collar. Though tattoos weren't neces-sarily frowned upon, they were more commonly associated with the Reinnairlei – an unfavourable affiliation to have in a place like Aethelind.

"It's a long story," Jasper said as he collected himself, shooting a meaningful glance in Dante's direction before the other man could offer a response.

Varus laughed, and the jovial sound was at odds with the intimidating display. "Oh, I'm certain. Haeyin mentioned you had an interesting encounter with a vagrant, I assume this is the very one." Dante shrank back in his seat, but Varus only laughed harder before addressing him. "You should have seen Haeyin that day, he nearly fell out of his chair when Jasper said it wasn't *him* that needed healing," Varus explained, winking in Jasper's direction.

Jasper was perplexed by his employer's cheery

behaviour. "Sir… you're not still angry with me?" he asked, leaning against the wall behind him.

The man shook his head, his expression sobering. "What needed to be discussed has been discussed," Varus offered simply. "I won't berate you further for an accident."

"But you…" Jasper cleared his throat, clenching and unclenching his fist as if to diffuse his anxiety. "I hadn't heard from you since. I thought maybe there was no more work for me."

Smiling crookedly, Varus crossed the room to take a seat beside Dante at the dining room table, which seemed to terrify Dante thoroughly. Jasper hadn't thought it possible for the man to look any more diminutive, but beside his employer Dante looked smaller than Charlotte. Then again, Varus had always been frightening on the best of days.

"Gods, I give you time off to *recover* and you think I'd washed my hands of you?" Varus replied, leaning back in his chair. Considering he'd never been inside Jasper's home, he seemed plenty comfortable here. "There's always work for you with me, Jasper. The number of people I can trust is growing smaller every day."

The back of Jasper's neck prickled at the words, so oddly similar to what Gideon had said earlier. "When do you need me?" he asked, somewhere between grateful he still had a job and worried by the connotation in the phrase.

"You can resume your regular dead drops tomorrow, if you're feeling well enough for it," Varus replied evenly, removing one of the daggers at his belt to examine the blade. Dante looked as if he might faint. Just as Jasper was about to deflate at being demoted back to his old routine, Varus continued, "And then in a month or so, I may have a more specific assignment."

Jasper perked up at the promise of something more exciting than a dead drop, proof that he hadn't completely ruined his chances. "Yes?" he prompted for more details, taking a seat at the table opposite Varus and Dante.

With a glance towards Dante seated beside him, Varus let out a soft chuckle. "Your company has been charming, but these are matters best not discussed outside of my inner circle."

Dante needed no further invitation. He muttered something under his breath about retiring early for the evening, darting away from the table towards the staircase leading to the loft. Jasper stifled a laugh as Varus shook his head, seemingly unable to stop himself from smiling crookedly in return. As he began to speak again, however, his expression grew quite serious.

"I don't suppose you know this, but the Aethian underworld is in a bit of a ... delicate situation, at present," Varus explained, sheathing his knife. "The arrival of the Valedian king has stirred up tensions above ground, but my position in the trade has become perilous with a few rival clans threatening to usurp me in certain territories.

"There will be a meet this summer, on a date that has yet to be determined," he continued, drumming his fingertips against the wooden table as he spoke. "Generally, these progress smoothly, and we fight amongst ourselves for the best pick of the litter, like proper gentlemen. However..."

Jasper blinked. "Do you... do you have doubts this will go smoothly, sir?" he probed tentatively.

Varus smirked, those hellfire eyes twinkling in the dim light of the oil lamps. "Surely I don't need to remind you I am not well liked, even amongst those of my standing," he offered plainly. "It's not that I have doubts it'll go smoothly, it's that I'd be a fool to think it would."

Swallowing thickly, Jasper nodded. "So then… I would be accompanying you?" Jasper guessed. "I don't understand – why *me*?"

He knew, deep down somewhere in the back of his mind, that nobody ever asked *why* Varus Emery requested their assistance, and yet he'd done so twice in less than a month. Questioning his reasons would at best irritate him, at worst result in far greater punishments. But even Jasper was not so inept at social graces that he could not sense that something had shifted for the better in the relationship with his employer. Perhaps it had something to do with carrying Jasper's half-dead body through the streets.

Luckily for Jasper, he appeared to have read someone correctly for once. The man's eyes crinkled at the corners as his smile deepened, though the set of his jaw remained tense. "What I am about to tell you, you do not repeat to anyone, aye?" he said sternly. When Jasper nodded gravely, he continued, "I need you at my side – at my *left* side – because I can't see a damned thing out of this eye."

Jasper blinked in surprise, scanning Varus' expression as the man pointed towards the left side of his face. There was nothing about his outward appearance that could confirm what he'd suggested; his eyes seemed perfectly identical, with no indication of any sort of visual impairment. For half a moment, Jasper focused his vision, as if he might peel through a glamour — but Varus was waiting for a response, his dark gaze fixed intently upon him.

Chewing his lip, Jasper nodded slowly. "So… I become an extension of your vision, in a sense."

"Exactly. Normally Haeyin, Cary, or even Nadine would take up that position, but… well, they have other responsibilities, unfortunately. And you are the only other person on this gods-forsaken bit of rock that I trust with this weakness."

Jasper opened his mouth to speak, to insist that Varus was one of the deadliest people he knew whether he had two good eyes or one, but his words failed him as he processed the rest of what his employer had said. Varus waited patiently in silence as Jasper shuffled through the noise between his ears, trying to sort his thoughts into a sentence.

"You trust me enough for this? After what happened last time?" he stammered.

Varus leaned back in his chair. "I saw you outside, you know," he offered thoughtfully, brushing his hair back from his face. "You fight well with a sword. You never mentioned having that in your repertoire."

Jasper flushed darker still, wishing he could shrink. "I prefer hand-to-hand, generally," he said quietly.

"You fight so well, in fact, that I might have been convinced you'd been professionally instructed," his employer continued knowingly. When Varus' dark eyes bored into his own, Jasper was forced to look away. "What's a chap like you doing working for me when you can fight like that? I recognize that lad you fought, he's the bloody captain of the guard. If I had to guess, you'd been trained similarly."

His gaze fixed at the table, Jasper shook his head. "Ancient history," he croaked, hoping his employer wouldn't press for details.

Varus was silent for a moment, the weight of his gaze heavy on Jasper's face for a little longer before he at last stood from the table, grunting slightly with the effort. "It's none of my business," he said at last, crossing the room to retrieve his coat from where he had hung it loosely over the banister of the stairwell. "In truth, it really doesn't matter where you come from, Jasper. What matters to me is that if you can fight like that with a practice sword in a field, I could really use someone like you at my side at the meet."

Burying the sinking feeling of shame that lingered in his gut, Jasper finally lifted his head to meet his employer's gaze. True to his word, there was no inkling of judgment in the man's dark eyes. If anything, Varus' gaze was painfully neutral, with only the faintest glimmer of that curious amusement in the corner of his mouth as he smiled crookedly. Perhaps it was that strange warmth that fanned in Jasper's chest, perhaps it was his desire to prove himself after having been reminded of his failure, he couldn't be certain – but in the end, Jasper found himself nodding in agreement.

"Of course, I'll do it," he said at last.

Varus' smile widened. "Excellent," he said approvingly. "I'll let you know when the lot of them have decided on a proper date." With a flourish, he tugged on his travelling coat, pausing to add, "And you can let that charming young man upstairs know that if he's looking for work, I may just have a position opening for him."

Without another word, Varus melted away into the shadows. Groaning, Jasper dragged his hands down his face, his appetite forgotten. His muscles were beginning to ache from sparring with Gideon, and even though there was time before the meet, he was dreading what protecting Varus would entail. Gangsters were not kind to their enemies.

The stairs creaked nearby as an ashen Dante crept back down from the loft. "Is it safe?" he asked timidly, his dark eyes wide.

"As safe as it gets in Caelfall," Jasper muttered as he

made his way towards his living room. "How much of that did you overhear?"

Dante shook his head too vigorously. "None of it," he insisted, waving his hands frantically. After a moment's pause, he amended, "Some of it. It didn't make a lot of sense to me. Who was that man? I'm sure I saw him at the harbour the other day."

Flopping down on the weary old sofa nearby, Jasper groaned as he sank into the plush fabric. "You probably did," Jasper agreed, closing his eyes. "He's... an entrepreneur."

The couch protested as Dante took the cushion beside him. "Was he being serious?" Dante asked tentatively. "About... about having work for me?"

Jasper's eyes snapped open. Moving as little as possible, he craned his neck around from his limp position on the sofa to stare openly at Dante. The man's condition had improved significantly since recovering from the gunshot wound to his shoulder the other day. Despite being too pale and too thin, Dante was beginning to look less like he had one foot in the grave and more like a living, breathing person. Jasper hated the thought of putting him in a position that might change that.

"I imagine so," he confirmed hesitantly. The ghost of hope in Dante's eyes was concerning. "I should warn you, his work is... difficult. And not necessarily legal. And possibly even a bit dangerous."

Dante gave him a wide, dimpled grin that brought even more life to his olive skin. "If you've forgotten, I was living in a cargo ship for about a month. I don't mind dangerous as long as it pays well... besides, I don't want to take advantage of your hospitality forever."

He managed to chuckle in response, even as his cheeks

flushed. "Yes, because you're absolutely eating me out of house and home," Jasper noted dryly, rolling his eyes. "You're not taking advantage of my hospitality, you're recovering. There's a difference."

Now it was Dante's turn to blush, his cheeks darkening as he hugged his knees to his chest, as if he could make himself smaller still. "Even so... it would be nice to have some form of employment." Shuffling where he sat, he added quietly, "Now, if you wouldn't mind, I would like to get some rest. You're in my spot."

Jasper grunted. "You can take the bed. I'm not sure I could get up if I wanted to."

Dante made a spluttering noise that sounded roughly as if he might have choked on his own words. "But—I couldn't, that would be *really* taking advantage of your hospitality."

"Are you planning on carrying me up the stairs? I don't think you could even if you wanted to. Besides, when was the last time you slept in a bed?"

It grew very quiet for a few moments. When Dante spoke up at last, he said softly, "Are you... are you sure you don't mind?"

Jasper nodded as much as his neck would allow with him leaning against the sofa. "Go now before I change my mind," he threatened teasingly, smirking as he closed his eyes. As he heard Dante slowly climb off the sofa, making his way towards the loft, Jasper felt the events of the day beginning to catch up with him. It felt as if his form weighed a thousand pounds, the exertion of forging blades and sparring with Gideon beginning to settle into his weary muscles. Jasper was out before he heard the last step of the staircase creak.

CHAPTER
SIX
DANTE

HAVING BEEN APPREHENSIVE WHEN JASPER HAD MENTIONED
potentially unsavoury work, Dante had been pleasantly
surprised by the offer that had been made. While it seemed
Jasper was cut out for more intensive physical labour, the
position offered to Dante was much more in line with his
current capabilities as he recovered. The Valedian embassy
was in dire need of staff, having been forced to accommodate King Fenyang and his council earlier than anticipated.
How Jasper had connections with the people who ran the
embassy, Dante hadn't a clue – but he wasn't about to look
a gift horse in the mouth.

Grateful for an opportunity that might allow him to find
his footing in this unforgiving kingdom, he had scrubbed
every inch of himself, determined to make a good impression. Despite his blacksmith host's best efforts to lend him
the smallest clothing he owned, Dante still had to roll the
sleeves of his burgundy shirt repeatedly in order to main-

tain use of his hands, a belt securing his trousers around his worryingly narrow waist. Perhaps his first paycheque would be put towards new clothing.

He was collected from Jasper's flat by the strange man who had visited the blacksmith's home the night before, in attire Dante recognized. Unlike the armour from yesterday evening, the man was clothed in a maroon three-piece suit with a matching top hat. Leaning leisurely on an oiled wooden cane outside a sheltered carriage, he looked extremely out of place in Caelfall. Dante immediately felt underdressed.

The man removed his top hat, bowing slightly towards Dante. "Good morning, lad," he greeted him. "I'll be escorting you to the embassy."

Dante stiffened at the formal greeting, unsure of how to proceed. He turned towards Jasper, hoping for some sort of social cue, but Jasper seemed equally perplexed. "Good luck," he offered Dante, eventually tearing his eyes away from the well-dressed man. "You're welcome back here any time."

Feeling his face heat at the sentiment, Dante mumbled a goodbye as he made to clamber into the carriage. He owed Jasper for his hospitality, and despite the smith's insistence otherwise, he couldn't stand to be a burden on a friend's shoulders.

The well-dressed man climbed into the carriage after him with some difficulty, owing to what Dante assumed was a bad knee. The carriage door shut behind him seemingly by itself, and the man signalled to the driver by knocking twice against the wall behind him. A few moments later, the carriage was moving towards Briardeen, leaving Caelfall and Jasper's smithy behind them.

"We haven't been properly introduced, Dante," the stranger began, breaking the silence.

Dante shifted in his seat, feeling uncomfortable with the cramped proximity. He was momentarily unsettled by the fact that the man knew his name – but then, Jasper must have said something. "You're Mr. Melicus, aren't you?" he replied, recalling the scene in Dornkeep, the almost reverence the dock workers had shown the man. He wanted to be on equal footing with the stranger, not suffering an imbalance of knowledge.

There was a curious gleam in his eyes, and the man chuckled in response. "You may call me Eodan," he offered, leaning on his cane idly as he regarded Dante. "You're... familiar with me?"

He wasn't keen on revealing how exactly he had heard the man's name, and Jasper hadn't once mentioned it at all yesterday evening. "In a sense," Dante offered evasively. "Jasper described you as an entrepreneur."

The corner of Eodan's mouth tilted into a smirk, as if laughing at some private joke. "I don't deserve half the respect that lad holds for me," he quipped with a sigh. "But yes, one might call me that. I invest in things I believe to be worthwhile, one of which being the embassy."

Dante schooled his expression as he listened to Eodan speak, mentally noting as many details as he could. He was no closer to identifying the man's curious accent than he had been at the harbour, and his outward appearance betrayed no secrets either. His attire was painfully Aethian, but beyond that Dante was mystified. With his ink-black hair and dark eyes, Eodan might have hailed from Siatha... but his intimidating height and russet skin suggested Valedian origin.

His analysis had not gone unnoticed, it seemed. While

Dante leaned back in his seat, he had the uncomfortable feeling that he wasn't the only one making assumptions. "What else do you know about me?" Eodan asked neutrally.

It was a deceptively benign question, but a similarly harmless answer would be difficult. Most of Dante's knowledge of the man came from eavesdropping, a fact he was not keen on revealing. "Not much, other than what Jasper's told me," he replied. The best lies were borne from half-truths. "He had warned me off working for you when I'd first showed an interest. Said something to the effect of danger and dubious legality."

His dry remark had succeeded in making Eodan laugh, but he was distinctly aware he was not out of the woods. "Honest to a fault, that one. And that wasn't cause for alarm?"

Dante shrugged his shoulders casually, glancing outside the carriage window for an excuse to look away. They were crossing over the first bridge towards Aerindale now, the gauzy interior curtain concealing them from view of the pedestrians walking alongside them. Eodan had fallen silent, and as the quiet stretched on, Dante fell ill at ease.

"You know… Jasper calls me many things, but he doesn't call me 'Mr. Melicus'," Eodan pointed out thoughtfully. "I saw you at the harbour the other day, didn't I? When the Valedian king arrived, you were aboard that old cargo freighter."

This information had been delivered casually, and yet Dante felt his heart stutter in his chest. It meant nothing, him knowing this detail. Before he could interject, Eodan shook his head.

"Don't fret, I'm not about to turn you in," the man

insisted, crossing his legs. "Rather, I think your specific skillset will be invaluable in the days to come."

Dante waved idly at the air, as if he might hurry Eodan along. "And that would be... what, exactly?" prompted Dante. The man's knowledge of his vantage point during the event set his teeth on edge, and he didn't enjoy feeling he was at a disadvantage. He knew there was no point in Eodan mentioning this without motive, whatever it was.

Removing his top hat, Eodan regarded it carefully before picking a speck of dust from the brim, discarding it on the floor of the carriage. "If you were close enough to hear my name, then you probably had a grand seat for viewing the confrontation that preceded my arrival," Eodan explained simply, placing the hat firmly back on his head as he leaned back in the carriage seat. "Relations between Aethia and Pharsat are strained on a good day, and King Fenyang arriving ahead of the accords' anniversary has done little to set them at ease. The Aethian king is ill-tempered at the best of times, so I doubt this will have improved his mood very much."

Pursing his lips, Dante mirrored the other man's posture as if he might place as much distance as possible between the two of them. "I am aware of the tensions, yes," he agreed dryly, rolling his shoulders. His injury had healed, but the muscles remained tense with anticipation long after the incident at the docks. "I was immensely curious as to why the dock workers held greater respect for you than towards a monarch from a neighbouring nation. The war explains the animosity towards King Fenyang, but it doesn't answer for their reverence of you – especially if you supposedly run the embassy of a country they're intent on despising."

Eodan gave him a wry, crooked smile. "You haven't

asked the question, but you've laid the groundwork. Why don't you just say it?"

Good, he was content to be direct. "Who are you, Eodan?" Dante asked, his voice carefully even as he held the man's stare.

He chuckled darkly in response before falling silent, regarding Dante with a shrewd expression. His dark eyes were unlike any that Dante had ever encountered, seeming to shift from a dark olive green to a yellow-gold hazel, before settling into the black of a moonless night. After what seemed like an eternity, Eodan finally spoke.

"The freighter you'd been hiding on had been docked for quite a while," Eodan mused, idly regarding the wood grain on his cane. "When I checked the ship's records, it had last stopped in Vol Ciacci some weeks ago before failing the maintenance check in Aethelind, where it has remained grounded ever since."

Dante's heart thudded in his throat, but he struggled to keep his tone flippant and casual. "Is this a noteworthy observation? I don't understand why you're so curious." It meant nothing.

He regretted speaking when Eodan leaned closer, smiling in a way that was more menacing than before. "I'm curious because it's not every day you find a young Fraecathan man hiding in the shipyards, lad. If it weren't for your tendency to gesture with your hands as you speak, it was your port of origin that gave you away. Judging by your nationality, your ability to remain hidden for extended periods of time, an evidently high pain tolerance, and you being exceptionally light on your feet..."

Trailing off, Eodan leaned back once more, as if permitting Dante to breathe in the reduced proximity.

"Who am I, Dante? Perhaps the better question is – who are you?"

His blood stilled in his veins. Dante weighed his options as he sat in the anxious, charged atmosphere of the carriage. If he took a chance and leapt out of the wagon now, he had absolutely no idea where they were at present. The guards may very well still be looking for a man fitting his description, and Jasper would be too far away to assist him. His heart hammered in his throat with the urge to hide, to run, to do anything other than exist inside of this carriage with this man.

"I'm not trying to frighten you," Eodan interrupted his train of thought, as if he knew exactly how frightened Dante was. "The truth is, it matters little to me who you are. No one is anyone here in Aethelind – look at the Valedian king, a hero to his people, yet treated like scum by the working-class citizens of Dornkeep."

Dante's voice sounded thin and weak to his ears when he spoke. "Why mention any of this?" he asked irritably, his hand pausing halfway through an exasperated gesture.

"To ensure you understand not to fuck with me," Eodan remarked smoothly, and those words set Dante's teeth on edge more than the suggestion that the man might know who he was. "Jasper trusts you, and I trust Jasper's judgment, but he has *worked* to earn that. Please, do not make accusations you don't understand. We hold the same allegiances."

Dante opened his mouth to speak, but something in his vision flickered. His attention was drawn to what appeared to be an illusion, a glamour frayed at the seams. For a moment, Dante permitted his senses to trickle forward, past the barriers he kept around his mind… only to collide with a wall of stone.

"GET OUT OF MY HEAD."

He recoiled at the barest hint of Eodan Melicus that had emanated from behind that impenetrable shield, at the retaliation he had not anticipated. There was something grim and cold that Dante couldn't name, couldn't fathom, as if he spoke not to a man but to the darkness at the depths of the ocean.

Fair enough. "You've made your point quite clearly," Dante spoke at last, withdrawing his senses with a snap. "What is it you want from me, then?"

With a sigh, Eodan adjusted his position on the carriage seat, extending his bad leg as much as the cramped space would allow without touching Dante. "You're going to be working as staff for the embassy on a surface level only," he began, his gaze falling to his hands. "The king has arrived for his own purposes besides the accords, reasons I will let him explain to you directly. He is aware of how much turmoil Aethelind is in at present, and the embassy has been recently... *upgraded* to ensure his safety."

Dante frowned, searching the man's face for the words he would not say. "You're preparing for the worst, I take it," he noted plainly.

"I would be a fool not to," Eodan insisted. "Your true position is to become an extension of King Fenyang's council – whether that means defending him with your life or assisting with the accords, I expect you to do it."

As the carriage door opened, Dante struggled to swallow with a throat that had become increasingly dry. It shouldn't have been a difficult request – what was his life worth now, anyway? "If you'll permit my curiosity, I have one question," Dante said quickly, sensing the end of the conversation. "With how much animosity Aethians hold for the Valedian king, as you say... why is it you're so keen to ally with him? To devote so many resources to protecting him?"

Eodan chuckled darkly under his breath, leaning on his cane as he exited the compartment. Turning his face to the wind as he adjusted his hat, he called behind him in response, "My dear boy, do I look Aethian to you?"

The Valedian embassy had been redesigned with its occupants in mind, furnished with what Dante could only assume were comforts from home. The stone floors and wooden panelled walls were distinctly Aethian in design, but the furnishings were ornately carved wood of Valedian make, the plush shag carpets and artfully preserved animal furs arranged meticulously across the floors as if to cover as much of the cold stone as possible. There were trinkets and talismans hanging from each threshold, Dante noticed, all of them turned to face the west.

As Dante struggled to recall their purpose in Valedian culture, the talismans shuddered precariously. In the distance, he could hear an argument taking place in a room down the hall, where the crackling of a fire undercut the bickering voices. He turned towards Eodan, not wanting to venture without permission.

Beside him, Eodan paused in his removal of his top hat and his jacket, his eyes glazing over in a way that suggested this was not the first time such an argument had occurred. The man muttered something inaudible before stalking into the room, with Dante following along behind him with no small measure of trepidation.

The lounge that Dante beheld at the end of the hallway appeared to be quite crowded, with King Fenyang and the entirety of his council within. The king was relaxing rather casually over the loveseat nearest to the fire, one of his council members sprawled beside him in a manner intimate enough that Dante felt the need to avert his eyes. The two older women amongst the council members were seated nearest the window overlooking the front of the embassy gates and the district streets beyond, sipping delicately from cups of spiced tea.

One of the council members was in a heated discussion with a woman that appeared to be one of the embassy's staff. He recognized the woman in question from the dock, her thick braids scraped back from her face with a sturdy leather band, the silver charms clinking together with each angry gesture she made.

"I meant no disrespect, my lady," the embassy staff member insisted in a tone that implied otherwise. Her back was turned to the hallway, and she hadn't yet noticed Dante and Eodan's arrival. "Mr. Melicus is a strange man to be certain, but I assure you that your dislike of him is misplaced."

"A strange man!" Eodan echoed in amusement. "Is this how my employees speak of me when I'm not here?"

The poor woman seemed to suffer a heart attack at his presence, spinning so severely she stumbled. "A—apologies, sir, I—I..." she stammered in response, but Eodan interrupted her with a gentle hand on her shoulder, shaking his head with a breathy laugh. He dismissed her with a nod towards the hallway behind them, and the woman fled after a rushed curtsy.

The council member with the beaded hair turned sharply to meet Eodan's gaze, her amber eyes darkening with recognition. "*I* called you strange," the Valedian warrior corrected. As her hawkish stare darted towards

Dante, he barely resisted the urge to cower at the intensity. She was taller than any woman Dante had met before, almost matching Eodan's intimidating stature. Her assessment of him completed, she directed her wrath towards his employer once more.

"You sequestered us within this embassy without so much as an explanation, alluding to vague issues of tension in this miserable place," she spat accusingly as she jabbed a finger in Eodan's direction. "We demand answers."

Though she claimed to speak for everyone, Dante noticed the council's attentions seemed divided. The elderly women seemed to be deeply invested in whatever they saw outside, pretending not to notice the conversation happening around them. The king watched on in amusement as the woman draped over him whispered something in his ear, his watchful stare sliding past Dante before he spoke.

"Benkaei, let the man breathe a moment," King Fenyang chided his council member. Even without the bulk of his armour or his furs, Dante was in awe at the sheer size of him, this mountain of a human being. "I trust Eodan, and that should be enough for you for now."

Eodan bowed his head gratefully in the king's direction. "I understand your frustrations, truly," he assured them, his tone firm but respectful. "My priority has always been your protection."

There was a prickle against his mental walls, and Dante became aware of the heavy undercurrent of magic in the room. His eyes darted between the council members, struggling to identify the source. Though he could detect a trickle of energy from the older of the two crones sitting by the window, it was the woman seated beside King Fenyang that had tentatively brushed against the shield around his mind. She might be considered beautiful, Dante thought to himself. Her dark, wavy curls framed a fair and freckled face, and her eyes were the colour of coffee – eyes that seemed strangely unfocused as she stared through him.

As if alerted by an unseen signal, the warrior named Benkaei turned towards Dante once more. "And who is this?" she questioned, glancing him up and down.

"A new staff member for the embassy," Eodan offered before Dante could stammer out a response, glancing towards him briefly before continuing. "With what information you were able to provide me, I believe he may be able to assist with your… predicament. He comes highly recommended by an associate of mine."

After the alarming confrontation in the carriage, Dante was uncertain how to respond to what seemed to be a *compliment*. "A pleasure to meet you all," he stammered awkwardly, bowing towards them.

Benkaei's stance had relaxed somewhat at Eodan's words, but her expression remained guarded. To his surprise, she bowed her head quickly towards Dante before continuing. "Is he aware of the 'predicament'?" she asked Eodan, crossing her arms over her chest.

Shaking his head, Eodan leaned against the wall, and Dante noted his cane had been forgotten by the front door. "I thought it more appropriate that you be the ones to explain it, considering the circumstances," he offered neutrally. Benkaei raised an eyebrow, nodding slowly.

Despite Eodan's invitation, there was a terse moment of silence. The council glanced back and forth amongst themselves behind Benkaei, none of them daring to speak first. After several moments, the Valedian king gently patted the woman beside him on her arm, signalling for her to shift as he rose from the armchair to his full height.

"Pharsat is currently suffering one of the worst droughts in our history," King Fenyang explained as he stood beside Benkaei, exchanging a concerned look with the warrior. "Normally, a drought isn't such a cause for concern... our people have studied the desert long enough to know when to stockpile, when to rest and recover."

The king paused as he glanced towards the eldest of the two women seated beside the window, a weary-eyed old woman in robes of pale lilac, with coarse, wiry hair as white as snow. A similarly white line had been painted from her bottom lip to the base of her throat, and Dante vaguely recognized the mark of a master healer, a rarity in Pharsat. "This drought has lasted longer than any before it," the crone supplied in a husky, even voice. "At first, we thought perhaps our calculations had been incorrect, that we had misinterpreted the signs and that our dry season was merely beginning later than expected... but it has been many months still, and our way of life is in danger."

"The effects of this drought will be deadly if we do not have some means of sustaining our people," King Fenyang continued gravely. "The accords demand an equal give and take, but Pharsat cannot sustain our side of the bargain when our people live on rationed supplies. Those of us who survive starvation are at risk of contracting the sand fever."

At the mention of the unique airborne malady, Dante shivered involuntarily. He had heard accounts of the sand fever, a plague that had haunted the children of the southern deserts for generations. Curiously, there was no modern medicine that had been found to treat it, and even magic was ineffective beyond surface level pain relief. The only thing to be done was to wait and pray that the children who contracted it were strong enough to survive, as King Fenyang himself had once been.

"I am truly sorry to hear that," Eodan replied, and something in the roughness of his voice told Dante that his empathy was genuine. "I had heard of the drought, but I admit I had no idea it was that severe."

After exchanging a terse glance with her king, Benkaei spoke up. "There's more. This drought is... unnatural. Some say it is a higher power that condemns us to death, but we have reason to believe otherwise."

King Fenyang glanced to the council member still seated in the loveseat behind him. "Huda?" he prompted her in a gentle voice.

Shifting where she sat, the woman named Huda turned her head towards Dante and Eodan's approximate location. "There is magic involved," the woman admitted quietly, her voice soft and sweet. "I have smelled it on the air, tasted it in the water. Something or someone is manipulating the weather."

"It speaks to you," Dante agreed grimly. As each person in the room turned to stare at him, his heart hammered in his chest. "It has—magic has a signature of a sort, right? Almost as if the person who cast the spell signed their name on their work."

Eodan raised an eyebrow in what might have been approval. Huda beamed at the affirming remark, clasping her hands excitedly. "Yes, that's exactly it," she enthused. "That's how I know this drought is magic-borne!"

"We don't *know*," the white-haired healer insisted, but doubt rested in the lines around her eyes. "But we suspect."

"This is a heavy accusation," Eodan warned, but his concern seemed less with the veracity of the claim and more directed towards their environment. "You will be hard-pressed to prove such a thing."

"Proving it for ourselves will be simple enough," King

Fenyang insisted, reaching back towards the loveseat to brush his fingers against Huda's forearm. "Huda and Verdis tell me that they will be able to recognize this magic should they come into contact with it again. Proving this to King Gustaf, however…"

Dante resisted the urge to raise his hand for permission to speak, waiting for a break in the discussion to interject without interrupting anyone. "You could… you could file for an investigation for a contravention of the mage laws," he found himself blurting out. As he felt the weight of several sets of eyes staring at him, Eodan included, Dante cleared his throat loudly. "It would be classified as—as an unlawful magical act, committed in bad faith for political gain. It was the argument made in Empress Farida's favour, during the trial for the… I think the twenty-fourth attempt at contesting her rule."

"Aethelind's courts will not follow the same laws as those in Siatha," Benkaei cut in, but her expression was curious.

Nodding quickly in agreement, Dante gestured towards Benkaei before mentally cursing the instinctive movement. "No, but the mage laws are not unique to Aethelind," Dante explained quickly. "The mage laws are international, they're as valid in Aethia as they are in Castavar."

A slow smile spread across the king's face as he regarded Dante. Taking a step closer, he asked, "What did you say your name was?"

I didn't, Dante realized, mortified. Somewhere, he could sense his mother cringing with embarrassment on his behalf. "Dante, Your Majesty," he introduced himself, bowing again.

"Dante," King Fenyang repeated, and something about

hearing the name in that Pharasathi accent nearly made Dante shudder. "You're certain we can pursue this?"

"I think so—*yes*," Dante corrected himself quickly, glancing towards Eodan to ensure he wasn't overstepping. "I would... I would have to read more into the specifics of the case, but I do remember the verdict. The courts ruled in the Empress' favour after an investigation determined a mage had been tampering with her memory."

The healer stood up from her seat beside the window, careful not to spill her tea. "We are still rushing forward with the assumption that this is indeed a drought of Aethelind's doing," Verdis warned with a stern voice. "Even if we can prove this..."

The woman beside her steadied the contrite healer as she stood as well, her short hair a steel grey. "One thing at a time, Mother," she interrupted with a gentle tone. "My son does not approach anything with haste, certainly not this."

As if amused by this remark, King Fenyang chuckled under his breath. "First, we seek the evidence we require when we meet with King Gustaf and his council," he decided, addressing everyone in the room. "Once we can confirm our suspicions... we can determine how best to proceed."

∾ ☀ ∾

When the council dispersed from the sitting room, Eodan gave Dante an informal tour of the embassy – and the various secret passageways and traps that had been installed. Dante was only mildly alarmed as he was led through the massive building, with his employer announcing the first floor kitchens and dining rooms. As they proceeded upstairs towards the second level, Dante half-expected to be shown his accommodations when presented with the servants' quarters. Instead, Eodan was leading him up to the third level, towards the first door on the right.

"The library has two entrances, one on the second floor and one on the third," Eodan explained as they entered the vast room, gesturing to the ornate wooden bookshelves. "The third floor has more desk and office spaces, which may be more useful to you while you're here."

Taking in his surroundings, Dante was filled with a childish sort of glee. There were shelves upon shelves of books, crammed with tomes of every size, shape and colour. The third floor entrance opened onto a balcony, and Dante could see the lower level of the library beneath them, staff members shelving assorted books below. The long, intricate windows on the far wall bathed the library in a dim glow, illuminating the fine dust that accumulated in the air wherever old books were kept. He hadn't seen a library so vast and so rich since…

His heart sinking, Dante took in the scent of old books, a scent that made him feel terribly homesick. He hadn't realized how much he'd missed it until now.

"How many books are kept here?" he found himself asking, an entirely inconsequential matter.

"I don't keep count," Eodan admitted, rubbing the back of his neck. The collar of his shirt just barely concealed the tattoos that Dante had spotted the night the man had visited Jasper. "I acquired a great many books over the years, salvaged from public libraries before they could be destroyed or sold for a profit. I can't keep them all at home, so I donated them here."

Dante wasn't sure what to say in response, somewhat surprised to have discovered that Eodan was a bookworm.

His thoughts were interrupted by a noise nearby, startling Dante out of his reverie. "Hello," a woman's small voice spoke up from one of the desks nearby. She appeared to be another of the king's council members, her rich and colourful silk attire setting her apart from the embassy staff.

"My name is Akila. It is an honour to work with you," she said earnestly. Dante tensed up instinctively as she bowed towards him, but he was slowly becoming accustomed to what appeared to be a normal Valedian greeting.

"The honour is mine," he half-mumbled in response, still a bit flustered.

As if sensing that Dante was very close to passing out on the spot, Eodan cleared his throat. "Let me show you to your quarters," he said, reaching forward to place a firm hand on Dante's shoulder. "There'll be plenty of time to hit the books later."

Akila beamed, nodding in response. "Of course," she agreed brightly. "The books won't be going anywhere."

Dante laughed weakly in response, waving goodbye as he was steered out of the library back towards the hallway. He made towards the staircase, intending to seek out the servant's quarters on the second floor, but Eodan redirected him towards a door to the left of the library. "Sir...?" he trailed off in confusion.

"This room is a spare," he offered by way of explanation. "The king insisted on having Huda share his own bedchambers, so you may as well take this one."

Dante was about to protest, but as Eodan opened the door to the room, he momentarily forgot what he was about to say. The room was roughly the size as the main floor of Jasper's flat, with a large, plush bed and white cowhide rug. From what Dante could tell, the room had been designed with a woman in mind, a large wardrobe and a vanity sitting adjacent to one another on the opposite wall. A padded bench sat beneath the bay window on the far side of the room, with a door leading to what might have been an ensuite bathroom.

Clearing his throat again, Eodan closed the door behind them. "For your first day on the job, I'd say you've outdone yourself," he offered, scratching idly at the side of his neck. "Huda quite enjoyed your remarks on magic having a trace, I expect."

The memory of his outbursts in the sitting room caused him to flush again, mortified anew. "I'm so sorry, sir, I don't know what came over me, I just—I just blurted it out, I couldn't help myself," Dante rambled along, gesturing wildly as he began to pace across the bed chamber.

"Dante," Eodan said sharply. When Dante turned to face him, there was a small, kind smile on the man's face. "I appreciate what you said."

He stared in naked shock. "I... I thought you'd brought me in here to threaten me again," he replied honestly.

Eodan blinked once before bursting into laughter, and Dante found himself even more startled than he had been before. "I suppose I owe you an apology," he sighed, shaking his head. "I'm sorry our introduction was so tense. I hope you can forgive how guarded I am with strangers, with the existence I lead. Perhaps now you understand what I meant, when I said I required your skillset."

Feeling his face heat, Dante turned away once more. He was wary of revealing too many details about himself, even if Eodan probably knew who he was. "Could you find no other charge with my level of schooling?" he remarked.

"No, none with your equivalent stealth and perception," Eodan offered in response. "And it seems my choice has paid off – that was some quick thinking, remembering the

Empress' case. I daresay I stopped paying attention after the eleventh."

"I always found it rather fascinating, how many times her rule was contested," he half-lied, fidgeting with the collar of his too-large shirt. "I think I was slightly obsessed as a child, I almost memorized most of her court cases."

"The woes of the late emperor fathering nearly a hundred children, poor woman needs a break," Eodan muttered, shaking his head. He eyed Dante with a keen expression, his lips still curled in a crooked smile. "As do you. Take some rest, you'll have a lot of work to do."

He left without another word, latching the door behind him. Dante exhaled a lungful of anxiety he hadn't been aware he was still holding in, crossing the room to flop face first onto the comfortable mattress of the embassy bed. Dante felt quite strongly that he was working himself into a quagmire he would struggle to free himself from, each lie he told threatening to drown him. Even when he told the truth, his knowledge was just as damning. Eodan's analysis of him still irritated the corner of his mind, and Dante wondered how long it would be before the council found reasons to distrust him after all.

Rolling over onto his back, Dante stared at the ceiling, the silence of the solitary, private room deafening. He had almost gotten used to sharing the little flat above the blacksmith shop after a month spent living in abandoned ships, and now that he finally had a room all to himself, Dante found himself sorely missing a certain blacksmith's company.

CHAPTER
SEVEN
CHARLOTTE

THE SOUNDS OF THE CATHEDRAL BELLS REVERBERATED throughout the church halls, between stone parapets and across stained glass windows. The churchgoers gathered before the statue of the three-faceted goddess, marble carved into the forms of maiden, mother, and warrior. Charlotte sat beside Eleni and Maya at the front of the group, the rest of the church choir surrounding them as they waited for their signal to begin the first hymn.

Charlotte had never considered herself a strong speaker, always feeling her voice tremble in her throat the moment any sort of attention was directed towards her. Years spent reciting prayers and teachings before the crowds that gathered in the church, seeking guidance for their woes and whims, had not instilled the skill of speech within her. A talent Charlotte did possess, however, was her singing ability. Her father had always claimed that Charlotte's voice would put a siren's to shame, a gift she had inherited from her mother.

Singing in the church choir had brought her some comfort over the years. Sometimes, it felt like the last connection she had with the mother who had left her. Charlotte's only surviving memory of her mother was the lullaby she once sang for her daughter at bedtime. After all these years, she truthfully couldn't remember the cadence of her mother's voice, but Charlotte could never forget those words.

Sing me a lullaby, sing me a sweet goodnight
We'll be safe and sound come the morning light
Darling, dry your eyes, it's goodnight and not goodbye
There's a place for us in the dark and the light

Genysa had left Aethelind when Charlotte was a child, kissing her husband and daughter goodbye in their sleep and vanishing without a trace. There was no denying that existing in Aethelind was difficult for a woman of Pharsat, but Charlotte often wondered how different her life would be if only her mother had chosen to take her daughter with her.

As the voices of the choir singers rose around her, bathing her in music, Charlotte found herself looking down at her hands, at Eleni's and Maya's on either side of her. This was where she had first met her two best friends years ago, when Eleni had taken her and Maya under her wing. The kinship she shared with the pair of them had been almost instantaneous, a common understanding that despite their differences, they each struggled with fitting into this cold society. Despite worshipping three goddesses representing unity, Aethelind was quick to cast out the undesirable.

She looked to that three-faced marble statue, pondering the goddesses she had been raised to worship; the winged, blindfolded Deltori, the scarred siren Eirodys, and the bold warrior Xiska. The church itself was conducted and maintained by the acolytes of Deltori, the goddess representing the eternal war of the spirit – which explained why Charlotte and the rest of the choir found themselves donning deep emerald robes over their civilian attire, a colour Charlotte found clashed horribly with her complexion.

Moreso than the church's horrid taste in colour palettes, it was difficult to subscribe to teachings weaponized against her, against the heritage she had never been permitted to connect with. The people of Pharsat worshipped Xiska alone, while Aethelind worshipped all three goddesses in connection with their combined form they had once existed as – the Mother of all things, Miagne.

It was strange to think on how much blood had been shed in the name of religion.

The song shifted, and it was Charlotte's time to shine. Eleni and Maya led her into the theme, their voices harmonizing as they echoed through the church. Charlotte buried her anxieties as she took a deep breath, adding her own melody to the chorus of the song. Her voice rang out across the stone halls, and if Charlotte could be confident in anything at all, it was that her voice could silence the masses on the first note.

The hymn told the ancient story of Evelyn, the daughter of Gwenhwyfar Drakewind and the Mother Miagne herself. When the goddess fractured into her three personas, it had been Evelyn who volunteered her demigod spirit to sustain Eirodys while she healed. Hers was a tale of duty and loyalty, a legend even Charlotte was enamoured by.

As the song progressed, Charlotte was displeased to recognize a familiar face amongst the crowd, staring directly back at her. No, not at her – Varus Emery was staring at *Eleni* as she sang beside Charlotte, seemingly unbothered.

In all fairness, Varus cleaned up rather well. If Charlotte pretended she didn't know who he was, she might have thought him a tall, dark, and handsome stranger. His black hair was combed neatly back from his face, his skin a shade or two deeper than Charlotte's own. He wore a three-piece indigo suit, a choice Charlotte found quite odd as she had never seen him in anything so proper. As his gaze remained fixed on Eleni, Charlotte found herself glaring at Varus even harder.

Once the morning mass had concluded and the church-goers had exited the cathedral, Charlotte wasted no time in escaping her emerald prison garb. The black skirt and dark blouse she wore beneath was perhaps a fashion faux pas, a colour scheme typically reserved for funerals, but Charlotte found it was one of the few palettes she felt comfortable in. She chucked her robes unceremoniously into the basket one of the Deltori acolytes held out for collection, ignoring the remainder of the congregation as she waited nearby for Eleni and Maya.

Eleni deposited her choir robes with far more grace than Charlotte had, silver cuffs catching the light as she readjusted her blonde curls — as if they hadn't remained in perfect condition while removing the garment. Glancing around to gauge the level of attention being paid to them, Charlotte waited until the choir had dispersed somewhat to tug on her friend's sleeve.

"I'm not sure if you'd noticed, but you seem to have had an admirer amongst the patrons today," Charlotte noted, unable to keep the accusation from her tone.

Eleni stared at her with wide blue eyes, searching her face with feigned confusion. "I'm sure I don't know what you're talking about," Eleni replied, her beaded earrings jingling as she shook her head.

"What are you two gossiping about?" Maya asked as she approached, having finished bidding a few of the churchgoers farewell. Her loosely braided hair framed her face where it was draped over her shoulders, concealing most of the scars that crept along her cheeks. Unlike Charlotte, Maya seemed to suit green very well. Either it was her favourite colour, or the church insisted on clothing her in it regularly, as her choice of dress today was nearly the same shade as the garment she had just discarded.

"Eleni's newest romantic conquest," Charlotte offered with a wry smile, watching in amusement as Eleni's expression changed from confusion to exasperation.

"No, Charlotte, not—"

"Oh, the man in the fifth row?" Maya piped up, wheeling herself closer. "He was staring at you the entire time."

Her cheeks colouring, Eleni cleared her throat. "Oh, fine… He's a friend," she said dismissively, examining her manicured nails as if she had stated it was raining and not that she was casually acquainted with a gangster.

Maya was seemingly unaware of Varus' identity, instead delighted at the prospect of Eleni having a romantic partner. "Oh, come on, 'Leni. Do tell us more."

Eleni made a sort of strangled hissing noise, her eyes darting back and forth at the lingering acolytes of the church. "Not here," Eleni offered simply. Though Charlotte had initially been teasing her, she suspected her observation was closer to the mark than she had thought.

Seemingly insistent on hearing this story, Maya shifted in her seat. "Would you help me back to my room, please?" the girl said suddenly, her voice loud enough to be over-heard. One of the acolytes looked over, her militant expression fixed on Charlotte, but she seemed to decide not to press the matter. Charlotte seized the opportunity to break eye contact with the old woman, gently grasping Maya's wheelchair as she began to steer her towards the hallway, away from the atrium. Eleni followed along, glaring daggers at Charlotte all the way.

The main structure of the cathedral was dedicated towards the main hall, where mass was conducted daily but usually only attended on weekends. What little space remained on the main level was used by the church kitchens, private rooms for confession, and the minister's personal chambers. The second and third levels were devoted for the acolytes' quarters, Maya's included. For reasons unknown to Charlotte, they seemed to be insistent on torturing the girl, giving her a room on the highest level closest to the resonant bell tower.

As Maya was unable to use the stairs, Eleni and Char-lotte led her towards the single, solitary lift at the end of the hall. The cage-like structure was large enough for the three of them to enter with Maya in her chair, Charlotte sliding the door shut with some difficulty. Eleni snapped her fingers, a small spark of lavender light trailing from her hand into the mechanism that powered the lift. With a jerk, the three of them ascended, the shuttered lights from each level casting long, slanted shadows across their faces.

"Speaking of romantic conquests, Charlotte, how is your blacksmith doing these days?" Eleni commented dryly.

"Oh, sod off."

With a creak and a shudder, the lift stopped at the third floor. The three women exited the lift quickly, not wanting to test their luck with the rickety contraption as they followed the narrow corridors to the room at the far end of the western side of the cathedral. Eleni was ready, her hand outstretched to receive the key that Maya palmed into her hand, opening the door as she stepped aside to let Maya pass—

"Maya! Where do you think you're going?"

All three of them jumped in alarm at the voice that echoed sharply along the corridor; Sister Margerie, a foul-tempered old hag who seemed to have it out for Maya, was walking quickly towards them, her deep emerald robes billowing with the speed.

"Maya, you are thirty minutes late for your lesson this afternoon," she thundered, and Charlotte felt her blood boil when she saw Maya flinch out of the corner of her eye. "Where do you think you're going? You will report to the archives at once for your training."

The effect on Maya was instantaneous, and Charlotte hated the way her friend withdrew into herself. "I… I'm sorry, I…" Maya stammered a response, her hands trembling as she struggled to gather her thoughts. Fortunately, it was Eleni who cut in, physically stepping between Maya and the nun.

"How can that be?" she asked pointedly, a hand on her hip. She was a head shorter than Sister Margerie, but Charlotte had seen Eleni make grown men quake in their boots with her wrath. "You say she is thirty minutes late, but mass ended only ten minutes ago, if that. Are you purposefully scheduling Maya for engagements she will inevitably miss?"

Sister Margerie made an odd sort of scoffing noise. "Be

that as it may, her responsibilities as a ward of the church require her to attend these lessons promptly," she continued, waving a hand as if to swipe Eleni out of the way. "If that is all, I will be collecting her now."

"With all due respect, Maya needs a break after a long service," Charlotte interjected. Sister Margerie's gaze cut to her with a snap. "Unless you would rather her struggle to focus during these lessons, I suggest you permit her this."

"I will determine what she needs, Miss…" Sister Margerie waved her hand again, as if expecting Charlotte to offer up her name, both of them knowing very well that they had met several times before.

"Please, I've had… I've had a feminine emergency that requires my immediate attention," Maya squeaked out, her hands still trembling. Charlotte reached from the back of Maya's wheelchair to give her shoulder a little squeeze, the girl's gaze fixed on the floor in front of her.

The sister narrowed her eyes, scanning the three of them even while her cheeks reddened. It seemed she'd heard enough to know this was a losing battle. "Very well," she said at last, sighing heavily. "See to your needs and meet us in the archives in ten minutes. You would do well not to dally, young lady."

She turned and stalked off without another word, and Charlotte wasted no time in wheeling Maya into her room, Eleni promptly slamming the door shut behind them. The chamber was only slightly larger than most living quarters in the cathedral to account for a wheelchair. The stone walls were otherwise unremarkable, but the room had been filled with various articles that were all undeniably Maya. She had been born obsessed with reading and would pore over anything she could get her hands on – especially if it wasn't meant for her eyes. Charlotte had found all manner of journals, schematics, and complex missives she was certain should not have been in Maya's possession.

"What an awful, twisted old wretch," Charlotte cursed under her breath. With a level of care she reserved for Maya and her belongings, she gently pushed the form of an old, threadbare plush lion to the side, perching on the edge of her friend's bed. "I can't believe they force you to study under her."

"I don't care for her," Eleni agreed, which was the closest thing to an insult she would offer here. Her maternal instincts seemed to be at war with her innate desire to attempt to tidy up as she regarded Maya. "Do you need me to fetch you anything?"

Turning her chair around to face the two of them, Maya gave them a shy smile. "I'm fine, honestly," she replied quietly. "I just figured it was the one reason I could give her that she wouldn't refute."

There was a moment's pause before Eleni and Charlotte burst into laughter. "Maya!" Eleni gasped, sounding equal parts surprised and impressed. "You lied to Sister Margerie?"

"I'm pleased," Charlotte noted, giggling. "Though I fear I may have been a bad influence on you."

Maya giggled, and the expression lit up her face in a way that inspired Charlotte to make her laugh every single day. Always a shy, quiet girl, Maya did her best to hide as much of herself away as possible. The tiny scars on her face would often be concealed by her hair, her residual limbs hidden beneath the layers of her heavy skirts. Every so often, however, Charlotte or Eleni succeeded in breaking through Maya's shell, and it was always rewarding.

"Well then, we haven't got long," Maya continued, her hands clasped together. "Eleni, tell us everything."

Charlotte had almost forgotten Varus' presence at the mass that morning, and her mood soured. Eleni seemed to pick up on this, idly rubbing her arms as she responded, "Truly, he is … he is just a friend."

"So, you *are* familiar with the man who was staring at you so intently he practically bored holes into your skull," Maya continued, a wicked gleam in her eyes. She seemed to live vicariously through Eleni.

"You seem dead set against him, Charlotte, so you must know who he is as well," Eleni replied coolly, but there was a knowing smile teasing against the corner of her mouth.

Charlotte found herself flushing, realizing with some dismay that she didn't know how best to explain her own complicated relationship to the man. "I… sort of, yes," she admitted finally, throwing her hands up in exasperation. "But only through Jasper, he's—he works for him, sometimes."

"Your blacksmith boy?" Maya teased, leaning on the arm of her wheelchair.

"Not mine," Charlotte corrected softly, her cheeks blushing darker.

"Perhaps the four of us should all meet up sometime," Eleni remarked dryly.

Charlotte shook her head, feeling her curls bounce against her neck from where they were frantically escaping the pins in her scalp. "No, no, and no again," she retorted, voice rising. "Eleni, I'm serious, you do not want to be involved with someone like that."

"And yet you are involved with him, by association?" Eleni prompted.

"Unwillingly," Charlotte said through gritted teeth.

Maya glanced back and forth between the two of them,

appearing quite confused. "Help a friend out, I know who Jasper is, who is this… strange man?"

At that moment, Charlotte and Eleni responded at the same time, but offered completely different answers.

"Varus Emery."

"Eodan Melicus."

There were several moments of silence as the three of them looked from one person to the other, all of them a bit alarmed at what had just happened. "I'm sorry, I'm a bit lost," Maya chuckled nervously, twirling the end of her braid between her fingers. "This is the same man, yes?"

Charlotte was desperately combing through her memory, but she was certain it had been Varus Emery she had seen seated in the church pews. "You're… certain that's his name?" she asked Eleni. "Tall, dark, frankly quite terrifying man with criminal underworld occupation?"

"Eleni!" Maya gasped, clapping her hands over her mouth.

"I… did not know him by that name," Eleni replied finally, seeming a bit flustered. "But I am aware of his occupations, yes. In addition to that, you might be interested to know he is a merchant in Dornkeep. He owns most of the harbour."

"He can't be both people," Charlotte insisted. "He's Varus Emery, he's a bloody kingpin."

"Well, clearly one of those names is an alias," Maya mused, tapping her chin thoughtfully. "Or perhaps both of them. Say, which one is technically employing your blacksmith boy, then?"

"Eleni, I'm begging you," Charlotte warned, ignoring Maya's question. She crossed the room, taking Eleni's hands and squeezing them with a gentle urgency. "Please, I have a bad feeling about that man. I don't like the hold that he has over Jasper, and I trust him even less knowing that 'Varus Emery' may not even be his real name. Please, promise me if you consider pursuing him, you will be cautious."

"Who is to say that I would pursue him?" Eleni returned. As both Charlotte's gaze and her grip remained unrelenting, however, she sighed and shook her head. "Fine, fine. I will be cautious in my romantic endeavours, should I choose to act upon them."

Somewhat satisfied, Charlotte released her hold on Eleni with a sigh. She leaned back against the dresser placed beneath the solitary window, a newspaper crinkling beneath her elbow as she did. Frowning, she twisted around to look at the headline of *The Aethelind Times*. The newspaper was more popular in Briardeen than anywhere else, and very rarely made it so far as Caelfall; even if it did wind up out there, it was usually used for handling fried fish before it was thought of as reading material. This copy's headline was particularly distressing, depicting the sketched remains of a ruined airship.

CARGO FREIGHTER DESTROYED IN DORNKEEP –
ARSON SUSPECTED

"Why haven't I heard anyone talking about this?" Charlotte pondered, leaning closer to skim through the article.

Eleni waved a hand towards the window. "We're in Briardeen, Charlotte," she sighed. "People here don't care about anything that happens outside of their own city."

"But even in Caelfall, no one's... no one's said anything," Charlotte explained, following the direction of the tiny, smudged print with her finger. It looked as if it was fairly harmless, with no reported injuries or casualties, but

Charlotte was vaguely horrified by the fact that this was the first she was hearing of it.

How long had she been unconscious this time? Had Jasper or her father kept it from her, not wanting to worry her?

"They might not know," Maya offered simply, as if reading Charlotte's mind. She had unwoven one of her braids and was beginning to weave it back into submission, her long brown hair spilling into her lap. "That's only today's paper, and it isn't well circulated outside of Briardeen and Aerindale."

"Or well liked," Eleni noted. "They practically invented biased journalism. Caelfall and Dornkeep may be waiting on the 'real' newspaper's take on things."

It was true enough that the southernmost districts relied on their own local journalism, but Charlotte couldn't shake the kernel of doubt in her stomach, the quiet dread that had come over her. Something about the article seemed amiss, and the fact that this was the first she'd heard of it disturbed her.

"Now that you mention it... I had dreamt something rather peculiar," Maya trailed off, tapping her chin as she stared off into space. "I'd forgotten it until now, but I'm certain I dreamt I was on a ship as it burst into flames."

"Goddesses, Maya. That's not a dream, that's a nightmare," Charlotte corrected her chidingly, even as she shuddered.

Seemingly oblivious of Charlotte's discontent, Maya sighed as she tied off the end of her braid. "As much as I hate to admit it, I should probably get going." She leaned back in her chair, crossing her thighs beneath her skirts as she rolled her eyes. "I'd love to ditch that old bat, but she'll probably assume I've hemorrhaged if I don't get going soon."

"First you lie to her, and then you insult her behind her back," said Eleni, shaking her head in mock disapproval. "I'm so proud of you."

Charlotte was admittedly proud of Maya as well, though it didn't make the task of handing her over to the horrid acolytes in the archives any easier. "Shall we drop you off, then?" she offered politely, struggling to put the image of the ruined freighter out of her mind.

Sighing dramatically, Maya leaned back in her chair. "I suppose so," she moaned as Charlotte opened the door for her, wheeling herself out of the room. "But don't you think I've forgotten about our conversation today, ladies. I will expect a full report on this Eodus Varemy, or whatever his name was."

The night air was cool by the time Charlotte ventured out from the bakery a second time, a shawl wrapped around her neck and shoulders in an effort to keep out the chill. The sun was beginning to dip over the horizon, the bright orange clouds hanging low in the sky as Charlotte walked as quickly as her joints could manage towards Briardeen.

When the princess had invited her over for tea that evening, Charlotte had been tempted to decline. The last time she'd seen Aurelia had been in the cathedral kitchens, when Charlotte had proceeded to faint after a comedy of errors. However, Aurelia had promised there was something she wanted to share with Charlotte, and on a night where Jasper was working for Varus, she found herself in need of some company.

Fortia met her at the castle gates, silencing the royal guard on duty with a wave of her hand and escorting Charlotte to the courtyard gardens. As they approached, she was startled to recognize the sensation of wards as she passed through them, but Fortia offered no commentary. They found the princess sprawled on a massive tartan blanket amidst a full tea set and a picnic basket, lying on her side with her head perched on her hand. Her powder blue dress was hitched up enough to reveal her bare feet, her shoes discarded elsewhere. In the twilight, Aurelia carried neither her dark-tinted spectacles or her parasol; it was the time of day where she could finally shed some of her daily protections.

"Charlotte, you came!" said the princess as she arrived, grinning as she looked up at her with bright, fluttering eyes. "Come, have tea with me."

"I brought my own," Charlotte offered apologetically, withdrawing a small sachet of the herb mixture Haeyin had supplied her with. After the last incident, Jasper had practically begged her not to leave home without it in the future. "Hopefully to avoid another situation like last time."

Aurelia smiled sadly, nodding as she slid a delicate teacup towards Charlotte. "I did, too," she admitted with a sheepish giggle. "And I think Fortia may have brought something stronger."

Fortia pretended to look wounded, her eyes crinkling at the corners as she poured boiling water with great care and attention. Charlotte stifled a laugh as she unpackaged her tea, her hands trembling as she pried open a small metal tea strainer she'd salvaged from home to brew her medication with. Aurelia's seemed to be a sort of powdered milk tea, and Charlotte watched with some envy as the princess merely poured it into her teacup to stir it in with a spoon. It smelled a fair bit sweeter as well, leading Charlotte to wonder exactly what herbs were included to give Aurelia the effects she needed.

"So, Charlotte... I have a confession," Aurelia began, watching Charlotte intently with wide pink eyes while she stirred her tea soundlessly. "I may have invited you here with an ulterior motive."

Raising an eyebrow, Charlotte mimicked the princess' posture as she stared back with open curiosity, wiggling her pocket tea strainer in her cup. "Well, you have my attention."

Grinning wickedly, the princess pulled the picnic basket closer to the three of them, lifting the lid to reveal... sandwiches.

"That's not quite the ulterior motive I'd anticipated," Charlotte admitted, struggling not to laugh in case she spilled tea down the front of her dress.

"I wish that was all that was in there," Fortia muttered into her own teacup.

Her gaze still fixed on Charlotte, Aurelia reached deeper within the basket, withdrawing a newspaper she had concealed beneath the food. She tossed it gently, the paper landing beside Charlotte's lap where she sat with her tea, frozen as she read the header for *The Jackdaw Herald*.

"Where on earth did you get this?" she hissed, unsure whether she should scramble to conceal it or burn it. "Just having this here is as good as treason!"

"Don't worry so much, Charlotte," Aurelia reassured her with a gentle hand on her knee. "Fortia was kind enough to ask Cary to keep an eye out for us, and Gideon's on patrol tonight."

That explained the wards, Charlotte thought to herself. It was one thing to know that Cary would be watching out for them, but the concept of Gideon being aware of this, of his patrol offering security for what the princess was doing… somehow, it was more horrifying than comforting.

"Your Highness—*Aurelia*," she whispered, glancing around nervously. "Involving me could land me in the dungeons! Who even gave you this?"

"I did," Fortia replied, much to Charlotte's surprise. She held her teacup with all the grace of a queen even as she sat cross-legged in men's trousers beneath her armour. "The princess has tasked me with keeping her… well-informed of the matters of the kingdom."

"My father refuses to involve me in any of his council meetings, even the ones concerning the accords," Aurelia continued in an uncharacteristically glum tone. She chewed on her cheek in a way that reminded Charlotte of Jasper, as if she were deciding what best to say next. "I don't know if he intends to keep me in the dark for some grand purpose, but I do not wish to be ignorant any longer. I asked Fortia to source the rebel newspaper for me, since the *Times* is rubbish."

The rebel newspaper. Charlotte couldn't help but laugh to herself; in Caelfall, *The Jackdaw Herald* was the only news-paper. Its origins were a mystery, kept secret to protect the authors from retaliation, as they tended to write genuinely career-ending articles with every issue. Charlotte was about to protest further, keen on sleeping in her own bed rather than a cell in the dungeons, when her eyes fixed on the front page.

KING GUS MAKES SCAPEGOAT OF BURNING VAGRANT LODGING

Career-ending articles, indeed.

"That was the airship that the *Times* reported on," Charlotte noted as she leaned in, careful not to spill her tea as she took a tentative sip. Though almost scalding, she felt near immediate relief as it settled in her stomach. "They said it was arson."

"There's more," Aurelia explained, her eyes lighting up again. "Fortia tells me there's a broadcast password hidden somewhere in this!" Rummaging further in the basket, the princess retrieved a clunky, rectangular object that Charlotte had only seen in shop windows in Briardeen.

Before she could ask, Aurelia was explaining. "This is a sort of miniature radio," she said as she handed the strange little box to Fortia. "I've been working on it for at least a week. It only receives signal, it can't transmit anything, but it'll serve our purposes for this evening."

Charlotte was still convinced the two of them were mad. She had no idea what manner of punishment the princess and her guardian might receive for dabbling with the *Jackdaw*, but she was certain for an ordinary civilian like herself she wouldn't see sunrise. Even as she opened her mouth to protest, however, she found her eyes drawn to the print where Aurelia had opened the newspaper up to the third page.

"That word there," she interjected, leaning forward to point it out. "The letter 'o' has been replaced with a zero."

Aurelia muffled a delighted squeal with her free hand, startling Charlotte with her excitement. "That's brilliant! I knew you'd be a great help with this, I can barely tell the difference in this lighting."

She resisted the urge to point out that reading at twilight might not be easy for anyone, never mind Aurelia with her poor eyesight. Sustained with tea and sandwiches, the three of them set to work skimming through the newspaper to find a sequence of numbers. Fortia explained this as the "password", while Aurelia elaborated the numbers would be the frequency needed to listen to the broadcast. The princess conjured three glowing orbs of light that floated around their heads, earning a soft, "Good work, Your Highness," from Fortia as they read long after the last rays of the sun had vanished.

After about ten minutes, as Charlotte's teacup was drained and her eyes were beginning to cross, Fortia ended her misery. "I think I've got it," she said triumphantly, fiddling a bit with the long, thin piece of metal that extended from the top corner of the box – the antenna, she'd explained. With a few twists and turns of the knobs and dials on the front of the machine, Charlotte was startled by the sudden sounds of the infamous pirate radio broadcast.

A man's voice, thickly accented and distorted with static, emanated from the radio. "... a grounded Siathan airship was set alight earlier today. Who's to blame?"

Charlotte felt her stomach drop. She'd recognize that tone anywhere, having only met one person with that cadence. How was Varus Emery haunting every area of her life?

Another man's voice, an Aethian one drenched with sarcasm. "Anonymous arsonists, clearly. Who else?" Charlotte had a sneaking suspicion that it might have been Haeyin, but it was difficult to tell.

A husky female voice laughed, though it sounded like a snort through the crackle of the radio. "What a surprise," she drawled. "Does the police commissioner have no leads to investigate the cause of such incidences? Arson seems to be frightfully common in Aethelind."

"So it would seem," Varus quipped. "Naturally, I felt

the need to investigate. It feels a bit odd, don't you think? This is Dornkeep that was affected—an industrial area, hardly a place of riots and such. You're more likely to see that in Caelfall."

Charlotte felt a heavy weight settle on her chest. There was a reason Caelfall had the reputation it did, but it didn't hurt any less to hear her city stereotyped in such a way.

"You raise a good point," possibly-Haeyin mused. "And specifically the harbour, an area under extremely tight watch at all hours of the day. These must be some professionals we're dealing with, to evade notice."

The woman scoffed. "You're missing the best part of this story," she insisted. "Do you know where that Siathan freighter was parked? Take a guess."

"Oh, you mean directly beside the Valedian council's airship?"

With a jolt, Charlotte's gaze snapped up to the princess. Aurelia was already looking at her, her eyes wide. It seemed she had come to the same conclusion, though Charlotte felt truly horrid even assuming such a motive.

"Precisely, my darling," the woman replied sweetly. "Now, it's outright treason to damage or destroy a vessel commanded by the King of Valedia himself, He Who Rises, long may he reign, etcetera. But if you merely destroy the airship docked next door, well… that sure as hell sends a message."

"I would also like to point out that this so-called 'arson' occurred immediately after some poor sod was caught living in the rafters," said the man who may or may not have been Haeyin. "Making this the … fourth time this month that vagrant lodgings have been conveniently destroyed by 'arsonists'."

"Bit bloody convenient, I'd say," Varus almost growled. "Kill two birds with one stone—"

Fortia leaned forward abruptly, grasping the volume control and quickly muting the broadcast. "I hear something," was all she said before the girls quickly packed up as much of their illegal reading material as they could, stuffing the radio and the newspaper beneath the tea set in the picnic basket. As the distant sound of footsteps drew nearer, Charlotte held her breath as a figure came into view. Their midnight-dark boiled leather armour was nearly invisible, the surface rubbed to a matte finish that seemed to swallow what little light reached their form.

"You should get going," the stranger warned in a soft voice – a voice that Charlotte recognized. *Cary...* She had never seen her in armour before, and the woman's face was almost entirely obscured by her thick, dark hood. Cary met Charlotte's eyes only briefly, glancing away as she continued, "I spotted the king's advisor skulking about the grounds. Best you get back to your chambers before he sees you, Your Highness."

"Thank you, Cary," Aurelia said, slipping back into her discarded shoes nearby. Fortia was already folding up the picnic blanket, basket looped through her other arm. The princess turned to Charlotte as she stood up, giving her hands a gentle squeeze. "Thank you for joining me, Charlotte."

"Thanks for having me," Charlotte replied numbly. She was still shocked by what she'd heard, the accusations of the *Jackdaw* broadcast ringing in her ears. "Your Highness... Aurelia, what are we going to do? How do we deal with—with any of what we just learned?"

"We lie low, for now," Fortia warned quietly, placing a hand on Charlotte's shoulder. The entirety of the picnic

set seemed to be tucked under her other arm, giving Charlotte the impression it was all lighter than air. "The broadcast has raised some important questions, but for now all
of this is speculation. I will gather more intel for the
princess to study. You are more than welcome to join us, if
you like."

The threat of being executed for treason still weighed
heavily on Charlotte's mind, and yet she found herself
nodding immediately. "I think I might like that," she replied
quietly. "Perhaps I'll see if I can find anything myself."

Aurelia looked delighted. "Be safe, Charlotte," she whispered in the near darkness, releasing her hands. "I'll send
for Gideon to take you home."

⚬⚬ ☼ ⚬⚬

After being scolded for a near-miss by Gideon for a good
twenty minutes, her friend deposited her safely back at the
bakery. He waited just long enough she thought he might
have had something to say, but the captain of the guard
merely waited until she was safely inside the bakery before
heading off. After sitting in the solitude of the entryway for
a minute, Charlotte had a change of heart in how she
wanted to spend her evening.

Satisfied that Gideon had departed and that Charlotte
wasn't being pursued by shady characters, she locked up the
bakery before crossing over to the smithy next door. She
rapped her knuckles against the door, hoping that Jasper
was still awake. When he finally opened the door, Charlotte
had to stop herself from laughing at his dishevelled appearance. He was wearing one of his larger sweaters, hanging
haphazardly off his form in a way that suggested he'd lost
weight recently. His sunset-coloured hair was sticking out in

all directions, his ever-so-slightly pointed ears uncharacteristically exposed.

"Charlie?" he asked sleepily, rubbing his eyes. "What's going on? Are you all right?" He automatically stepped aside once he realized it was her, letting her enter the flat as he shut the door.

Charlotte took the stairs slowly, pacing herself as she eased up one step at a time, her knees aching from the day of walking. "Did you know… your dashing employer seems to have… a few extracurricular activities?" she asked between steps.

From behind her, she could almost hear the gears turning in Jasper's head. "Mr. Emery?" he returned, audibly confused. "What are you talking about?"

Pausing for a minute on the main level before she attempted to venture up to the loft where Jasper slept, Charlotte leaned against the banister for support, her hips aching. "Earlier today, I saw him at the cathedral during mass," she explained. "He was staring at Eleni the entire time, and when I asked her about it, she knew him by a different name entirely – Eodan Melicus."

Jasper paused, frowning as his sleepy stupor began to ease. "Funny you mention that," he replied, crossing his arms as he leaned against the railing opposite her. "The other day when Dante was leaving for the embassy, Mr. Emery showed up to collect him with a carriage of all things, dressed in a *suit*. I've never seen the man in anything but a trench coat and armour."

At the mention of his friend, Charlotte offered him a coy smile. "Am I ever going to meet this friend of yours?" Charlotte teased him, beginning to brave the next set of stairs. "I can't believe you let him sleep in your bed but you haven't even introduced me."

She didn't need to look behind her to know Jasper was blushing redder than his hair. "I—he was—you were ill!" he stammered in protest as he followed her up the stairs, pausing behind her every time she faltered as if preparing to catch her. "You were sleeping all day and *he* was sleeping all day, and—"

"Jasper, I'm only teasing you," Charlotte interrupted him, unable to keep herself from laughing. "I'm sure I'll meet him eventually, whenever he gets a day off at the embassy."

This loft was smaller than the one above the bakery, accommodating a solitary bedroom. The only window faced east, which was incredibly unfortunate with Jasper's preference of sleeping in. All of his furniture had seen better days, and he had made countless repairs to each item – the dilapidated old wardrobe that had belonged to Zeke, a nearly broken desk, and a three-legged chair balanced on a wooden box. Another, similar crate served as his bedside table, a lone oil lamp providing a gentle light. He was perpetually untidy, managing to wash clothing and dishes but ultimately failing to put anything away. The untouched side of his bed was covered with hastily folded clothing he'd managed to bring upstairs, at least.

As if realizing there was a distinct lack of space to sit, Jasper stooped to collect the clothes piles from the bed, making room on the desk for them. "As much as I'm always happy to see you, I'm sure you didn't come over just to tell me Mr. Emery might be using a different name," Jasper noted as Charlotte took a seat on the bed, gratefully sinking into the surface of the mattress.

"Well, that's the other thing," Charlotte continued, remembering the remainder of the day's events. "Did you know *The Jackdaw Herald* has a broadcast?"

"I… I did, yeah."

"Have you ever listened to it?" She already knew the answer, mentally kicking herself as Jasper sat down beside her.

He chewed his cheek, looking down at his hands as he fidgeted with the uneven hem of his sweater. "Not really a good format for me," Jasper explained softly. "I don't… I miss out on a lot of the words."

He had explained to her some time ago why conversations were draining for him, how he struggled to piece words together from the sounds he had heard. Charlotte had noted in their conversations that Jasper often watched her mouth when she spoke, deriving meaning and tone from her facial expressions. Naturally, a radio broadcast wasn't exactly accessible for someone like him – and after what Charlotte had heard tonight, the crackly broadcast on Aurelia's project radio would have been entirely unintelligible.

"Tell me about it," Jasper said suddenly, meeting her gaze again. His green eyes were still weary, but he seemed to have perked up enough to hold a conversation with her.

She recalled the evening's events to the best of her ability, explaining the concerning headline of *The Aethelind Times* compared to *The Jackdaw Herald*. As she recounted sharing tea with the princess and Fortia – "I didn't realize you two had tea parties," Jasper had noted teasingly – Charlotte described finding the broadcast hidden in the rebel newspaper, tuning in to listen to none other than Varus Emery's voice.

"Huh," was all Jasper had to say at first, leaning back on his palms in the hastily made bedspread. "He's never mentioned it to me, but then again… Mr. Emery's really only just started discussing things outside of my normal work for him. Maybe pirate radio stations were the next topic on his list."

"I'm pretty sure the other person might have been Haeyin," Charlotte speculated, knocking her knee against Jasper's beside her. "And there was a woman, but I didn't recognize her voice. But how disturbing, to think that a ship might have been burnt down to threaten the Valedian king?"

"That, or trying to kill Dante," Jasper snorted. When Charlotte gave him a confused look, he offered, "He told me that was the airship he'd been sleeping on for a month before he got chased out here."

"Ah, so that's what they meant when they said 'vagrant housing' was being targeted," Charlotte mused.

Beside her, Jasper yawned loudly. "As much as I would love to stay up with you... I may pass out," he managed to say between yawns, rising from the bed as he began to shrug out of his sweater.

She managed a laugh, standing herself. "You and me both," Charlotte assured him. "I should get going."

He paused in his efforts to shrug out of his sweater, his gaze fixed on the floor while he chewed his cheek. "You're welcome to stay," Jasper offered without looking at her, tugging his undershirt down where the fabric had ridden up his back.

Charlotte felt her heart stutter at the offer. "If you don't mind," she stammered in response. "I'm fairly exhausted myself."

"I never mind," Jasper insisted, beginning to draw back the barely made bed covers. Charlotte removed as much of her overclothes as she could manage by herself, as much as she felt comfortable removing around Jasper, before easing her weary body into the bed as Jasper extinguished the oil lamp.

Curling up beside Jasper felt like the most natural thing in the world on nights such as these. In the darkness of the loft, Charlotte lay awake for some time listening to the creak of the old flat as the wind howled outside, the beginnings of a late spring storm brewing as droplets of rain cascaded against the window – and the soft sounds of Jasper snoring beside her. Amidst the sea of blankets strewn around them, at some point in the night Jasper rolled over in his sleep, his large form enveloping Charlotte in a warm embrace as he draped his arm over her side.

Her heart hammered in her throat loud enough she feared she might wake him, distinctly aware of every inch of skin that connected them. She all but held her breath at the sensation of Jasper's against her neck, and Charlotte was at war with herself. There was an immense guilt knowing Jasper was so obviously unconscious and unaware, likely to be embarrassed in the morning if he woke up to find himself in such a compromising position. Even so, Charlotte couldn't deny that it felt good to be so close to someone whom she cared so deeply about, the warmth of his body comforting against her back as she settled against him.

In the morning she would deny it had ever happened, insisting she had fallen asleep almost immediately after such an exhausting day. It was easily explainable with the side effects of her medication, and Jasper would have no reason to doubt her… but if he did, Charlotte would insist she saw him only as a friend, as she was certain Jasper saw her.

Tentatively, she shifted her hand to where Jasper's now rested beside her, brushing her fingers over the scars she had memorized along his knuckles. For tonight, Charlotte was content to pretend.

ACT II

SUMMER

AMENDMENT TO THE MAGE LAWS ACT (cont.)
As per His Majesty King Gustaf Edmund Davenport III:

At first indication of magical proclivity, a mage shall be registered by county census for record keeping purposes.

At initial registration, the mage shall be fitted with regulatory silver wristlets. Under no circumstances are the wristlets to be tampered with, removed, or destroyed.

The mage shall report to their regional authority for annual wristlet maintenance. Tardiness or truancy will not be tolerated.

CHAPTER

EIGHT

DANTE

As he walked through the smooth, polished streets of Briardeen, Dante struggled to blend in. Wearing a newly purchased linen shirt, his satchel slung over his shoulder in the gratefully clear weather, he strolled as casually as he could manage as he made his way towards his destination. Dante still hadn't let go of the constant paranoia that someone out here would apprehend him, despite his employment with Eodan Melicus ensuring that the incident down at the harbour had blown over entirely.

Of course, the freighter being burnt to cinders hadn't helped.

Dante had tried not to dwell on the suspected arson too much. King Fenyang and his council had discussed it at length with Eodan, agreeing that it was too great a risk posed to the king's life to assume it was a coincidence. Eodan had doubled the security at the embassy, hiring several people from varying backgrounds to stand guard outside as well as on the third level where the king and his council members slept. Ironically, the added presence made it even more difficult for Dante to sleep at night. Something about the situation felt off to him, and he couldn't shake the suspicion that perhaps there was more at play than merely a threat against Fenyang.

In an effort to assist the king and his council to the best of his abilities, Dante had been hard at work with his research. He'd received a recommendation from Eodan for a bookstore he hadn't yet tried, with the promise that the owner was trustworthy and well educated on the subject. *Hourglass Books* was located on the corner nearest the bridge leading towards Aerindale in the west, the grand hospital and the combat academy visible in the distance. Dante stepped inside, a little bell chiming at the entrance startling him as he walked in. Sun-blind from the late afternoon light, Dante collided with something warm and solid the moment he stepped into the store, a pile of books tumbling with a thud.

"Sodding Keepers—" he spluttered, reaching out blindly to catch the person he had just stumbled into. "I'm so sorry, forgive me, I didn't see you there." His fingers closed on the light blue fabric of a blouse, but he could see little else.

"No, no, that's all right," a woman's voice replied. Dante blinked repeatedly as he waited for his eyes to adjust, automatically stooping to collect the books that had dropped in the collision. The familiar cover for a book of fairy tales came into focus – no, not fairy tales, but *The Trials of Rhey'lu*. The legend of the Tide Keeper Celüne's godling son was a childhood favourite of Dante's, having begged his mother on many occasions to reread it to him. Seeing it here of all places was nostalgic and confusing;

who in Aethia would take such an interest in the myths of Fraecath?

As he stood upright once more, he regarded the brown and freckled face of the woman he had bumped into, her countenance reminding him of Huda. "Unusual choice of reading material," Dante noted, his curiosity demanding an investigation. "Here in Aethelind, I mean."

The young woman chuckled nervously, accepting the pile of books as Dante handed it back to her, *The Trials of Rhey'lu* balanced neatly on top. "Eleni's recommendations haven't failed me yet," she supplied, nestling the books safely within the crook of her arm. Her eyes were a bright and verdant hazel, and though Dante was certain he had never met this young woman before, those eyes coupled with her dark curls convinced him that a certain blacksmith had described her likeness.

"Forgive me, but… is your name Charlotte?" he asked.

The look she gave him was a mix of interest and trepidation, and Dante mentally cursed himself as he realized how frightening it must have been for a stranger to say such a thing. "Do I know you?" she asked warily, her grip on the books in her arms tightening.

Shaking his head, Dante offered his hand. "Dante. We have a mutual friend, Jasper."

Her eyes lit up the moment he said his name, as if she had been looking forward to this moment. "Oh, I'd been hoping to meet you!" Charlotte exclaimed, her lips stretching into a wide smile on his behalf. Adjusting her grip on the books she carried, she angled her arm to shake his hand quickly. "Yes, I'm Charlotte. Apologies, I'm not exactly accustomed to people knowing my name."

Chuckling nervously, Dante held up his hands in a gesture of surrender as the handshake ended. "No, no, I definitely could have phrased that in a less… unnerving manner," he offered in reply. "What are you doing here? Is Jasper with you?"

"No, he isn't. His… employer has him working on something, and the less I know of that the better," Charlotte replied with a shake of her head, curls bobbing as she sighed. "I dropped by to exchange a few books, myself. What brings you here?"

The way she commented on Jasper's employer made her distaste apparent, and Dante briefly considered lying about his true intentions – but then, what a horrid impression it would make to meet Charlotte and immediately lie to her, should she find out otherwise from Jasper.

"Well, I'm… I'm not sure if Jasper mentioned this, but I'm working at the embassy now," he explained, clearing his throat as he waved towards the bookshelves. "Eodan sent me here for a book. I mean—of course I'd be here for a book… I'm looking for a *specific* book."

Charlotte gave him a wry smile in response as he tripped over his words. She was certainly beautiful, and Dante thought he could understand why Jasper was so enamoured with her. She gestured for him to follow with a nod of her chin, leading Dante further into the store, past rows of finely polished wooden bookshelves. He noted that Charlotte walked with a slight limp, and he resisted the urge to comment on it as they approached a checkout counter.

An ethereal woman with blonde hair stood behind the nearby counter. She looked up from her records with a calculating blue stare, her gaze darting back and forth between Charlotte and Dante. "I didn't expect you to finish those so quickly," she remarked teasingly towards Charlotte. A black and white mottled cat was perched on the counter beside her, staring at Dante as if he were a great threat to the bookstore.

Charlotte laughed sarcastically in response. "Dante, this is Eleni," she offered, gesturing with her free hand. "Eleni, this is Dante. He's a friend of Jasper's, and… employed at the Valedian embassy by Eodan."

Adding that last detail with some trepidation, Dante wondered if Eleni also knew Eodan, and what their relationship was. Surely they were on amicable terms if the man had sent him here? The blonde-haired woman stood and smoothed the crimson floral-patterned gown she wore, gracefully walking around the counter to greet him more appropriately. As she extended a bejeweled hand, Dante struggled not to balk at the sight of the mage's cuff on her wrist, forcing himself to shake her hand as he was met with the scent of lavender.

"A pleasure to meet you, Dante," Eleni greeted him warmly, blue eyes sparkling. "What is it that Eodan's sent you for?"

Clearing his throat once more, Dante withdrew his hand as she released him. "I was hoping to find as close to an original copy of the mage laws as possible," he explained.

Humming thoughtfully, Eleni tapped her chin. "I think I can help," she replied eventually, gesturing for them to follow as she ventured further into the bookstore. Dante followed along with Charlotte in tow, seemingly curious herself. "You would be hard-pressed to find or read an original draft, however. The mage laws were written by the Tyiadai Daru."

The black and white cat darted ahead of them, causing Dante to bump into the neighbouring shelves as he struggled not to trod on her. "The—the mage laws were drafted in Thelind by Gwenhwyfar," he stated blankly. Thelind, the kingdom Aethelind had once been, long before the war with Valedia, before Castavar had all but sunk beneath the waves entirely.

Eleni turned her head slightly to look back at them, a bemused expression on her face as she walked. "Darling, whoever taught you your history lessons? Thelind was founded by Gwenhwyfar Drakewind, and she was the last princess of the Tyiadai Daru – the shapeshifters."

It was rare that Dante encountered a missing facet of knowledge in his education. He chanced a look back at Charlotte to see if he was losing his marbles, but she appeared to be as confused as he was. They arrived at the section of magical law, Eleni stopping abruptly ahead of him. Dante struggled to come to a halt before he crashed into the back of Eleni's head, Charlotte letting out a small huff as she collided with the back of him.

"That's for bumping into me earlier," she muttered teasingly as she steadied herself. Dante mumbled an apology as he stifled a laugh.

The cat was meowing incessantly, and oddly enough Eleni seemed to be communicating with her. "Yes, I do know this… Well, there's nothing to be done about it… and what would you know about that, Mo?" Dante elected not to inquire further.

"At the risk of sounding ignorant, what exactly are these mage laws?" Charlotte piped up behind Dante. She had set her stack of books on the floor, now leaning against one of the shelves heavily. "I hear about them all the time, but I've never actually learned what they *are*."

Dante was admittedly curious himself. Though he was familiar with the global application of the mage laws, Aethia's take on the legislation seemed far more militant than Fraecath. Nowhere else had he seen mages sporting silver cuffs, the requirement unique to Aethia and its citizens.

"They're a series of … well, *rules*," Eleni explained with a dismissive gesture that jostled the cuff on her wrist, her eyes scanning the books along the shelves. "They were drafted when Thelind was founded because it became a sort of harmonized community. So many different cultures, all with different views on magic… the intention was to set some common ground and avoid any disagreements.

"Take Valedia, for example," she continued as she removed one of the books from the shelves, skimming through it briefly before frowning deeply at whatever was inside. "Magic is incredibly uncommon in Pharsat, and what magic-users they tend to produce thrive in elementals or necromancy. Fraecath believes the latter to be an affront to the Keepers. You can see how a difference in opinion on the topic of magic might prove deadly, if certain conditions were met."

Dante struggled not to shudder at the mention of necromancy. It *was* an affront to the Keepers, as far as Fraecath were concerned – no one in their right mind ever dabbled in matters concerning the Soul Keeper. Even the temporary borrowing of such power was blasphemy. There were countless horror stories of what happened to those who were foolish enough to cross Rhanigan, Lord of Chaos.

Charlotte squeezed past him, plucking a book from one of the shelves to skim through it. "That sounds awfully well-intentioned," she noted as Mo the cat began to sniff at her shoes timidly. "I can't imagine how that turned into a way for the royal family to control who uses magic here."

Straightening up, Eleni gave a long-suffering sigh as she

closed the book in her hand. "Those in power fear anyone that might usurp them," she offered darkly, her blue eyes shuttered. "King Gustaf has never been well-liked amongst our people, and a few decades ago his rule inspired a rebellion. The mages suffered the worst for the crimes of a collective. As punishment for their involvement, the king decreed that all those born with magic be registered with the kingdom for record-keeping purposes... and so that we would be shackled."

She raised her free hand for emphasis, that heavy silver cuff catching the light. "You know, I was in line last year to have my cuffs checked," Eleni began wistfully, regarding the metal closely. "There was a woman ahead of me, waiting in line with a baby... but the mama didn't have any cuffs, and she was well past the age that her magic would have manifested. No, the child was the one receiving cuffs that day."

Dante and Charlotte stiffened in unison, startled by the casual tone in which Eleni had delivered such a horrifying statement. She let her hand fall, her eyes tracking back towards the pair of them as she continued. "That happens sometimes," Eleni replied simply, a sadness in her voice as she smiled. "Your daughter laughs and flowers blossom, or a hearth fire rages when she cries. It's rare, usually only occurs when you have a strong magical bloodline from one parent or the other. Imagine that, welding metal onto a baby's wrists because they dared to be alive."

His mouth felt dry. "Do... do the cuffs ever come off?" Dante found himself asking. "What happens when the baby outgrows theirs?"

It seemed Charlotte already knew the answer, but Eleni replied anyway for Dante's benefit. "Ironically, the cuffs are enchanted... they grow with you," she replied with a wistful sigh. Eleni extended the book she held towards Dante, gesturing for him to take it. "It's not the original translation, but it's as close as you'll get while still being able to read it. It's transposed into the 'common tongue', or what was considered such back then."

Wrinkling her nose, Charlotte leaned closer to Dante to get a better look at the book he now had in his hands. "That is… not readable."

It *wasn't* readable, not exactly. Dante squinted at the front cover, the header and subtitle of the massive textbook giving a good impression of gibberish. The more he skimmed over it, however, he thought he could pick up bits and pieces of other languages he *did* know.

Eleni shook her head, crossing her arms over her chest. "Technically, it's what we would call Theian," she offered apologetically. "It's a language that evolved from the Tyiadai Daru dialects when Thelind was founded – linguistics-wise, it's a bit of a bloody mess. If you find yourself fluent in what we would call *our* 'common tongue', Fraeling, Pharasathi, and Siatch, then you might be able to read that."

That made more sense; it was a language Dante's father had once referred to as "that bastard tongue", often used in bazaars or marketplaces where strange merchants were commonly met with stranger customers. "Thank you," said Dante earnestly, dipping his head in Eleni's direction.

She regarded him warily for a moment, her eyes narrowed as she examined his face. "What is it you're up to that you're invested in magical law?" Eleni mused.

He could feel Charlotte's eyes on him as he flushed dark red once more. "N—nothing," he stammered, straightening up. "It's just… it's an assignment for Eodan, er… Mr. Melicus."

Eleni laughed dryly. "Oh, I am familiar with Eodan,"

she explained darkly. "You can tell him to stop by at some point. No need to be a stranger."

He had the distinct suspicion that there was some sort of inside joke he was missing out on, because Charlotte was also chuckling sardonically, for whatever reason. Eleni cast her a withering stare before turning her attention back to Dante, gesturing for him to head back to the front of the store. He turned towards the register, but that black and white cat was perched on top of it, as if barring anyone from using it.

"Shouldn't I… shouldn't I be paying for this?" Dante wondered aloud. He panicked internally, realizing that Eodan hadn't given him a budget for this book.

The bookstore owner clasped her hands as she regarded the cat now curled up on top of the register, her eyes beginning to droop shut. "Well, if Mo doesn't seem to think you need to, who am I to refute her judgment?" Eleni pointed out, sighing dramatically. With a conspiratorial wink, she added, "Friends of ours can consider this a library if not a bookstore. I'll only charge you if you destroy it, and then you're banned for life."

Dante didn't know whether to balk or laugh. His eventual reaction was a horridly awkward braying that barely passed for laughter. Thankfully, Charlotte drew Eleni's attention away from Dante's panicked noises with a snort under her breath, muttering something to the effect of, "Don't give Jasper any of these, then."

He bowed his head towards Eleni again, the book clenched tightly between his hands as he tried to shove it as gently as he could into his satchel. "Thank you, Miss—Eleni, ma'am," Dante stuttered, unsure of how to address the woman.

Waving a hand, Eleni only smiled. "Don't mention it,"

she insisted. "Who knows, perhaps I may be in need of a good scholar in the future. Good luck with your research – and do give Eodan a good telling-off for me."

Dante must have visibly paled at the prospect of telling his employer off, because both Eleni and Charlotte broke into fits of laughter. "I might not survive very long afterwards, ma'am," he chuckled nervously, wishing the floor might swallow him up.

"Don't be silly, darling," Eleni chided him, her voice honey-sweet. "If Eodan sent you here, he must like you. At least a little bit."

His satchel heavier and his face redder, Dante was forced to consider Eleni's words as he exited the bookshop. Bidding Charlotte farewell as she made her way towards the cathedral, Dante began the walk back to the embassy in silence.

The following morning, the Valedian council was bundled into the largest carriage that Eodan could summon, Dante among them. He had done his best to dress as smartly as he could in the hopes of blending in with the council's formal attire; having filled out somewhat once he had started eating regularly again, Dante had been able to source new clothes that fit him, for once. Though still too long for him, his dark hair had been combed back from his face, freshly washed and curling around his collarbones.

The king himself sat opposite Dante, wearing a silk tunic embroidered with gold, detailing the goddess Xiska and her legendary wolves along the collar and hems. The queen mother Hasima and the king's grandmother Verdis sat on either side of Dante, their stern faces and distinct perfumes making him feel quite claustrophobic. Benkaei, second in command, seemed quite displeased to be sharing a seat with King Fenyang and Huda. Dante could only assume that Huda was either the king's bride or his concubine by his gentle but possessive hand on her thigh. The shy, quiet Akila was seated by the window, her eyes filled with sympathy for Dante's seating situation as she smiled at him. Each council member was clothed in silk and leather brought from Valedia, and Dante was all too aware of the way his attire paled in comparison.

"Are you nervous, Dante?" King Fenyang asked suddenly, startling Dante from his thoughts.

"Very much so, Your Majesty," Dante admitted.

To his immense relief, there was no amusement at his admission. Akila addressed him first, tucking a twisted lock of hair behind her ear. "This is my first time attending an accords meeting, as well," she admitted with a shy smile.

Benkaei was silent for a moment, as if debating the benefit of being kind to him. "This is only my second time attending," she admitted with a sigh after a moment's pause.

"Just follow my lead, Dante," the king offered, and there was a distinct kindness in the monarch's eyes that made Dante almost uncomfortable. He was accustomed to thinking of royalty as a distant, cruel force, and an unkind childhood spent disappointing his parents led to Dante having a distinct distaste for authority figures. Despite his status, King Fenyang was remarkably ordinary – an honourable, ordinary man.

Gripping his knees, Dante did his best to calm himself, but the thought of being in this council meeting before the Aethian king was terrifying to him. He struggled not to panic, not to imagine fictional scenarios where he failed his task before he even began. After all these years, Dante still remembered his upbringing, the failures he had been made to remember. His father had been insistent on drilling his mistakes into his head, as if an iron brand in his memory might better serve him.

There is something broken inside of you that cannot be fixed, it can only be destroyed.

The fabric of his trousers felt damp beneath his palms as Dante clenched his fists, digging his fingernails into his skin. He could not fail the king today.

A quick, rapid knocking against the carriage door alerted them to their arrival at the castle, and the council began to exit the carriage. It was a muggy, overcast day in Aethelind, and within the short walk through the castle courtyard Dante had the distinct impression he had expired. He missed the dry, temperate climate of Fraecath. He missed the countryside, the scent of the ocean on the wind... he missed home in so many ways, ways that had nothing to do with home at all.

He was grateful for the cool interior of the castle as they entered through the main gate, the great oak doors already opened wide for their arrival. The ancient wood had been carved to depict the three goddesses, splitting down the middle along Xiska's face. If there was some affront to the Valedians there, Dante could not detect it in their expressions.

The main entrance hall was decorated in the proud colours of Aethia, their ancient dragon insignia emblazoned on emerald banners hanging from each stone pillar. Castle Fraecath was partially hewn from the very mountain it resided in, smooth stone floors and walls lovingly carved by their ancestors. To see gleaming stone bricks polished and cut, towering high above his head in a grand domed ceiling... he wondered how long such a feat had taken.

A withered old man met them in the entrance hall, bowing stiffly. If his violet robes were not symbol enough, the flowering crest of Eirodys across the front of them proclaimed the goddess he devoted himself to. "Your Majesty," the man greeted the king, his jaw moving as rigidly as his body seemed to. "Allow me to escort you and your council to the meeting room."

"Thank you, Aloysius," King Fenyang replied, startling Dante with his familiarity with the decrepit old man. He had to be a member of the Aethian council. As Aloysius led them from the entrance hall to a grand staircase stemming from the northeastern corridor, he eyed Dante warily.

"Is this a new council member of yours?" the old man inquired, his misty eyes narrowed on Dante's face.

King Fenyang responded smoothly, as if he had anticipated the question. "This is Dante Styvacino. He is acting as a consultant for my council."

Dante felt his face heat. Styvacino was a city in the northeast of Fraecath, with the convention of adopting the district of birth as a surname being reserved for children born out of wedlock. He had neglected to provide Eodan and King Fenyang with a full name for himself, but he wasn't sure he liked the alternative of being perceived as a bastard.

Composing himself, he bowed briefly towards Aloysius. "A pleasure to meet you, sir," he managed to mutter.

The old man made a noise in his throat that might have been approving. "Well, I hope you've trained him well," he scoffed as he made his way up the stairs, leaving Dante to simmer angrily behind him. Akila placed a reassuring hand on his shoulder as the king and his council made their way up the staircase, crossing the large atrium above the main entrance hall. Aloysius led them along another corridor before coming to a stop outside a relatively plain-looking wooden door, left open for them as they entered the meeting room.

A wide, round table filled with maps and scrolls had been stationed in the centre of what appeared to be a small study, the walls on either side lined with bookshelves. A quick glance confirmed for Dante that the assortment of tomes seemed to be legal texts and historical accounts, ideal for an accords meeting. A single large window on the far wall illuminated the dusty air as the Valedian council wandered into the room.

"You may seat yourselves," Aloysius sniffed, still eyeing Dante as he entered the room. "I will summon the king shortly."

Once Aloysius had departed, the council members made quick work of inspecting the room. Benkaei was particularly vicious in her search as she examined the table, each chair beneath it, and as many books as she could in search of weapons or traps. To Dante's surprise, Huda seemed to employ an alternative tactic. He watched as the woman began to weave a dark string of her power into a web, stretching it between her fingers as she spoke in a hushed voice. It made sense for a sightless spellcaster to verbalize her intent, but it was not the whispered Pharasathi incantation that made Dante uneasy.

The web grew wider and wider until it encompassed the entire room, each of the council members enveloped in that thread. A sharp pang of horror sliced through Dante as that energy made contact with him, that chilling and powerful magic that tasted of the dead of winter and grave-yard dirt. Huda was a necromancer.

"There are no wards or enchantments in this room, Your Majesty," Huda confirmed, oblivious to Dante's analysis. She chuckled to herself, as if laughing at some private joke. "None that I can detect, at least."

"Thank you, Huda," the Valedian king replied, leading the woman towards one of the chairs. Seemingly noticing Dante dissociating nearby, the king addressed him. "Are you all right, Dante? Come, you will sit beside Huda on my left."

Dante schooled his expression immediately, not wanting to betray his aversion towards the woman's actions. She had done nothing wrong, and he refused to make anyone aware of his intolerance for death magic. He was just about to take his seat when footsteps sounded from the hallway, and Dante met the king of Aethelind.

From the moment that Dante had first seen King Fenyang, the man had never worn anything resembling a crown. As King Gustaf entered the room, his brow was adorned with a golden crown beset with emeralds, his steel-grey eyes examining each member of the Valedian king's council with a calculating stare. He was tall for an Aethian, clothed in finery so dark that Dante could not immediately identify it as blue. He was notably older than King Fenyang as well, with a wind-worn face and dark hair threaded with silver.

"His Majesty, King Gustaf Edmund—" Aloysius began in a stiff voice, but King Gustaf waved a hand.

"Let's get this over with, shall we?" the Aethian king began dismissively, taking a seat directly opposite King Fenyang across the table. A flustered Aloysius sat to the right as another man entered the room, shutting the door behind him before seating himself to the left of King Gustaf. Judging by his age and the armour he wore, Dante guessed he was the king's general. As he realized no one else would be joining them, Dante glanced towards King Fenyang, uncertain of how to proceed.

Meeting Dante's gaze, the Valedian king smiled politely. "Good day to you, as well," he said plainly as he sat down, gesturing for Dante and his companions to follow. "Will the rest of your council not be joining us today?"

King Gustaf reached for the nearest scroll from the middle of the table, casually skimming it before he responded. "My other associates are indisposed," he offered in explanation without looking up. "The accords decree a minimum quorum of three members of each nation, including the monarch. This meeting can continue without them."

Dante blinked. What could possibly take precedence over the accords? Were there no alternative members to attend? He knew King Gustaf had a daughter around Jasper's age, but the princess was also suspiciously absent from the meeting.

"The accords also state that there shall not be an imbalanced attendance between the two parties," King Fenyang warned, his brow furrowed. "You should have warned us your full council would not be present, and we would have made arrangements to match our numbers."

With a dismissive wave of his hand, the Aethian king shook his head. "The council of Aethia will waive this requirement with your concurrence," King Gustaf supplied, settling into his chair as he regarded another of the scrolls before him. "Our first matter will be trade, of course. Pharsat has not met the accords-decreed requirement to provide their quota of goods... Is there an issue in the supply chain?"

The Valedian king laughed, but there was no humour

in his tone. "Straight to business, then," he muttered. Clearing his throat, he continued, "You can hardly expect us to continue regular trade when we have been plagued with drought for nearly a year."

The general scoffed, leaning back casually in his chair. "Do you not live in a desert? I thought you might be better prepared for such weather patterns."

"This past spring was supposed to be our rainy season," Verdis interrupted, her husky voice commanding attention with ease. Her face was freshly painted with the stark white healer's markings, intensifying her stern expression. "A damned dry one it's turned out to be."

"My people grow hungry on the remnants of last year's rations," King Fenyang continued, nodding in agreement. "They cannot survive much longer if you demand the same exports as you would have of others in safer, more fertile lands."

The general leaned forward where he sat, his eyes narrowed. "You're well aware our nation faces a similar plight," he pointed out, as if everyone in the room could collectively pretend it didn't rain every other day, the reservoirs full to bursting.

Aloysius cleared his throat, silencing the general with a wave of his hand. "What General Byron means is that our smallfolk are also at a disadvantage," he attempted to clarify. "Though different in nature, our people are also affected by food scarcity."

Judging by the way Benkaei's expression sharpened at the man's words, Dante suspected she was similarly aggravated by the false comparison. "This is not food scarcity due to poverty or classism," Benkaei cut in, her tone leaving no room for disagreement. "If you wish to maintain this alliance, the people of Pharsat are in dire need of support."

"Is that a threat?" General Byron demanded, standing up so abruptly his chair screeched back behind him.

The Aethian king raised a hand, his expression unchanged. "Byron, that won't be necessary," he said smoothly. The general sat back down. "Though I admit I don't care for your tone, madame."

Benkaei bristled, but her king spoke for her. "My second-in-command speaks the truth," he insisted, tossing her rank into the conversation as if to quell any complaints from the other side. "The accords call for a give-and-take when it comes to our exports. Valedia has given what little we have, but Aethia has not."

The withered mage spluttered, crossing his arms over his robes. "Are you accusing us of not holding up our side of the accords?" Aloysius hissed.

"Is that not what *you're* doing?" Hasima asked baldly.

King Gustaf sighed, raising his eyes from the scroll to eye the Valedian king at last. "The accords are clear in their description of acceptable reasons not to uphold them," he explained slowly, as if he were disciplining a child. "Most of those reasons all pertain to war, as you well know. Drought and other inconvenient weather phenomena do not qualify."

"Have you ever visited Pharsat?" Akila piped up suddenly. As all eyes turned to face her, she cleared her throat, chewing her lip before she continued. "You may recall the dry season generally lasts throughout the summer months, lingering into the autumn. It is a difficult time, but it is rationed for accordingly – Valedians even conduct their ritual pilgrimage during the hottest, most dangerous months of the year, for that is how they test their mettle against the goddess' most formidable obstacles."

"I don't recall asking for the history lesson," King

Gustaf replied stonily. Dante blinked, struggling not to visibly recoil from the king's response, as if the scathing words had been directed at him instead of Akila. For the first time during their meeting, King Fenyang seemed aggravated.

"The point is to demonstrate that we *are* prepared for droughts, for our dry season," he explained in a carefully even tone, the set of his jaw tense. "We are prepared when they last three to four months, as they always have. Not nine, not longer."

Aloysius was turning an unsettling shade of red, clearly preparing for another enraged response. Dante was distracted from the discussion by Huda beside him, sniffing primly as she crossed her legs. He glanced over at the movement, at the way her hands had been delicately folded on the table... her forefinger subtly pointing towards the withered council member.

"Regardless of the length of the drought, we cannot rewrite the accords," King Gustaf insisted, shaking his head. "You know how vitally important it is we maintain these. They are clear in their acceptable terms, and weather patterns simply do not qualify."

There was something about the way the Aethian king spoke in that moment, something about that smug cadence that set Dante's teeth on edge. King Gustaf reminded him of his father, the way he would phrase refusals as if he were genuinely trying to help but was otherwise unable to. He could hold his tongue no longer.

"An extended drought is not merely a 'weather pattern'," Dante found himself cutting in, his anger overruling his judgment. "And I think you'll find that magical intervention in climate changes *will* qualify."

The brief silence that fell around the table was satisfying, but also incredibly intimidating. Aloysius turned a shade of purple so deep Dante feared he might be choking, and the general stood up again so quickly his chair clattered backwards behind him. "How dare you accuse Aethia of such a thing!" Byron roared. "We would no sooner violate these accords than declare war on the goddesses themselves!"

King Gustaf's gunmetal gaze was fixed on Dante, but he refused to balk, refused to wither beneath that hateful glower. "The accords, and moreover the mage laws themselves, are clear in their condemnation of magical acts for political gain," Dante continued, and he held the monarch's stare as he spoke.

The Aethian king laughed. Dante was too stunned to even be offended as the sound reverberated in the silence. "Have we truly strayed so far from the Three that we claim to know the origins of the weather?" he chortled, his voice dripping with sarcasm.

Dante wanted to scream. He wanted to throw his chair, he wanted to point out to the stupid Aethian king that he was from Fraecath and he believed in the Keepers, *thank you very much*, but to his immense relief it was King Fenyang who responded.

"We have had this drought assessed by our own experts," he explained. "Magic leaves a signature, as unique as our fingerprints. If we were to identify the person who cast the spell causing or extending a drought... that would be classified as an act of war."

The Aethian king's laughter died down as he regarded the Valedian monarch with cold hatred in his eyes. "You would do well not to accuse anyone of war crimes at this table," said King Gustaf in a low voice. Aloysius remained silent, offering no words to aid his defense.

"We are not accusing anyone of anything just yet," Verdis cut in, casting a quick glance towards her grandson. "While this may be an act of war, it remains to be seen who is guilty."

The Valedian king stared at the monarch sitting across from him, the man who represented the nation that was supposedly their ally. "In light of recent events, the kingdom of Valedia requests an official investigation into an alleged unlawful magical act," King Fenyang announced. He turned towards Dante, nodding approvingly as if waiting for him to continue.

Dante cleared his throat. "If it is found that the drought has been cast in bad faith for political gain… you will forgive Pharsat for not meeting their export quota and you will provide immediate aid for the citizens affected." He was pleased his voice did not quiver.

"And if we are found innocent?" Byron spat, still standing. He leaned on the table, eyeing each of the council members as if they might jump up to strike him. "What punishment will Valedia suffer then?"

"You will receive the full amount of the goods owed to Aethia," Benkaei offered before Dante could speak up. "As well as a formal apology from Valedia, her king, and each of his council members."

King Gustaf shook his head, a smile crossing his face. It was not a pleasant smile, and Dante suddenly had a very, very bad feeling about this. "No, that isn't good enough," he disagreed. "If we are found innocent, Aethia will consider this an act of war."

"How dare you!" Hasima hissed. The queen mother stood, with far more grace and poise than Byron was apparently capable of, scowling in the Aethian king's direction. "On what grounds?"

"How would this be an act of war?" King Fenyang asked calmly, gesturing for his mother to sit back down.

"You know what's at stake, and you would threaten our alliance with false accusations," King Gustaf warned.

"If they truly are false accusations, then you have nothing to worry about," the Valedian king reasoned, leaning forward on his elbows. "I respect our alliance, and the accords. But I must protect my kingdom, and that includes being thorough. As our allies, Aethia should see the merit in assisting us as we work to uncover the culprit behind such acts."

"I will not be *slighted*."

Dante's head was spinning. This felt like an outcome he should have foreseen. He glanced up at King Fenyang, wanting to say something—anything to plead his case, to insist that King Gustaf was wrong, that their defense was solid.

To his surprise, the Valedian king was smiling, his words even and calm with an undeniable authority to them. "The kingdom of Valedia will proceed with the investigation," he began. "A neutral party will determine the truth of the allegations by means of detecting the magic's origin. There will be no trial, only the determination of a mage's evaluation. Is this agreeable to you?"

A terse silence hovered over them, the air thick with emotion. Huda turned her head ever so slightly towards Dante, her hand still pointing towards Aloysius where it rested on the table. Following her lead, Dante allowed his senses to trickle out from behind his walls, tentatively reaching towards the old man across the table... his mental probe found only a fortress of iron, but Dante still recoiled at the power he felt rippling from beyond that stronghold.

As his senses withdrew, Dante's eyes narrowed. He had

not analyzed the drought as Huda and Verdis had. Sensing the depth of the energy within that horrid man, however... an immense amount of magic and skill would be required to initiate or even extend a weather pattern, and Dante knew innately that Aloysius was capable of it. He had encountered only one other person with a mental shield that strong. Unlike Eodan, however, Aloysius seemed rather worse for wear, as if the physical strain of the weather magic had caused him to wither beyond normal human aging.

Shifting on his chair, Dante angled his foot to tap Huda's ankle gently. Her lips curled into a demure smile as she withdrew her hands, folding them delicately in her lap. The monarchs at the table stared at one another for a few seconds more before King Gustaf leaned back in his seat, exhaling slowly.

"You leave me little choice," he replied at last, drumming his fingers against the wooden surface of the table. He seemed agitated, his mind far away. "Very well. The sooner we commence, the sooner this foul affair can be done away with."

"Of course," King Fenyang agreed. Dante could hear a flicker of surprise in his voice, but he wasn't sure if the Aethian king would have caught onto it. "I wouldn't have it any other way."

Their host stood from the table, adjusting his finery with a detached expression. Aloysius, still red in the face, followed suit along with the general. None of them looked particularly pleased with the way the meeting had gone today.

"It seems the meeting of the accords cannot continue until this investigation is concluded," Aloysius offered stiffly, fidgeting with his robes as he stood. "Which is permitted, of course, under acceptable delays for... extenuating circumstances."

"Of course," King Fenyang repeated. He stood with a slow grace that Dante found impressive, both for Fenyang's height and for the lack of composure witnessed across the table. As he stood, his council members rose in unison around him, Dante scrambling to join them.

"We shall consider this meeting adjourned then," King Gustaf continued to no one in particular, his eyes on his sleeves as he adjusted the fastenings at his wrists. "I have other business to attend to. We will be in touch."

Without another word, the Aethian king and his companions exited the room, leaving the Valedian council to their own devices. Once she was certain they were out of earshot, Benkaei spat out, "Pale bastards."

"What did we do wrong?" Dante asked immediately, raking his fingers through his hair. "I—we researched this for hours, I looked at every possible angle. It's an entirely reasonable defence, given the circumstances..."

Akila gave him a sympathizing look, reaching to squeeze his shoulder gently. Dante noted with some dismay that none of the council members seemed surprised by how the meeting had ended. "This was... not unexpected," was Hasima's response, smiling apologetically.

"I greatly enjoyed you wiping that smirk off his face," Verdis muttered under her breath. "Bloody cheek."

"But Your Majesty, he—he can't speak to you that way!" Dante protested, waving at the spot where King Gustaf had been sitting.

With a sigh, Fenyang dragged his hands down his face in an uncharacteristic display of vulnerability. It was the most human gesture Dante had ever witnessed from the king, and it did a strange thing to his heart. When the Valedian king turned to meet his stare, his golden eyes were weary.

"Dante... this is behaviour we are accustomed to receiving from Aethia," King Fenyang explained softly, sounding quite exhausted. "I likely should have warned you to expect such animosity from him, but in truth I worried it might hinder you to know you might be arguing with a brick wall."

"You did very well," Benkaei replied stiffly, crossing her arms over her chest. Dante was even more startled by the compliment coming from her.

Shaking his head, Dante buried his face in his hands. "Accusing you of an act of war... what have I done?"

"You have given us a chance where we had none," King Fenyang insisted, and there was no refuting the authority in his voice. His honey-brown gaze was intense as Dante looked up at him, and he understood why the king did not wear a crown; he never needed to remind anyone *why* he was king. Pharsat had chosen him as their ruler, and that was enough. "Gustaf would have responded poorly no matter our defense, but you have assisted us in providing a solid, factually driven case against him. I could ask for no better outcome."

His council members were nodding in agreement, and even Huda had turned in his direction to offer a shy smile. Dante could not be convinced, however. As his gaze fell back to the wooden table before them, an uneasy feeling settled in his gut. Somehow, despite Fenyang's reassurances, Dante couldn't shake the feeling that he had talked them all into a battle they couldn't win.

CHAPTER
NINE

JASPER

It was a humid afternoon as Jasper went to retrieve the latest shipment, uncomfortably warm even with the sleeves of his light shirt rolled to his elbows. The summer dance of the volatile Aethelind weather was in full swing, and the sticky, sunny day signalled another thunderstorm would follow later that week. Everyone around him seemed to be equally agitated by the weather, which did little to help the brewing tensions in the city.

The accords meetings were highly secretive affairs, so naturally the anxious gossip spread like wildfire. Jasper didn't pretend to understand political matters as intimately as Dante evidently did, but his friend's hushed explanation of the proceedings was chilling. The meeting had not gone well, and the discussions for the accords were apparently on hold indefinitely. Caelfall especially was fraught with anxiety and fear, for the last war had done little to ease the already poor economic status of the district.

Jasper had thought about the potential implications of a conflict and had ultimately concluded that he might very well be in trouble. A blacksmith was always a necessity, but he wasn't certain whether his talents as a smith or his ability to fight would be more important in a time of war. He had no love of combat or violence, however often he seemed to be called to it, and Jasper was not keen on being reminded of why he had never become a knight.

Even the opiates business seemed to be suffering. There was no shortage of product, but as Varus had predicted there were tensions below ground as well. Jasper had already found a dead bird in one shipment, a note pinned to it that he hadn't bothered reading before he buried the animal. It seemed a bit early for him to retire, but the business was beginning to take a toll on him emotionally, oftentimes leaving him too drained to speak to Dante or even Charlotte once he'd finished for the day.

As Jasper inspected the latest package of opiates in the horse-drawn wagon, taking a little extra care to ensure there weren't any unexpected surprises in the form of more dead birds, a voice startled him from behind. "Looking for anything specific?" said Cary teasingly as she approached, and when Jasper looked up, he had to blink repeatedly to ensure he wasn't hallucinating. Cary was clothed in a fine jacket and trousers, her long dark hair secured beneath a bowler. Had he not heard her voice, he might not have recognized her. With the aid of a glamour, Cary's appearance leaned into a more masculine presentation.

"Misplaced my marbles," he stammered after an uncomfortably long pause. Securing the thick textiles that concealed the nature of the shipment, Jasper straightened up as he cleared his throat. "What, er… what brings you here?"

She raised a brow beneath the brim of her hat, a hand on her hip as she leaned casually. "Haven't you noticed? You seem to have a few admirers in town today. I figured you might need a hand."

Jasper's mouth went dry, his gaze remaining fixed on Cary as he took notice of the several pairs of eyes currently trained on him. He may as well have been a signal flare, a red-headed flag waving back and forth for all to see. "Admirers for me, or admirers for the product?" he muttered in mock wonder, rubbing the back of his neck. "Glad you showed up."

"Let's be off then," Cary urged him gently. "The sooner we get out of here, the better."

Nodding his head, Jasper decided against mounting the horse in favour of remaining on foot, guiding the mare at his side in a nervous trot through Caelfall. He was uncomfortably aware of the attention that followed them as they made their way towards Haeyin's clinic, wishing he had a weapon on his person. Cary kept pace with him opposite the mare, and Jasper knew from experience that her eyes were watching every potential threat, her hands clenching her knives where they had been casually shoved in her pockets.

In the corner of his eye, he watched as one by one, strangers stood up from bistro tables, abandoned produce stands and shopfronts as they began to pursue them doggedly through the streets. The sound of the wagon wheels against the uneven cobblestones almost drowned out their footsteps as they approached, and Jasper could see the glint of steel in Cary's pocket out the corner of his eye as she began to withdraw her knives.

His heart pounded in his ears as he kept his gaze fixed straight ahead, mentally counting each body he could see in his peripheral. One, two, three... five he could see, and however many were behind him. Not good – Jasper and Cary were outnumbered, and that was without the precious, highly illegal shipment they were forced to try and protect.

His grip on the reins tightened, and he forced himself to remain as calm as possible while he maintained pace, struggling not to frighten the mare. Ahead of him, a woman with strawberry blonde hair was watching them, her piercing green eyes tracking the movement of their pursuers. To Jasper's left, a man with a scar along his cheekbone revealed a sharp dagger—

"... by order of His Majesty, King Gustaf Edmund Davenport III... you have been sentenced to death for the heinous crime of murder of the first degree against a citizen of the sovereign kingdom of Aethelind..."

Jasper froze involuntarily, Cary pausing with her knives withdrawn, hooked around her fingers. Their pursuers seemed equally startled by what they'd heard, several heads turning in unison towards the source of the noise. Ahead of them, some twenty yards away in the market courtyard, a confrontation between a group of soldiers and a lone woman was taking place, scattered spectators watching nearby. Despite the precarious situation he found himself in, Jasper knew their stalkers wouldn't attempt to murder him and Cary in the presence of so many authority figures. He breathed a sigh of relief, though he wasn't out of the woods yet.

The subject of the accusations was an elderly woman with silver hair and watery eyes, her face browned and lined by the sun. Looking quite startled by the charges made, she stared blankly at the soldiers who faced her, the knight who led them. Feeling sick to his stomach, Jasper wondered briefly if it was Gideon.

But no—it was not a knight that led the soldiers, but a templar of the Order of Xiska, distinct from the royal guard by his black armour and scarlet cloak. Templars were set apart from even knights as being the most prestigious of fighters, pupils of the highest graduating class of the combat academy. The bold wolf's mark of the warrior goddess was engraved in his cuirass, and there was a perverse sort of irony in the fact that a templar was delivering a death sentence to a seemingly harmless old crone.

"I will ask you again," the templar spoke. "Do you have any last words?"

The question sparked a change in the old woman, and a sudden ferocity bloomed across her expression. She stepped forward, much to the soldiers' collective alarm. They half-raised their rifles as if to strike her down, but the templar halted their actions with an outstretched hand once he saw the woman had taken only two steps towards them.

"What is she doing?" Cary hissed. Still mostly occupied with the retreating pursuers, her knives were partially exposed as she prepared to strike at the slightest provocation.

Jasper could only watch, a sensation of dread settling over him. He had encountered many criminals in Caelfall – the strangers who had been following him and Cary today were a good example. In truth, the woman who had been accused did not look like a murderer. She still wore a flour-dusted apron, her hands coated in confectionery. He couldn't be certain, but in a place like Caelfall, he knew the odds were high that he had met and talked to this woman before.

Cementing her feet where she stood, she raised her fist

to the skies in a gesture of defiance. The crowd gasped audibly where they watched nearby, murmurs making their way through the courtyard to Jasper's field of hearing. "I would rather die on my feet than live on my knees before a false king," she declared loudly, her age-roughened voice rumbling across the crowd. Jasper nearly stumbled at the power in her statement, the influence an otherwise unremarkable woman seemed to command.

The rest of the crowd seemed to be struck by the same reaction. The murmuring grew louder, some shouts of agreement joining in as their shock evolved into a wave of righteous anger. Jasper was about to abandon his horse and run over to the woman, to do something, to do *anything*...

Her executioner seemed momentarily stunned before scoffing cruelly. "Very well." The templar, his hand still raised to signal the men behind him to hold, brought his arm down in a vicious swing, and a cacophony of gunshots echoed across the courtyard. Screams rang out as the soldiers' rifles ricocheted, pottery smashed and baked goods pulverised by stray bullets as those nearest the accused ducked for cover. The woman's body recoiled horribly, many of the shots landing their mark across her chest, her face – she fell to the floor in a heap, the pigeons that scavenged across the city taking flight in alarm, fleeing the scene in a scattered cloud of anxious flapping. Jasper's horse panicked at the sound, pulling at the reins and the confines of the wagon with a frantic whinny.

"Come on, Jasper, we have to go!" Cary hissed, tugging the reins from his hands as she pulled the horse away from the scene, struggling with the anxious animal. Their "admirers" were nowhere to be found, having fled the scene of the altercation. "Help me, we have to leave *now*."

Jasper was far away. He stared for what felt like an eternity, the world growing quiet as he stared at the woman's body. Her watery, empty eyes stared up at the sky above as blood spilled from her broken skull. The frantic thrumming in his mind was underlined by his rapidly accelerating heartbeat, thudding through his veins as he stared—

"*Jasper!*"

He startled, the horse beside him whinnying again as he involuntarily panicked it further. Leaning forward, Jasper stroked the mare's snout with as much gentleness as he could summon, his hands eerily still. Even as he felt himself coming apart at the seams, Jasper bit down on his tongue, bit down on that sick sense of dread and horror that bubbled from within him. Whatever emotions he felt, whatever shock his body was falling into, Jasper buried it deep within him, packaging it somewhere in his mind where it couldn't hurt him.

The mare calmed enough to be led away from the scene, and Cary and Jasper departed for the clinic as quickly as they could. Behind them, the citizens of Caelfall gathered to mourn openly for the woman who had died.

∽ ✲ ∾

Cary had insisted on dragging Jasper back to *Raven's Haunt* after they had dropped the opiates off at Haeyin's. The man had been actively stitching up someone's amputated fingers, blood up to his wrists, and yet had still found the time to worry over Jasper.

"You are very clearly in shock," he protested as Jasper tried to leave as quickly as humanly possible. "Please, at least let me make sure you're alright."

Thankfully, Cary had been around to assist. "I can take care of him," she assured Haeyin. "Maybe you can meet up with us for a pint when you're… when you're done here." Leaving the room very quickly before she could stare too much at the gore on the table, Cary had grasped Jasper by the collar of his shirt and directed him out of the clinic, steering him through the city streets towards *Raven's Haunt*.

The atmosphere was different today, Jasper noted. It was never particularly cheerful in *Raven's Haunt*, but today there was a distinct sorrow that hovered over the tavern like a cloud. Even Nadine's sunny disposition was dampened, her smile failing to reach her eyes as she pulled Jasper into an embrace he couldn't return.

"You look positively wrecked, Jasper," the woman worried over him, drawing back to search his face. "What's the matter?"

He was unable to voice a reply while her hands were on his arms, and Jasper was grateful when Cary responded for him. "We were privy to the nasty business that went down in the courtyard," she offered in response, her lips pursed as she regarded Nadine's hold on her companion.

Nodding slowly, Nadine withdrew her grasp. "What can I get you?" she asked quietly, her eyes darting from Cary to Jasper.

"Brandy, please," Cary began, removing her coat and her hat. Her dark hair tumbled free at once, and it was as if whatever glamour she had conjured to give herself the appearance of a man had vanished. "Don't bother with a glass, I'll take the bottle. And a cider for this one, if you wouldn't mind."

Nadine's eyes tightened as she nodded. "All right, love," she agreed in a soft voice, turning away quickly. Cary and Jasper made their way towards their usual table at the back corner of the room, but Jasper stopped abruptly as he saw a familiar face sitting at another, nondescript table nearby.

"Gideon?" he asked incredulously, doubtful.

He looked awful. His blonde hair half-scraped off his face in a loose knot, Gideon fit in well with the sombre clientele, which was not a complimentary comparison. It was strange enough to see him in his civilian clothes, stranger still to see the man so obviously in a state of despair. He turned to meet Jasper's gaze, a haunted look on his face.

"Jasper," he greeted him numbly, nodding absentmindedly. "I'd hoped I might see you here."

Very clearly drunk, Jasper noted. He took a seat tentatively beside the man, clearing his throat as he addressed Cary. She was staring at him, her pink eyes wary as she waited for some manner of clarification.

"Cary, this is… this is Gideon," he began, searching for something to add as if to say, *He's normally in much better shape than this.*

"I know," Cary replied, slowly taking the seat furthest from Gideon. Her eyes landed on the knight as she assessed his appearance, the stein of ale in his white-knuckled grasp as he leaned on the table for support. "We've met at the castle before."

"Oh, right," Jasper stammered in response, shaking his head. Of course, Cary's cautious expression wasn't a lack of familiarity – it was her wondering what the captain of the royal guard was doing in a place like this. "Gideon, what's the matter? Are you all right?"

It felt like a stupid question to ask when the man was clearly not all right, but Jasper wasn't sure how to address him. Typically, Jasper was the one whose life was in shambles; it was rare to see Gideon, perfect and handsome and honourable, in such a state of distress. The other man sighed as he stared into his ale, as if he sought some answer for his existential crisis in the bottom of the stein. There were lines beneath his eyes Jasper had never noticed before, the faded scars on his face unnaturally harsh in this lighting.

"I thought I was doing the right thing, becoming a knight," he said distantly, as if having a conversation with someone else entirely. "I thought I was protecting people, I thought I was on the side of justice."

Jasper stiffened at the man's words. The last time Gideon had spoken so candidly in front of him had been in a field beside the graveyard, the two of them alone at twilight. "Gideon, maybe we shouldn't talk about this here," he muttered, glancing around at the tavern patrons. Cary's eyes narrowed on Gideon as he spoke, idly toying with her mother's necklace at her throat.

"Did you see it?" Gideon asked suddenly, and he turned to face Jasper at last. The full force of that empty stare rocked him to his core, and Jasper had to force himself not to recoil as he felt pinned beneath that gaze. "Did you see that woman die today?"

The memory tugged at his heart, dragging that heavy grief deeper within his chest. "Yes," he whispered.

Gideon laughed, and it was a horrid, hollow sound. "Do you know what she was guilty of?" he asked, his voice gravelly. "She... she murdered a man, that much is true. But do you know *why* she did it? Bastard raped her daughter, and no one did a bloody thing about it, so she took matters into her own hands."

Cary loosed a pained breath, pinching the bridge of her nose. "Shadows..." she cursed under her breath.

The man took a deep gulp of his ale, swallowing it with a desperation Jasper had never seen him possess before. "I became a knight to protect people," gasped Gideon, his voice rough. "And yet when shit like this happens, I can't do a damned thing. I didn't kill her, but I sure as hell didn't protect her."

"Gideon... it's not your fault," Jasper insisted.

"Isn't it?" Gideon snapped in reply. "Am I free of sin solely because I did not pull the trigger?" As if noticing Jasper's automatic flinch at the rise in volume, or remembering their surroundings, Gideon lowered his voice once more.

"Jasper, I have—I have done things, you know? I have done... *horrible* things in the name of king and country. The things they have asked of me, I should have refused, I should have questioned it, but I just followed my orders like a good little dog. My hands are as bloody as the lot of them."

"You're aware of it, at least," Cary remarked as she leaned back in her chair, though her tone was not unkind. "That's half the battle."

Gideon laughed again, shaking his head. "But not the half that matters, is it?" he protested.

A thought crossed Jasper's mind, the words of the old woman lingering in his thoughts. "What did she mean when she said, 'a false king'?" he found the courage to ask, posing the question to Gideon and Cary, whoever would answer.

Gideon's brow furrowed at the comment, but it was Cary who answered. "There are rumours that Gustaf is not Aurelia's sire," she explained with a sigh, brushing her hair back from her face. "And as she stands upon the cusp of adulthood, there are some who take issue with the fact that Gustaf is only truly the king regent. They believe that Aurelia should rightfully be queen as the only living descendent of Evelyn Drakewind."

It seemed Jasper was always the last to pick up on societal gossip and murmurings, but he could see where the rumours had been sowed. Gideon grunted in a sort of laugh, raking his fingers through his dishevelled hair. "For crying out loud, it's albinism," he grumbled. "Doesn't mean anything at all – she could be his twin, but they wouldn't be able to see past her colouring."

"People will believe what they want to believe," Jasper murmured, thumbing the wood grain of the table as he recalled the whispered rumours he had overheard in his youth. Zeke had tried to protect him from many things, but he couldn't shield Jasper from their neighbours' gossip of his questionable parentage, the hushed word *changeling* passing their lips. His uncle had warned him never to show his ears, not wanting to add fuel to the fire.

Gideon's weary gaze slid over to Jasper, a war of emotions brewing in his eyes as he seemed to struggle to formulate a sentence. "You know, Jasper... maybe I was wrong to say you should have been a knight," he admitted finally, his voice ale-rough.

Jasper felt his hair stand on end at the remark. "What?"

"I wanted you there with me, selfishly," the other man continued, a ragged hopelessness entering his voice. "But all the reasons I thought you would be a good knight, your skill and your courage... you have a good heart, Jasper, and you do not belong amongst the monsters that follow the king's orders."

He wasn't sure whether to be offended or relieved at Gideon's words. Cary seemed to be in a similarly perplexed state, leaning forward on her elbows to speak more quietly. "Gideon, think about what you're saying," she said in a gentle but urgent voice, glancing at their surroundings. "This is not a conversation you would want overheard."

"This is Caelfall," Jasper pointed out as he mimicked her gesture, leaning towards the table. "Not exactly an appropriate place to point out your career."

"And it's the last place they'll look for me," Gideon noted glumly as he took another swig.

"Who's your friend, Jasper?" a deep voice rumbled, and Jasper started in alarm as none other than Varus Emery appeared behind him. He stood before them unobscured, to Jasper's immense surprise. Seeing Varus without a glamour in the wild seemed even more out of place than finding a drunken Gideon in *Raven's Haunt*.

How much had he overheard? A tremor of anxiety ran through Jasper like an electric current as Gideon looked up slowly, making eye contact with the kingpin. Cary seemed to be similarly on edge, evident in the way the muscle in her jaw tensed.

Gideon swayed slightly where he sat, leaning on his elbow. "Some friend," he murmured, his voice barely above a whisper. "I should have left with you, Jasper. Should have seen what it did to you when you were in training... Should have left then. None of this would have happened."

Jasper stiffened, chewing on his cheek as he pondered how damning Gideon's words had been. Cary cleared her throat across the table, and he could sense Varus standing over him, could picture the way his eyes would slide from Gideon to Jasper to Cary as he regarded the three of them.

"Mind if I join you?" his employer asked, his voice somewhere between curious and amused.

The knight stood with little grace or composure, sliding his stein towards the middle of the table. "You can have my seat, I think I'm done," said Gideon in a hoarse voice. "I... I need to get back."

"Will you be all right?" Jasper asked, unable to stop the

panic that leaked into his tone. Gideon's father was volatile at the best of times, and he had spent a large amount of his childhood avoiding the man.

His friend met his gaze, and Jasper hated how ghostly those blue eyes were. He managed a smile, and something about the expression was more uncomfortable than just eye contact alone. "I'll be fine, Jas," he murmured, nodding slowly. "He's too much of a coward to try anything these days." With a dismissive wave, Gideon stumbled out of *Raven's Haunt*, leaving the three of them remaining in a heavy, awkward silence.

Varus cleared his throat, taking the seat opposite Jasper. "Now that I think on it, he seems familiar," he pointed out neutrally, his gaze sliding from Cary to Jasper. "I recall seeing you sparring with him in the spring."

Beside him, Cary seemed to have relaxed. Jasper struggled to do the same as Nadine finally made her way over to the table with an earthenware mug of cider and an entire bottle of brandy for Cary. The normally friendly woman mumbled what might have been a "hello" to Varus before she skimmed off to deal with the next customer, the inn cat following along behind her as he mewled irritably. If Varus was surprised by her change in demeanour, he didn't let on.

Jasper took a gulp of his cider instantly, suddenly seeking the burn at the back of his throat after the day he'd had. Cary's gaze was directed towards him, but she didn't seem to be *looking* at Jasper as she uncorked the brandy, taking a deep swig herself.

"I heard about what happened," Varus noted, acknowledging he understood whatever trauma response was unfolding in front of him. Cary offered him the brandy, but he shook his head. Seeing Varus decline a drink dared to compete for the strangest occurrence that day. "I wanted to thank you both. I had reports stating you were pursued with today's shipment."

Jasper found himself laughing, distantly aware he sounded a bit like Gideon when he did. "They didn't last long," he explained simply. "Cleared off when... when it happened."

"Did you know her?" Varus asked.

"Might have seen her around once or twice," Cary offered, leaning back in her chair as she fiddled with the chain around her neck.

Varus shook his head, a dark expression on his face. "Just when I didn't think this place could get any worse," he muttered under his breath. "Kingdom's gone to the dogs if we're executing old women in the streets."

Shaking her head, Cary took another deep swig from the brandy before sliding the half-empty bottle towards the middle of the table. "I don't want to talk about this anymore," she murmured. "We should get going. I have an early shift in the castle." She stood up abruptly, her hands trembling in a way that Jasper had never seen.

Before Jasper could rise from the table to follow her out of the tavern, Varus interrupted him. "If you wouldn't mind, I'd like a word with you, lad," his employer requested. Turning towards Cary, the man nodded once. Her eyes tightened as she regarded Varus and Jasper at the table, but she did not refute the dismissal. Cary waved goodnight to him and Varus before she turned and made her way through the tavern towards the exit.

It was the first time he had been alone with his employer in a while, and Jasper felt a bit awkward sitting here. He still hadn't known how to confront the man after what Charlotte had discovered in the spring, unsure if the validity of the information changed his opinion of Varus.

He sat there for some time, sipping more of his cider as he debated whether or not to bring it up now.

"Going back to that companion of yours…" Varus drawled after a beat of silence, causing Jasper to tense up involuntarily. "Will you tell me how the two of you know each other?" He reached forward to shift the bottle of brandy away from the centre of the table, removing any obstacles between him and Jasper.

"Grew up together," Jasper offered simply. Varus' eyes remained fixed on him, as if urging him to continue. "We… the three of us, Gideon, Charlotte, and I. They're the closest thing I've got left to a family."

Something flickered in Varus' expression. "It's a bit odd that a lord's son would go to the trouble of sneaking to Caelfall. Surely he could find other playmates his age in Briardeen?"

Jasper's cheeks darkened at the logic, something he himself had truthfully wondered more than once. "I think he's always held a torch for Charlotte," he admitted softly. "I was just a part of a package deal."

His employer's expression darkened further at his words. "And did it ever occur to you how dangerous it is to be friends with a knight when you work for me?"

"In all fairness, we weren't speaking when I started working for you," Jasper clarified somewhat defensively. "It was after… well, some things had happened and I'd isolated myself for a bit. I kept him at arm's length for a while. He doesn't know."

Varus paused as he processed this information, as if reassessing the level of risk. "Tonight might have gone very differently if he knew who I was, you know."

For a moment, Jasper paused. Whether it was some aftereffect of the shock he had barely recovered from or a bottled courage he gained from the cider in his veins, he found himself with the nerve or the stupidity to voice a question that burned in his mind. "Is Varus even really your name?" he managed to ask, his voice low and soft.

To his surprise and relief, there was no visible animosity in Varus' face at the inquiry. If anything, a sadness seemed to cloud his eyes as he watched Jasper for several moments, as if he were debating how to answer. "It is one of the names I use," he conceded finally. "You can imagine why I might need to keep a low profile sometimes. It helps in situations like this, where I can walk up to a knight and he doesn't recognize me for what I am."

"Why didn't you tell me?" Jasper asked quietly.

"You didn't need to know," Varus replied simply. "And in all honesty, I probably would not have shared this information. I'm careful not to cross worlds. It might never have come up had you not introduced me to Dante, whom I'm assuming told you after he had worked at the embassy for a bit."

"Charlotte, actually," Jasper corrected him, his cheeks flushing at the mention of her. "She said she saw you at the cathedral, her friend knew you by a different name."

To his immense surprise, Varus seemed flustered by that knowledge. "Ah, right…" he murmured, clearing his throat. "Well, she's sharp as a whip, that one. Not surprised she'd pick up on that."

Jasper found himself bobbing his head in agreement, taking several moments to force his head to stop repeating the movement. "Should I still call you—what should I call you, sir?" he asked slowly, having difficulty forming his words.

Thankfully, Varus only smiled crookedly in response, the expression softening his features. "Let's keep things the same for now," he offered simply. Shifting in his chair, trying to get comfortable with his bad leg, he continued, "If we're clearing the air, I would ask one thing of you. A truth for a truth – will you tell me why it is you never became a knight?"

He could have asked any other question, and Jasper would have answered without hesitation – but the moment the words left Varus' mouth, Jasper found himself tensing up. "Mr. Emery—Varus, sir... I don't think you'd like that truth," Jasper insisted.

Varus' smile persisted. "You're a good man, and I've seen you in a fight," he offered, gesturing to Jasper. "You're more than capable, you're a bloody powerhouse. What went wrong?"

His wording, however unintentional, caused Jasper to wince. "It's a long story, sir," he protested.

"We have time," Varus assured him.

Jasper closed his eyes, feeling the effects of the cider swimming through him. He was at war with himself for a long time, debating whether or not this was a story he should tell. By all rights, explaining what had gone wrong felt like an adequate way of getting himself fired by Varus. With the kind of work he did for the man, Jasper would certainly not have hired someone like himself.

When he opened his eyes at last, Varus was still staring at him, those dark eyes neutral. Jasper took another swig of his cider as if it might sustain his courage. "I'm not," he insisted finally. "Not capable, I mean. That much was clear within a few weeks. Apparently, I can't wear armour."

His employer raised an eyebrow, searching Jasper's face. When it seemed apparent that Jasper wouldn't continue unprompted, Varus probed. "I'm not sure I follow."

Exasperated, Jasper dragged a hand through his hair,

his eyes tracking downwards to focus on the cider clenched in his other hand. "It was humiliating enough that I didn't know how to bloody talk to anyone," Jasper rambled, gesturing vaguely with his free hand. "That I couldn't deal with the sound, the constant noise. I'm always the odd one, I've always *been* the odd one, but that was nothing compared to the moment we all got suited up to practice fighting in real armour.

"I have a problem," Jasper admitted in a breathy laugh, incredulous that he was even saying this. "If something doesn't *feel* right, it's as if I'm on fire, like my skin is full of insects trying to break through. I don't know why it happens, but when that armour touched my body... it didn't take long before I lost my mind."

Varus' expression was guarded. "What happened?"

Swallowing the feeling of nausea that washed over him, Jasper leaned into the table in front of him, his gaze fixed on the wood grain. "I just... couldn't take it," he offered simply. "I don't really know how to explain it. Somewhere between the noise, the scent of sweat and iron, and the burning in my skin, I just started screaming. It was all just too much, I just—I lost my damned mind.

"It was Gideon who had to drag me from the training grounds, pry the bloody armour off of me," Jasper continued, rubbing his eyes. "Everything was on fire, just—my mind was on fire. When I finally stopped screaming, I couldn't speak for days, maybe even weeks. By the time I could articulate a sentence, it was clear I couldn't continue the training. And I couldn't look Gideon in the eye after he saw me like that."

He couldn't find it within himself to explain the parts of the story he had left out, purposefully. No matter how honest he was being, Jasper didn't want Varus to know how many days he had laid motionless in his bed, unable to eat or speak or even dress himself. Charlotte and Gideon were the only people who knew what had happened back then, and that was solely because they had witnessed his complete breakdown... and only Charlotte had ever been offered the raw glimpse into just how broken he had been. She was the sole person in his world who could empathize with his inability to complete his education. Jasper had never needed to tell anyone else, nor had he wanted to.

The silence that followed was deafening. It made Jasper's skin crawl as he wondered what his employer was thinking, now that he knew the truth about why Jasper had never become a knight. For all Jasper knew, he may have just talked himself out of a job.

"How long ago was this?" Varus asked finally, and the gentle tone of his voice caught Jasper off guard. He looked up from the table to meet his gaze, expecting pity or disappointment and finding... nothing of the sort. Varus' expression was still carefully guarded, but the warmth in those hellfire eyes seemed kind, even sympathetic.

"Last autumn," Jasper offered in response. "A little while before I started working for you." He dreaded the day his former class would graduate, free to spread rumours through the barracks of the man who had lost his mind during training.

Varus nodded slowly, rubbing at the beginnings of stubble on his chin. "I am sorry that you went through that, Jasper."

He hadn't expected Varus to take it so smoothly. Blinking, Jasper raised his eyebrows. "You're not... disappointed?" he asked warily.

Varus scoffed, shaking his head. "Disappointed?" he repeated, leaning back in his chair. "No, I'm not disappointed, Jasper. I was only curious, but I'm sorry to have brought up such a painful memory."

Something about the way Varus took the information so casually caused Jasper's chest to tighten uncomfortably. To be able to tell Varus what had happened, and to have it be received so smoothly, was unexpected.

Squinting at the dim light that made its way into the tavern from the dirty window nearby, Varus scraped his hair back from his face with a sigh. "It's getting late," he said suddenly, rising slowly to his feet as he tossed a few coins and crumpled bills onto the table. "I have somewhere I need to be, and you should get some rest. The date for the meet has been announced. They want us in the catacombs three days from now, half past nine."

Jasper reeled at the statement. "You... you still want me to go with you? After what I just told you?"

"Of course," Varus replied, as if everything Jasper had told him had no bearing on his decision whatsoever.

Nodding numbly, Jasper found himself without a response. "All right," was all he could manage after several beats of silence.

Varus smiled crookedly. "Get some rest, lad," he instructed him as he turned to leave. "I'll see you in a few days' time."

Gripping the table for support, Jasper nodded again even as he realized Varus was no longer looking at him. His employer paused in his exit, turning towards Jasper once more.

"You might find better success with leather armour," Varus called back to him. At Jasper's resulting confusion, the man cleared his throat. "You were wearing knight's standard plate armour, I assume. I never cared for it, myself. Boiled leather armour is a bit easier to wear, sturdy but still somewhat flexible. Less… overwhelming."

Jasper couldn't help but stare, mildly stunned.

"In the time that you've worked for me, you've never once disappointed me," Varus assured him, his gaze fixed on an empty chair nearby. "You're good at what you do, even if you do have a tendency to get yourself into trouble."

His ears burning, Jasper could only stare as his employer turned on his heel, exiting *Raven's Haunt* without another word. Eyeing the unfinished bottle of brandy, Jasper reached for the liquor. There was a kinship with Varus he had never anticipated, and Jasper couldn't be certain if it was the burn of the brandy or a comforting familiarity that bloomed in his chest.

CHAPTER
TEN
CHARLOTTE

Drowned in soft, well-loved sheets and linen blankets, Charlotte had spent what felt like days in a hellish place between consciousness and nightmares. She wandered through the dreamscape without a voice, calling out in vain for her father as she stumbled through nothingness, arms stretched wide as she reached out for something to guide her. There was a light ticking noise, too soft for her to distinguish from the thick silence she waded through, but loud enough for Charlotte to convince herself she had heard it. Accompanying it, a woman's voice—

War is drawing near, now
Which side will you choose?
The fallen are crying out, blind eyes search for you...

Charlotte spun on her heel, searching the dim light

around her for the speaker. She found only the near-silence of her mind, dark and empty. "Who's there?" she wanted to cry out, but from her throat only a small and soundless whisper escaped, the darkness offering no immediate reply.

As she reached ahead of her wildly, she crushed her fingers against the solid shape of a door in front of her. The ticking was louder now, loud enough that Charlotte thought the source might be directly behind this door. Scrambling for the doorknob, she wrenched it open – but it was just as dark and foreboding on the other side of the door, not an ounce of light to be seen. A distant, breathy laughter echoed from somewhere down below, and Charlotte found herself following it.

She stumbled as she walked blindly through the inky blackness around her, cold stone stairs leading somewhere deeper into the nightmare. Charlotte gathered her courage even as an icy fear took hold in her heart, a deep dread building within her.

Don't disregard your past, now
It will catch up with you
You may try to run and hide, but no good will
    it do…

There was a sudden, sharp intake of breath behind her, the sound of a hag cackling. Though she was soundless, Charlotte still clapped a hand over her mouth instinctively to silence the shriek that built up within her. Spinning blindly in the darkness, her heart pounding in her chest, she searched for the source of the laughter. To her dismay, the silent dark around her offered no trespasser or creature for her to see.

Eyes straining, Charlotte took several deep, steadying

breaths. She'd come so far now, she wouldn't give up – not when she felt so close to *something*. She couldn't be certain what she was searching for, but the noises and voices around her seemed to grow more frightful and malicious the further she descended the stairs, and she took that to mean she was getting closer.

How often do you wake, gasping out in cold
   shade…
Nightmares and hushed words, goddess' light has
   left her…

The sounds grew louder, more insistent in their rapid shouts and frantic whispers. Charlotte's shuddering breaths came quickly to her now, rushed attempts at gathering oxygen else she faint from the sudden terror that gripped her. She was running now, her bare feet numb with cold against the stone floor beneath her at the bottom of the stairs. Whether she was running away from some dark presence that cackled and shrieked behind her, or running towards the source of the song before her, Charlotte couldn't be certain – all she knew in that moment was that she could not stop.

Can you hear them screaming?
Can you hear them pleading?

She was close now, Charlotte could feel it in her bones, feel it in the oppressive ache of an unknowable, divine pressure in her chest. The ticking had evolved into a god-like rumble of thunder in the deep, resonating within her as she came to a sudden halt before a wall of solid stone. The laughter, the screeching, and the thunderous ticking all grew very quiet suddenly, and even the voice that sang to her in the darkness began to fade away.

> *Do not serve a false king, infernal ringing…*
> *What are you doing in the dark?*

"Come back," Charlotte pleaded, her voice a breathy croak in her throat. The darkness began to fade around her, and with a start Charlotte recognized where she was; she stood in the main hall of the cathedral, deserted and illuminated with a ghastly light. The three-faceted goddess loomed over her, Deltori's sightless eyes gazing down upon her. The once golden tears that had been painted on her face were now a vicious blood red, glazing unhurriedly down her stone cheeks.

The moment that divine ichor dripped onto Charlotte's face, she awoke with a start.

"I'm here," her father said soothingly, pressing a cold, damp cloth to her forehead. "It's okay, Charlie, I'm here."

She gasped as the world returned to her in a shock of light and sound, but it was nothing that threatened to harm her. It might have been late morning, she couldn't be certain, but the sun was high in the sky and she could hear the distant sounds of the bustling street outside.

"The shop," she protested, struggling to sit up in bed. "Who's watching the shop?" There was a hot water bottle propped up against her abdomen, the bedsheets were freshly changed, and Charlotte was dressed in a clean nightgown. She flushed at the thought of her father having had to change her while she lay ill, though she knew it wasn't the first time he may have had to do it. Samuel had been dealing with the woes of taking care of his only daughter's unusual afflictions for some time now.

"It's all right, sweetheart," he assured her, brushing her damp hair back from her face. He had his signature smile on, the sort that made his kind eyes twinkle, but Charlotte could still see the worry that lived within the lines on his face. "Jasper's watching the shop for a minute so I could come upstairs and check on you. He said he could afford to take the day off."

Her face flushed darker still. She wasn't sure whether it was better or worse if Jasper might have been the one to have had to change her clothes and her bedsheets, though he was undoubtedly as used to it by now as her father was. "How bad was it?" she asked softly. She didn't remember much of the day prior, though she vaguely recalled the familiar sensation of pain and managing to lie down on the floor before she passed out.

Chuckling softly, her father shook his head. "Don't you worry about it, Charlie," he insisted. "Nothing we can't handle."

It was bad, then.

Oblivious to her inner turmoil, her father leaned close to kiss her forehead, his beard scratching gently at her face. "You should try and rest some more," he instructed her sternly, even as his eyes retained their kind warmth. "Do you want something to eat? I can send Jasper up with a spot of breakfast."

Charlotte nodded against the pillows stacked beneath her head. "Yes, please," she replied. "Love you."

Her father seemed reluctant to leave her alone, at war with himself as he hesitated between remaining at her side and getting up to head back downstairs. After a moment's awkward pause, he finally patted her shoulder before standing up with a groan, his knees popping as he made his way back towards the staircase to return to the bakery.

With some difficulty, Charlotte struggled in her bedcovers, feeling the plush surface of several layers of soft, padded sheets beneath her. Haeyin carried them for surgical procedures to try and keep blood and other substances from spilling onto the clinic floor, though it seemed he always managed to make a mess regardless. After finding they functioned quite well as back-up bedsheets, he'd given Charlotte a few to use on her worst nights.

The loft had been converted into a sick room once more, a component of their regular routine. An empty teacup sat at her bedside table beside *The Trials of Rhey'lu*, the aged porcelain still smelling of the medicine that she must have consumed but had no recollection of drinking. There were lengths of clothesline hanging from the rafters, freshly washed and bleached bed sheets hanging to dry. An open window offered a pleasantly cool breeze despite the sunshine, but Charlotte shivered as the wind reached her damp skin. Retrieving one of her mother's old silken ties from the bedside table, Charlotte scooped her sweat-soaked curls off her neck and tied them back into a hasty knot.

There was a creak as the stairs signalled Jasper's entrance. True to her father's word, the blacksmith carried a tray of warm baked goods for her. Despite the state she must have been in, Jasper smiled brightly when he saw her.

"Good morning," he greeted her.

"Is it morning?" she asked genuinely.

Jasper's smile turned sheepish. "We can pretend," he offered, and she couldn't help but laugh as he placed the tray of bread rolls and chocolate scones in front of her. He shrugged out of a loaned apron, smelling of coffee beans and cinnamon as he draped it over a nearby chair. After seeing the inebriated state Jasper had been in the other night, it was comforting to see the blacksmith back to his usual self. The public execution had taken a toll on him, and Charlotte had been grateful she hadn't witnessed it, though it left her feeling empty and fearful all the same.

"Was it bad?" Charlotte dared to ask, knowing that Jasper would be less guarded than her father. She reached for one of the scones, nibbling at the edge of it.

Jasper readjusted his sleeves where they had been rolled up to his elbows, the scars along his hands and forearms catching the light as he moved. He had regained some of the muscle he'd lost that winter, and she could see it even in such a mundane movement. "Bad in the sense that you had me worried," he offered as he moved towards the little stove nearby, refilling the used pot with fresh water from the reservoir for another batch of tea. "But you must be used to that by now."

Pursing her lips, Charlotte curled up tighter on the bed. She was more than used to it. It was particularly taboo to discuss feminine needs so openly, especially with a man she wasn't married to. The nature of Charlotte's condition forced her to constantly explain her needs, however, when she had fainted in public frequently enough that people began to wonder if she was dying.

Ever since Charlotte was a little girl, she had been prone to all manner of injury, spraining her wrists and her ankles easily. When her first cycle arrived, it became apparent something else was wrong, some new batch of symptoms that couldn't be explained away as merely womanhood. The pain had proved so brutal, so all-consuming, that it had forced Charlotte to end her schooling prematurely. Her father had known Haeyin from when Jasper's uncle had been ill, and he had called upon the doctor for his assistance on multiple occasions. Haeyin had made several attempts to try and give Charlotte some semblance of long-term relief, but she had given the healer his first case of a malady that magic could not solve. Charlotte would never forget the devastation on the man's face as he discovered this, as he was forced to deliver the news that there was no cure he could provide.

Even so, Haeyin was determined to treat her pain to the best of his ability. The herbs that the doctor blended for her, the protective sheets on the bed, and several years spent carefully maintaining her health… all of it had helped, but ultimately Charlotte would always have her bad days.

And bless his heart, Jasper had always been so good to her. He never once complained, merely comparing it to the way Charlotte had looked after his own injuries, mopping blood from his arms when he injured himself at the forge. She was grateful for a friend like him, and yet resentful all at once. Every time Jasper brewed her tea for her, held her hair back when the pain made her retch violently, or changed her sheets for her… Charlotte was unpleasantly reminded that a man like him couldn't possibly love a woman like her enough to want a lifetime spent doing all of *this*.

"Is that still warm enough for you?" Jasper asked suddenly, pulling her from her recollections. He was pointing at the hot water bottle where it remained propped up against the pillows.

Charlotte shook her head as she handed it to him. "Father said you were taking the day off," she asked warily, mouth half full of food as she finished the scone – propriety be damned, she was starving. Charlotte fretted over her father being unable to run the bakery on days she was ill, though she had accounted for their finances and knew they had a bit of a safety net. On the other hand, Jasper had an

entirely different work schedule as a blacksmith. Charlotte
had no way of knowing if taking time off to look after her
would bankrupt him.

Returning to the kitchenette, Jasper filled the bottle with
the remainder of the boiled water he hadn't used for the
teapot. "I just finished an order for the harbour," Jasper
offered by way of explanation, as if he had known exactly
what Charlotte was worried about. "I have a few days off
before I have to get started on another batch for the
garrison."

"Well, that's good to hear," Charlotte replied as she held
her arms out for the revived water bottle, hugging the heat
close to her belly. She could feel the effect of the warmth
instantly as it soothed the aches deep within her; it was
often the only non-medicinal remedy that worked, and her
abdomen was covered with aging burn marks as a result.

"I'm glad to be done," he murmured with a frown as he
went to retrieve the teapot. He paused for a moment,
leaving Charlotte instantly wary as he poured another cup
of medicated tea for her. As if he couldn't keep the words
in any longer, he finally burst out, "And I have another job
for Varus soon."

Charlotte might have growled at that. "This is a Varus-
free space," she grumbled as she reached for another scone.

Sensing her displeasure, Jasper shook his head. Setting
the teapot down beside the cup on the bedside table, he
took a seat beside her on the bed. "It's not a drug-related
job," he offered. "I'm just escorting him to a meeting of
sorts. Bodyguard, if you will."

Raising an eyebrow, Charlotte regarded him as she
chewed her food. She had a hard time consolidating the
way she saw Jasper with the way other people did. Perhaps
it was because they had known each other as children, but

to her Jasper would always be a kind-hearted man who had never been anything but gentle with her. She knew he could fight, knew he had skill with a blade or with his bare hands… but as she looked at him now, his sea-green eyes bright and his red hair tousled, she couldn't picture him any other way.

"Even so," she said at last as she swallowed a mouthful of bread. "Please be careful, Jazzy-boy. Trouble seems to follow that man like a dark cloud."

Jasper offered an incredulous smile. "I'd say trouble follows *me*, but I suppose you have a point," he replied. Goddesses, she loved seeing that smile on his face, the way his chin dimpled with the expression. "I promise I'll be careful."

Perhaps it was an impulse, perhaps it was the exhaustion that weighed heavily on her mind, but Charlotte almost gave in to the urge to tell him everything in that moment. She wanted to admit how that smile made her feel, how she longed to have him in her bed, and not because one of them was playing nurse for the other. She wanted to give him every reason she could think of not to go with Varus, to stay in this room with her where it was safe.

Instead, Charlotte swallowed her feelings with the last of her scone, chasing her thoughts down with a swig of too-hot tea. The pair of them remained silent for some time until Jasper shuffled in his seat, the tell-tale look of a question burning on his tongue evident on his increasingly red face.

"Have you heard from Gideon recently?" he asked finally, and Charlotte was admittedly taken aback by the mention of their mutual friend. Setting her cup down again before she spilled tea on herself in shock, Charlotte shook her head earnestly.

"Not really, no," she admitted, her full attention on Jasper now. "I've seen him around the castle or the church occasionally, but we haven't had the opportunity to catch up." She paused momentarily, assessing the expression on Jasper's face. "Are you two talking again?"

His gaze was shuttered as he stared seemingly at nothing, and Charlotte knew him well enough to know he was parsing his response in his head before he spoke. "I don't know," Jasper replied eventually, painfully honest as always. "He's been trying to reach out, but it wasn't until recently that he... well, I don't know what's going on with him lately, but he was completely rat-faced the other night at *Raven's Haunt.*"

"Our Gideon?" Charlotte replied, unable to stop the frown that came over her face. Was this related to why Jasper had been so drunk that night? "That doesn't sound like him at all. Did you... Have you told him why you stopped speaking to him?" *Or that you're working for a kingpin on occasion?*

Jasper flushed, and Charlotte had a feeling her unsaid question was on his mind as well. "No, and I don't plan to," he said firmly. "It sounds like he's started to question the king's rule, the things he's been asked to do as a knight. I don't want to test how deep that rebellion runs just yet."

It was difficult to imagine Gideon questioning anything about the king. Even when they were children, he had always been the voice of reason amidst Jasper's parroted conspiracy theories he'd heard from his uncle Zeke. Charlotte thought back to the private meetings she'd had with Aurelia and Fortia, how both Cary and Gideon had been guarding their secrets. Perhaps it had been an easier deci-sion for him than she had initially thought.

"I should get going," Jasper said suddenly, straightening his clothes as he stood up. "I'll check back in with you later, all right?"

Charlotte nodded numbly as Jasper made his way towards the door, missing his presence immediately as she reached for her tea. Some days, when he cared for her and brewed her medication during her worst episodes, it was as if they shared a deeper connection than she could put words to. Others, it was like a chasm stretched between them, and Charlotte could only attempt to decipher the emotions Jasper didn't – or couldn't – share with her.

Today seemed to be one of those days.

Later that evening, Charlotte had been determined to venture outside of the bakery, in dire need of some semblance of normality. She hadn't heard from Jasper since he'd left the bakery that afternoon, and it had been a few days since she'd checked in with any of her friends.

Every afternoon, Maya had her schooling with the nuns in the cathedral archives. Though Charlotte and Eleni made an effort to visit her frequently, it was a rare occasion that between Eleni's store hours and Charlotte's varying health that the three of them were able to spend time together after Maya was available in the evening. Between making plans with Aurelia to derive meaning from the *Jackdaw*'s cryptic articles and broadcasts, spending every other weekend bedridden, and worrying over Jasper's safety, it had been a while since Charlotte had seen her friend.

The late sun cast long, daunting shadows across the

cold surfaces of the cathedral, dark fingers stretching along the floor towards the statue of the three goddesses in the main hall. The deities' eyes stared down at her, Deltori's golden tears glinting in the light. Charlotte felt a shudder ripple down her inflamed spine, involuntarily rubbing her bare forearms; her light summer blouse was fine outdoors, but the cathedral carried an unearthly chill she had never felt here before. Charlotte tore her gaze away as she forced her feet to carry her towards the stairs. The elevator wouldn't work for her without Eleni present, so Charlotte began the arduous walk up the steps, her hips aching all the way.

She was grateful the cathedral was otherwise deserted, Charlotte's efforts up the staircase unwitnessed as she struggled. At each landing, she took a small break to lean against the cool walls of stone behind her, closing her eyes. The way her muscles ached now, Charlotte knew she would probably need to rest most of tomorrow. She tried to ignore the pain as best she could, focusing instead on each measured, controlled breath she took, the sensation of the stone walls at her back, the distant sound of screaming—

Screaming?

Charlotte's eyes snapped open as she looked towards the last flight of stairs, her mind curious even as her body was exhausted. For half a second more, she wondered whether or not she had lost her mind. Hadn't she dreamt of this, once?

The screams continued in the distance and dread hooked a long finger through her stomach. Charlotte willed her feet to move, hauling herself up each step with her skirts gathered in her free hand. Charlotte could barely make out the voices that blended with the despair of her friend, loosely catching the words "awakening" and "scrying" – no, she mustn't have heard that right. There were sounds amidst the screaming, distant shouts in varying tones, an ugly current of scraping chairs and what might have been the impact of a hand against someone's cheek.

The closer Charlotte came to the archives, the cold dread in her heart hardened into something darker, something violent. She broke into a run, fearing the worst.

She didn't really have a plan for what came next. Charlotte could think of only one thing, one person as she pushed against the solid oak doors of the archives, the heavy wood swinging wide with a crash as she burst into the room. She could feel her ire crackling in her ears as she stared down the wide-eyed faces of the acolytes, startled into paralysis by her entrance.

"How did you—how did you get in here?" the one nearest her stammered, pale grey eyes blinking wildly. "You shouldn't be here, the archives are off-limits to civilians!"

Charlotte ignored him. She turned her attentions to Sister Margerie, standing at Maya's side where she sat in her chair opposite Charlotte, a long table filled with tomes and texts between them. "What is going on here?" Charlotte demanded, ensuring her voice resonated within the room.

"This does not concern you," Sister Margerie replied, her tone cold and biting. "You should not barge into meetings where you do not belong." She folded her hands as she met Charlotte's stare, having the gall to look as if she had done nothing wrong, and needed no remorse.

Charlotte had never seen Maya so distraught. The girl was prone to panic attacks on occasion, but Maya had screamed herself hoarse, her hands trembling where she pressed her palms into her eyes, as if she might block out the acolytes that surrounded her. Rage ignited in her veins as Charlotte took in the sight of her.

"What have you done?" she roared, several people flinching away in shock at the volume. Maya dropped her hands to look over in her direction, her brown eyes rimmed with red.

"This does not concern you, Charlotte," the old crone merely repeated, examining her fingernails.

"So, you do know my name," Charlotte spat in response. "I think we can all agree Maya is done for the day." She crossed the room quickly, but suddenly there were bodies moving in front of her to block her path towards Maya. Dull eyes and faces stared down at her as she attempted to pass through the sea of emerald robes.

"We'll be the judge of that," Sister Margerie offered in response, dismissing her with a wave of her hand.

Charlotte resorted to physically shoving acolytes aside, ignoring the mental voice that suggested eternal damnation as consequence. "What are you talking about?" she asked incredulously. "What do you possibly have to gain from torturing her like this?"

If Sister Margerie had been about to respond, the hag was distracted by another presence at the doorway. Her eyes narrowed on whoever stood behind Charlotte, a sour expression tugging at her face. "And what are *you* doing here?"

Charlotte craned her neck around to see who had vexed the nun – and to her immense surprise, Dante stood in the doorway, accompanied by a positively murderous Varus Emery. He was dressed more as "Eodan" today, wearing most of a suit of dark mauve and finely polished dress shoes.

"Is this church not welcome to all?" Varus asked dryly,

crossing his arms over his chest. His suit jacket absent, Varus' shirt sleeves had been rolled up his forearms, as if he anticipated getting his hands dirty.

"The archives are not for civilians, these are private affairs you have walked in on," Sister Margerie protested, gesturing towards Maya where she sat across the table. Abuse could apparently be chalked up to the guise of "private affairs", whatever that meant.

Dante took the opportunity to step forward, and Charlotte noticed he carried a heavy book under his arm. "Actually, a ward of the church is not a private matter," he offered, his voice eerily calm. "Not when Maya is eligible to be adopted."

For a moment, her heart fluttered in her chest. If Charlotte had thought she and her father could afford the price of adoption, she would have begged him to help her bring Maya home in a heartbeat. The thought of her friend being rescued from the hellish cathedral was a welcome relief, but to be adopted by Varus bloody Emery... Charlotte wasn't sure whether she hated Varus or Sister Margerie more, but she was terrified of the fact that her allegiances were leaning towards the former in this particularly horrid equation.

Sister Margerie's thoughts seemed to echo her own. "You mean to tell me that the elusive Eodan Melicus seeks to adopt a child?" she replied, her tone a mocking laugh. "You will understand that the church will seek a full background check before such a motion will be passed."

Charlotte's hopes seemed to have been dashed before they ever stood a chance, but the defiance in Varus' gaze hadn't so much as flickered. "Oh no, you are mistaken," he insisted, shaking his head. "I'm only here to facilitate as a witness and a sponsor."

Footsteps sounded from the hallway, and Varus stepped aside with a smile as Eleni entered the room with all the grace of a queen. Charlotte had never seen the triumphant fury that now dwelled within her friend's features, her blue eyes piercing as she stalked towards Sister Margerie. There was a missive clutched tightly in her hand, and Charlotte was immensely pleased by the way Eleni tossed the paper onto the table with a satisfying thunk.

"I will be adopting Maya today," Eleni announced. "The paperwork has already been processed."

Sister Margerie made a satisfying sputtering noise. "Well—this documentation will need to be verified, and—"

"You will find that the minister himself has already signed off on this adoption," Dante spoke up. "When we first brought this request to his attention, he was in agreement with our logic on the situation."

"And what might that be?" Sister Margerie spat.

Dante's stare was frigid. "There are two possibilities. Either Maya is of age, which is entirely possible considering, by your own testimony, her birth records were destroyed before she came to the church..." He tilted his head as he let his words sink in, the accusation he alluded to. "Or she is still young enough to be considered a ward of the church. In which case, Aethian adoption laws apply, and Eleni's request is deemed valid."

Charlotte could hardly contain the manic relief that bubbled within her. As if noting the shift in the room, the distinct realization among the acolytes that Sister Margerie could not refute this, Eleni turned her attention towards her. "Charlotte, would you be a dear and help Maya collect her things? We'll meet you both downstairs at the entrance when you're ready."

She didn't need to be asked twice. The acolytes did not

resist her as she shouldered through them, taking hold of Maya's wheelchair and exiting the room as quickly as she could without jostling the poor girl further. The silence was broken by Maya's occasional whimper, her chest still heaving in sobs that wracked her small frame. The long, eerie corridor seemed to stretch further and further ahead of them until finally they reached Maya's cramped living space, parking her wheelchair in the centre of the room. Unable to wait a second longer, Charlotte bent down and promptly threw her arms around Maya, the other girl leaning into the embrace as she buried her face in Charlotte's neck. Her own chest heaved as her eyes burned with tears she hadn't known she was holding back.

"It's okay now, it's all right... it's going to be okay," she whispered, stroking Maya's hair soothingly. Eleni's request to adopt Maya was a best-case scenario Charlotte hadn't known to hope for, and the thrill of her friend finally being free from this cathedral was beginning to feel more and more real. Maya wept into Charlotte's hair, her fingers trembling as she clung to her, breathing raggedly through her tears. Charlotte held her tighter still, as if the love she had for her friend might be enough to help her, enough to heal her.

She couldn't be certain how long the two of them sat there together, but their trance was eventually interrupted by Varus knocking at the open door. Charlotte's joints were aching when she unravelled herself from Maya's arms, faltering as she struggled to stand.

Wordlessly, Varus assisted her to her feet before addressing Maya. "Do you have something to collect your belongings, dearie?" he asked quietly.

Maya sniffled, nodding slowly as she pointed towards a trunk that lay in the bottom of the open wardrobe. Most of the girl's collection of personal effects were books in varying sizes, and Varus made quick work of slotting them into the trunk. Charlotte took to gathering all of Maya's clothing and the threadbare stuffed lion that lived on her bed. Somehow, without anything of Maya left in the space, the room seemed smaller still, barren stone walls and a bed without her little comforts.

As Varus made quick work of the clasps on Maya's trunk, Charlotte held out her hands in an offer to carry it for him. It was an instinctive reaction, recalling the man walked with a limp, but he merely shook his head as he carried the entire trunk with one hand. She watched with some shock as he left the room without another word, carrying all of Maya's possessions as if they weighed little more than a pillow – indeed, limping all the way.

A part of her desperately wanted to ask Maya what had transpired in the room prior to her arrival, but she couldn't bear the thought of traumatizing the girl further as she sat still sniffling, fidgeting with her hands. A piece of skin near her thumb seemed especially raw, so Charlotte was forced to draw on her imagination. "Maya, talk to me," she said quickly, hoping to interrupt the girl's self-destructive tendencies. "Tell me about something."

Sniffling, Maya tilted her neck to look at her. "Like what?" she asked in a small voice.

"Anything – but not another of your nightmares, please," Charlotte offered, nudging the brake on the wheelchair with her foot as she began to wheel Maya out of the tiny bedroom and back towards the elevator. "Tell me about... tell me about the shadow people, those old elf legends you used to read about."

There was only silence for a few moments as they made their way down the corridor towards the elevator, where

Varus had waited for the pair of them. Maya shifted in her seat, as if mentally preparing herself before she spoke. "The elf legends... the stories about the so-called fae are thought to refer to three factions of people known as the shadow folk."

"Go on," Charlotte urged her gently as they approached the lift, turning the chair around as she carefully led them in.

Maya gave Varus a nervous glance before she continued. "The shadow folk were the Reinnairlei, the Gwynti, and the Damhn," she recited hesitantly, fidgeting with the end of her braid as she recalled the information. "Long ago, there was a fifty-year war of shadow that nearly destroyed civilization completely. The Damhn were victorious, and they claimed the space deep beneath the surface as their kingdom. The Gwynti secured the caverns within the mountain ranges to the north..."

Charlotte glanced up at Varus, who had initially seemed quite bored with the conversation. It was only now that she saw he was listening intently, signalled by a muscle feathering in his jaw. Charlotte wasn't sure what to make of his reaction.

She became aware of the fact that the elevator wasn't moving around the same time Varus and Maya did. "It... it runs on magic," Maya offered quietly.

Varus turned to look at Charlotte then, and there was something of a question in his eyes, dark green in the harsh lighting of the elevator. Her gaze hardened as she returned the kingpin's stare, and it became apparent that Maya's escape might very well be delayed by the fact that none of them possessed magic... but Charlotte had seen Varus teleport in the blink of an eye, hadn't she?

After what seemed like an eternity, Varus gave a long-suffering sigh as he lazily gestured towards the elevator wall, an inky blackness firing from his veins towards the lift controls. The old mechanism seemed to shudder in response, but they finally began to descend. Charlotte's gaze on Varus hardened. She expected him to ignore her, or perhaps even to meet her stare with some defiance. He did neither; his expression as he looked down at Charlotte was one of weary discretion, as if he were asking—or pleading —that she didn't share what she had just seen.

It was the first time she had ever seen the kingpin look vulnerable, and she wasn't sure that she liked it. It wasn't as if she would rat him out. After all, with Haeyin as her doctor, what would it say that Charlotte might pick and choose which renegade mages she reported to the authorities?

Squeezing Maya's shoulder gently, Charlotte finally broke eye contact with the underworld leader beside her. "You were saying, about the elves?" she asked gently. "What about the Reinnairlei?"

Maya cleared her throat. "They surrendered, you see," she continued. "So, in return…"

"They were punished for it," Varus offered, to both Charlotte and Maya's surprise. They turned to face him as he continued, his voice low and solemn. "The Reinnairlei surrendered because they saw the atrocities committed by the Damhn for the sake of winning the war. The queen saw what remained of her people, and she chose them over victory. As punishment for her humanity, the Reinnairlei received Castavar as their homeland, the least desirable of all the territory that was up for grabs. Or so they say."

Charlotte was vaguely horrified by learning this ancient bit of history, but Maya seemed delighted. "I was never able to find anything specific about why they surrendered," she replied, her eyes wide and bright. "What were they so afraid of? There's so much we don't know about the Damhn and how they won the war."

Varus' gaze turned steely, his expression carved from stone. Just as Charlotte tensed up, ready to interject, his expression softened as he seemed to remember who he was speaking to. "I'm sure it's all just a bedtime story at this point, lass," he replied at last, and though dismissive his tone was not unkind. "After all, the Reinnairlei hardly resemble elves of legend. They're as human as you and Charlotte, and yet still live as outcasts for that story, for the magic they're gifted with."

If either Maya or Charlotte had wanted to press him for more details, they were interrupted by the elevator abruptly reaching the ground floor, as if whatever brand of magic Varus had injected into it had stopped short at the last few inches towards the bottom. Charlotte stumbled, the impact jostling her bruised knees, nearly toppling over before Varus grabbed her arm to steady her, his other hand dropping the trunk to stabilize Maya's wheelchair.

"Goddesses, whatever you did to it, it's never done that before," Maya exclaimed.

"My apologies," Varus murmured softly as he released Charlotte, stooping to pick up the trunk. Charlotte wheeled Maya out the lift as Varus continued, "If you want to know more about the shadow folk, I'm sure Dante would be happy to help you."

"Would I?" Dante asked as he appeared from around the corner, seemingly having taken the stairs with Eleni. She seemed a touch more breathless than Dante did, primly brushing flyaway hair back from her forehead. "I'm sure I would, whatever it is."

The pair joined the three of them as they made their

way towards the cathedral exit, the twilight barely illuminating the streets beyond the stone archways. The soup kitchen nearby was finishing up the dinner run, but the cathedral itself was largely deserted. Eleni turned to address Charlotte, squeezing her hand. She was wearing a dress Charlotte hadn't seen her in before, far more muted in colour and style than her usual choices, though it was hardly drab. The empire-waist cream was still more fashionable than most of Charlotte's own wardrobe.

"I ought to thank you for introducing me to Dante," she began, her eyes twinkling as she addressed Varus. "I wanted to ensure there was nothing those hags could exploit to keep her there, and he helped me with the application."

"How long have you three been working on this?" Charlotte found herself asking, glancing between her companions.

"I've wanted to adopt Maya for some time, but the price of adoption is a bit steep even for me," Eleni explained grimly. "Between the three of us, we were able to find the funds and the legislation respectively to make it work."

Charlotte found herself beaming at Dante, her chest swelling with pride for her friend. "Look at you, all busy and important." The young man's face split into a wide grin. As Charlotte turned towards Eodan – towards Varus bloody Emery, as she always thought of him – she struggled to find the words to thank him as well, to convey any sort of appreciation without it sounding sarcastic.

To his credit, the man only nodded, his expression guarded. It seemed Varus was well aware of Charlotte's opinion of him, and that this was only one step in the journey of changing that for the better. She nodded once in return; Charlotte could accept saving her friend from the cathedral, but she remained displeased with the fact that Jasper came to harm working for him.

They emerged into the quieting city streets as the last rays of the sun were illuminating Briardeen, and for half a moment Charlotte was entirely at peace. Her friend was safe, they were relatively alone and private in the almost empty streets, and the pleasant smell of bread and hearty stew filled the air as the soup kitchen began to close up shop for the evening.

"I'd best be getting back to the embassy," said Dante with a sigh.

"You're sure you won't join us at the manor for a drink, lad?" Varus offered, gesturing somewhere to his left. "Celebrations are in order."

Dante laughed quietly, shaking his head. "No, I don't drink," he explained apologetically.

"While I am grateful to be out of there, I'm somewhat curious where I'll be living from now on," Maya piped up suddenly. "You said you live in Dornkeep, right?"

An uncharacteristic flush crept across Eleni's cheeks, and Varus seemed suspiciously interested in a timepiece he'd retrieved from his pocket. "Well, you see... I had hoped to have a moment to brief you on this, but—" Whatever Eleni had been about to say, her words were cut off abruptly as she delicately raised a hand to her mouth. A startled expression crossed her face as she seemed to restrain the urge to discard the contents of her stomach, the colour having drained from her face as suddenly as it had appeared.

Dante's eyes widened, his hand hovering as if he were unsure whether or not to steady her. "Eleni, are you feeling all right?" he asked tentatively.

Despite her rather ghastly appearance, Eleni nodded

quickly. No longer pretending to be uninterested in the conversation, Varus was by her side in an instant, and all notions of pretense were dashed as he set down Maya's trunk on the cobblestones. He supported Eleni with an arm around her waist, entirely inappropriate for a man she claimed not to be pursuing.

"Do you feel ill?" he asked her, a quiet urgency in his low voice that Charlotte had never heard before.

"Please, darling, I'm fine," Eleni insisted softly, though her outward appearance suggested anything but. "Just— just the smell caught me off guard, I'm fine."

"Maybe you shouldn't be walking home," Varus suggested. "I can take you, it'd be quicker."

"Yes, because giving me *vertigo* will make me less nause-ated," Eleni managed to groan, her hand pushing at his shoulder ineffectually. "Just—give me a moment, I'll try not to reject my lunch."

Charlotte was at a loss for words. She glanced between Dante and Maya, as if either of them might have a shred of information that would provide some clarity on what was happening here, but the two looked just as perplexed as she was. In all the time Charlotte and Maya had known the bookstore owner, they had never once seen Eleni with so much as a cold, let alone feel ill at the smell of bread and soup.

Seemingly deciding she'd had enough of their cryptic conversation, Maya cut in. "Are you unwell?" she asked.

Had Eleni been in a better state than she currently was, she might have blushed at the forwardness of the question. As it was, the barest hint of a pink flush coloured her cheeks. Her gaze shifted towards Varus at that moment, and Charlotte became distinctly aware of the fact that he seemed to be concerned, but not at all *surprised* by what had just occurred. She glanced back and forth between Varus and Eleni, and the intimate manner in which the two of them looked at one another did not escape her notice.

Her thoughts drifted to Eleni's words back in *Hourglass Books*, the baby with the mage's cuffs she had described...

Whatever explanation either of them were about to supply was cut off by Charlotte's loud, exasperated groan. "Damn you, *Eodan*," she growled as she met the man's gaze. "I was just starting to like you."

CHAPTER

ELEVEN

JASPER

VARUS CAME TO COLLECT HIM FROM HIS FLAT AT TWILIGHT, arriving in attire that Jasper recognized; battle-scarred boiled leather armour and a black tunic, his arms bare except for his strange, asymmetrical gauntlets. His ever-faithful knee brace was strapped tightly over his trousers, foregoing his cane. The other man looked him up and down, nodding approvingly.

"You don't look half-bad," he noted. After several empty seconds of Jasper's visible confusion at the turn of phrase, struggling to decipher whether this was praise or an insult, Varus elaborated with a crooked grin. "It looks good on you, I mean."

Jasper felt his cheeks flush as he rubbed the back of his neck, fiddling with his attire. Following their conversation in the tavern, Varus had gifted Jasper with his own set of boiled leather armour. Gideon had been practically delighted when Jasper had asked to spar with him again, perhaps too excited by the prospect of coaxing Jasper out of his shell to question what he was wearing. It had felt decidedly strange the first few times he'd sparred with it on, heavier than his usual clothing but far lighter than steel armour. As he gradually became accustomed to it, however, he found himself more comfortable in the garments than his own skin. There was a satisfying weight and stability to the rigid leather that seemed to numb his overly sensitive nerves, dampening the constant white noise of hornets.

"It... it helps," Jasper admitted in a small voice. He still wasn't used to this closeness with Varus, this vulnerability he had never fully shared with anyone except Charlotte – who would probably not enjoy hearing about what would transpire this evening. "Thank you."

"You're welcome," Varus replied. "We should get going. Never good to be early to these sorts of things, but it would be in poor taste to be too late."

Mentally preparing himself, Jasper squeezed his eyes shut as he took Varus' offered arm, and the two were falling through space and time. It wasn't as unpleasant as it had been the last time, now that his insides weren't freshly stitched together with magic. The voices were still there, however, clearer than Jasper had ever heard them before.

Jasper...
Wake up...

Keeping his eyes squeezed shut, Jasper struggled to hear the murmurs around him. There was an unearthly roaring wind in his ears that drowned out the sound, and his mind could not decipher the foreign words without faces. He was tempted to open his eyes, just to see...

The ground jolted beneath him as they returned from oblivion, and his knees ached as reality welcomed them back with a dizzying sensation of nausea. Jasper opened his eyes slowly as he released Varus' arm, taking in their surroundings. They stood in the church gardens, the cemetery stationed behind the cathedral where the folk of Briardeen could ignore the headstones of their forgotten dead.

"We're meeting at the church?" he wondered aloud.

Varus laughed quietly, shaking his head. "No, no… though I would find that hilarious," he noted, gesturing for Jasper to follow him as he led them through a winding path between crooked headstones and manicured grass. "We'll be meeting in the catacombs."

Though he probably shouldn't have been surprised by anything Varus said at this point, Jasper was still startled by this information. "Seriously?" he asked incredulously. "We used to play down there as children. You're telling me this is where drug lords meet?"

Varus paused in his efforts to limp through the cemetery gardens, giving Jasper a dull stare. "I am thoroughly impressed you reached adulthood, sometimes," he remarked dryly.

Jasper struggled not to laugh inappropriately in the silence as they wove through the headstones towards the goddess statue situated in the centre of the gardens. Unlike the polished marble kept within the cathedral, this one had fallen into disrepair in Aethelind's damp climate; moss covered every inch of the aged stone, the features of the goddesses' faces worn to faint lines, the idea of a deity rather than the depiction of one. Varus led them to a mausoleum behind the decrepit statue, the ancient structure equally covered in moss and sprawling ivy.

Varus grasped the heavy padlock securing the mausoleum doors. "I must admit, I am curious how you got in here as a child," Varus mused, rummaging in his pocket with his free hand.

"Picked it," Jasper admitted immediately. "With Charlotte's hair pins." If his overly sensitive ears were good for anything, it was listening to tiny, nearly undetectable sounds.

Varus laughed, shaking his head. "Figures," he muttered, but he did seem genuinely amused. Retrieving a key at last from the depths of his pocket, Varus unlocked the weathered padlock with a rusty click, the chains binding the mausoleum doors falling to the floor with a dull, heavy rustling. Sweeping them aside with his foot, Varus eased one of the doors open. Despite its age, it swung open easily and soundlessly, as if it had been oiled recently.

As they crept into the ancient mausoleum, Jasper glanced around at the vaguely familiar surroundings. It had seemed so much larger in his youth, thrilling and frightening with its dark, gloomy atmosphere. "Is there a reason we're using this entrance specifically?" Jasper asked, shutting the door behind them. "For the catacombs, I mean."

Occupying himself with a single, large coffin in the centre of the cramped space, it took a moment for Varus to respond. "We can't all arrive together," the kingpin explained casually, grasping the large stone slab that covered the decrepit coffin. "Imagine how out of place that would be, a herd of criminals all headed towards the church. Confession's not that popular."

Jasper had half a mind to assist his employer with the task of moving the stone lid, but Varus had already shifted it, setting it aside with care. "That seems logical," he agreed, frowning at the slab. In hindsight, Jasper had no idea how he, Charlotte, and Gideon had once removed the coffin lid to expose the narrow staircase concealed beneath. Perhaps Varus was right to question how Jasper was still alive.

"As for why we're using the mausoleum specifically... well, truth be told, nobody else cared to use this one," his employer admitted, gesturing for Jasper to follow as he carefully began to descend the staircase within the coffin. "Fearful of booby traps, I reckon. Mind your step, I'm sure one of these activates something."

"The seventh from the bottom," Jasper said automatically. He vividly remembered tripping on it as a child, and he thumbed the resulting scar on his chin absentmindedly.

Varus chuckled low in his chest, the sound resonating within the confines of the staircase. "Maybe it's a good thing you had a death wish as a boy."

The pair of them gingerly made their way down the staircase, dodging the step Jasper had previously knocked himself unconscious falling off of. The catacombs expanded at the base of the stairs, but the corridor was still only just wide enough for Varus and Jasper to walk side by side. The walls were filled with the silent remains of hundreds of nameless bones, a testament to wartime, plague, and famine. Jasper had been here a dozen times in his childhood, but walking through the near darkness of the tombs, illuminated only by the dim glow of the sparse oil lamps... only now did Jasper sense the foreboding presence that people claimed to feel in places such as these. He'd heard rumours that people *lived* down here, though he had yet to encounter any catacombs-dwellers.

"What exactly should I expect?" Jasper asked in a low

voice, as if speaking too loudly in such a place would draw attention to them.

Varus didn't appear to be as tense as Jasper felt. If anything, the edges of him seemed to blur into the darkness around them, as if he belonged to it. "The heart of the northern catacombs connects somewhere beneath the town square in Briardeen. Think of it as a political meeting without the pretence or poise. We're here to keep things the way they are."

"If it's a political meeting, what figureheads are there?" Jasper continued, his gaze catching on the empty eyes of a humanoid skull staring blankly ahead.

"Well, let's see…" Varus hummed low in his throat, assessing a fork in the catacombs ahead of them before gesturing for them to take the left path. "The leader of the fighters' guild will be there, Rasmussen. The Madame from the brothel Cary works at will be there as well, I reckon. I would be surprised if we saw anyone from the Twilight Dominion, but Morgan sometimes makes an appearance."

Jasper regretted asking. "Is there a… king? Queen? Lord?" he gestured vaguely as he attempted to convey his meaning. "A leader of this group?"

Frowning into the darkness, Varus seemed to be eyeing the walls around them carefully as if he were looking for some sort of landmark. "Of a sort," he conceded, though Varus hesitated long enough that Jasper guessed he was attempting to find a way around the question. "There is a person known as 'Azrael' who is generally considered to be the leader."

"Can't say I've heard of them."

Varus chuckled again. "That is sort of the point," he explained. "More myth than anything. You ask any of the people here tonight, they'll tell you they've never seen him."

"Have you?" Jasper asked, finding himself immensely curious.

Varus paused in his efforts, chewing on his lip. "Aye," he said at last. "And for what we're hoping to accomplish tonight, it'd be best if we *don't* see him."

Seemingly having decided which direction to go in next, Varus led them down another fork, this corridor so narrow that Jasper was forced to follow along behind him. He had a thousand questions, but he didn't feel it was a good time to ask any of them. They were travelling deeper and deeper into the catacombs, farther than he had ever been with Charlotte or Gideon, and Jasper was forced to bite down on his anxiety as it thrummed through his chest.

After some time, the corridor widened into a vast chamber illuminated by several oil lamps. There were others already occupying the chamber, some already seated at a wide, round stone table, others mingling amongst themselves in various pockets throughout the room. Varus had underemphasized the number of attendees; there were at least forty, maybe fifty people around them.

Beneath the skylight was a statue Jasper didn't recognize. Instead of the three goddesses, there was a solitary woman carved from stone. Her lovely face was hewn from expressionless marble, her arms open in what might have been an embrace.

"What is this place?" Jasper murmured.

Varus followed his gaze, a muscle twitching in his jaw as he regarded the statue. "Gwenhwyfar's sepulchre." Jasper must have looked sufficiently shocked, as Varus looked over at him and added, "Don't worry. She isn't buried here."

A familiar chestnut-haired woman strode towards them, flanked by two figures in dark armour. "Varus, you finally showed up," the woman purred, extending a bejeweled hand towards him. She was one of the few people not wearing some variety of protective clothing, swathed in a purple satin overcoat that hugged her form.

"You know I don't arrive anywhere quickly, Madame Rosaline," Varus offered playfully in response, pressing a kiss to the woman's hand. Jasper vividly remembered the magic he had seen that hand conjure. The Madame's gaze narrowed on Jasper, though not in a manner that suggested hostility. If anything, Jasper had the distinct impression he was being assessed. He struggled to stand up as straight as he could manage, the rigid leather armour aiding his posture.

"Who is your charming companion, Varus?" Rosaline asked, intrigued. "I feel we've met before..."

Varus gestured towards him. "Madame Rosaline, this is Jasper," he returned, something akin to pride colouring his voice. "You may have seen him in Cary's company at *The Raw Diamond* before."

Somehow, the verbal confirmation that Jasper had once been in a brothel was mortifying, mostly for how poorly he had handled it. Rosaline did not seem to share his feelings on the matter; rather, her eyes lit up as she clapped her hands together, assessing Jasper in a new light. "Ah, yes – darling boy, you were trying to defend my dear Cary, I remember you now."

Beside him, Jasper's employer hummed in agreement. "Nice of you to join us after all, Cary," Varus noted approvingly. "I admit I feared the evening would sour without your presence."

Jasper almost didn't recognize Cary at the Madame's side, the woman giving him a subtle wink beneath her hooded garment. Curiously, neither Cary nor the woman stationed opposite Rosaline contributed anything to the conversation, not even a laugh at Jasper's expense. As he regarded Cary now, Jasper could have sworn the presence of a glamour flickered in his vision. He blinked rapidly to try and see through it, but his attention was drawn elsewhere before he could investigate further.

"Rosaline, is that you?" a new voice called. "My, they really do just let anyone in here, don't they?" A willowy woman with harsh features strolled up to them, manicured hands perfectly balancing a wine glass that held something too viscous to be wine. Her black hair was scraped off her face in a high ponytail, lending to the severe expression on her face.

Whoever the unfamiliar woman was, Rosaline's disposition changed entirely. "Clearly, if they permitted a parched corpse such as yourself to take part, Tassa," she remarked dryly.

The woman named Tassa sniffed, looking down her nose at Jasper. "Varus, I see you've recruited a new friend," she mused, wiping an imaginary speck of dust from the sleeve of her form-fitting black dress. "Are you old enough to sit at this table, dear?"

Before Jasper could process her words long enough to bristle in indignation, Varus was already prepared to respond. "Bold words from a woman who employs children to please men," he retorted. His stance shifted ever so slightly, as if he might shield Jasper from her. "Remind me, how old was the last girl who died in your brothel? Twelve?"

Jasper resisted the urge to shudder at the thought of a child so young being employed at a brothel. Tassa's stare glazed over, the smug look finally fading from her features.

She turned on her heel soundlessly, stalking away to some other corner of the room to socialize elsewhere.

"I'd best meander as well, lest the rest of the congregation think we're conspiring," Rosaline sighed, tucking a stray lock of brown hair behind her ear. "Talk soon, Varus."

As the large, elegant Madame began to sway towards other groups of people within the sepulchre, mingling with the various factions, Varus leaned in close to whisper to Jasper. "You've obviously met with Madame Rosaline before," he explained in a low voice, speaking slowly for Jasper's benefit. "She runs the brothel in Caelfall, but she is also the head of the Silent Sisterhood, which by now you may have figured out that Cary takes part in."

Jasper nodded slowly, analyzing his employer's mouth as he spoke to better hear the man amidst the din of voices that echoed within the room. "That explains the... the silence, I guess," he stammered in reply. "Who was that other woman?"

Varus made a low noise in his throat. "Runs another, similar establishment in Aerindale," he offered, his eyes scanning the room. "Rosaline... cares about her people. Tassa seems to have little regard for human life beyond what kind of profit she can make off it."

His mouth dry, Jasper flexed his hands. He had been distantly aware before, but now he had confirmation that the people here weren't merely petty criminals. Tassa couldn't be the only person who had killed someone in here, directly or by association. Somehow, the thought of being amongst strangers who had taken lives was far more daunting.

There were people from all walks of life in the sepulchre. Jasper vaguely recognized two or three lords and ladies from Briardeen, influential families with their fine clothes who didn't seem to belong here, chatting and mingling with the rest of them. Instinctively, Jasper turned away the moment he caught sight of Lord McClelland, not wanting to risk being recognized by Gideon's father. Amidst cutthroat pirates with weaponized prosthetics, battle-hardened warriors with scars and missing teeth, and individuals clothed in hooded darkness and a preternatural stillness… Jasper was acutely aware of how green he looked in comparison.

And yet, Varus had chosen him. That had to count for something.

There was an inexplicable shift in the room as Varus gently nudged him with his shoulder, leading him towards the stone table. Gradually, each group of people dispersed throughout the sepulchre began to make their way towards their seats. When everyone was finally seated, Varus cleared his throat.

"Thank you all for coming," he began, his voice carrying in the relative silence of the chamber. There was a murmur of voices, nodding heads around the table. "It's about time we collectively got our shit together. What the hell was that stunt in the markets? Since when does the fighters' guild care about the opiates trade?"

There was an awkward rumble throughout the congregation, and even Jasper was taken aback by Varus' brazen introduction. "Since when does the Silent Sisterhood get to steal our contracts?" a cold, hoarse voice cut in. One of the hooded patrons spoke up, similarly clothed individuals stationed on either side of them. "We have an agreement. The Dominion owns targets in Aerindale and Briardeen."

"This issue has been discussed, Morgan," Rosaline

replied, her voice a weary sigh. "The targets that wander across boundaries are still *our* targets."

"The moment they wander over that bridge, they should be ours," the Dominion's leader retorted.

Rosaline was not deterred. She laughed loudly, shaking her head. "Ah, yes – the grand plans of the Twilight Dominion revealed," Rosaline snorted. "The moment we agree to that, you claim every poor bastard who lives in Caelfall and works in Briardeen. I think not."

"We've yet to hear your piece, Rasmussen," Varus interrupted, his voice a threatening growl. "Care to supply any defense for harassing my envoy and trying to steal my property?"

A man in dark, weathered armour stood up on the other side of the table, and Jasper was displeased to recognize the scarred pursuer he'd seen in the Caelfall markets. Rasmussen raised his hands in a gesture of defeat, though his gaze remained steely. "You threw the first punch, Varus," he warned. "Burning down our freighter was a declaration of war."

"You think I would stoop to setting alight to ships?" Varus barked.

"I just think it's pretty rutting convenient that the only ship damaged in Eodan's shipyard was the one containing *our* product," Rasmussen retorted.

The next response was too quiet for Jasper to hear, and after he strained his ears to pick up what the new speaker was saying, he realized their speech was not Aethian. An elderly Siathan man sat a few people away from him on his left, a silk scarf wound around his throat and a single tattoo of an eye on his forehead. The woman seated beside him nodded slowly, listening to his thoughts as he responded in rapid Siatch before she interpreted.

"I think you mean *our* product," she replied coolly, gesturing towards Rasmussen. Her nails had been sharpened to points, a detail that the scarred man did not miss. "Or have you forgotten that you still owe us for that shipment? We do not take kindly to being cheated, Mr. Rasmussen."

"He is the reason that shipment was destroyed!" Rasmussen protested, pointing at Varus again.

"You would do well not to accuse me of something so petty as arson, Rasmussen," Varus warned.

"But perhaps we *should* accuse you of other things, Varus," came Tassa's silky voice from nearby. Her wine glass was half-empty, her lips disturbingly dark as she leaned casually in her seat. "You seem to be growing careless in your old age… sloppy, even. Perhaps you have other, more pressing matters that are consuming your attentions? Trouble at home, perhaps?"

Varus grew very still. "Choose your next words carefully, Tassa," he said slowly.

Tassa laughed, a high-pitched, girlish sound that did not match her outward appearance at all. "I mean no offense, truly," she insisted, though there was a wicked gleam in her eyes. "I merely thought it worth mentioning how *complicated* your personal life must be right now. Tell me, have you heard that your darling doctor has a sordid love affair with that bookstore owner? Did you know he's due to be a father?"

The terse silence was preceded by a few noises of surprise and curiosity. This was certainly news to Jasper, but he didn't dare look back at Varus now. He could practically feel the ominous rumble of power resonating beside him, and he refused to show any visible sign of how startled he was.

"You've lost your touch, Varus, and it shows," Rasmussen saw his opportunity amidst the silence. Several people around the table gasped as Rasmussen dug into his pocket, withdrawing a revolver. "Step down, and we'll divide your territory as we see fit."

Rosaline was enraged. "Have you lost your minds?" she demanded, gesturing wildly with her adorned hands. "Have you forgotten how it was before Varus, how disorganized we were? We *own* Aethelind now. I will not go back to the way things were."

There were murmurs amongst the congregation, some in agreement and others shaking their heads. The Siathan man was speaking rapidly once more, his interpreter listening intently before she spoke. "And have you forgotten who owns this organization?" she offered, leaning forwards to gaze around at the faces staring back at her. "Azrael is clear on one thing – there is to be no blood spilled in this sepulchre. Are we no better than beasts, resorting to violence and threats?"

Rasmussen waved the revolver around wildly, addressing the group. "Do you see our fearless leader among us?" he demanded.

"Don't do this, Rasmussen," Rosaline warned quietly.

Varus still hadn't moved. Jasper dared a glance at his employer, half-expecting him to bare his teeth or growl as he had witnessed on occasion. Instead, as Rasmussen aimed at the kingpin's face, his finger squeezing the revolver trigger, Varus remained motionless.

Pure instinct took over, and Jasper was moving faster than he had ever moved in his life. He barely rose from his seat as he lunged, grasping his employer as he all but tackled Varus to the floor. His ears throbbed with the sound of the revolver as it fired once, twice – he prayed to every god he could name that he was faster than a bullet.

They collided with a crash on the stone floor, and Varus grunted as Jasper landed on top of him. His employer's face had been grazed by a passing bullet, but he was otherwise very much alive and with his head intact. Adrenaline surged through Jasper as he drew his sword, clambering to his feet.

"For the Dominion!" Morgan called out nearby, and pandemonium erupted around the table. Overlapping shouts echoed throughout the sepulchre as violence broke out. Rosaline had grappled for the revolver, and she and Rasmussen were presently fighting to the death. The assassins of the Twilight Dominion dispersed in the chaos, the guild of fighters drew swords and pistols, and Tassa's dark lips were stretched wide to reveal unnaturally sharp teeth. She locked eyes with Jasper as she cackled, vanishing in a cloud of smoke.

"Get up, Varus, *get up*," Jasper urged, reaching to help his employer to his feet. The hair on the back of his neck was prickling, and Jasper moved just in time to block one of the assassins, a shift in the air his only warning before a dagger was aimed at his heart. He shoved the attacker with the full force of his weight before slamming the hilt of his sword into their head, dropping them in an instant.

"Varus!" Jasper called, spinning on his heel. The other man was on his feet finally, his own swords drawn at last. "We need to get out of here!"

Varus was silent for a moment, a resonant anger rippling in the air around him. "We can't leave yet," he insisted, his eyes scanning the crowd. He moved, seemingly by instinct, to stand at Jasper's right side. "I can't abandon the people who are loyal to me."

He couldn't fault his employer for that. "Fair enough,"

Jasper agreed, even as his heart sank. "Stay with me, then. I need you focused."

Through the chaos, it was difficult to decipher friend from foe. Those who stood with Rasmussen seemed to be the entirety of the guild of fighters and the Dominion. The lords and ladies of Briardeen had fittingly vanished. On Varus' side, Rosaline fought with the Silent Sisterhood in the dim light, launching lightning at her opponents. The grizzled pirates seemed to be fighting for them as well, gratefully, though they still seemed to be outnumbered.

Jasper blocked several incoming strikes from the fighters, each armed with crude weapons – hammers, crowbars, and lead pipes. What they lacked in polish and finesse, they more than made up for in ferocity. To his surprise, Varus fought in a manner similar to his own, and it was almost second nature for Jasper to parry several would-be lethal blows towards the kingpin's blind left side. All around them, members of each faction fell to the floor in bloodied heaps, electrocuted or impaled or worse.

Just as Jasper was about to knock out a disarmed assassin, Tassa emerged from the fray, slamming her drained wine glass into the side of his face. Jasper recoiled instinctively, squeezing his eyes shut as he felt glass in his skin. Her arms were around him in an instant, nails like talons digging into his throat as the woman restrained him. His soul nearly left his body entirely at the sensation of a tongue dragging along the side of his face, lapping at the blood now streaming from his temple.

"What a rare and curious flavour," Tassa purred in his ear, her teeth nicking his skin. "Fret not, little one. I will savour you, every last drop…" Blinking blood out of his eyes, Jasper struggled to open one of them enough to orient himself, writhing in her grasp.

Their allies dwindling, Varus was left surrounded by mutinous Dominion assassins and guild members, with Rasmussen closing in. Noticing Jasper's distress, his employer made a fatal mistake. As he turned to face Tassa, taking in her grasp on his bodyguard, Varus did not see Rasmussen sauntering towards him, the murderous gleam in his eye.

"Varus!" Jasper called out, his voice strained by Tassa's death grip on his throat.

Faster than Jasper could process, Varus spun on his heel. He grasped the revolver in Rasmussen's right hand, jerking it out of the way at the last second as the gun went off, the sound deafening as it reverberated throughout the sepulchre. Rasmussen wasn't finished, however; from his pocket, the man withdrew a dagger he promptly buried in Varus' flesh.

"No!" Jasper roared, the nails at his neck drawing blood as they pricked his skin. Behind him, Tassa cackled.

Time stood still as Varus was silent, one hand wrapped around Rasmussen's revolver, keeping it pointed skyward, the other on the dagger wedged into his abdomen. "I never could stand the way you talked down to us," Rasmussen snarled between gritted teeth, dragging the dagger up through Varus' gut. Varus made a strangled noise as he struggled to arrest Rasmussen's efforts to eviscerate him, his entire body seeming to tremble with rage and pain. "Always thought you were better than us, eh?"

Breathing heavily, Varus looked up at Rasmussen, and Jasper didn't need to see his face to know the wrath in those hellfire eyes, the depth of the ire directed at the other man at this moment. "Rot in the void, you dried up maggot," Varus snarled.

Rasmussen's determination flickered in his eyes. Quick

as lightning, Varus headbutted the other man once, twice, three times – with so much ferocity that Jasper flinched. After the first, Rasmussen dropped the revolver with the shock, the weapon clattering to the floor. With the second, he took a half-step back as he faltered, blood dripping from a cut on his nose where Varus' brow had connected. By the third, Rasmussen was sprawled in a heap on the stone floor, out cold.

His hand still clenched around the dagger buried within him, Varus tore it from his stomach with a war cry that made even Tassa shudder. The exertion sent his employer to his knees, and Varus spat blood as he heaved a ragged breath. It stained black against the stone floor of the sepulchre, black against his skin as it dripped down his face from his split forehead, soaked through his tunic, and for a moment Jasper was stunned.

Not once in his entire life had he encountered someone whose blood was not red.

Everyone seemed frozen in time for a moment, watching as Varus panted on his knees, one hand clutched at his abdomen in a vain attempt to stopper the blood that spilled from him. Madame Rosaline looked on in horror, her magic sputtering from her fingers. Cary and the other hooded sister were poised on either side of her, prepared to strike the moment the action resumed, but many of the mutinous coalition seemed to be eagerly waiting to watch the kingpin die.

Varus tilted his head back, breathing slowly as he did. For a moment, in the dim light, he looked very young. Exhaling slowly, the man looked towards Rosaline in the crowd, a barely perceptible nod before he turned to face Jasper. A savage grin spread across his lips, revealing unsettlingly sharp canines set in his lower jaw.

"Close your eyes, Jasper," he instructed him quietly. "Please."

Jasper was too shocked to argue. He screwed his eyes shut, knowing that when his employer asked him to do so it was for his own good, some horrifying bit of magic Varus didn't want him to see. He felt, rather than *heard*, the shift in the room, the way his bones ached as that dark energy began to emanate from where Varus knelt nearby. His employer's voice deepened into a guttural snarl, and the sepulchre erupted into a cacophony of screaming.

When Jasper came to, his head was throbbing and there was a warm pressure on his chest. He gingerly opened his eyes, expecting to find himself captured or buried beneath the aftermath of the mutiny – but to his surprise, he was lying on a soft surface, and someone was pressing a cool, damp cloth to his stinging face. He was disoriented, but with some difficulty he remembered what had transpired before blacking out.

"Varus!" he cried out, sitting upright. The pain surged in his head and he winced audibly, stars dotting his vision as Jasper swayed. There was an irritable hiss as an animal that had been sitting on his chest was promptly dethroned from its perch.

"Don't move so quickly," a woman's voice warned, a pair of hands on his shoulders steadying him. "You hit your head fairly hard, you might not want to sit up just yet."

Jasper was in no position to protest, the woman's hands guiding him back down to where a soft pillow had been propped up beneath him. "Is… is Varus okay?" he dared to ask. "Did he make it?"

As his vision began to clear, his eyes focused on the woman seated beside him. Her blonde hair was loosely plaited over her shoulder, the short sleeves of her white nightgown exposing a pair of silver mage's cuffs. "He'll be okay," she assured him, a warm smile on her face that made her blue eyes twinkle. "Haeyin is with him in the other room."

Jasper exhaled slowly, feeling a tension in his bones relax at her words. The woman resumed cleaning his face, gently wiping the blood and dirt and gods knew what else from his temple. "I feel like I know you," he said finally, having given up on trying to remember her name.

The animal that had been sitting on him — a black and white cat with green eyes — seemingly forgave Jasper's transgressions and resumed her perch on his chest, purring with enough vigour that he felt the sensation through his entire body. The woman paused for a moment, studying the cat with an amused expression on her face.

"It seems Mo has taken a liking to you," she offered approvingly. "My name is Eleni. I'm a friend of Charlotte, but you and I have only met in passing."

Whether due to his terrible memory for names or his probable concussion, Jasper's recollection of the woman returned slowly. "Eleni... yes, I remember now," he replied after a moment, absentmindedly petting the cat on his chest. "I'm sorry, I'm not myself."

"Don't be silly," was all Eleni offered in response before returning her focus to his face. "Hold still, this might hurt a bit."

Through his shuttered gaze, Jasper could see the soft, violet glow of the woman's magic. As Eleni's hand hovered over the side of his face, he could feel the sting in his skin start to fade as the energy knitted his temple back together.

Her magic felt different to Haeyin's, a warm, vast ocean instead of a blazing fire. His face resonated with that warmth after she had moved her hand away, and Jasper was relieved to find his head no longer pained him.

"It's not very pretty, I'm afraid," Eleni explained apologetically. "If you had gotten here sooner, I... maybe if I'd cleaned it out a bit more..."

"It's fine," Jasper insisted hurriedly. In truth, he was incredibly unsettled by the fact that he had no idea what state he was in visually; he had grown accustomed to his scars, and the fact that he seemed to be perpetually collecting them, but he had a fixed idea of what his *face* looked like. It was strange not to instinctively know his appearance anymore.

If Eleni disbelieved him, she said nothing. "Can I get you something to eat? Something to drink?" she asked.

Shaking his head, Jasper tentatively began to sit up so as not to anger Mo the cat a second time. Growling mournfully, the animal seemed to accept her desired seat was no longer available, retreating to the arm of the sofa. He was in a grand sitting room, every wall inlaid with bookshelves filled to the brim with tomes. A fireplace crackled in the wall behind him, but Eleni did not seem as distressed by the proximity to the books as Jasper was. He could only assume he was in Varus' home, the manor in Dornkeep owned by the mysterious "Eodan Melicus".

"Can I see him?" Jasper asked. "Varus?"

"Of course," she replied. "I'm sure he'll want to see you." She stood slowly, gesturing for him to follow. She was barely taller than Charlotte, but from the looks of her she could have thrown Jasper on his back. Jasper followed with some trepidation as she led him into the hallway, Mo's watchful stare following them all the way.

The manor was exquisite, if somewhat lacking in décor; the dark, polished wood floors and gleaming brass candelabras were lovely, but the walls were entirely bare. There were no portraits of deceased family members as there were in Gideon's ancestral home, nor were there any potted plants, crockery, or embroidery that Jasper was accustomed to seeing in Charlotte's loft. The sitting room seemed to be the only place with any ounce of Varus' personality.

That was before Jasper followed Eleni down the hall into the kitchen, and he saw the chaos. The kitchen might have been beautiful on any other day, boasting a concerningly large liquor cabinet that occupied much of the wall adjacent to Jasper. Seated at the kitchen table, Haeyin was currently at work suturing up Jasper's employer, covered in that strange, black blood up to his wrists. Varus lay on his back upon the table, his shirt discarded to reveal the full expanse of his intricate tattoos, the first time Jasper had ever seen all of them on display. They stretched from his elbows to his shoulders, arcing along his sternum and extending across his collarbones.

As they entered, the doctor glanced up from his work to smile wearily at Jasper. "Oh, good," he said by way of greeting. "I'm glad only one of you was eviscerated. It's lovely to see you in good health, Jasper."

Spluttering at the blunt remark, Jasper struggled to respond. Gratefully, Eleni spared him from parsing a sentence. "How is it going?" she asked conversationally, as if this were a perfectly normal occurrence. If any of what Tassa had said at the meet was true, perhaps it *was* normal for them.

Propping himself up on his elbows, Varus sat up as much as he could. Haeyin paused in his efforts to resume stitching the man up, turning his head as he gave Varus a withering stare until the man laid back down. Crossing his ankles casually, the kingpin was seemingly unaffected by Haeyin's irritation as he turned his head to face Jasper.

"Well, I think," Varus replied. "I'm in good hands." His face was unblemished, with no evidence of the bullet graze or the split in his forehead from headbutting Rasmussen. Jasper couldn't help the pang of jealousy that splintered through him, still struggling with the knowledge of his altered appearance.

"Rather, you have good hands in you," Eleni quipped casually, with Jasper managing not to choke as he restrained his laughter. Varus chuckled as well, much to Haeyin's chagrin, but even the doctor was struggling to hide his amusement.

"Every bloody week, one of you puts my abilities as a surgeon to the test," Haeyin muttered under his breath, occupying himself with what remained of the wound to Varus' abdomen. From what Jasper could tell, Haeyin was suturing the man shut layer by layer, weaving his employer back together. It made him a bit nauseous to look at the spot where Varus had been mortally wounded, so he looked away.

Varus noticed his discomfort. "Are you all right, Jasper?" he asked gently.

Forcing himself to focus on the man's face and not his cadaver half, Jasper couldn't help but laugh. "Am I... I'm fine," he insisted. "*You* were nearly disemboweled, and you're asking me – is this how you feel when I say I'm fine after I've nearly died, Haeyin?"

"Yes," Haeyin replied immediately. Eleni covered her mouth with her hand, attempting to hide her laughter even as her shoulders shook.

"While I am relieved that you aren't dead, and that

we're having this conversation… how are you still alive?" Jasper asked finally, gesturing vaguely to the minced meat that Haeyin was trying to coax back into a torso. "I *saw* what happened to you, I thought you…"

Something flickered in Varus' eyes, an emotion Jasper couldn't name. He turned away, his gaze towards the ceiling. Though he seemed to be in better shape than he had been back in the catacombs, his breathing was still laboured.

"I'm sure you have many questions," he noted, his voice rough. "And you've more than earned an explanation. Let's start with the obvious – you may have already suspected this, but I am… not like you. Not human."

It was the first time in Jasper's life that someone had referred to him that way. Normally, he was referred to by others as distinctly *not* human in some way or another, for his sometimes stiff and awkward behaviour or his aversion to touch and textures. Something about his employer's words sent a chill down his spine, the confirmation that Varus himself stood starkly outside of humanity.

"You may not be human, but for the love of Celüne, you need to be more careful," Haeyin interjected before Jasper could question Varus. He seemed to have finished cramming the man's intestines back into his stomach cavity, suturing the wounded flesh as he went. "It's not *easy* performing surgery on you by any means."

"Varus is very difficult patient," Eleni murmured in Jasper's ear, her lips curving into a smirk. "We can't sedate him because his tolerance is astronomical, so he just talks the entire time Haeyin's working. He can't stand it." Varus offered Eleni a dull stare in return for her betrayal, but she only winked at him.

Eleni's words sparked more questions than they

answered. Frowning as he regarded the sparse streaks of white in Haeyin's hair, Jasper finally realized what was so jarring about the scene before him. "Why aren't you using magic?" he asked.

Haeyin paused in his efforts, his eyebrow raised in silent question as he looked towards Varus, as if waiting for permission. The kingpin loosed a weary sigh. "You've seen my abilities, aye?" Varus began. When Jasper mumbled in agreement, his employer continued. "It doesn't... play well with others, shall we say. Haeyin could exhaust himself trying to heal me, and his magic would be swallowed whole before it could accomplish anything."

"'Doesn't play well with others' is an understatement," Haeyin grumbled as he finished the last of the stitches in his partner's abdomen. "I tried to heal him normally *once*, and the next thing I knew I was being helped up from the floor."

Clearing her throat delicately, Eleni gestured towards one of the wooden chairs not currently covered in blood and medical supplies. "Perhaps, now that the crisis has been averted... you might be inclined to tell us what happened down there?" Eleni suggested. Her voice was gentle, but she spoke with the conviction of a detective investigating a case. Jasper found himself compelled to sit down.

Haeyin seemed equally invested in this story, crossing the kitchen to scrub his hands thoroughly in the sink. "Yes, please tell us," the doctor agreed, rejoining them as he dried his hands on a fresh towel. "I'm curious to know why you thought it was a good idea to bring *the boy* to this." Realizing he was "the boy", Jasper's face heated.

Varus seemed unruffled, as if he were used to being interrogated by his partners. With some difficulty, a hand pressed to his newly stitched wound as if it might prevent him from tearing a stitch, he swung his legs over the side of the table. "It was worse than I thought it would be," he admitted in a low voice, gingerly sliding down from the table as he made his way over to the liquor cabinet. As he turned, Jasper was startled to see even more dizzying spirals inked into the man's skin, the patterns reaching across his shoulders to connect at the base of Varus' neck.

"What happened?" Eleni prompted, taking a seat beside Jasper on a mostly clean chair.

Haeyin seemed very concerned about the bottle of liquor Varus was reaching for. "What have I told you about drinking when you've—you know what, never mind," he conceded with a huff.

As if he hadn't heard his partner, Varus tore the stopper from a dark glass bottle, the contents nearly invisible within. "Rasmussen thought we burned down the Siathan freighter," Varus explained, taking a concerningly deep drink from the bottle. He paused for a moment, as if waiting to see if it spilled out of his freshly mended stomach, then carried on. "They were keeping stock on that ship."

"Do we know who *did* burn down the freighter?" Jasper asked, unable to keep the question in his head any longer. He was already pleased with himself for not blurting it out during the meet.

"No," Haeyin answered quickly, shaking his head. "Not a sodding clue. Most concerningly, we have no idea what their intentions were, whoever they are. The more we find out, the more convoluted the situation becomes."

"Aye, and with little evidence, there's not much to prove our own innocence," Varus added, grunting as he eased himself into one of the chairs, still holding his gut for good measure. "I was prepared for *tensions*. I didn't expect a bloody mutiny."

"How many?" Haeyin asked wearily, rubbing the bridge of his nose.

Releasing his wounded abdomen, Varus began to count their enemies aloud. "Rasmussen, obviously… I assume the entirety of the guild will remain loyal to him. The Dominion allied with him as well, so they'll be none too pleased with us. Tassa did a number on Jasper."

Haeyin seemed to jerk awake. "You let the vampire attack Jasper?"

"The *what?*" Jasper startled.

"He's fine," Eleni insisted, as if this was not the noteworthy detail Jasper and Haeyin seemed to think it was. "Who else?"

Varus shook his head. "The Briardeen bunch made themselves scarce when the fighting broke out, so I'm assuming they'll ally with whomever they fear most," he continued dryly. "Rosaline and the Sisterhood remained on our side, as well as the Siathan smugglers and the pirates, so… there's that, I suppose."

"Are they okay? Rosaline and Cary?" Jasper interjected. With a pang of guilt, he realized he hadn't thought of their allies since he'd woken up.

His employer took another swig from the bottle in his grip, nodding slowly. "Aye, they're all right," replied Varus. "The Sisterhood suffered some casualties, but Rosaline and Cary made it out, that much I know."

"What does this mean for you?" Eleni asked warily. She was seated very close to Jasper, though she seemed to be careful not to touch him. He wondered if Varus and Haeyin had briefed her on his aversion to physical contact.

Varus was silent for a moment, dragging a hand down

his face. "I don't know," he admitted after a moment. "The underworld hasn't been this divided for twenty years. With any luck, what happened tonight will dissuade others from trying anything, but I wouldn't rule out retaliation."

With a pained expression on his face, Varus glanced up at last, his eyes darting between Haeyin and Eleni. "They... they knew about you, Eleni," he added after a moment's pause. "I fear you may no longer be safe here."

Jasper hadn't wanted to ask, but Varus' words confirmed the partial truth in Tassa's taunts. Haeyin's face betrayed his concern, but Eleni's remained carefully guarded, with only the barest hint of strain in her eyes. "We've discussed this," she replied simply. "I'm not afraid of them."

"Whether or not you fear them won't deter their efforts," Varus warned, and Jasper noted the way his knuckles were taut on the bottle of liquor he clutched, the set of his jaw as he spoke. "*This* is what we're up against, *this* is what they will attempt to exploit."

"Let them try," was all Eleni offered in response, a sense of finality in her tone.

Varus' grip on the bottle in his hand remained white-knuckled, but he said nothing as he met Eleni's level gaze. Before either of them could continue, Haeyin stretched audibly, several of his joints cracking in response. "Well, whatever the case may be, neither of *you* should try anything stupid any time soon," the doctor scolded pointedly. "You're damned lucky the pair of you are evidently so hard to kill."

Varus' eyes glazed over in a dull stare again, and Jasper was unable to stop the bubble of laughter that rose up from within him. It had arguably been an awful, terrible evening, and he would probably have nightmares for weeks – but between Haeyin's dry wit, Eleni's soothing presence, and the familiarity of Varus' general persona, he was beginning to feel more and more at ease. Gradually, the impending meltdown that had been building up within his chest was slipping away.

"As for you, my dear," Haeyin continued, crossing the room to where Eleni sat beside Jasper. "You'd best try and get some rest, you shouldn't be exerting yourself so much."

Even as she rolled her eyes, Eleni was unable to hide her smile as she took Haeyin's offered hand. "If it's not one of you fretting over my safety, it's the other fretting over my health," she mused, sighing deeply as she stood. "I'm not dying, you know."

"I know," Haeyin replied, pressing a kiss to her temple. He offered her his arm, leading her out of the kitchen towards the hallway. Eleni glanced back at Jasper, giving him a wave before the pair of them left the room.

Jasper became aware of his employer watching him from across the kitchen. "It's getting late, lad," Varus agreed, though he made no effort to follow his partners to bed. "Normally, I'd offer to take you back home, but Haeyin will probably kill me if I rip a stitch."

He found no reason to argue, the weight of exhaustion sinking into his bones even as Jasper found himself craving his own bed. "He might very well do that," Jasper agreed, nodding sleepily.

"I had my butler prepare a guest room for you," offered Varus, stretching out his bad leg beneath the kitchen table. "East wing, second door on the left side of the corridor."

"Thank you, sir." He stood up from the kitchen chair, his joints already beginning to stiffen with exertion and fatigue. As he was about the cross the threshold of the kitchen into the hallway, Jasper found the courage for one last question.

"Varus, if you don't mind me asking…" Jasper began, leaning on his arm against the archway. "You said you aren't human, but… what are you, exactly?"

Gratefully, Jasper's clumsy wording only caused Varus to chuckle under his breath, shaking his head. "A fool cursed with longevity," he replied in a low voice. He met Jasper's eyes, raising his bottle with a crooked smile. "It's a long story, my boy. We'll have time for it another day."

CHAPTER

TWELVE
CHARLOTTE

As Gideon escorted Charlotte towards the castle to meet with the princess, she tried not to dwell on where Jasper was that evening. Dante seemed to be under the impression that "Eodan Melicus" was on a business trip to the mainland below, while Maya had told Charlotte that the man was visiting family. She knew neither scenario could be accurate while Jasper was involved, but it was impossible to derive any truth on the matter when no one seemed to know otherwise – or if they did, weren't inclined to share it with her.

"You're awfully quiet tonight, Charlie," Gideon noted. She startled at the sound of his voice, glancing up to meet his piercing blue stare.

"Sorry, just… thinking," Charlotte said dismissively. "Not that you're one to talk. You've barely spoken to me for months, now."

It was the most up front she'd been with Gideon

about his recent change of heart, observed only by Jasper. It wasn't so much that she didn't think she was close enough with Gideon for him to confide in her, but Charlotte rarely saw the man in a situation where she could ask him about it. Even now, as the twilight settled over Briardeen, there were still far too many people for a comfortable conversation about the crumbling state of the kingdom.

Gideon looked around conspiratorially before he responded, as if he too was gauging whether it was safe to discuss anything with her. "I... I'm sorry, Charlie," he replied eventually, turning his gaze back towards the street. "It's nothing you've done. I just have a lot on my mind."

"You and me both," Charlotte agreed. "You're... you're safe, yes? You'd tell me if things were bad again?"

He smiled at her, and something about the way Gideon smiled lately bothered her. It was never a true smile that brightened his eyes, but a sad sort of smile as if he were putting on a brave face. "It's all right, Charlie," Gideon assured her. "Things at home have been... stable."

She didn't know whether she believed him. "You know you can always talk to me, right?" Charlotte continued, nudging him with her elbow. "Even if I can't help, I can always listen." She wondered if she spoke too baldly then, if she had given him a reason to think she knew more about his current plight than she let on. Would he be cross that Jasper had divulged details of his conversations to Charlotte?

At that moment, however, all the streetlights illuminating Briardeen promptly spluttered and died. Charlotte blinked in the darkness, the thinned crowd around them equally surprised as they stood in the insufficient light of the dwindling sunset.

"That can't be good," she murmured as the lights remained out.

"It's been getting worse," Gideon agreed, offering his arm as they carried on towards the castle. "No one wants to talk about it, but…" He trailed off, leaving Charlotte to ponder in silence as he led her towards the castle gardens in the near-darkness. At some point, as they crossed through the castle gates, the streetlights in the distance finally flickered back to life.

Gideon escorted her from the courtyard entrance into the gardens, clearing his throat. "Don't stay out too late," he instructed her. "There's trouble afoot tonight, apparently."

She frowned, searching his guarded expression. "What's going on?" probed Charlotte.

Shaking his head, Gideon shifted in his armour, as if it might make the suit more comfortable. "Nothing for certain, but we heard rumours of a criminal gathering taking place somewhere in the kingdom," he offered. "Extra patrol in case we catch anything amiss."

Charlotte felt her eyes glaze over in what she could only reason was an instinctive reaction. "Good luck, then," was all she could say. Jasper had promised her he'd be careful… this sounded as if he were doing exactly the opposite.

Gideon seemed not to notice her chagrin, or perhaps didn't think it warranted comment. He gave her a little wave before he left her to her own devices in the gardens, easing through the presence of Cary's now familiar wards. The princess had invited Charlotte here urgently, her letter reading quite distressed when Cary had delivered it to her this afternoon. She wasn't sure what discovery the princess might have made, but Aurelia clearly thought it urgent enough to summon her that night.

She found the princess pacing beneath a delicate cloud of conjured fireflies, shaking her hands out as she murmured to herself. Fortia was perched nearby on a stone bench, eerily calm in comparison. "You shouldn't say such things, Aurelia," said Fortia, her tone one of warning.

As usual, the princess was not heeding her guardian's advice. "It's impossible the two things are not related," she insisted, flapping her hands as she spoke. "If the— Charlotte!"

Charlotte barely had time to say "hello" before the princess beckoned her over. She must have been particularly anxious, her eyes trembling more severely than they did usually. "What's the matter, Aurelia?" Charlotte prompted her gently.

"I… I think I may have discovered something terrible," the princess admitted, gesturing at Fortia frantically. The Reinnairlei woman sighed before she stood up, a folded copy of the *Jackdaw* in her hands. "The front page, take a look."

Charlotte did as she was instructed, unfolding the worn newspaper with trepidation. The first page was an article detailing the upcoming investigation into what had delayed the accords meeting; an accusation of magical warfare that had extended Pharsat's dry season to the extent of a soon-to-be lethal drought. Some of the information that had been provided Charlotte was already aware of, either through what Dante had been willing to share with her or from what gossip had reached Caelfall – but one detail caught her eye.

"Your father is responsible for this?" she hissed. "Aurelia—"

"By proxy," Aurelia elaborated quickly. "He has… he has this advisor, Aloysius. He's one of the most powerful mages I've ever met, he used to train me to use my magic before... well, that doesn't matter anymore." She waved her hand dismissively, but her face betrayed the fact that perhaps this mattered still.

"Aurelia believes that Aloysius is responsible for this magical warfare," Fortia continued, her tone weary. The woman didn't sound as if she disbelieved the princess, but to Charlotte it seemed as if Fortia was wary of making such an accusation, regardless of the verity of it.

"Charlotte, I'm certain of it," Aurelia insisted in a hushed voice, her rosy eyes wide. "Listen to me – you've said before, you have mage friends, yes?"

She half-choked, fearful of outing her renegade doctor. Eleni was her only "mage friend" who was registered by the kingdom census. "Y—yes," she stammered, but Aurelia pushed on.

"Now, you're aware of the... the physical symptoms of magical overuse, yes?" Aurelia prompted her. When Charlotte nodded slowly, the princess took a deep breath. "Aloysius has been unwell for... quite some time. Nearly a year, I'd reckon."

Blinking, Charlotte waited for her to continue. When a moment or two passed, she replied, "Is that all?"

Aurelia began to pace in the gravel once more. "At first, I'd thought it was just... he's just old, right? The man was ancient when I was born. But in the last year, he's been especially unwell, and just acting strange all around. His hair has been falling out, he's constantly excusing himself from meetings and the courts on account of coughing fits and nose bleeds. I've walked in on him bandaging his hands on far too many occasions."

"So he's old, and he's probably dying," Charlotte

insisted, not wanting to believe a person was capable of such things.

The princess paled further, an expression Charlotte hadn't thought possible. "It's not just physical symptoms," Aurelia continued, fidgeting with her hands. "Magical overuse can cause psychosis. It's rare, and every single mage is taught to avoid it at all costs, but with some varieties of magic — and some *quantities* of magic — it's inevitable."

Charlotte shuddered with a sudden chill. "What are you saying?"

Aurelia exchanged a grim look with Fortia. "I've caught him talking to himself on numerous occasions, now," she admitted softly. "He's forgotten my name a few times, how old I am... that can all be chalked up to old age, but talking to the walls? I'm hard-pressed to find an alternate explanation for that."

Her thoughts turned to Haeyin, the number of times she'd seen or heard of his hands blistering with magical exertion. She had never seen Eleni use that much of her magic, but the thought of either of her friends succumbing to such a thing... "Are you sure?" Charlotte breathed.

"We can't be certain of anything," Fortia warned, her hand on the princess' shoulder.

"But how could it be anything else?" Aurelia demanded in an exasperated hiss. "The amount of effort it would take daily to maintain something like that... it's unprecedented, I've never heard of one man sustaining drastic climate change that long. There must be something he's consuming to bolster his magic, the exhaustion would kill him otherwise—by all accounts, it *is* killing him."

"Aurelia, *why* would your father order this?" Charlotte whispered. "We're supposed to be allies with Pharsat, the accords are meant to maintain that peace. What does he gain from another war?"

The princess took a shuddering breath. "There's something else," she continued. "Something I wasn't supposed to find out. I didn't know with certainty until this morning, but I was supposed to—"

"Quiet, I thought I heard something," Fortia said suddenly, and the three of them jolted where they stood. Charlotte was motionless as the Reinnairlei woman turned in a slow circle, surveying their surroundings. Aurelia extinguished her fireflies, squinting in the darkness as well. There were a few terrifying moments of near silence as the three of them waited for another sound, another sign that they were no longer alone in the gardens. Her breath catching in her throat, Charlotte became aware of the absence of Cary's wards, the magical presence she had come to feel safe within.

A hand grasped the back of her head, fingers threading through her curls as Charlotte was yanked backwards with a force that made her yelp with shock more than pain. Her assailant shoved her roughly into the dirt, her face smashing into the gravel hard enough to break her nose. She inhaled a lungful of dirt and blood, choking as she was pinned against the ground by whoever had grabbed her. The folded-up *Jackdaw* bounced and rolled away, damning her as it lay exposed in the clearing.

"Don't touch her!" Aurelia was shrieking nearby. "I demand you release her at once."

At the sound of the princess' voice, there was no reaction. The pressure against her shoulders, the weight of her aggressor's knee on her back did not let up at the command. Charlotte felt tears prick her eyes as the distant sound of gravel crunching drew nearer and nearer, and

Aurelia's protests quieted. She craned her neck as best she could, catching sight of an armed Fortia standing between the princess and the castle guards who had caught them. It was clear from their stances they would not be gentle with Aurelia either, if not for the presence of her guardian.

Her heart sank as the nearing footsteps came to a halt, with none other than King Gustaf standing before them, his crown almost glowing in the light of the moon. Charlotte had seen him from a distance in the past, occasionally at the church, but to see him up close was something else entirely. There was a cold, calculating fury in the man's steel-grey eyes, the hard lines in his face unforgiving. She couldn't help but think on how little Aurelia resembled her father.

"I had thought after our last discussion you would cease this nonsense, but it seems you have yet to learn your lesson," he began, the low timbre of his voice sending chills down Charlotte's spine. "Have you put her up to this, Fortia?"

"Father, please – let Charlotte go, she had no part in this," Aurelia pleaded, her vermillion eyes wet with tears. In some distant part of herself, Charlotte realized how truly powerless the princess was in this scenario, and the thought filled her with a strange sort of grief. If Aurelia couldn't protect her, there was no hope of mercy from the king.

At the mention of Charlotte's name, the king's gaze dragged over her, painfully slow in its pace. Those cold eyes seemed to roam over her form, and it took all of Charlotte's strength to hold that hateful look and stare him down in retaliation. "What rebel bitch have you dragged into your game now, Aurelia?" King Gustaf said wearily. "Is this how you got your hands on *The Jackdaw Herald?*"

"No!" Aurelia shrieked. "No, I swear to you—she had nothing to do with this, let her go!"

"To the dungeons with her," someone said nearby, another of the guards that had apprehended them communicating with the person that pinned Charlotte to the ground. She was hauled roughly to her feet, her shoulders aching in her sockets where her arms were held unnaturally taut behind her back. Her momentum was halted by the king as he raised his hand, and the guards watched and waited.

"Your Majesty?" prompted a voice behind her as the guard waited for orders.

King Gustaf's cold gaze pierced through Charlotte as his eyes narrowed. "To my chambers," he instructed, dismissing the guards with a wave of his hand as he turned to address his daughter.

There was a ringing in Charlotte's ears as she struggled to process the information. *To your chambers, not the dungeons?* Aurelia was screaming her name now, Fortia being forced to restrain the princess more than she was protecting her. There was blood in Charlotte's mouth, her face stinging as she was dragged by the guards.

She would not be executed, not yet. But she would be punished.

"Know this, dear daughter," the king said in a low voice behind her, his voice growing faint as Charlotte was pulled further and further away. "What happens to her now... it is because of you and your meddling. You had a choice, and you did this."

Charlotte had never been this deep within the castle walls. After some time being pulled down stone corridors, Charlotte was simply without the energy to struggle further, a bone-deep weariness settling in as she tired. She was powerless to resist as the guards who carried her brought her to a grand hallway with a solitary, ornately carved door at the far end.

If the guards stationed at either side of the archway thought it odd that a young woman was being dragged towards the room, their expressions revealed nothing. How many women had suffered a similar fate, for this to be such a routine affair? With a stiff, nodded salute, the guards merely stepped aside, the wooden doors swinging wide as Charlotte was shoved roughly into the entryway. She stumbled, her newly freed arms struggling to balance her weight as she crashed to the floor again, the carpet beneath her burning her palms. Charlotte turned as quickly as she could, hoping to catch a glimpse of whoever it was that brought her to her punishment, but the guards were already closing the doors behind them.

As the grand doors slammed shut with a bang, Charlotte shot to her feet, renewed with a surge of adrenaline as she became vividly aware of how little time she had left. Her eyes scanned her surroundings, searching for something she could use to escape, or defend herself. The guards were far too calm about whatever would happen to her; she would find no assistance from the men who served the king. She crossed the opulent chambers towards the study, searching for anything she might use – and her eyes settled on an ornate, polished letter opener.

As she retrieved it from the king's desk, Charlotte tested the weight of the letter opener in her hand as her fingers closed around the metal. She was no warrior, but she had learned a thing or two from Jasper and Gideon. The letter opener was too blunt to lacerate, but anything could be used as a stabbing implement with the right amount of force. It would have to do. Lifting her skirts, Charlotte tucked the letter opener into her boot, fidgeting with it against her ankle until she could walk normally. Smoothing her dress back down, she darted towards the bed chambers to search for—

The door burst open, and Charlotte's brief burst of energy faltered in her veins as she spun around to face the source of the noise. Her eyes locked with the king as he entered the room, the doors slamming shut behind him once more as he sauntered towards her. Though she knew him to be human, the man before her moved with an eerie stillness, a silence no ordinary person could maintain. His features cut from stone and iron, the king's expression was unchanged – but there was a hunger in his eyes that Charlotte didn't like one bit.

She stood frozen to the spot as he approached, terrified that King Gustaf might somehow know what she was up to, what was concealed within her boot. Instead, the king grasped her chin roughly, and Charlotte winced audibly as his fingers met her bloodied chin. Now she heard some small sign of life from the king, even and slow breaths from his barely opened lips as if what he was doing—what he was about to do—were entirely mundane for him.

"Unacceptable," he murmured, and Charlotte had the unpleasant suspicion she was being evaluated. "What were they doing, shoving your face into the dirt like a common criminal?"

Charlotte stood motionless, too afraid of what her defiant tongue might say if she permitted herself to speak. The king turned her face as he inspected her injuries, and she could only imagine how she must look – her face throbbed in his grasp, her skin stinging with only the slightest change in the air.

"It is amusing, how I have overheard the guards and the men of the court discuss your appearance," King Gustaf continued, releasing her chin carelessly. His gaze had drifted down from her eyes. "As if you could ever be linked to a Valedian witch. You are far too lovely to ever be insulted with such a comparison."

If there was intended to be a compliment woven into his remarks, it was lost in the vague horror that men in Briardeen gossiped about Charlotte, the insult to her mother and their shared heritage. Charlotte prayed he could not sense her revulsion as she resisted the urge to wrinkle her nose, to pull away from his cloying gaze. She was all too aware of how her clothes had torn and wrinkled in the assault, feeling as if every curve of her were on display for this foul man.

"Are you mute, girl?" King Gustaf said suddenly, his tone causing Charlotte to flinch. He was far too close, close enough to smell him – for him to smell *her*, and she wasn't sure which was worse.

"Kind words, Your Majesty," Charlotte commented dryly, managing not to stammer. She cursed herself for her sarcasm, but gratefully King Gustaf seemed too distracted to notice. The king's hands moved down from her throat to trace along her collarbone, and as his fingers came to a rest down her side Charlotte realized what a hopeless situation she was in. Every inch of her screamed in protest, in agony at the thought of being touched by anyone who wasn't Jasper. She had visualized such caresses, such moments of improper closeness, but with hands scarred and calloused and sun-stained. This was not what she wanted.

But who was she to refuse a king?

The hand at her hip grasped her roughly, forcing her to turn away from the king as she was shoved roughly towards the bed. Charlotte's heart leapt into her throat at what may as well have been a cell in the dungeons, the dim light casting long, dark shadows across the chamber. Despite his chagrin that her face had been shoved into the gravel, King Gustaf was not gentle with her as he directed her towards the mattress, pushing her to bend over the side of it as he came closer still.

a silence came over her

pressed against the unyielding surface

unable to move

at the small of her back

a bitter feeling of helplessness

a sadness taking hold

her mind adrift in a thoughtless ocean

fresh wounds, aggravated

the pain, a distant distraction

through a broken nose, gasping for air

tears stinging down her ruined face

jarring imperfections in the tapestry

of a royal family heirloom

she was far away from here

washed away, her thoughts drifted

a red-headed boy

with kind, green eyes

would she see him again?

be allowed to survive?

Jasper...

in the distance

Charlotte felt

the weight of the letter opener

wedged against her ankle

calling to her

How many women?
How many girls?

she only had one opportunity

permit him to finish

a chance to overpower

overwhelmed her in weight and height

if she was careful with her aim

the letter opener could do enough damage

if she waited too long

the king would dispatch her once he tired

Could Charlotte kill a king?

a grunted moan behind her

fixed her gaze on the opulence

lamps that had not once flickered

century-old furniture that did not creak

the force of the weight slammed against it

Yes, perhaps she could.

Her arm concealed by the skirts that had been shoved roughly up her back, Charlotte reached for the letter opener in her boot. As her fingers tightened around the polished metal, she whipped her arm around with as much force as she could muster. The metal dug deep into the man's flesh, twisting through cartilage and sinew as she forced it deeper into his knee. The king screamed as he stumbled backwards, giving Charlotte an opening to scramble away with a renewed vigor. The man collapsed against the bed side table, knocking the lamp aside to shatter on the floor beside him. The letter opener remained wedged horribly beneath his kneecap where Charlotte had struck him, and his fingers clawed hopelessly at the offending object.

Time seemed to slow to a crawl as Charlotte considered her options. She was likely already a dead woman, and there was no scenario she could envision where she made it out of this endeavour alive. Gathering her courage, Charlotte felt rather than heard the scream that crackled out of her throat as she tore the letter opener from the man's leg, embedding it deep in his chest. Blood spurted from the king, spattering her face as he roared in agony.

There were distant shouts from the opposite end of the king's chambers, muffled yelling and banging from the other side of the door. Ripping the letter opener from the king's body once more, Charlotte stalked to the other side of the room, determined not to go down without a fight. The wounds she had sustained slowed her pace, but a fire had been kindled in her soul that refused to die out.

The doors to the grand hallway swung wide, and Charlotte raised her crude weapon—

"Charlotte!"

Her childhood friend stood before her, his plate armour spattered in dirt and blood as he cleaned his sword. The guards around them lay motionless, disturbingly still, and it seemed at last that Gideon had chosen a side.

Her heart stopped momentarily, the letter opener clattering to the floor as her grip loosened in her shock.

"Gideon?" she breathed, her voice barely above a whisper. As her anger subsided, something acrid and ugly began curling its fingers in Charlotte's stomach, something she couldn't name.

Gideon was at her side in an instant, tugging his helmet from his head and casting it aside as he examined her, inspecting her visible wounds. His gloved hands on her face were far gentler than the king had been, but Charlotte still flinched, unable to meet his bright blue stare.

"Are you all right?" he asked, taking in her appearance. "Whose blood is this?"

From behind Gideon, Fortia stepped towards Charlotte, her calculating gaze fixed on the scene behind her as she sheathed her daggers. "His, I'd expect," she noted grimly. "We have to get her out of here."

The moment Gideon released her, a small white form darted forward. "Charlotte! I'm so sorry, I'm so sorry—" Aurelia's words were interrupted as the princess embraced her, seemingly heedless of the blood on Charlotte's clothes. The warm comfort of a friend embracing her, after the last comparable physical contact Charlotte had endured, was almost too much. Her eyes began to burn.

"It's okay," Charlotte found herself saying, her voice sounding distant and thin to her own ears.

The princess pulled back, clutching Charlotte's shoulders in a startlingly firm grip. "Did he hurt you?" Aurelia demanded, her fluttering eyes searching Charlotte's face.

"No," she replied too quickly. "I'm fine."

Her friend seemed oblivious to her turmoil, almost melting with relief at the lie. "Thank the goddesses, we made it in time," Aurelia breathed. "I was worried we were too late, that he might have—"

"I'm fine," Charlotte repeated, her fingers growing colder.

"Your Highness, we have to get Charlotte out of here," a fourth speaker interjected, and Cary stepped over one of the prone forms of the motionless guards in the hallway. Her eyes met Charlotte's gaze, and something almost pitying resided in that stare. *I hope you never do.*

The princess stepped back from Charlotte, nodding profusely as she assessed the people surrounding her, the witnesses to the terrible incident that had occurred. "Gideon, you and Cary should get her somewhere safe," Aurelia instructed, a determined gleam in her eyes. "Fortia and I will handle this."

Leaving the princess and Fortia to address the grisly scene within the king's chambers, Charlotte found herself without the strength to argue. She allowed herself to be led away, Cary's fingers threading with her own as Gideon led them out of the castle, away from the mess she had made.

⚬ ☀ ⚬

Charlotte couldn't go home. She couldn't bring herself to face her father, because she was faced with an impossible choice – tell him nothing, or tell him everything. She wasn't sure which option terrified her more, which option would be the least painful. There was a thrum of white noise between her ears, a low vibration that unsettled her even now, long after the danger had subsided.

Charlotte didn't know whether she was comforted by Cary and Gideon's presence or mortified by their shared knowledge of what had transpired. The wounds in her soul had filled with a deep, inescapable shame, the blood on her face drying even as her heart continued to weep. She wasn't sure if the alternative would feel more comfortable, whether it would be better or worse to be alone in this moment. There was a howling deep within her, a whistling wind that begged to be heard.

Charlotte had been numbed into silence when Gideon had asked her once, twice, a third time if she was certain she didn't want to return home. Cary, bless her, didn't push Charlotte for further details. Instead, the Reinnairlei woman led her somewhere she insisted it would be safe for her to remain, at least until they determined the fate of the king and what it meant for her. She hadn't asked if the king was dead. She wasn't sure which outcome she preferred, which option would alter her future as little as possible. Within Charlotte's ribs, a hurricane was building, a storm she struggled to contain.

While Gideon and Cary maintained constant vigilance of their surroundings, Charlotte was far away. It was as if she were in a trance, floating through an existence she was only vaguely aware of, tethered to her body by a single, fragile string. No amount of pain could make Charlotte feel more connected to her flesh in that moment; her entire life she had been in pain, had grown too used to it.

The shape of a manor, dark and mysterious, loomed in the distance behind a foreboding gate of twisted iron. Having been instructed to stand guard at the entryway, Gideon had hesitated for several moments while he stared down at Charlotte, as if warring with himself over whether or not to leave her side. She couldn't look him in the eye, couldn't meet that blinding blue gaze as Cary led her past the gate, escorting her to the entrance of the estate.

Charlotte hadn't known what to expect, but she was unpleasantly startled as the door to that grand dwelling opened, revealing none other than Varus Emery. His harsh gaze shifted from Charlotte, to Cary, to the distant form of Gideon at the edge of the property. When he glanced back towards her, he looked about as shocked to see Charlotte as she was to see him.

"I didn't know where else to take her," Cary was explaining before Varus could so much as open his mouth, and yet he stepped aside immediately. "She... she had an audience with the king."

It was a kindness, Cary's discretion with Varus, but Charlotte still found herself cringing as she was led into the manor. Such a pleasant, tame description of the evening that had transpired. *Did he hurt you?*

There was a dark expression on the kingpin's face, as if he knew exactly what manner of audience had transpired. "The bathroom on the ground floor is the largest," Varus offered quickly, directing Cary and Charlotte down the corridor to his right. "East wing. Should I fetch Haeyin?"

Cary paused for a moment, and after a few seconds of silence Charlotte realized she was waiting for input from her. She was moving in slow motion, her movements and her words addled as if she were wading through mud and slime just to function.

Eventually, Cary replied for her. "Not yet," she said warily.

Varus' eyes were heavy, so very heavy on Charlotte's face. "Let me know if you need anything," was all he said before he turned and hobbled down the hallway in the opposite direction, leaving Cary and Charlotte to their own devices as she was led towards the bathroom.

It was the nicest she had ever been in, Charlotte decided. The floors were smooth stone tile, the features all crafted from porcelain. Without instruction, Cary left her side to start the bath, turning the taps with a manner of ease that suggested she had used it many times before. The tub was large enough for two, maybe three people, and suddenly Charlotte was possessed by an urge to scrub her skin raw.

Turning back towards her, Cary hesitated. "Do you want help?" she asked, her hands hovering as her pink gaze settled on the remnants of Charlotte's clothing.

Her voice failing her, she nodded numbly in reply, managing not to flinch while Cary's hands made quick work of the surviving fastenings. Her hands were gentle, feather-light where they made contact as she worked. As the layers of fabric fell away, Charlotte barely had the sense to be embarrassed as she stood before Cary in her under-garments.

Sensing her discomfort, the woman averted her eyes. "I'll send for a change of clothes," she offered, crossing the room towards the linen closet nearby. "There's an empty bedroom directly across the hall, you'll be able to stay there tonight." Retrieving a pile of fluffy white towels, wash-cloths, and a similarly plush bathrobe, Cary deposited the bundle on the bathroom counter before pausing, scanning the room as if she were searching for other tasks to be completed.

Charlotte swallowed. "Thank you," she whispered.

The woman appeared to be warring with the same conflict Gideon had struggled with, the indecision between staying with Charlotte or leaving her to her own devices. After a few moments of silence, Cary excused herself with a soft, mumbled goodbye, shutting the door behind her. The room became unbearably warm as the steam from the hot water enveloped the room. With trembling hands, Charlotte shucked off her ruined undergarments, wishing she could burn them as she stepped into the bath water.

The temperature offered her none of the comfort she would normally find, for the pain Charlotte sought to alleviate was far deeper than merely her joints.

She set to work, taking a washcloth to her arms and legs, rubbing her skin until it was raw and red. There were ghosts in her flesh, it seemed, remnants of a man she was struggling to forget. The water stung and burned every wounded inch of her, but Charlotte wasn't done. She cleaned every fold, every crease, every bit of skin she thought he might have touched, might have looked at, might have thought of. When she nearly drew blood from her knees, Charlotte's hands were shaking so badly she dropped the cloth into the dirtied water. She pressed her knuckles to her mouth, as if she might suppress the shout that was begging to be released, building up within her ever since she had been led into that castle.

Plunging her head beneath the sullied water, Charlotte opened her mouth and screamed.

When the water grew too cold for her to tolerate it any longer, Charlotte emerged from the tub shivering. Grabbing the bathrobe Cary had set aside for her, Charlotte eagerly bundled herself in the plush fabric. As she secured the tie around her waist, she was startled by a knock at the bathroom door.

"Charlotte?" came a familiar voice. "May I come in?"

"Yes," Charlotte managed to rasp, her throat hoarse from howling.

The door opened to reveal Eleni, gingerly entering the room with an offering of pyjamas and a housecoat folded in her arms. The expression on her face was nothing short of devastated. "Oh, Charlotte," she breathed as she set the clothes down on the counter, crossing the room and gathering Charlotte in her arms, heedless of her wet hair. "My dear, I'm so sorry. You're safe now."

The word "safe" did something strange to Charlotte's heart, her eyes welling with tears. "I'm fine," she murmured weakly. Pulling back to assess Charlotte's face, Eleni pursed her lips. Her eyes tightened with doubt, but she did not question Charlotte's words.

"Let's get your face healed up, all right?" she instructed more than suggested. Taking Charlotte's hand, she tugged her gently towards the bathroom sink, taking a fresh washcloth to dampen beneath the faucet. Charlotte was silent while Eleni worked, delicately wiping at the cuts and scrapes that she had forgotten about while focusing on the skin between her fingers.

"We had another visitor this evening," Eleni offered, cleaning her face with a gentleness Charlotte had not reserved for herself. "Your blacksmith boy."

It was a mark of the state Charlotte was in that she didn't protest at the term. "Where is he?" she asked, though in truth the thought of seeing Jasper in her condition was terrifying.

"He's in the bedroom opposite Maya," Eleni replied as she summoned a soft plume of lavender light in her palm, gliding it across her injured face as Charlotte closed her eyes. "He arrived recently enough that he's probably still awake."

Charlotte nodded numbly in response, her face heating beneath her friend's magic. It was as if she could sense Eleni's concern through her power, that endless ocean of energy tasting of the woman's aching heart. As she felt the warm glow of the magic fading, Charlotte opened her eyes to see the lilac glow fading from Eleni's irises.

"Is he all right?" she found the courage to ask. When Eleni offered no immediate response, Charlotte shook her head. "Jasper. I know about the meeting. Is he all right?"

Pursing her lips, Eleni rubbed the reddened palm of her hand. "He is," Eleni explained with a frown. "Eodan— *Varus* fared worse than he did… I healed Jasper's face for him, but there were no mortal injuries for him this evening."

Even after everything she had been through that evening, Charlotte heaved a sigh of relief. "Thank the goddesses for small miracles," she murmured.

Eleni was examining Charlotte's face, as if trying to find a reason to stay with her, to keep her focus on her. After a few moments of silence, she seemed to give up. "I'm sorry, darling," she conceded. "I want to stay up with you, but I'm afraid I'm exhausted."

A wave of guilt washed over Charlotte as she remembered her friend's early pregnancy, how drained Eleni must have already been. "Of—of course," she stammered, shaking her head. "I'm so sorry, I forgot, I wasn't even thinking—"

"Charlotte," Eleni silenced her with a gentle squeeze of her shoulders, her stern expression offering no room for argument. "Don't you dare apologize. Just try and get some rest."

Even with the kindness in Eleni's voice, Charlotte's eyes burned with tears. She nodded slowly as her friend leaned in to kiss her forehead once before she turned to exit the bathroom, leaving Charlotte alone with her thoughts. She gratefully accepted the pyjamas that Eleni had brought, a simple set of delicate silk only slightly too large for her.

She dared a glance in the mirror, examining Eleni's handiwork. Charlotte hadn't seen what state she had arrived at the manor in, but she could accurately guess based on how it had felt. Eleni had washed and healed the cuts and scrapes Charlotte had felt stinging on her cheek and her jaw from having her face pushed into the dirt, the fracture to her nose from the impact. If there had been any swelling from the injury, Eleni had undone it all. Looking at the mirror now, Charlotte's outward appearance gave no indication of what had happened, each of her freckles and features exactly the same as they had been the day before. She glanced away, unable to meet her reflection's gaze as she donned the housecoat Eleni had provided, burying herself in the warmth.

Exiting the bathroom, Charlotte made her way towards the opposite door before she paused. A familiar black and white cat was seated in front of the door to the bedroom she had intended to use, Mo's knowing gaze resting heavily on Charlotte as she barred the way with her tiny body. Her eyes travelled against her will, landing on the door to her right; opposite Maya's room, Eleni had said.

Maya… Maya would likely be asleep at this hour, and no matter how broken Charlotte felt, she couldn't bring herself to be so selfish. But Eleni had specified that perhaps Jasper would be awake, and the glow that emanated from beneath the closed door suggested he hadn't retired for the night just yet.

She was conflicted, torn between wanting to be alone and desperately wanting the comfort of her best friend. Even while her head deliberated, her heart knew what Charlotte wanted. Her feet carried her towards the other bedroom, not bothering to knock before opening the door. Just as Eleni had promised, Jasper was alive and well within the room, halfway through tugging a shirt over his head, the sun-speckled skin and the stretch marks along his back exposed. He wriggled out of the fabric ungracefully, tossing the garment to the floor as he did. As Charlotte shut the latch behind her, Jasper turned around at the noise. He looked shocked and delighted to see her, and it did strange things to her heart.

"Charlie?" he asked incredulously, his voice soft with consideration for the late hour and the manor's sleeping occupants. "What are you doing here?"

It was such a simple question, such a harmless beginning to a conversation, and yet Charlotte found herself at a loss for words. She stumbled over her thoughts, trying to come up with some tame explanation for what had happened to her as Jasper crossed the room to greet her. Her eyes found their way back to his face, and she froze.

She had memorized Jasper's face, burnt every line and contour into her memory. She could recall each detail, each little scar and freckle and the way his entire face right up to his curiously pointed ears turned bright red when he was embarrassed. She did not remember the new scar that he now wore, the jagged red line that cut deep along his temple towards his left ear, not quite concealed by his too long hair.

"Your... your face," was all she managed to say after an uncomfortable silence.

Immediately, Jasper chewed his lip, his hand reaching to fluff his hair in a vain attempt to hide the new injury. "I... I haven't looked yet," he admitted in a low voice. "Is it bad?"

Charlotte shook her head, electricity crackling in her veins. "How are you always so casual about these things?" she breathed. "You just... you keep getting yourself into trouble, time and time again. You promised me you'd be careful."

Something shuttered in his expression, and a different version of Charlotte would have cracked at the wounded look in his eyes. "Charlie—"

She pressed on, ignoring the way her heart tightened at the sight of him. "I know what you were up to with Varus," Charlotte continued. "Yes, because news of your little underground society meeting made it up to the castle, you know. Gideon was on patrol, looking for anything amiss. You *knew* how dangerous it would be, you—Jasper, what were you *thinking*?"

"Charlotte, listen to me," Jasper interrupted her, taking a step towards her. "It wasn't meant to be violent. We were ambushed, there was a mutiny—I was being honest with you when I said I'd be careful. Neither of us expected it to get that bad."

She found herself laughing then, dark and biting to her own ears. An anxious overflow of frustration built within her, some manic energy that she could no longer contain, and Charlotte could not stop the words that rolled out of her mouth.

"You don't get it, do you?" she said softly, clenching her fists in a vain effort to stop her hands from shaking. "You don't bloody *get it*. Do you know how many nights I've spent awake, biting my nails to the quick because you haven't come back home yet? How many days I sit and wonder if I should have memorized our most recent conversation, if I should have saved the last letter you wrote? I've spent hours in a panic because I've forgotten what you last said to me, because I'm afraid I'll forget the sound of your voice, too."

The wind was howling between her ears again, her heart thrumming through her chest as she struggled to remember to breathe. She couldn't look Jasper in the eye, couldn't meet his gaze while she spoke, while the words poured from her errant lips.

"I love you, you know that?" Charlotte snapped, her voice trembling. "I love you, Jasper, and I have loved you for years – but this is not how I wanted to tell you. I wanted to wait until the moment was right, I wanted to *show* you that I love you when we were both ready... but now, I'm afraid if I don't tell you I'll have run out of chances!"

Forcing herself to lift her head, Charlotte locked eyes with the boy she was berating. There was something fractured in his stare, something so vulnerable and fragile in his face that it broke her heart. She wanted to take back her words, wanted to reel her argument back and swallow it, but she couldn't stop the tidal wave that escaped her.

"I can't live like this, Jasper!" she exclaimed, her voice breaking as a new round of tears spilled from her eyes, trailing down her freshly healed face. Even though the wounds had been mended, those tears scorched her skin all the same. "I can't spend my life worrying whether or not the man I love will make it home, do you understand?"

I can't die knowing I never told you how I feel.

Charlotte pressed her fists to her brow, hating the way her eyes burned as she sobbed, hating the words that had spewed from her mouth, the pain her tongue had wrought. Every sensation in her body was too much, every nerve on fire as she finally processed how close she had come to oblivion – Charlotte had been so certain she was about to die, so certain her efforts to incapacitate the king had been to take him with her, and yet here she stood. Charlotte had spent her life in pain, but this felt far worse. The reminder of her own mortality, and the reality of her continued existence, was a greater agony than she could bear.

How many women? How many girls?

A pair of calloused hands tenderly pried her balled up fists from her face, and Charlotte couldn't stop herself from flinching at that touch. Jasper was not deterred, however, his grip warm and firm. He waited patiently, cradling her hands until she found the strength to meet his gaze. Those green eyes were exactly the same as she always remembered them, bright and open and so utterly Jasper.

"I'm sorry," he replied at last, his voice soft. "I'm so sorry, Charlie. This isn't how I thought things would turn out... this isn't what I wanted for us."

She looked up at him, confusion addling her thoughts... until she realized that Jasper didn't know what had happened. Eleni and Varus hadn't told him what had transpired, what Charlotte had endured — and so Jasper was apologizing for his crimes, oblivious to her own.

"I don't know what I was thinking, looking back," Jasper continued, unaware of her inner turmoil. "I... when it was obvious becoming a knight wasn't going to pan out, I thought—I *knew* I couldn't offer you much on a black-smith's salary. I thought working for Varus would be a temporary thing, just to get back on my feet. I wanted to have something to my name before I asked you to marry me."

As each of his words sank in, a new wave of tears spilled down Charlotte's cheeks. All these years, she had managed to delude herself into believing that Jasper couldn't possibly return her affections, couldn't possibly love a woman who needed so much physical care and attention. After all this time, knowing the truth was as devastating as the innocence she had lost that day – that not only did he love her still, he wanted to spend his life with her.

He released her hands then, calloused thumbs brushing

the tears from her freckled cheeks. Charlotte found it within herself to laugh incredulously, feeling the last semblance of her sanity beginning to crumble. "Goddesses, you're a fool," she murmured, unable to shake the tremble from her voice. "You're an absolute fool, Jazzy-boy."

"A fool for you," he offered immediately, and Charlotte couldn't stop herself from rolling her eyes, laughing more genuinely this time. "I am sorry. I know I've hurt you."

He was trying his best to make her feel better, and everything he was saying made her feel worse. Her tears returned, her chest heaving in sobs at the guilt and shame that ate away at her wounded heart. And Jasper, her darling blacksmith boy, hesitated for only a moment before folding her into his arms in an uncharacteristic embrace. She clung to him as tightly as her weary body would allow, the warmth and the strength of him a life raft in a tumultuous storm, and Charlotte sobbed herself hoarse once again.

"It's okay, Charlie," Jasper whispered in her ear as he held her. "It's okay."

CHAPTER

THIRTEEN

DANTE

GENERALLY, DANTE WAS NOT ONE FOR EAVESDROPPING.

Rather, this was what he assured himself as he sat motionless among the rafters above the Valedian king's chambers, silent as he listened to the conversation that unfolded beneath him. Exploring the embassy's secret passages had become a personal activity for him, determined to familiarize himself with the layout of the building not accounted for in the blueprint. Arriving here had been an accident entirely, and now Dante was stuck in a rather uncomfortable position.

King Fenyang was quiet as he sat on the edge of his bed, unfastening the garments he was wearing. Huda appeared to be assisting him with some of it, feeling her way along the seams of the leather to find the ties and clasps. Benkaei was pacing back and forth from the desk to the wardrobe, her stance reminding Dante of a prowling wolf.

"We were supposed to receive word from King Gustaf by now," she noted irritably. "It speaks to his guilt that we remain waiting with no news."

"It speaks to nothing," her king insisted diplomatically. The visible tension in his jaw and his shoulders suggested he agreed with his second-in-command, even if he wasn't inclined to voice his opinions.

"Our people are dying," Benkaei continued, gesturing angrily. "They are suffering while this pale bastard squanders our precious time, prolonging our investigation unnecessarily."

King Fenyang sighed, his braided hair falling across his face. "I am aware of this," he noted.

"Every civil investigator we have suggested has been denied, only to be replaced with someone who will most obviously side with him!" she continued, unaware of the king's growing irritation. "We can't even prove our case because he refuses to proceed—"

"Do you think I don't know what kind of man he is?" Fenyang demanded, whipping his head around to face Benkaei. Beside him, Huda flinched backwards from the sudden movement. The room was silent for several seconds before the man continued. "Gustaf showed me his hand a long time ago."

Benkaei narrowed her eyes. "What do you mean?" she asked. Dante leaned forwards as if he might better hear their discussion.

The Valedian king paused for a moment more, gently caressing Huda's thigh where she sat beside him in apology. She leaned against his shoulder as she calmed at the touch. "A few years ago now, I received a missive from the Aethian king," he explained. "We agreed that the accords had secured an uneasy peace, but that a union might forge a more sustainable alliance. He offered me his daughter's hand, and I accepted."

Benkaei seemed more irate by this knowledge than Huda. "You never told me this," she scoffed, sounding wounded.

"Because it was reneged before it came to fruition," the king continued with a sigh, beginning to remove his shirt. "My sources tell me that Gustaf now plans to wed his daughter to Prince Vincenzo of Fraecath."

Dante felt the shift in the room as the two women digested the information that had been offered to them. "But to what end?" Huda asked calmly, seeming unsurprised by the king's admission.

"What other end can there be?" said Benkaei. "Aethia does not want to align themselves with Pharsat. They want to fortify their offense by allying with Fraecath."

Even the Valedian king, ever the diplomat, could find no retort to dissuade his second-in-command from her conclusion. "So it would seem," he agreed at last. Huda assisted him in tugging his shirt over his head, and Dante couldn't help but stare in mute shock at the sight of the man's bare back. The expanse of skin that had been revealed was pox-scarred, spanning the wide breadth of his shoulders down to the small of his back.

Dante had heard rumours of Fenyang's bout with sand fever as a small child, surviving the infection that had taken his twin brother. As he stared at the scars on the king's back, Dante felt immensely guilty witnessing something clearly only intended to be shared with Benkaei and Huda. He should have turned away, but if he left now, he might alert them to his presence with the sound of his retreat.

Stop lying to yourself, he thought with a soundless sigh, his temple pressed against the wooden beam beside him. There were many things Dante couldn't escape, his heritage being one of them. Stealth and subterfuge weren't simply what he'd been trained for, they were in his blood. He knew very well that his escape would be silent, just as he knew how incriminating it was that he could not take his eyes off the Valedian king.

"I haven't heard any manner of gossip on a betrothal with Fraecath," Huda noted quietly.

King Fenyang shook his head, his hand returning to her thigh. Somehow, the simple gesture was the most aggravating part of this exchange. "Whatever motive the Aethian king had in keeping the announcement under wraps, I doubt his intentions were pure," he continued. "But I imagine the prince's disappearance has complicated things."

"Come again?" Benkaei snapped. "He's *missing*?"

"Allegedly," the king clarified, though the set of his jaw implied he was not hopeful. "Some manner of vampire raid gone wrong. Those Cacciatores have a knack for biting off more than they can chew."

Dante found himself scowling in the darkness. To speak ill of the Cacciatore di Anima family was frowned upon in Fraecath, but in Valedia... theirs was not a traditional monarchy, and their so-called kings and queens were elected by the public. Perhaps speaking ill of the royal family was not regarded with such scrutiny.

"What does King Gustaf plan to do with his precious daughter in the interim?" Benkaei sneered. Despite the acidity of her tone, she leaned rather casually against the wall opposite the bed, crossing her arms over her chest. "He's obviously desperate to marry her off."

"Who can be certain with a man like him?" the Valedian king replied wearily, dragging a large hand down his face. Even though Dante knew the man to be ten years his senior, Fenyang typically did not look his age, blessed with an unfairly beautiful countenance. As Dante watched him now, however, there were shadows and lines beneath his eyes that he had never seen before, a weariness that settled into each pore.

Leaning towards him, Huda found the man's cheek-bone with a brush of her fingertips, pressing a gentle kiss against the king's face. "Whatever our next steps, it won't do to stay up all hours of the night worrying over such things," she said calmly. She was taking the news of King Fenyang's almost-betrothal much better than Benkaei, Dante thought. "We should all be getting some rest, in the event the king decides to meet with us tomorrow, after all."

As the necromancer exited, her fingers trailing along the perimeter of the wall to guide her, Dante began to shuffle away soundlessly. Whatever would transpire in the king's chambers after Benkaei left was not something he wanted to spectate. He crept down the ladder that led from the crawlspace into one of the unused storage closets. The embassy was deserted as he re-entered the hallway, tiptoeing towards his quarters.

"You seem to vanish almost as well as Eodan does."

The voice behind him startled Dante so badly he nearly tripped on the carpet beneath his feet, his arms waving wildly to balance himself. He cursed his carelessness; he should have waited for Huda to return to the room before he'd ventured outside.

"Huda," he breathed, crushing his palm against his chest as if he might slow his errant heart. "I didn't see you there."

In the darkness, Huda smiled. "In all fairness, I didn't see you either," she mused. Before Dante had a chance to curse his choice of words, she continued. "I was on my way to use the facilities, when I noticed a familiar presence flickering to life like a candle… as if you appeared out of thin air."

Dante searched his mind for some sort of excuse. "I sleepwalk," he offered. "It's a lifelong affliction. I usually lock my door, I'm sorry to have disturbed you."

Even with his senses reeled in tightly, he could sense the wintry aura of death that hung around the woman as Huda took a step closer to him. "You're a good man," she began, her voice quiet in the darkness. "I think I speak for everyone when I say that the work you do is greatly appreciated."

Swallowing his anxiety, Dante tried to smile. "My pleasure," he replied.

"That doesn't mean I trust you."

The air around them seemed to grow colder still, despite Dante's walls locked tightly around his mind. There was no magic permeating his shields to make him shudder, only Huda's judgment. "I… I'm sorry?"

She took a step forward. "I don't trust you," Huda repeated herself. "That's a clever trick of yours, that barrier you keep around yourself. I know you can sense my magic. I know what it *means* that you can sense my magic."

"If you know what it means, then you know why that barrier is in place," Dante snapped. Huda recoiled from his tone, and he instantly regretted his words.

She frowned at him. "How long have you been lying to yourself about who you are?" Huda asked quietly, so quietly he thought he might have misheard her.

The question was innocent enough, and yet still Dante bristled at her words. "I know what I am," he hissed. "You shouldn't concern yourself with that."

Nodding slowly, Huda said nothing as she began to back away. "Forget I said anything, then," she replied solemnly before walking away, her hand brushing along the wall to guide her in the eerie silence. As the crushing solitude settled on Dante's shoulders, he was left with nothing but the echo of her words as he made his way back towards the fortress of his chambers.

At an especially heinous hour of the morning, a messenger from the Aethian king arrived at last to invite the Valedian council back to the castle. Dante was awoken abruptly by a very apologetic Akila knocking on his door with the frequency of a rabbit thumping the ground, not pausing her efforts until he wearily opened the door.

"Something's happening downstairs," a wide-eyed Akila announced, practically vibrating as if consumed with a nervous energy.

Rubbing his eyes wearily, Dante struggled to gather his composure. "What's happening?" he probed.

Shaking her head, Akila was already heading for the stairs. "I don't know!" she called back to him, her curly head of hair disappearing behind the banister.

While still groggy and disoriented, Dante had at least been startled awake thoroughly enough to throw himself into warm, soapy water and a clean set of clothing. It had been some time since they last heard from anyone regarding the accords, and none of their updates had been positive. As Benkaei had noted in the conversation Dante was not a part of, King Gustaf had been particularly unhelpful in procuring an investigator who would remain neutral. As much as Dante wanted to be hopeful that today's meeting would prove a turning point in their struggles, there was an uncomfortable sensation in his gut that disagreed with him.

Almost thirty minutes later, Dante trudged wearily downstairs to find the rest of the Valedian council, pleasantly surprised that he was awake as well. Verdis and Hasima seemed to be the only two people well-rested and ready for the day, fanning themselves idly. Akila seemed more manic than rested, and Benkaei was impossible to read beneath her signature scowl. King Fenyang led Huda towards the carriage, assisting her up the wooden steps.

They rode towards the castle in near silence, the grim clouds overhead threatening rain at any moment. Outside the carriage, Dante could distantly hear the bustle of the marketplace, and he found himself missing simpler days when he traversed Briardeen on foot, seeking an unusual tome from a particular bookstore. He missed Jasper and Charlotte, whose company made him feel normal and at ease with himself.

Fenyang's golden gaze settled on Dante, and in an instinctive reaction he found himself testing his mental fortress for weaknesses. There were none to be found, no fractured beams or crumbling bricks for anything to leak through, yet still Dante found himself unsettled by that stare. Whatever demons that had been prevalent on the king's face had been eradicated by a short rest; he was as flawlessly handsome today as usual, much to Dante's despair.

"We should try to proceed as diplomatically as possible," King Fenyang offered suddenly in the quiet, stuffy atmosphere of the carriage. "That means we refrain from immediately shutting down whatever prospect they offer as investigator."

Benkaei shot him a withering stare. "Define 'immedi-ately', Your Majesty," she retorted brazenly.

"Try to follow my lead, and hopefully we'll make some progress today," he continued, ignoring Benkaei. "Dante, can you think of anything in your homework that might assist us today?"

Struggling not to jump at the sound of his name coming from the king's mouth, Dante shook his head. "Nothing I haven't mentioned already," he explained. "The chosen investigator cannot be a named member of any known faction allied with either party, but King Gustaf knows this. He's been trying to find ways around it with every person he's suggested."

The Valedian king nodded, and though this was not a new discussion Dante still found himself disheartened by his own inability to remedy the situation. The council disembarked wordlessly as they arrived in the castle court-yard. The sky above was a dark grey, the first tentative rain drops falling as another summer storm rolled in. Dante exited behind the council, his steps silent as they connected with the flagstones beneath them. He assessed their surroundings, finding the last thing he had expected them to receive as a welcome.

The king's general stood before the main entrance to the castle, his hands clasped behind his back as he stared straight ahead at the Valedian council. As he took notice of their environment, Dante became aware of the fact that they were surrounded; dozens of Aethian soldiers were strategically positioned around them, emerging from behind the courtyard foliage and stone décor. No, not soldiers, Dante realized – these were templars of Xiska that circled them, the goddess' wolf insignia almost mocking them as they stood in defiance of the Valedian king. The gates screeched shut behind them with a sense of finality, the noise reverberating across the courtyard.

The Valedian council did not react visibly, giving the impression that they were unsurprised by this turn of events. Only Benkaei had a tell visible to Dante, her jaw clenched as her hand fluttered, desperate to reach for her concealed weaponry.

"That was some trick," Byron called out to them across the courtyard, a smug smile on his face. "Caught us all by surprise, that's for certain."

King Fenyang blinked. "Forgive me, but I have no idea what you're talking about," he said plainly.

"Sending your Valedian bitch to try and assassinate the king," the general retorted, taking a few steps closer. "I see you had the good sense not to bring her with you today, but fear not. We saw that gesture for what it is."

The Valedian king grew very still. "All of my council are present with me today, General Byron," he responded firmly, gesturing to his allies around him. "And I can personally vouch for their innocence in the matter you speak of."

Byron still had that awful smirk on his face, that smug expression that Dante hated more and more with every second. "Save your breath, Your Majesty," said the general, shaking his head. "This is not a trial."

One by one, each templar surrounding them drew their swords, forming a wall of steel that served to box them in further. The men standing abreast of the general drew long, polished firearms, aimed towards each member of the Valedian council. Dante vividly remembered his last experience with a gun, and he did not care to relive it.

"What is the meaning of this?" he demanded, hearing his voice echo across the flagstones. "It was *you* who claimed that violating the accords was to declare war on the goddesses themselves!"

"It was your allies who threw the first punch, little one," Byron taunted. "Are we not to defend ourselves against the would-be assassination of our beloved king?"

Dante bristled with anger. "You would stoop to this, during the season of the accords? Do you *want* another war?"

Byron tilted his head, withdrawing his own pistol and firing a single shot in Fenyang's direction. The resulting bang echoed across the courtyard, between Dante's ears, within each chamber of his heart. He flinched automatically, his hand clapping over the pitted scar tissue in his shoulder, instinctively preparing himself for a wound – but his hand came away bloodless, moistened only by the increasingly heavy rain.

The queen mother had leapt in front of her son, absorbing the wound intended for the king. Her fingers were surprisingly still as she regarded them, rain mixing with the blood on her hands as she slumped against King Fenyang.

War on the goddesses, indeed.

"What have you done?" Benkaei screeched. She and the king were supporting Hasima, her strong hands attempting to apply pressure to the gunshot wound in her abdomen.

The general had the gall to look indifferent to the damage he caused, to the pain he wrought. "Perhaps we need another war," he responded at last, meeting Dante's gaze. "Maybe we should finish what we started."

The Order of Xiska began to advance, and Dante was struck by the horrible realization that he had caused all of this. He glanced between Hasima, having fallen to her knees on the flagstones, and Byron's wild expression, the righteous fury that had overtaken the general. Huda had begun whispering frantically under her breath, and Dante did not miss the minute movements of her hands as she wove a spell. Her voice too quiet for him to hear completely, "shield" was the only Pharasathi word Dante could recognize. The rain fell harder, his hair plastered to his throat as he counted the templars that surrounded them, weighed their odds of survival as he assessed their surroundings.

Is this how I am fated to die?

In the temples of Fraecath, the opening prayer was one of resignation and acceptance – *All that begins, all that ends, all shall return to the Soul Keeper*. It was one of the few songs that Dante could always remember off the top of his head. Rhanigan was associated with all of the divine Chaos that had muddied their world, but they were also the Soul Keeper. The godly shepherd of souls was said to collect and carry the spirits of the dead into the afterlife, the pool of rebirth, or the pits of eternal damnation. The hymn spoke of a man who accepted his demise and walked willingly into the lands of the dead, and that one line had stayed with Dante all his life – *is this how I am fated to die?*

The courtyard grew eerily silent as the templars stared at the Valedian council, their eyes wild with a fury reserved only for their mortal enemies. He looked at the faces of his allies, prepared to die for their king and country. As he felt the trickle of his life force weave through the cracks in the walls around his mind, Dante grit his teeth as that hymn echoed over and over and over again in his thoughts.

Is this how I am fated to die?

And the answer offered within that silence was a resonant *no*.

From within him burst a tempest Dante could keep

buried no longer, a whirlwind of energy as dark and cold as the winter solstice. His hands shook with the effort of containing it, shaping it into something other than a lethal tidal wave, directing the energy in a focused stream. Magic seared his skin in arcing patterns of silver light as the ground shook, earth cracking and shifting as bare, boney hands broke through the dirt. Long dead soldiers rose from unmarked graves, ancient beasts crawling from the dirt towards their assailants, their empty and expressionless faces confronting the templars.

"What—what is this?" Byron called out, his face white as a sheet. He fired round after round at the undead soldiers that stalked towards him. The bullets ricocheted off worn armour and bleached bones, shattering ribcages but ultimately failing in their efforts to stop the reanimated army. He wailed as a skeletal hand dragged sharpened fingers through his face, slicing his cheek to ribbons.

The templars recognized the source of the cadavers' power, seeking to end Dante before his deadly onslaught could continue, but at that moment Huda's spellcasting was complete. A shield of her power slammed down around the Valedian council, preventing their enemies from reaching them. Out the corner of his eye, Dante could see King Fenyang directing the rest of the council, ushering them back towards the carriage.

There is something broken inside of you that cannot be fixed, it can only be destroyed... Even as his father's words echoed in his mind, Dante persisted. He focused on maintaining the magical energy he poured into the ground, into the skeletal forms of his soldiers. There was something so utterly wrong about what he was doing, something infernal and hellish, and yet for the first time in his life Dante felt liberated. There was a flood of power in his veins that he had never felt before, a lightness in his chest that made him question how he had ever lived without it.

From where he drew his strength, Dante could not be certain – he was terrified and exhausted, his arms shaking with exertion. Corpse after corpse emerged from the dirt, swinging ancient swords and worn battleaxes towards their opponents. When their weapons struck true and their lethal onslaught felled their opponents, the freshly deceased templars stood at his command as well. Dante felt his entire body shudder as his bones ached, his palms raw and red from the exertion.

A small, delicate hand covered Dante's, fingers interlocking with his own. Dante startled as Huda stepped towards him, lending him her power as her veins emanated a shadowy resonance. Without the impenetrable barrier of his mental fortress, he felt her voice in his mind, her uninhibited magic mingling with his own power. "*Come on, we have to go,*" Huda urged him, tugging on his arm. Only then did Dante see the fruit of his efforts; while he kept the Order of Xiska distracted, Fenyang and Benkaei had assumed control of the carriage once more, ready to flee.

He nodded absently, slowly backing away from the battle ahead of him, maintaining the skeletal army while Huda kept them safe behind a wall of impervious energy. As he reached the transport, Benkaei reached out to assist Huda into the carriage, yanking Dante in behind her. Stumbling into the seat, Dante kept his frostbitten palms facing the battlefield, kept those undead soldiers upright as long as he possibly could. Only when Huda blasted apart the courtyard gate, allowing the carriage through to the streets of Briardeen, did he allow himself to release the magic at last. Dozens of reanimated corpses collapsed into piles of bones and viscera, and Dante promptly fell into darkness.

⚬⚬ ✺ ⚬⚬

"Dante?" a small voice beside him spoke quietly, a pressure on his shoulder nudging him awake. "Dante…"

The first sensation he was consciously aware of was a throbbing pain in his temple, his mouth tasting of ash. Gingerly opening his eyes, his vision slowly adjusted to the light of the embassy sitting room. He had been sprawled across the largest sofa, and to his dismay the Valedian council appeared to be seated all around him, watching him intently.

Beside him, Akila had been perched on the edge of the couch, her amber eyes bright as she regarded him. "You're awake, thank Xiska – are you feeling all right?"

"No," Dante rasped weakly. Someone must have anticipated how poorly he was feeling; a pitcher of water had been left on the coffee table in front of him, along with a few slices of toast and some fruit. He eagerly reached for a glass, the cold water feeling rather splendid against his wounded palms through the bandages someone had applied. Each of the council members were sitting on the edge of their seats or leaning against the furniture as they regarded Dante with apprehension.

The Valedian king was seated directly across from him, a mischievous glint in his eyes as he regarded Dante. "You're looking better already," Fenyang noted approvingly. He couldn't have been much to look at in his current state, and Dante found himself flushing in embarrassment.

"That was an impressive stunt you pulled back there,"

Verdis agreed nearby, nodding stiffly. "I doubt the general was expecting that."

"*Nobody* was expecting that," Benkaei emphasized, leaning casually in the armchair nearest the fire. She seemed to fare the worst with the damp and the cold, two things that were unfortunately bountiful in Aethelind. "You've never once mentioned being a mage before."

Dante felt his face heat as he flushed darker still. He was spared from responding by Huda, who was seated beside King Fenyang with a sad smile on her face, her dark curls still partially damp from the rain. "Necromancy is forbidden in Fraecath," she offered by means of explanation. "Perhaps this was Dante's first attempt at ever utilizing his magic."

"Is it forbidden, truly?" Akila asked, her eyes growing even wider in astonishment than Dante thought possible.

"It's not... *forbidden*, per se," he found himself clarifying between deep gulps of water. "But it is frowned upon. And I had a... very, very traditional father." From across the room, he glanced towards Huda, knowing he owed her an apology.

"I hope you know we hold no such judgment in this room, Dante," Fenyang replied, his voice stern. "You saved our lives, and all of us are grateful."

Dante nodded slowly, unable to find the words to acknowledge the king's appreciation. "Is your mother—is Hasima all right?" he asked, desperate to steer the conversation away from himself.

The king nodded, but it was Verdis who spoke, the elderly healer addressing Dante with an appreciative nod. "She will be fine, thanks to you," she replied. "I was able to dig the bullet out with the time that you bought us."

He wasn't sure he needed that much explanation.

Despite the relative safety he found himself in, his heart still thudded in his chest, in his ears. "What do we do now?" Dante wondered aloud, glancing between the faces of the council members. "What... what *can* we do? The general said someone tried to kill the king, and they think *we* did it. I doubt I've been much help to dispel that rumour."

Benkaei snorted. "They would have found a way to pin that on us regardless of your stunt in the courtyard," she noted.

The king nodded in agreement, chuckling under his breath despite the situation. "We've likely put a wrench in their plans by avoiding a would-be execution," he mused, chewing the inside of his cheek. "They might be hard-pressed to explain what transpired without admitting fault, which hopefully buys us some time."

Whatever Dante might have offered in response, his attention was drawn instead to the still water of the pitcher placed in front of him, no longer stagnant. There were ripples cascading across the surface of the water, the droplets of condensation trembling down the glass. Dante felt the distant, rhythmic thudding in his chest, and with a sinking sensation of dread he became aware of the fact that it was not the beating of his own heart. Surging to his feet, Dante bolted across the room to the curtained windows, pulling back the coverings to expose the outside world – and the mob beyond the embassy's gates.

"Sodding Keepers," Dante swore under his breath.

Akila had followed him to the window, peeling back the curtains to get a look for herself. "Your Majesty, we may have a problem."

From beyond the gates, Eodan's hired security struggled to grapple with a group of irate townsfolk, loyalists who seemed intent on breaking through the gates surrounding the embassy. As few of them caught sight of the signs of life within the sitting room, launching a flaming object at the glass. It struck and bounced away, succeeding only in cracking the window, but Dante had mere seconds to react before the makeshift explosive fired. Grabbing Akila by her waist, he all but tackled the poor girl to the floor, shielding her as the window promptly shattered with the impact. The council cried out as glass sprayed into the room, ducking beneath furniture for cover.

The thudding noise grew louder, the townsfolk having succeeded in breaking through the embassy gates with their makeshift battering ram. His face stinging, Dante tugged Akila to her feet, supporting her as she stood shakily. Through the windows on either side of the grand front door, Dante could vaguely make out several concealed bear traps springing forth from the front gardens, dirt and flowers flying as the mob thundered straight into them. Distant shouts and cries of agony followed them as the council ran through the embassy hallway, and Dante had to look away as one of the townsfolk landed face first into an open bear trap, twitching grotesquely.

Benkaei was grappling with a hidden compartment in the hallway, a concealed cabinet springing open to reveal a bell. She rang the alarm with an urgent fervour, the bell managing a startling level of volume as it signalled the evacuation. His stomach dropped as Dante struggled to remember the embassy blueprints that Eodan had given him, his weary mind unable to recall the evacuation protocol.

Gratefully, it seemed not everyone had lost their heads in the panic. "To the kitchens, everyone!" Fenyang instructed as a surge of embassy staff descended the staircase from the upper levels, two of them assisting Hasima as she rejoined the council. She managed an impressive vigour despite her near-death experience, powering through the hallway with the assistance of her cane. The Valedian king guided Huda as he ushered everyone along towards the kitchens, the ominous thud of the battering ram growing louder as the embassy doors began to succumb.

As the wooden doors creaked and splintered, the floor of the entryway opened up in response to the onslaught of irate loyalists. A large contraption unfolded, the stone tiles coming apart neatly to reveal an expanse of lethal spikes. A handful of the townsfolk fell to their doom as the traps mortally wounded them, their followers quickly stepping over the impaled bodies to continue their pursuit.

Ahead of the stampede, the embassy staff had revealed another hidden door behind a cupboard in the kitchens. The structure had rolled aside to expose a stairway cloaked in shadows, so deep and so dark that Dante couldn't see the end of it. Despite the Valedian king's insistence to stay behind, he and his council members were ushered towards the doorway, descending along the staircase that seemingly led to nowhere.

"Single file, keep moving," a butler named Etienne urged, standing to the side as he gestured for the council members to traverse the ominous staircase. Despite the instructions, Dante found himself hesitating. Even if they escaped, it would all be for nothing if the mob followed them down the secret stairwell. Eodan had hired him to be an extension of the council, to defend Fenyang with his life if necessary...

He turned on his heel, raising his hands as he stretched his senses across the embassy, reaching for the fresh corpses he knew littered the floors. At the attempt to use his magic, Dante's head throbbed with the exertion, his vision stuttering as he almost blacked out a second time. He had expended more of his energy today than he had in years, and he had almost nothing left to give… almost.

As if sensing his intentions, a familiar presence prodded at his mind. *"Dante,* don't – *come quickly, we can still get out of here!"* Huda all but screamed at him. The embassy's traps continued to activate in the distance, thudding and clanking noises erupting throughout the building. They didn't have much time, but if Dante could just summon the dregs of his power—

A hand on his shoulder tugged him backwards, urgent and yet gentle. "Go," an aged voice commanded, and Verdis stepped in front of Dante. "Go, now."

Her presence startled him, having been certain he'd seen her escape through the stairwell already. "I can do this," Dante insisted breathily, exhaustion weighing on his bones. "I need to hold them off—"

A makeshift bottle explosive hurtled towards them, and Dante instinctively ducked to avoid the impact. To his immense surprise, Verdis' arm whipped out ahead of him, catching the container with surprising agility. Her hand clamping around the glass bottle, the crone hurled it back towards the mob with a vicious accuracy.

"Go!" she bellowed, and Dante could see the old woman's magic thrumming in her veins with a white-hot light, sputtering in time with her heartbeat. After her efforts to heal Hasima, she must have been exhausted as well. Horror sank in his gut like a stone as Dante realized he and Verdis had shared the same instinct.

"Verdis, *stop,* you're going to burn out," he protested. "Verdis!"

The wizened healer turned to face him, and Dante felt the back of his neck prickle at the proximity of that raw energy. Her irises were already clouded over with the ghostly glow of magic running wild, and she smiled the smallest, saddest smile Dante had ever seen. Every vein in Verdis' face was illuminated with power, the very last of her power.

"Go," she said once more, her voice so quiet Dante barely heard her. "*Live.*"

She rose into the air, her head rolling back as she glowed brighter still. Dante struggled to tear his gaze away from the scene unfolding ahead of him, the imminent explosion of the king's grandmother. Her physical form was shuddering in and out of existence, blurring into a shapeless energy. The butler Etienne grabbed his arm, all but hauling Dante towards the staircase as he reached for the false cupboard door—

The impact of the burnout sent a shockwave reverberating through the embassy, the force of a bomb erupting in the kitchen. Dante lost his footing halfway down the stairwell as the walls shook, tumbling down the stairs with the butler behind him as the healer unravelled. He landed hard on his back, every inch of him seizing up in protest as the butler proceeded to collapse on top of him. The aftershocks of the explosion seemed to last for hours, his ears ringing as Dante struggled to catch his breath.

Etienne wasn't especially heavy in any sense, but as he struggled to his feet Dante found himself able to breathe at last, shutting his eyes in the darkness as he tried to calm himself down. He didn't *feel* as if anything was broken, but adrenaline did strange things to a person; for all he knew, he might have wrecked every bone in his body.

A soft, recognizable voice spoke to him in the darkness. "Come on, up you get." The king's face was hidden in the dim light, but Dante could recognize him only by the cadence of his voice, as familiar to him now as his own. "On your feet, Dante. We have to keep going."

It was the most kingly he had ever sounded, and Dante had the sense that Fenyang wasn't merely referring to their continued escape. He squinted in the shadows, their environment only vaguely illuminated by a small fire a young servant girl cupped in her hands, the tiny flames casting eerie shadows.

"Where are we?" Huda asked, her fingers brushing the faded stone reliefs around them.

"The catacombs," Akila explained while Dante gathered his bearings. The young woman seemed to be assessing her surroundings with a keen interest. "They stretch for miles underground, I hear."

The description gave Dante pause. "Underground?" Dante asked incredulously. "Wait, but—this is *Aethelind*. There's not much 'underground' here."

King Fenyang laughed despite the situation, and Dante was grateful no one could see him flushing in the darkness. "There is enough for catacombs, I assure you," the king explained, running his hand along the far wall. At his touch, a doorway opened in the darkness, and he gestured for Etienne to lead their party forward. "Don't worry, *d'viin*, we aren't in any danger of plummeting into the ocean just yet."

The unfamiliar word stood out, a Pharasathi term that Dante hadn't previously encountered. He had half a mind to ask, but his heart was still too heavy with guilt. "Your Majesty…" he continued after a pause, the king leading them deeper into the catacombs. "Your grandmother, Verdis, I—I'm so sorry."

His voice trailed off, unable to find words of comfort or explanation for what had transpired. There was a heavy silence that followed, and none of the council members seemed to be able to continue the train of thought. After some time, it was Hasima who finally spoke, Benkaei supporting the queen mother's weight. "My mother died bravely," she said quietly, her voice rough. "We should not dishonour her sacrifice by perishing in these catacombs. We must press on."

The king nodded sagely, ducking his head with the low ceiling of the tunnel they walked towards. "Stay together," he instructed. "I don't want anyone getting lost down here."

Resuming his post as evacuation warden, the butler led their party through the catacombs, the girl cradling the tiny flames following closely behind. To Dante's surprise, he caught snippets of text engraved in the stone walls around them, surrounding each hewn grave – *Mother Moon, guide us to an easy slumber*. It was strange to think that some of his people had been laid to rest as far away from home as Aethelind.

"I didn't think there would be Fraecathans buried here," Dante wondered aloud, his fingers brushing the worn stone.

"I hear there are all sorts of people down here," Huda replied, much to Dante's surprise. It seemed she had recovered from the fall more quickly than he had, gliding through the tunnel with her hand brushing along the wall to guide her. Then again, Dante supposed that Huda was accustomed to traversing without visibility.

Dante mimicked her movements, using his sense of touch to guide him through the dim lighting. He cleared his throat, still uncomfortably aware of how poorly their last conversation had gone. "Huda… I owe you an apology," he began in a low voice. "I had no right to speak to you the way I did last night, I'm sorry."

"Correct, you did not," Huda agreed, but there was no animosity in her tone. "How bad was it, back home?"

He shuddered involuntarily at her words, grateful she couldn't see his reaction to such a simple question. "I… It was bad," he admitted at last. Despite the quiet atmosphere of the catacombs, the rest of their group had spread out enough along the tunnel that Dante felt safe to speak on the subject. "It manifested before I'd even learned to speak. My parents were horrified. Tried to beat it out of me in any way they could."

Huda hummed in reply, nodding her head. "That explains why your barrier is so strong," she noted softly. "I've never encountered one so… intense. It blocked your very life essence from my own magic."

He nodded in the darkness before remembering Huda wouldn't see it. "I had to keep it up all the time," Dante elaborated. "Even while I slept. There was a sort of… a family shame to it, in a way. Nobody knew for certain, but there were plenty of rumours. I had to constantly ensure I was keeping it locked away."

She was silent for a moment, the only noise around them the echoing footsteps of the servants and the council members as they navigated the tunnel. "I'm sorry, Dante," Huda replied after a few moments of silence. "You didn't deserve that."

It was a strange validation, and yet even after all he had suffered at his parents' hands, Dante could not find it within himself to believe her. He had spent two decades believing he was wrong, that he was broken, that there was something cursed and beastly about what he was capable of doing. It would take more than one day with a fellow necromancer to disprove that.

"I'm not a monster," Huda said suddenly, her voice

quiet as she turned to face his general direction. "You do know that, don't you?"

Dante was at a loss for words momentarily. "I don't think you're a monster, Huda," he insisted.

She hummed in agreement once more before facing forwards again, still guiding herself forward with one hand along the wall and careful, measured footsteps on the uneven ground. "And if I'm not a monster, Dante... then neither are you," she said firmly. Taken aback by her words, Dante was stunned into silence.

The tunnel stretched on for some time before their group arrived at a second hidden door, with the Valedian king unlocking this one in a similar fashion. The passage beyond widened into a small room, and Dante quickly began to feel somewhat nauseous at the concept of being trapped. An enormous, ornate mirror was positioned at the far end of the space, adorned with dust-covered cobwebs. Fearful of what he might find, Dante reached out tentatively with his senses – and recoiled the moment he felt the magic within the luminescent glass.

"What is this?" he asked in disgust.

"This is our exit," the Valedian king explained simply, stopping to stand beside the mirror. The servant girl's tiny flames illuminated the angles of his face, his eyes glowing molten gold. "When Eodan orchestrated our renovations, it included an escape route should the worst come to pass. We'll be safe through here."

Dante stared at the portal, an infernal instrument he had been taught to fear before he could speak. Much like necromancy, imbuing an inanimate object with magic was incredibly taboo, and a portal mirror was no exception. It was "frowned upon" in that attempting such magic was an excellent way to be disinherited – assuming you weren't spliced across dimensions in a failed attempt. He had never seen one in person, let alone used one. Perhaps today he would unlearn more than one prejudice he had been raised with.

Etienne leaned forward, flicking the surface of the mirror with his gloved fingers. The reflection rippled as if it were a pool of clear, viscous water, and Dante shuddered in revulsion. The butler assisted each of the council members and the embassy staff through the portal, the silvery surface of the mirror swallowing them one by one. Dante stood rooted to the spot, his throat dry as he watched his companions leaving the catacombs without him.

Finally, he was left standing alone in the darkness with only the Valedian king and Etienne, the servant girl extinguishing her conjured flames before slipping through the portal herself. Noticing Dante's distress, the king leaned over to the butler to whisper something in his ear.

Looking quite alarmed, the butler glanced back and forth between Dante and the king. "Are you quite certain, Your Majesty?" Etienne stammered. "It's against the evacuation protocol, Mr. Melicus will be—"

"Let me deal with Eodan," King Fenyang assured the butler, directing him towards the mirror. The man seemed quite panicked, but he eventually managed an awkward bow before darting through the mirror himself.

With the pair of them left alone in the catacombs, the king turned towards him. "It won't bite, you know," Fenyang chided him, a hand on Dante's shoulder.

Dante was grateful for the shadows concealing the visible embarrassment on his face. "I know," he insisted too quickly. "I… it's difficult not to be wary of something you've been taught to believe is sacrilege, you know."

"I do know," the king agreed.

"And portals are possibly the worst, most catastrophically dangerous of all enchanted objects," Dante prattled on, gesturing manically at his rippling reflection in the giant mirror. "There's a dozen things that can go wrong in the initial enchantment alone, and a dozen more that can go wrong even if you manage to get everything right, and then—"

"Dante."

He paused immediately at his name in the Valedian king's voice, shivering in a way that was entirely inappropriate. "Sorry," he mumbled, his hands dropping to his sides. "It's foolish, I know."

"I didn't say that," Fenyang insisted. His hand came away from Dante's shoulder, brushing his arm as the king took his hand. Every nerve in Dante's body burst into flame as the man interlaced their fingers, lightning thundering through his body as that warm, calloused hand engulfed his own. He was immediately self-conscious of every detail he could think to point out about himself, the wounds on his palms from where his own magic had damaged his skin. But the Valedian king said nothing about them, his grip carefully avoiding the blisters as he held Dante's hand.

"I…I'm…" Dante opened and closed his mouth, struggling for words only to find none available to him, his heart thundering in his chest.

"I'll go with you," Fenyang offered, giving his hand a gentle squeeze. "If it helps."

"Please," he managed to blurt out in reply. "I would… yes, if you don't mind."

The Valedian king smiled in the soft light of the mirror. Dante decided in that moment that if Fenyang asked it of him, he would follow the man to the end of the world. Squeezing his eyes shut, Dante took a tentative step into the rippling surface of the mirror, the king following along in unison. A cold layer of magic washed over Dante, and for a brief moment he was in a void without warmth or sound or air. He choked on his own breath with the shock, the freezing cold sinking deep into his bones, chilling his very soul. He clung to that warm, solid hand in his own like a lifeline, an anchor preventing him from drifting away in an endless ocean.

He stumbled as his foot connected with solid ground once more, but Fenyang was there to steady him. "That wasn't so bad, was it?" the king asked, a hint of amusement in his voice. They had landed in an ornate bedroom, all of the furniture pushed to the far side of the room to give them a large space to exit the portal mirror. The servants and the other council members were nowhere to be found, but the bedroom door was open to reveal a corridor beyond.

Dante turned to face the king, intending to conceal his embarrassment with some witty remark. The moment he looked up at King Fenyang, however, it was as if all semblance of thought promptly exited his mind. They were standing far too close, and he had to lean back just to make eye contact with the king. Those whisky-gold eyes were searching Dante's face, as if the most important thing in that moment was ensuring that he was all right.

"Where... where are we?" Dante managed to ask, finding his voice once more.

Before the king could answer, a familiar figure entered the room, rolling his shirt sleeves up to his elbows. Eodan Melicus walked into the room as if he owned the place — knowing him, he probably did. The man grinned crookedly as he regarded Dante and Fenyang.

"About time you showed up, Your Majesty," he drawled. "Is that everyone?"

"That's everyone," the Valedian king affirmed. He withdrew his grip to flick the surface of the portal mirror once more, and Dante found himself missing the sensation of the king's hand in his own immediately. "I must thank you again for the escape route — looks like we needed safe passage after all."

"My pleasure." Without warning, Eodan walked across the room to retrieve an old, dusty ornament from the end table that had been shoved into the corner. Faster than Dante could process what was happening, Eodan chucked the paperweight unceremoniously towards the mirror, promptly shattering the now solid glass.

The king turned to admire the man's handiwork. "I hear that's seven years' bad luck, Eodan," he mused.

Their host laughed darkly, gesturing for them to follow him into the hallway. "I'll take my chances. Better I be cursed more thoroughly than risk anyone following you through that portal. Besides... my estate really, *really* can't handle any more visitors these days."

CHAPTER

FOURTEEN

CHARLOTTE

Following her arrival at the estate, Charlotte slept poorly. After her first disastrous attempt at sleeping alone while Jasper was at work, Charlotte had resorted to staying in Maya's room. Even with the comfort of a physical presence beside her, however, sleep had evaded Charlotte tonight. She lay awake for what must have been hours, imagining patterns into the ceiling of the estate bedroom as she waited for exhaustion to overpower her frightful imagination. Just as it seemed Charlotte might finally find rest at last, Maya began to cry out in her sleep.

In the years that Charlotte had known her, she was well-accustomed to dealing with Maya's nightmares now. Sitting upright in the bed, Charlotte reached over to where the girl lay sleeping nearby, her hands balled up in the sheets and a frown on her face. It was second nature for Charlotte to embrace her friend, gently pulling her from the nightmare.

"Maya, wake up," Charlotte whispered, squeezing the

girl's shoulder. "Maya—you're safe, you're all right. Wake up."

Her eyes opened wide in the darkness, Maya gasped for air. "The man with two faces," she breathed, releasing her hold on the tangled bedsheets to grasp Charlotte's hand. "He betrayed the conquest."

Charlotte had no response for this information. "The man with two faces?" she repeated slowly.

As her breathing settled, Maya rolled onto her back. Frowning, she met Charlotte's gaze in the dim light. "Now that I hear it out loud... it doesn't make much sense, does it?" she replied, a sheepish smile easing onto her face.

"Not at all," Charlotte agreed, biting her lip to keep from smiling herself. Her discipline dwindled as Maya's face split into a grin, her hand pressed against her mouth as if to suppress the laughter that bubbled up within her. Charlotte ended up burying her face in the pillow beside her, lest she wake their chaperones upstairs with hysteria.

When she could draw in a full breath, Charlotte managed to speak. "Who was this man with two faces?" she questioned.

Shaking her head, Maya sighed as she sank back against the pillows. "I don't know," she admitted, wiping at her eyes. "That's all I remember."

Propping her head up with her arm, Charlotte regarded her friend in the dim light. "At least you can remember something that made you laugh," Charlotte offered, reaching to brush Maya's hair back from her face where it had escaped her braid.

"I'm sorry I woke you," Maya whispered, her expression sobering. "I'm all right, really."

"Don't be sorry," Charlotte chided her. "You didn't wake me."

Maya was quiet as she searched Charlotte's face, the barest hint of dawn illuminating her profile. "You can't sleep?" she prompted.

Charlotte shifted in an effort to get comfortable on the tangled bed sheets, humming a non-committal noise of agreement. "Don't worry about me. It's still early, you should try and sleep some more."

Her friend's eyes narrowed at her words, and she knew Maya would stay up if she asked, sorting through the complex feelings that were keeping Charlotte awake. Instead of discussing them, Charlotte kept stroking the girl's hair back from her face, reciting the lullaby her mother had once sang for her on sleepless nights. Maya's eyes fluttered closed at the sound of her voice, her breathing slow and even.

After some time, her friend had fallen fast asleep once more, but Charlotte knew she would find no rest in the vast bed they shared. The uneasiness in her heart made rest difficult, her waking thoughts and her dreams eerily similar in their darkness. Gently, Charlotte climbed out from the tangled bed sheets, leaving Maya to sleep while she bundled herself in a borrowed housecoat to wander the manor.

She didn't much care for the estate, Charlotte had decided. It was a fine, grand establishment, with imported wooden floors and bannisters, rich golden light fixtures and ornaments. For all its features, however, it felt so unbearably empty. Other than the kindly old butler named Derek, Varus had almost no staff. Everything was so dark and so quiet at this hour of the morning, without even a ticking clock to mark the beats of silence as she walked.

Her wandering led her up the staircase to the second floor, each step creaking beneath her. No matter the quality of the materials used, it seemed no house could survive the wrath of Aethelind's miserable climate; several parts of the manor seemed to ache and groan in protest. It was all well and good when Charlotte heard the stairs beneath her, but when something creaked on the opposite end of the house it startled her every single time, as if she half expected a familiar man to step from the shadows to claim her once more.

A soft mewl in the darkness startled her, but it was only Eleni's cat perched at the top of the stairs, regarding Charlotte with what might have been curiosity. The cat's gaze shifted towards a solitary open door, Mo's eyes casting an eerie glow with the sliver of light reflected in them. Charlotte found herself walking towards that open door instinctively, her feet seemingly moving of their own accord.

As she drew closer, she could hear voices from within, and Charlotte realized that this was Eleni's room. From what little she could see with the door ajar, this room oozed more personality and light than the entirety of the estate. In here, it was soft and bright, the lamp light illuminating a dozen half-finished canvasses of rich violet and cerulean paints, Eleni's pet projects she hadn't yet found the time to finish. She could smell the dried lavender Eleni loved to keep, hanging it in front of every open window she could find. As Charlotte drew close to the door, she halted at the sound of hushed conversation inside.

"I'm fine, darling," Eleni's voice insisted, gentle as always. "I'm sorry I woke you." Such an eerily similar conversation to the one Charlotte and Maya had had earlier.

"Don't worry about that. Can I get you anything?" The low, accented voice set Charlotte's teeth on edge — but then, whose voice had she expected to hear?

The door wasn't opened wide enough to see the room's

occupants directly, but Charlotte could see Eleni's vanity on the opposite end of the room. Her angle from the doorway permitted her to view the reflection of the conversation she could not witness. In the ensuite bathroom, Eleni leaned against the wall beside the toilet, a half-dressed Varus seated beside her. Haeyin remained unconscious in the bed nearby, somehow undisturbed by the hushed conversation of his partners.

Eleni smiled up at Varus, somehow managing to look radiant even when she was visibly exhausted. "I've got everything I need," she insisted, her hand sliding along the folds of her delicate lilac nightgown to rest against her abdomen. "I think she's settled down now."

Smoothing her sweat-dampened hair back from her face, Varus kissed her forehead. "Let's get you back to bed then. You need your rest."

Charlotte was distinctly aware she was witnessing a terribly private moment, and yet she found herself unable to tear her gaze away. There was an ugly, twisted thing coiled within her, something dark and monstrous and evil. Her only reaction to the joyous turn her friend's life had taken should have been a positive one, or at least concern for Eleni's wellbeing. Instead, envy rooted its fingers deep within Charlotte, and she could not say why – she could only say that it was not joy that filled her in that moment, but a cloying sorrow.

At that moment, Mo seemed to have decided she wanted in. She strolled past Charlotte's ankles, causing her to jump in alarm, aggravating her aching hip. The dreadful manor creaked with the sudden movement as the cat yelled at the occupants within the room, as if to announce their visitor. Hearing the noise, Eleni and Varus' reflections turned towards the door. Charlotte had to clap her hand over her mouth to stop the gasp that bubbled up from within her, for the man seated beside Eleni did not have Varus' face. It was certainly *Varus*, of that she was certain; he had the same hooked nose, the same dark hair and russet skin. The man's face, however, was ravaged by scars Charlotte had never seen before, scars that twisted his face into something she could not recognize.

She stumbled in alarm, nearly tripping over the hem of her housecoat as she scrambled backwards, unsure of what she had seen. There were more hushed voices, careful footsteps from within as Varus promised to investigate while Eleni went back to bed. Moments later, the lamp light was silhouetting Varus as he stood in the hallway, his face hidden in shadow.

"Charlotte?" he whispered. "What are you doing awake?"

The corridor stretched around her, the walls impossibly wide and narrow all at once in that darkness. She didn't know what she had seen. She didn't know what to make of it.

"Are you all right?" asked Varus, tilting his head. He appeared so ordinary now, entirely mundane.

"I couldn't sleep," she admitted in a breathy whisper, her throat feeling tight. "I'm sorry I startled you."

Varus shook his head. "You don't need to apologize, Charlotte. On the contrary, it seems I've startled *you*." He closed the door behind them with care, the fractured light tracing his silhouette vanishing in an instant. "Come with me."

He took about five laboured steps forward before he noticed Charlotte was not following him. She stared wide-eyed in the dim light, her hands scrunched in the fabric of her housecoat. "Where are we going?" asked Charlotte, forcing her voice not to squeak.

He might have smiled, judging by the noise he made. "Somewhere I go to disappear," he offered. "When I find myself unable to sleep."

Against her better nature, Charlotte found herself following Varus down the corridor. Disappearing sounded wonderful at the moment, she thought to herself as they ascended a staircase to a third floor she hadn't visited yet. This level was smaller than the rest, with only the elevator entrance to their right and a lonely door at the end of the hallway. The dawn light barely illuminated Varus' form as he led her towards that door, curious lines of ink barely visible beneath the white cotton of a hastily donned shirt.

He led her into what appeared to be a vast study, part library and part workshop and entirely chaos. There was an old typewriter perched on a grand wooden desk ahead of her, an easel nearby hosting a half-forgotten sketch with several others scattered into a loose pile on a table beside it. A grand piano stood opposite, an entire corner of the room devoted to it, with a thick wad of music sheets strewn across the bench. There were half a dozen mismatched book-shelves surrounding them, carelessly organised and clut-tered with seemingly random paraphernalia.

Charlotte forgot herself, wandering towards those books as if compelled by what secrets they held. She ran her fingers along the spines, feeling the mismatched texture of cloth and leather. These tomes were not for show; they had been new once, had fallen into disrepair, but it was clear they had been well-loved in their time. The corners were bruised and the pages were battered, dog-eared and stuffed with little notes and additions, as if someone had read them and had many thoughts needing to be documented.

"I never took you for a reader," Charlotte noted, finally finding the courage to turn back and look at Varus' face. There was no trace of the scars she had seen, his umber skin as unblemished as always, dark hair falling loose to his collarbones. The rumpled shirt he wore was haphazardly buttoned up partway, revealing unintelligible symbols inked along his sternum. He regarded her with those dark eyes, as if he were assessing her as well.

"You could say I have a great deal of free time," Varus offered dryly, but his lips curled into a crooked smile. "I've certainly had my share of sleepless nights."

Charlotte eyed the half-finished sketches, the messy scrawl of handwritten music sheets, the chicken scratch additions to otherwise neatly typed documents. "It seems you're having one right now," she noted plainly.

The man laughed half-heartedly, brushing his hair back with his fingers. "Takes one to know one, I suppose," Varus murmured. "Why can't you sleep, Charlotte?"

She glanced away, crossing the room towards the easel and the unfinished sketches. Varus had a messy, erratic style; every line was the amalgamation of about seventy, as if he began with stuttering scrawls that evolved and took shape as solid lines. He drew landscapes, he drew maps, he drew Haeyin. Charlotte looked away, suddenly feeling as if she were intruding on something private.

"I'm afraid," she admitted at last, either to herself or to Varus. "I have nightmares of monsters, and then I awake to the memory of them. At least when I'm awake, I know that I'm not there anymore."

A half-truth that sounded silly to her own ears, but Varus made no chiding remark. Instead, he gestured around the pair of them. "You're welcome to come here whenever you might need to," he offered, and his tone seemed sincere. "Sometimes, I find I just need… something to distract me for a little while. Somewhere to get the thoughts out of my head so I might find some peace."

She was unaccustomed to receiving kindness from Varus, someone she had dedicated herself to being opposed to. Her eyes burned, and she wiped away the traitorous wetness with the back of her hand, her gaze fixed on the threadbare rug beneath them. "Does it get any easier?" asked Charlotte, unable to keep the bitterness out of her tone.

"Yes," Varus replied immediately, catching her off guard. Her eyes snapped towards him, ready to bite back, ready to spit acidic words in his face, but Varus continued. "I know it seems impossible, and I know it feels as if you're drowning, and every thought and every word is too loud and too heavy to bear. I know it feels as if everything is collapsing in on you, and I know it feels as if you're alone in a great, empty void, all at once.

"I can't pretend to know… *exactly* what you've been through, Charlotte," Varus continued, those intense eyes heavy and serious. "But I can tell you that this isn't forever. One day you'll wake up, and that noise between your ears will still be there, it might always be there. But it will be quieter, and you will be stronger."

She stood there for what might have been hours, staring at him in silence. There was no jest in Varus' face, no cruel joke to be played on her. Charlotte opened her mouth, but she had no words, no vile retort to cut him down at the knees with. Whatever beast that lurked within her had been declawed in that moment, left without a response.

"You know… I still don't like you, Varus," she managed to choke out at last, unable to stop the manic laughter that bubbled up as her eyes burned.

Varus seemed to be amused by her remark, a breathy laugh leaving his lips. "That's entirely fair," he agreed with her, smiling crookedly. He gestured around them, taking a step back towards the door. "Have a seat, have something to read. You might find it will clear your head, replacing that noise with… something comforting. No one will bother you up here."

He left her in that grand study, shutting the door behind him. Charlotte was left alone with her thoughts in that silence once more, but it was different here. It was as if the air around her was softer, gentler. The creaks and groans of the manor did not reach her ears in this room, and the altitude offered her a view of the sunrise through the open curtains. True to Varus' word, this did seem to be a place she could come to disappear.

She took the oldest, most damaged book from the bookshelf, the one filled to the brim with annotations and notes, and Charlotte began to read.

~∘~ ⚙ ~∘~

It was well after noon when Charlotte awoke, curled up in the old armchair of Varus' study with the book open halfway on her lap. She couldn't be certain when she had fallen asleep, but she vaguely recalled having opened a folded critique Varus had carefully tucked inside *Gods of the Old World*. His scribbled notes had remarked on inaccuracies in the origin of the Lutaidhr, the god of the void. He was a decidedly strange person, his earlier kindness weighing on her heart. Begrudgingly, Charlotte was forced to accept he was just all right.

Carefully placing the book back amongst its peers, Charlotte made her way down to the main level. She was aching for a bit of food and sore from sleeping in an armchair. To her astonishment, she found the atmosphere of the manor had changed entirely. The building had gone from painfully empty to impossibly crowded seemingly overnight, and Charlotte was suddenly surrounded by strangers. She was distinctly aware of the fact that Varus kept no staff, and yet people in uniform filled the estate.

She ducked and tip-toed through the throngs of people towards the kitchen, hoping she might be able to swipe a bit of breakfast from whatever leftovers remained. She unintentionally crashed headlong into one of the newcomers, and Charlotte was sent promptly to the floor.

"Oh!" was the only sound she managed to make, landing roughly on her backside. Just as quickly as she had fallen, Charlotte was gently lifted to her feet by a pair of strong arms, righting her with great care.

"My apologies, I didn't see you there," a deep cadence replied. When Charlotte looked up at last, she nearly strained her armchair-stiffened neck. He was the tallest man she had ever met, towering over her as she stared up at him. He had a kind face, his golden eyes searching her for injuries as he steadied her. He was Valedian, that much was certain — his skin was deeper than her own, his dark hair intricately braided.

If she had been about to say anything, a familiar voice interrupted her train of thought. "Charlotte!" was all she heard from Dante before she was gathered in his arms, consumed in a bone-crushing embrace. She was too startled to process what had happened, finding herself awkwardly wrapping her arms around him in return.

"Dante? What are you doing here?" she managed to ask him as he released her. As her vision focused on his face, her stomach dropped. "Goddesses, what happened to you?"

Dante shared a glance with the giant man beside them. "To cut a long story... *very* short, the Valedian embassy has been obliterated," he replied slowly, rubbing at his neck with a bandaged hand. His face was a patchwork of scrapes and bruises, shallow cuts along his brow and his cheek. "I see you've already met King Fenyang."

Upon realizing the identity of the stranger she had crashed into, Charlotte nearly fainted. "*Oh*—Your Majesty!" she managed to croak, stumbling into a curtsy so clumsy that Aurelia would have choked on her tea. "Please forgive me, I wasn't looking where I was going."

The Valedian king laughed, and it was a kind, joyful sound. "There is no need for that," he replied simply, and Charlotte was struck by how jarringly different King Fenyang was from the other monarch she had encountered. All the same, Charlotte found herself crossing her arms over her chest, painfully aware of how much of her skin was exposed by Eleni's loaned nightgown and housecoat.

Clearing her throat, Charlotte glanced back towards the kitchens. "I was hoping there might be some leftover food?"

Nodding, Dante gestured for her to follow, leading her away from the Valedian king. "You have good timing, we just cooked up a batch after everyone arrived," he explained as they exited the hallway.

The kitchen seemed enormous, perhaps simply because it was the only room that wasn't overcrowded at present. As promised, the countertop was filled with plenty of food left-over from the breakfast that had been cooked up for the new arrivals. Dante wasted no time in filling up a clean plate for Charlotte, spooning scrambled eggs, bacon, and fresh fruit onto the dish.

"I feel like I haven't seen you in forever," said Dante, handing Charlotte the plate. She took it gratefully as she settled into one of the chairs at the wooden kitchen table, her stomach grumbling as she sat down.

"It *has* been a while," Charlotte agreed, eyeing the bandages on his hands as he poured two cups of tea. "Are you… is everything all right? What happened to you?"

Seating himself opposite her, Dante chewed his lip as he slid a cup of tea across the table. "I'm not sure where to start," he admitted, his voice uncharacteristically rough. "Truthfully, I'm still processing everything."

Her heart fractured at his words. "I can understand that," Charlotte offered, nibbling on a bit of bacon. Her eyes landed on his bandaged hands as they left the teacup, a sight she was all too familiar with.

Noticing her gaze, Dante's expression sobered. "That's part of it," he agreed, acknowledging Charlotte's unspoken question. "I'm… not ready to talk about that in detail."

Shaking her head, Charlotte managed a smile for him. "We don't need to talk about it," she assured him. "I'm just glad you're safe. When did you get here?"

Testing the cup of tea, Dante sipped gingerly at the hot liquid. "About an hour ago. Eodan had rigged up an escape route through the embassy, it led to one of the rooms here."

The name jolted her, unfamiliar with referring to Varus as such. She wondered when the topic of their host's conflicting identities would come up. "You had to escape the embassy?" she replied, picking at the sliced apple on her plate.

Dante laughed breathily, an awkward sound that Charlotte was immeasurably fond of. "Yes, that's… that's an even longer story, to be honest," Dante admitted, rubbing idly at the uninjured side of his face. "General Byron accused us of trying to assassinate the king. After that, things got messy."

Charlotte dropped the slice of apple, blanching at Dante's words. His eyes narrowed as he regarded her, Dante's brow furrowing as recognition dawned on his face. "Keepers... It was you, wasn't it? You're the one the general was talking about."

She winced involuntarily. "Does everyone know?" Charlotte asked glumly.

Shaking his head, Dante sipped at his tea. "I've only just put two and two together," he explained, waving with his free hand. "Something General Byron had said, that the would-be assassin was Valedian... and given how fond you are of Eodan, I assume you'd have good reason for staying here, of all places."

Charlotte pursed her lips, picking at her scrambled eggs for an excuse to break eye contact with her friend. "We're on better terms now, I suppose," she offered, swallowing a lump that formed in her throat. "But... you're correct in your assumptions."

She could feel Dante watching her, silent for a moment as she played with her food. "Good on you, the bastard had it coming," he decided at last, nearly causing Charlotte to choke. "He'd been a complete twat with our negotiations, and he tried to have the Order of Xiska murder us in a courtyard. It should be blasphemy, treason. Instead, the kingdom's outraged with the Valedian council."

She was taken aback by how baldly he spoke of the king, of the Order — but then, Dante wasn't an Aethian citizen. Insulting the king wasn't an affront to his patriotism, it was merely political commentary. Managing a brief smile at his words, Charlotte dared to ask the question that had been sitting on the edge of her tongue, a hot coal lodged in her throat.

"Is he... is the king still alive, then?" she whispered.

As Dante nodded slowly, her heart sank. "Yes, as far as I know," he offered. "Injured enough that we've not seen or heard from him since, but alive."

Charlotte set down her fork, exhaling softly as she processed the information. Part of her was disappointed to learn that the king hadn't succumbed to his injuries... part of her was relieved she hadn't murdered another human being, no matter how horrid a man the king had proved to be. Regardless, the outcome for her would be the same; she doubted *attempted* regicide would be a lighter sentence than successful regicide.

Dante eyed the food on her plate. "Not much of an appetite?" he asked gently.

Charlotte stared longingly at the bacon in front of her, finding any semblance of a desire to eat had vanished entirely. "Is Haeyin still here?" she asked suddenly, her gaze snapping back towards Dante.

He blinked, shaking his head. "No, I think he's at the clinic," Dante admitted. "Did you need him?"

She tried for the eggs again, losing the motivation halfway through the motion of scraping some onto the fork. Exasperated, she brushed her hair back from her face with her hands, heaving a sigh. "I—yes, I needed... my medication is all back home," Charlotte explained, and it was mostly true. "I can't go back home, so I need him to procure a fresh batch for me."

Bless his heart, Dante did not question her. "Well, you shouldn't be wandering towards the clinic alone," he noted, leaning back in his chair. "Which raises a bit of a conundrum, since most of the people you're currently residing with are wanted fugitives, in some form or another."

Nodding in agreement, Charlotte ran through a mental checklist of everyone she knew would be willing to accompany her, and there was a staggering amount who were in fact fugitives. Those who weren't were otherwise occupied; Jasper was likely already at the forge, and while Eleni or Maya might be willing to join her, Charlotte could not forgive herself if she endangered them with her presence. She knew Varus was capable of getting around Aethelind unnoticed, but the thought of spending more time with the man still made Charlotte uneasy.

"I'll go with you," Dante offered suddenly.

Charlotte raised an eyebrow as she met his gaze. "Aren't you also something of a fugitive at this point in the game?" she asked, unable to keep herself from smiling.

Dante laughed that awkward, loveable laugh again. "You aren't wrong," he conceded, but there was a mischievous glint in his eye. "Trust me, I am very good at going unnoticed when need be."

Travelling through Aethelind with Dante turned out to be a nerve-wracking experience. Charlotte had spent most of her life blissfully unaware of her surroundings when she was idly making her way through the city, unless she was walking home at night. Dante seemed to portray that nightly hyper-vigilance during every waking second of his life, and it was both intriguing and exhausting. He was aware of threats Charlotte hadn't even picked up on, guards and templars in half-baked disguises she would never have noticed. He even seemed to walk soundlessly, the soles of his boots making nearly no noise at all as they traversed the cobblestones.

"I realize now I took living so close to the clinic for granted," Charlotte groaned as they neared the ammunitions factory, having finally been given the signal she could relax by the way Dante exhaled a lungful of anxiety. All of that walking made her hips and her knees ache, and she was disheartened by the fact that she knew she still had to walk all the way back.

Dante had noted her discomfort, evidently having resisted the urge to comment until now. "Are you sure you wouldn't rather just go home?" he suggested. "You're right next to Jasper's, aren't you? It'll be a shorter walk back than the manor."

"No," Charlotte blurted out immediately, swallowing her nervousness as it bubbled up her throat. Dante waited patiently as she collected her thoughts, clearing her throat before she spoke again. "No, I... I can't, not right now." Guilt tugged at her heart as she thought of her father managing the shop by himself, unaware of her turmoil. She knew Jasper would have told him some story or another, perhaps that she was staying with Eleni and Maya; a half-truth, the best attempt at lying that her blacksmith could manage without turning scarlet.

Pursing his lips, Dante seemed to weigh his curiosity against his loyalty, ultimately deciding not to pry. "All right," he agreed simply, following closely as Charlotte entered the clinic.

The wards pressed against Charlotte's skin as they crossed the threshold into the ancient factory, the recognizable sensation of Haeyin's warm, comforting power. The magical presence glided over Charlotte and Dante as the wards accepted their presence. The clinic was unusually deserted for this time of the day, and Haeyin was nowhere to be seen. It was Cary who greeted them in the space that passed for a waiting room, wearing a brown leather vest over a loose, pale shirt. It was strange to see her outside of her castle servant garb, or even the armour Charlotte had grown accustomed to seeing her wearing.

Emerging from a teetering pile of supply crates, there was a wary look in her rosy eyes. "Charlotte, good to see you," Cary noted with a nod of her head, running her fingers through her dark, loose waves. "And who's this?"

Her brisk demeanour, after how considerate she had been with Charlotte at their last meeting, felt like whiplash. She bristled at the woman's words, though admittedly Charlotte was uncertain if a familiarity with Cary would make her feel better or worse about what had transpired.

"This is Dante," Charlotte offered, clearing her throat. She was keen to be finished here, to head back to the manor and hide for the remainder of the day. "Is Haeyin available?"

"He has his hands full at the moment," Cary trailed off, craning her neck around to see what Haeyin was doing in the other room. Following her gaze, Charlotte watched as a familiar auburn-haired doctor crossed the space, and her eyes locked on the form of the patient lying on Haeyin's operating table, too quiet and too still. The man's dark hair was peppered with silver along his temples, a small scar along his brow visible before the doctor covered the patient's body with a plain linen sheet.

She averted her gaze, the man's body seeming too private and too grim to be witnessed. There was a conversation occurring beside her, Cary and Dante exchanging small talk, but their words were inaudible to her ears. It was only when Haeyin emerged from the operating room at last that Charlotte could focus again, the doctor drying his hands off on a clean towel.

"Charlotte, Dante, how lovely to see you," Haeyin greeted them, but his small smile did not meet his eyes.

There was a weariness there, his whisky-gold gaze uncharacteristically dimmed.

"What happened?" she found herself asking, though she knew the answer already.

The doctor turned to look at the patient behind him, that heavy exhaustion settling into his shoulders. "He arrived too late, unfortunately," he explained with a sigh. "By the time we admitted him, he'd already lost too much blood."

"I'm sorry," Dante offered immediately, sincerity lacing his words.

Haeyin merely shook his head. "It is an unfortunate part of our work here," he replied. "You can't save them all."

Charlotte's gaze seemed fixed upon the deceased stranger, the horrid stillness beneath that sheet. "What… what happens to him now?" she asked absentmindedly.

Cary was watching her gaze, her expression unreadable. "Normally we would attempt to notify family, but he has none we are aware of."

The doctor murmured in agreement, crossing his arms over his chest. "We try to deliver the remains to family members for a proper burial, but when there are no next of kin…" Haeyin trailed off, shaking his head. "Well, as you might imagine, there are some difficulties associated with an apostate clinic disposing of unnamed persons. We have an associate who works in the Aerindale morgue who collects the bodies on a need-to-know basis, gives them the sort of nondescript burial reserved for plague victims."

Dante nodded slowly, his expression sombre. "That is… that is good, at least," he managed to reply.

As if sensing the topic of discussion was bringing down the tone of the conversation, Haeyin pivoted. "Now, then," he cleared his throat, clasping his hands together. "What can I do for you today?"

Dante turned to Charlotte, encouraging her with a gentle nudge. Charlotte was presently dying, or what felt like dying. It seemed as if her ribs were enveloped in chains, encased in iron that stoppered her breath. "I was... I was hoping to... can I have a word with you?" she managed to croak out, sniffing. "Privately?"

Haeyin turned, looking back at the still form of the nameless person on his makeshift operating table. Sensing this was no longer an ideal place for a living patient, he gestured for Charlotte to sit down on one of the mismatched chairs in the waiting area. Unprompted, Dante nudged Cary with his elbow before gesturing for her to follow him, exiting the atrium to give Charlotte some privacy.

"Is everything all right?" Haeyin asked the moment they were alone.

His amber eyes were bright, too bright for her to meet his gaze. Charlotte found it easier to focus on her palms, the callouses from years of burning herself at the bakery. "Would you be able to give me an early refill?" asked Charlotte.

The doctor seemed taken aback. "Of course," he replied, crossing his legs. "I'm afraid I don't have it ready for you yet, but I could have it delivered to you."

"Could you deliver it to the manor?" Charlotte asked. "Just as I—I'll be staying there for a little while, it seems."

She could see Haeyin nod slowly in her peripheral vision, but he did not prompt her for further details. There was more she needed to ask, more she needed to tell him. The words were stuck, a scathing coal lodged in her throat that Charlotte couldn't swallow. She needed to spit it out.

"Did Varus tell you?" she managed to whisper, her voice threatening to fail her. "Or Eleni, or… or Cary, I suppose. Do you know about what happened?"

Haeyin was silent a moment longer, and she could feel that molten gaze on her still as the doctor nodded once more. "Yes," he confirmed.

Her heart sank at his words, as if somehow Charlotte had held onto hope that there was someone in her life who didn't know about something so private. It was better, she told herself, that Haeyin already knew, for Charlotte didn't have the heart to explain to him what had transpired in the king's chambers.

"I've been having nightmares," she began, her voice low and uneven. That lump of coal sat lodged between her jaw still, threatening to burst out of her if Charlotte did not speak quickly. "So I stay awake as long as I can, and… and I'm just frightened and angry all of the time, and…"

"It's very normal, what you're going through," Haeyin offered gently when Charlotte trailed off. "It's a terrible, dreadful thing that happened to you, and it should never have happened at all. But how you're handling it? That is completely normal, Charlotte."

Closing her eyes, Charlotte absorbed those words, absorbed the weight of that comforting sentiment. Her chest ached, iron chains digging into her lungs as she fought to breathe, struggling to make eye contact with the man beside her. His face was open and sincere, compassion oozing from those eyes, and she appreciated it and hated it all at once.

"I can handle the nightmares," Charlotte stated, and somewhere within her, even when she felt so broken, she knew it was true. "But… I need to know that the nightmares are all that's left of him, Haeyin."

The silence that followed was physically painful as Charlotte waited for the doctor to respond. His brow furrowed as his gaze wandered to the floor, idly rubbing at his chin. She could almost see the gears turning in his mind while Haeyin pondered her words, contemplating every possible outcome.

"The tea you take should prevent any... unwanted side effects," Haeyin replied at last. "It's not its intended purpose for your condition, but it does function as a contraceptive."

The relief that washed over Charlotte was nearly as painful as her trepidation, her eyes burning with tears. She squeezed them shut, fearing that if she opened the flood gates now, she would be sobbing all the way back to the estate. She could feel her lips contorting, and Charlotte covered her mouth for good measure as if she might stop herself from falling apart entirely.

"If it doesn't..." Haeyin continued, glancing back towards Charlotte. "If it doesn't, you should know that I am here for you, whatever it is you may need. You're not alone, Charlotte."

She could only nod in response. Haeyin reached for her free hand, squeezing it gently, and Charlotte swore the man was channelling magic into her skin. His palm was warm and his grip was firm, and the longer he held Charlotte's hand it was easier and easier for her to breathe. She recalled Varus' words from that morning – *it will be quieter, and you will be stronger* – and somehow, Charlotte started to find herself believing them.

There was a sudden flurry of footsteps, and for a moment Charlotte panicked that something was wrong, and that Cary and Dante were hurrying back to warn her to run. She and Haeyin were on their feet in an instant –

but to their surprise, it was Jasper and Gideon who bolted in through the front entrance, nearly colliding with the supply crates as they staggered to a screeching halt.

Her heart thudded in her chest at the sight of them, and Charlotte swallowed the last lump of coal threatening to burn her throat. Gideon was covered in blood and bruises, half of his left shirt sleeve ripped away and hastily wrapped as a makeshift bandage across his face. His expression softened as he looked at her, and Charlotte hated the pity in Gideon's eyes as her name left his lips in a hushed whisper. She focused instead on Jasper, who looked at her as if the sun shone from her face, as if the world had changed but she had not.

"Jasper?" she breathed in response, her voice still trembling. "What's going on? What happened?"

Jasper gestured weakly towards Gideon before clasping his knees again, as if he might lose his balance at any second. "Need... to get him... to Dornkeep. V—Eodan. Guards... *everywhere.*"

Having evidently heard the commotion, Cary and Dante emerged from the back, narrowly avoiding a collision with the furniture. Dante's relief at seeing Jasper was short-lived as he took in the sight of an injured Gideon beside him, but it was Cary who spoke.

"Well... this is a surprise," the Reinnairlei woman trailed off, her eyes narrowed. Her hawkish stare scrutinized Gideon's presence in the clinic, but Haeyin interjected with a raised hand before she could interrogate him further.

"Cary, help me make some space for our friend?" Haeyin interjected, his amber eyes locked on Gideon. The woman's frown deepened, but Cary did not argue as she scooted past the group to clear the operating table.

Following their intentions, Gideon gave them a dismissive wave as he shook his head. "There's no need for that," he insisted. "It's only my eye."

Despite the situation, Haeyin managed to laugh dryly at the knight's words. "By the Three, 'only my eye', he says... must be a friend of yours, Jasper," the doctor scoffed, pinching the bridge of his nose. "At least have a seat here then, won't you? Let me take a look at that."

With some hesitation, Gideon eventually took a seat beside Haeyin, his movements slowed by whatever unseen injuries he had sustained. Charlotte moved over to stand beside Jasper and Dante as they spectated.

Clearing his throat, Dante waved his hand towards the group of them. "So... care to explain what happened?" he began, glancing meaningfully at Jasper. The blacksmith hesitated before he responded, either for fear of incriminating Gideon or as a result of the exertion still apparent in his laboured breathing.

Eventually, it was Gideon who provided the details. "I was eavesdropping on a conversation between the king and his advisors," he explained casually, unravelling the makeshift bandage from his head. "They didn't take kindly to a knight spying on them, in addition to my recent infractions."

Charlotte stiffened at his words, at the implication. Having overheard Gideon's refusal of the operating table, Cary had opted for dragging a spare surgical lamp into the waiting area, positioning it beside Haeyin as he examined the man's injuries. With the temperamental electricity that Caelfall received, the device's power switch required multiple attempts before the lamp finally turned on. As the last of the fabric fell away from Gideon's face, there was a collective gasp at what was revealed beneath the harsh light.

"*Keepers*," Dante hissed as he slapped a hand over his

mouth. Cary promptly left the room again. Charlotte noted that Jasper was very wisely staring at the wall opposite them.

Gideon, to his credit, seemed to be taking this rather well. "I'm accustomed to stares when I remove my helmet, but usually that's a complimentary thing," he mused, his battered face managing a self-deprecating grin. The man looked to have been in a good fight at the very least, bruises spreading from his brow to the bridge of his nose. His right eye was horrifically swollen beyond recognition, blood leaking from the corner with the absence of his makeshift bandage.

The only person without any sort of visible reaction was Haeyin, who appeared to be analysing Gideon's injury with the same inquisitive expression Charlotte had seen a few minutes earlier. "Well... well, damn," he offered finally, his shoulders sagging in a weary sigh. "I doubt I can save that eye, I'm afraid."

"Just so long as I don't die of an infection, I'm satisfied," Gideon insisted.

Pushing a cart of medical supplies, Cary returned from the operating room once more with an assortment of tools and cleaning products. As she straightened up, Cary's rose-hued gaze slid from the gore on the knight's face to Jasper, eyeing the blacksmith warily where he stood off to the side. He was still staring anywhere but at Gideon.

Hesitating where he surveyed the knight's face, Haeyin's expression was conflicted. "I am happy to treat you, but... you must understand that our establishment caters to the socially vulnerable," Haeyin explained to the knight, retrieving one of the antiseptic-soaked cloths from the cart beside him. "I need to know that you won't report this."

"He helped me, Haeyin," Charlotte offered in his

defense, her voice rough. "That night, after… at the castle. We can trust him." She could feel Gideon staring at her, but she kept her gaze trained on Haeyin as she spoke. Nodding appreciatively, he set to work on cleaning the blood and muck from her friend's face.

Gideon winced as the antiseptic touched his wounds. "You have my word. If it's legal action you're wary of, might it help to know I've been unofficially relieved of my title?" he offered dryly. Charlotte felt her chest tighten uncomfortably, knowing what it meant to Gideon to have lost his title as a captain.

The doctor's brow frowned almost imperceptibly, continuing his work. "It does, admittedly," Haeyin conceded after a moment. He gave the man's face a quick once-over before continuing, discarding the antiseptic cloth in favour of utilizing his magic. The doctor's hand hovered over Gideon's eye, and Charlotte watched as that familiar energy glowed in his veins, his irises. Her friend tensed at first, either from shock or from the heat of that magic on his ruined face. The golden light illuminated his profile as the magic began to knit his flesh back together, and eventually Gideon seemed to relax into the sensation.

As if noting Haeyin required no further assistance, Cary sashayed across the room to stand beside Jasper. Charlotte frowned as the Reinnairlei woman stood uncomfortably close to her friend, Cary leaning in to whisper in Jasper's ear.

"You're planning on bringing your handsome young friend to Dornkeep, then?" she mused, barely loud enough for Charlotte to pick up.

Jasper nodded slowly, his gaze drifting towards Charlotte as he spoke. "I need Eodan's assistance," he explained quietly. She noted the choice of persona, as if Eodan

Melicus were a more tolerable person to introduce to a knight — *former* knight — than Varus Emery.

"And how will Eodan feel about this?" Cary retorted, her tone soft but urgent. There was a warning in her rosy gaze as her shoulder brushed against Jasper's back, and Charlotte did not miss the way he edged away from the contact. "I doubt he will take kindly to your friend's occupation."

"I'll deal with it," said Jasper grimly, stepping closer towards Charlotte. He murmured a soft, mumbled apology as he bumped into her, his fingers brushing against the back of Charlotte's hand. Before she could pull away, to give her blacksmith space, Jasper reached to interlace her fingers with his own. She blinked, startled at the rare proximity, but Charlotte did not withdraw her hand. She could feel the tension dissipate from Jasper as his shoulders relaxed, and Charlotte's grip on his hand tightened in response.

Clearing his throat again, Dante addressed Gideon as the golden light of the doctor's magic faded. "What is it you need from Eodan?" he asked, interrupting Cary's barrage of questions.

Gideon scrunched his nose as he stood up, Haeyin still regarding his handiwork with a measure of concern. The doctor had done a rather remarkable job on her friend's face, Charlotte thought. Even with Haeyin's talents, however, there was only so much his magic could heal. Beneath the blood still matting his hair, a single scar along his lid was all that remained of the wound that had irreparably damaged Gideon's eye.

His remaining eye tracked each of their faces, as if testing what was left of his vision. "Gustaf's out of his damned mind," Gideon explained, and Charlotte flinched at the name.

"Fair enough, but what else is new?" Jasper mumbled under his breath. Charlotte managed a small laugh, and it was a testament to whatever change Gideon was undergoing that he spoke so openly, so negatively about the king. He chuckled darkly under his breath, shaking his head before he continued.

"He's ordered a curfew for this evening," Gideon elaborated. "What he's neglected to mention is that the curfew has been moved up by *three hours*. That's what I'd overheard before... well, before this." He gestured blithely towards his right eye, a ghostly, milky white in comparison.

"Three hours?" Haeyin repeated. "A nine o'clock curfew? That's unheard of, even in Caelfall."

Gideon shook his head, frowning. "That's the point," he insisted grimly. "They're trying to trap people out on the street. They're giving orders to detain anyone they catch outside after hours."

"That's ludicrous," Dante fumed. "On what grounds?"

Her friend paused, his gaze hovering over Charlotte as if he were deciding how best to phrase his response. That haunted stare made her blood run cold as Gideon replied, "They're looking for the Valedian council... and they're looking for you, Charlotte."

CHAPTER

FIFTEEN

JASPER

As the fireplace crackled and spat in the sitting room of the Melicus estate, Jasper was forced to consider the possibility that he had overestimated his rapport with his employer. They had arrived at the estate only moments before, a borrowed cart from the community stable serving as a discreet method of transportation for three fugitives. Now that they were obliged to meet the wrath of Varus Emery, Cary had opted to linger back at the threshold of the hallway as she watched the confrontation take place.

Since he had last been at the manor, it was as if the population had tripled overnight. Jasper was startled by the onslaught of foot traffic in the estate, though Dante and Charlotte seemed unsurprised with the sudden influx of inhabitants. When they flagged Varus down in the sitting room, their host was not alone, deep in conversation with three people Jasper didn't immediately recognize. The taller of the three strangers was a handsome albeit intimidatingly

354

tall man, his deep complexion and amber-coloured eyes suggesting he was Valedian. The two women beside Varus were vaguely familiar to Jasper, a warrior standing beside one of the upper-class ladies of Briardeen, the battle-scarred armour at odds with the delicate lace of floral-patterned fabric.

Varus looked up at them with a shrewd stare as their group bustled into the sitting room, his eyes skimming across each of their faces. "Jasper," Varus began, his words dangerously quiet. "Please, tell me I have misunderstood something. Tell me you haven't brought a knight into my home." The man's jaw tightened as he spoke, the only tell that betrayed his raw desperation.

"Please, sir—hear me out," Jasper began to protest. "It's a long story, but…"

His employer halted Jasper's attempt at explanation with a gesture of his hand, recognition dawning on his face as he stared at Gideon. "It was you that night, wasn't it?" Varus asked calmly, his brow furrowed. "You brought Charlotte here, with Cary."

Before Jasper or Gideon could confirm the kingpin's words, it was Charlotte who replied. "Yes," she assured Varus, her voice so soft that Jasper scarcely heard her. Her hand remained entwined with his own, having only let go of him briefly to board the cargo hold of the wagon they had taken here. He had not missed the way Gideon's stare had followed the movement, the way the man had glanced away rapidly as if he had stared directly at the sun.

Sensing an opening in the conversation, Dante gestured towards the tall, handsome man for Jasper and Gideon's benefit. "As you may have already gathered… Eodan is currently hosting the Valedian council," he explained, his cheeks tinged with pink.

With a smirk, Varus nodded towards his guests. "I would like to introduce you to King Fenyang, He Who Rises," the kingpin remarked casually. After a moment's pause, he added, "And you may be familiar with Princess Aurelia and Fortia."

At this piece of information, the lady beside Varus turned to face their group, removing the dark glasses obscuring her eyes. Her light hair was the colour of sun-bleached bones, artfully woven back from her face. Her pale red eyes were constantly moving, her gaze flickering back and forth as she eyed the newcomers. The warrior beside her surveyed the group with similarly scarlet eyes, scanning each of them with a calculating stare.

"I can vouch for Gideon, for what it's worth," Princess Aurelia spoke up, addressing Varus. "He was a knight in my father's employ, but Gideon has been working privately for me for some time now. He had been standing guard for Charlotte and I that evening, and he was instrumental in her escape."

They had not discussed what had transpired prior to Charlotte's arrival at the manor, and Jasper hadn't wanted to ask. What details he had picked up on were devastating, and his thoughts drifted to the nameless woman that Varus had mentioned only briefly that spring, the reason that Jasper had been recruited for the assignment with Cary. The thought of such a terrible thing happening to Charlotte... his fingers tightened around her hand at the princess' words, wanting nothing more than to whisk her away from this room to someplace safe. And to commit regicide, potentially.

Gideon stepped forward, lowering himself to one knee as he bowed his head towards the princess and the king. "Your Majesty, Your Highness... I sought out Jasper to pass along a warning," he explained solemnly. "I cannot atone for what sins I committed serving King Gustaf, nor can I undo the harm done to the Valedian council, but I can offer you information. In order to justify searching Caelfall for the survivors of the explosion at the embassy – and the king's attempted assassin – Aethelind will see a nine o'clock curfew this evening, without warning."

The princess and the Valedian king exchanged glances. "You may rise, *Sir* Gideon," Princess Aurelia replied, a small smile on her beatific face as she emphasized his rank. "It seems you and I arrived here with similar intentions. I must confess I had sought to pass along the same information."

To Gideon's apparent shock, King Fenyang bowed his head towards the man, his hand over his heart. "It is no small feat, to betray your superiors in order to do what you believe is right," the Valedian king noted gratefully.

Pursing his lips, Varus crossed his arms over his chest. "I can see this information was hard-earned, lad. It should go without saying that we all appreciate you risking your neck not once, but twice in the last few days. This brings us to a crucial point, however... what are our next steps?"

"I would strongly recommend safely transporting the king and his council from Aethelind," Gideon emphasized. "Your Majesty, you were attacked in the courtyard under the guise of an accords-related meeting. I fear you are no longer safe here."

A voice spoke up from the threshold, sufficiently startling Jasper as he remembered that Cary was still present. "Forgive me, but I thought it was a direct violation of the accords to leave before a resolution is reached?" she interjected.

Frowning, Dante turned to the woman who leaned

casually against the threshold of the sitting room. "The accords have already been breached," he explained slowly. "Whatever the kingdom may be led to believe, General Byron has well and truly violated the accords by nearly having us *killed* – and by the Order of Xiska, no less. There is no salvaging this."

The words did not sit well with Jasper; "us", and not "them". It made sense that Dante would have been at the embassy during the aforementioned explosion, but what had transpired beforehand...? In a span of days, Jasper had nearly lost his closest friends, his family. It was a troubling thought, one that impacted him even more than the confirmation that there would be another war between Pharsat and Aethia.

"The curfew will be disastrous for Caelfall," Charlotte remarked quietly, drawing the attention of everyone in the room. "We have to warn as many people as we can. Can we use the *Jackdaw* broadcast to spread the word?"

A vein throbbed in Gideon's forehead as he turned towards Jasper. He could only shake his head subtly in response as Varus pondered the question, rubbing his chin idly. "We can, we've already distributed the frequency with the paper," he thought aloud, his stare distant. "But we don't air until eight, and that may not be enough time."

"I could pass along the warning to the Sisterhood," Cary suggested from the doorway, a pensive smile on her face. "Information circulates well amongst the brothel and its clientele."

Before the knight could question another nugget of information, Jasper interrupted. "Haeyin also said he'd notify anyone who came into the clinic today."

The Valedian king seemed troubled, even with the

suggestions that had been made. "What is the population of this district?" he asked the princess.

Shaking her head, the young woman appeared mournful. "Large enough that despite all of our combined efforts, I fear we will be at a disadvantage," Princess Aurelia pointed out.

"The city guard will be authorized to use whatever force they deem necessary," Gideon said slowly, purpose lacing each word as he held Varus' gaze. "The townsfolk won't stand a chance."

"Quite right," Varus agreed immediately, and Jasper was familiar with the determined expression on the man's face. "Our only option may very well be to fight."

There was a terse beat of silence as each of them pondered Varus' words, knowing what it meant to willfully strike against the king's men. There would be no turning back from this, no amount of apology that could excuse what would be considered treason.

King Fenyang appeared to be deep in thought, formulating a plan. "Forgive me, but I am unfamiliar with the layout of this city," he admitted, searching the faces of their allies. "Do we have safe houses that civilians can be directed towards, should we encounter them on the streets tonight? Our priority should be removing as many people from harm's way as possible."

"I should emphasize that *you* will not be taking part in this raid," Varus pointed out, gesturing towards the king. "I appreciate your enthusiasm, but we gain nothing if you're captured or killed tonight."

Beside the princess, Fortia raised an eyebrow as she regarded the young woman. "I couldn't agree more," she added pointedly, as if this was a conversation that had already transpired between them.

Sighing, Princess Aurelia idly rubbed at her temple. "Regrettably, I fear I mustn't take part for similar reasons," she replied in begrudging agreement. "It further harms our shared goal for peace if we perish in the affair."

Dante raised a hand tentatively, as if seeking permission to interrupt. "Eodan, would it be possible to house civilians here? How many people can we accommodate in this manor?"

"We have room for more," Varus assured him, nodding slowly. His brow remained furrowed, and Jasper guessed the dilemma before his employer continued. "We need something localized to Caelfall, though. Getting everyone across the bridge into Dornkeep could prove difficult."

A thought crossed Jasper's mind, and he cursed himself for not having mentioned it sooner. "The cellar of the bakery, could we keep people there safely?" he asked Charlotte.

Something flashed in her eyes, but it was gone before Jasper could attempt to process it. "Yes, that could work," she agreed softly.

"There are also entrances to the catacombs scattered throughout Caelfall," Gideon suggested. "Not ideal for the elderly or those with impaired mobility, but there's an option as well."

The flames crackled in the background as Varus exchanged glances between King Fenyang, Fortia, and Princess Aurelia, his face lined with consternation. "This was not what I had hoped would come of this," he emphasized in a low voice.

Shaking his head, King Fenyang clapped the kingpin on the shoulder. "I still have hope yet that we might see peace in my lifetime," he said earnestly, and despite the circumstances surrounding them, the king seemed sincere in his optimism. "I will advise my council and the embassy staff of our plans, they may wish to volunteer for our rebellion as well."

Affixing her dark spectacles over her trembling eyes, the princess bowed her head towards the Valedian king. "As always, I share this hope and I will never cease in my efforts to achieve it," Princess Aurelia assured them. "I must take my leave, but I will do what I can."

The warrior offered the princess her arm, guiding her around the furniture in the sitting room as they made their exit. Passing Cary in the doorway, Fortia met the woman's eyes with a subtle nod of her head, and the assassin followed her and Princess Aurelia out of the manor. King Fenyang exited the room shortly afterwards, presumably to seek out his council.

Before leaving the space himself, Varus paused before Jasper and his friends. Conflict and dread warred in his expression as he regarded the four of them, raking his fingers through his hair as he heaved a sigh. "I would not think any less of you, should you decline to take part in this," Varus addressed them. "This is no small feat, and you can still help our cause if you remain in the safety of the manor and help with whatever injured civilians are brought here."

Not expecting an immediate response, their host left them alone with their thoughts in the now quiet sitting room, the last embers of the fire smouldering softly. Jasper turned his head to glance down at Charlotte, finding her eyes were already trained on him. He had promised her that he would be careful, and her pained words from the night she had arrived at the estate had haunted him ever since.

She seemed to understand his despair, as she always did.

Her eyes glittered with unshed tears even as she nodded slowly, a pained smile on her face. "What choice do we have?" Charlotte replied shakily, and he knew that she understood. He could not stand aside and do nothing, not when their home was in danger.

Dante glanced back and forth, rubbing his arms with his bandaged hands. "Perhaps this reflects poorly on my self-preservation, but I have every intention of fighting," he admitted in agreement.

Gideon laughed at the remark, crossing his arms over his chest. "I never thought I'd say this, but if I die defending citizens from the wrath of an unhinged king, I would consider it my highest honour."

"If we need to use the bakery as a safehouse... someone needs to brief Samuel on this first," Jasper said slowly.

To his dismay, the prospect of the task seemed to incite a panic. "I don't—I can't... I can't go back," Charlotte stammered at his side. His heart sank at the despair on her face, and Jasper struggled to parse a sentence that would honour what his best friend, what his *person* was going through.

Gratefully, Dante seemed to have a better mastery of words than Jasper possessed. "It doesn't have to be you," he offered at Charlotte's apprehension, stepping forward to place a tentative hand on Charlotte's shoulder. "We can talk to him on your behalf. Besides, I'm sure he'd appreciate an update that you're safe."

Her lip trembled as she regarded the three of them, her eyes lined with tears. "I don't want to hide while you risk your lives," Charlotte protested. "I want to help."

"Charlie, you stabbed the king," Gideon pointed out, his face spreading in a dimpled grin. "You've already done more for this rebellion than most."

"That just made everything worse!" she moaned, but a small smile had made its way onto her face.

Shaking his head, Dante squeezed her shoulder. "He was never going to make it easy for the Valedian council," he explained sullenly. "No matter what we did, he would have found a way to cheat the accords."

Heaving a shuddering breath, Charlotte squeezed her eyes shut as she shook her head. "He doesn't know what happened," she whispered softly. "My father. He'll be so angry."

"*At the king*," Gideon emphasized. "And rightfully so. There's not a person in this room who doesn't want to finish the job for what he's done, to you and to others."

There was a question on Jasper's mind, a question he knew would hurt but demanded to be asked. Meeting his gaze, it seemed Dante shared his thoughts. "Do you want us to tell him what happened?" the man asked hesitantly. "If you don't want him to know, we won't say anything. But... seeing as we're headed out that way, if it's easier to have someone else talk to him about it..."

Charlotte was silent for a moment as her friends watched and waited for her decision. "If he asks... please don't lie to him," she instructed at last. "And tell him that I'm safe, and that I'm here at the manor doing my part to help."

He loved her. He had never loved her more. As he regarded the bravery in her eyes, even as Charlotte was coming apart at the seams, Jasper decided then and there that he would do anything to protect her, to keep her safe. It was the easiest thing in the world to tug on her hand, to pull her into the circle of Jasper's arms as he embraced her. There was no sensation of hornets between his ears at her touch, no agitated thrum of anxiety in his chest. There was only the warmth of Charlotte, his mind comfortingly quiet as they stood there together.

When Jasper, Dante, and Gideon were certain that Charlotte was stable enough to be left alone, the three of them departed for Caelfall once more to recruit a certain baker to their cause.

It had been one of the most uncomfortable conversations he'd ever been forced to have with Charlotte's father. Samuel *had* asked, and Jasper had been forced to explain in as kind words as he could manage what had transpired. He was endlessly grateful to have had Dante and Gideon at his side, for the moment Samuel learned what had happened to his daughter, he was understandably furious. He was livid at what King Gustaf had committed, but also that Jasper had lied to him about what was going on.

"It wasn't our business to share," Dante had protested, seeking to settle the antagonistic tone of the conversation. "Charlotte has been dealing with this the only way she knows how, and she hasn't even verbalized what happened to her – we've just pieced it together."

After several moments spent witnessing a father's despair at what fate had befallen his daughter, Samuel's rage settled into a smouldering grief. The bakery was closed briefly while they explained the issue of the curfew, the need for a safe shelter for civilians affected by it. Jasper watched as a man he had known all his life took on a demeanour he had never seen before, a darkness entering his eyes as his resolve was fortified.

"You're certain Charlotte is safe at that manor?" Samuel asked in a hoarse voice.

"Safe as houses," Gideon had insisted solemnly.

When Dante and Jasper agreed with Gideon's senti-ment, the baker nodded once. "Then you can send whoever you need to here. My door will be open."

What little time remained of the afternoon was devoted to whatever preparations the men could take. Jasper had recently finished another garrison commission, and he'd volunteered the completed weapons to put towards the armoury Varus kept at the manor. His recently washed laundry was shoved into a satchel, as Jasper had every intention of remaining at the Melicus estate with Charlotte until she was ready to return home. While Dante and Gideon gathered the weapons into crates to take back to the manor with them, Jasper made one last trip up to the bedroom of his flat for a frivolous, personal venture.

Setting down the satchel at the doorway, Jasper kneeled down before his dresser to rummage in the bottom drawer. There was one more thing he wanted, one thing he half-recalled the location of. Buried amidst old belongings and clothes, there was a small box swaddled amongst the rest of his uncle Zeke's belongings. It had remained there since his death, a dead dream too painful to be remembered.

The stairs creaking behind him revealed Gideon's arrival before the man spoke. "We're just about ready to go," he announced from the doorway. Jasper could picture the way the man's brow would furrow as he paused, analyzing whatever it was he was witnessing. "What's that you've got?"

Opening the box, Jasper regarded the two rings nestled snugly within the satin lining. "Zeke made these for my parents," he explained in a low voice, as if even now his uncle might scold him for touching something that wasn't his to touch. He'd never understood as a child why Zeke had kept the rings, why his parents had been buried without their wedding bands. It wasn't until after his uncle had passed that Jasper had understood that he was conceived out of wedlock, that what should have been a declaration of love was simultaneously a shameful secret.

Shoving the drawer shut, Jasper pocketed the ring box as he stood. Gideon had gone quiet, standing very still as his gaze followed that box. "We should get going," the man said at last. He turned and exited the room, descending the steps ahead of Jasper. They met Dante outside with the weapons and supplies stocked in the loaned wagon, and the three of them made their way back to Dornkeep.

Good evening, everybody… before we begin our regular broadcast, a warning for any of you planning to be out late this evening. Without warning or notice, our dear, dear King Gus has decreed a most unusual curfew this evening, at the tender hour of nine o'clock tonight.

His Majesty would have you believe that such a decision is in the interest of safety, an abundance of caution as the kingdom tirelessly searches for the culprit behind the monarch's attempted assassination. However, this is a lie. In truth, dearest Gustaf searches for the witnesses to his own crimes – his savage mistreatment of the Valedian council, his repeated abuse of vulnerable women.

To those of you listening, I implore you to stay home, if you can. To those of you who can't, fear not. You will have allies in the streets this night, and we will do everything in our power to protect you.

Do not serve a false king.

. . .

Night settled over Caelfall swiftly, a premature darkness brought on by the swollen storm clouds that obscured the setting sun. The smell of impending rain was prominent as Jasper stood beside Gideon, the sensation of his leather armour grounding him even as worry threatened to consume him. Their warnings had reached as many people as they could, but there was more work to be done.

After their host at the Melicus estate had briefed their allies, Varus had been forced to consolidate his two personas. Gideon had not taken the news of Jasper's employment by a kingpin very well, but begrudgingly agreed it was neither the time nor place for that discussion. Despite Dante's surprise, Jasper noted that the Valedian king seemed not to be startled by the information that had been delivered.

Varus and King Fenyang had divided the district into zones, with volunteers being assigned to defend their neighbourhood and direct civilians to wherever their nearest safehouse was located. Jasper and Gideon had immediately partnered up, with Cary volunteering to join them. Another Silent Sisterhood assassin named Sasha was allocated to complete the group, and the four of them were assigned to the same area of the marketplace where Jasper and Cary had once witnessed a public execution. The assassins were tasked with defending the entrance to the catacombs in their zone, while Jasper and Gideon would direct citizens towards the safety of the underground. In the distance, Jasper could see the forms of Varus, Haeyin, and Rosaline where they patrolled the town square. The Madame had insisted upon joining their cause the moment she was alerted to the curfew dilemma.

There was an eerie quiet that settled over the city at night with the absence of the townsfolk. He and Gideon had directed as many civilians as they could towards the safehouses before the curfew officially began, and Jasper could only pray it would be enough. While Cary was spinning one of her knives idly around her fingers, Jasper was thumbing the hilt of a sword of his own make. It was strange to think he had changed so much, that at the beginning of this year Jasper would have insisted upon fighting with his bare hands rather than a weapon... yet here he was, fidgeting with a sword to ease his anxiety.

The thought of change brought the skeletal image of Death to his mind, a half-remembered dream from another lifetime. As Cary wandered nearer, Jasper found himself asking, "Cary, do you still have those cards with you?"

The woman's face was almost entirely obscured, a mask up to her nose and a thick leather hood revealing only her rose-hued eyes. She regarded Jasper with what might have been a quizzical expression, tilting her head as the silence stretched on. Jasper was about to ask again, to offer more details as if he might jog her memory – but of course, Cary was at work as an assassin of the Silent Sisterhood.

"Never mind, I... I forgot about the whole silence bit," he murmured under his breath. He could have sworn Sasha was silently laughing at him nearby, but Cary's eyes never left his face.

As if sensing that this would be the only peace and quiet they saw this evening, Gideon gently nudged Jasper with his elbow to draw his attention. "How long have you known all these people?" he asked quietly, nodding his head towards the town square where Varus and his group were patrolling in the distance. The former knight was sporting a loaned eyepatch, courtesy of Varus; it contributed to what

Jasper could only describe as an overall intimidating appearance.

Jasper paused as he sifted through his memories. "Some I've known longer than others," he explained. "You might have already heard of Haeyin, since he's been Charlotte's doctor for a few years now. We met Cary while she was working at the clinic with him, and we crossed paths with her on the food drive as well. As for Varus... I'd never heard of him until last winter." He declined to divulge meeting Madame Rosaline at *The Raw Diamond*.

The other man nodded slowly, deep in thought. He regarded Jasper with a conflicted expression, as if he were assessing him before he continued. "This was... after the incident at the academy, I take it?" Gideon guessed.

Jasper could feel his face heating in the darkness at the shameful memory. "Yes," he admitted, turning away. "Not immediately, but... yes, after."

His friend was silent for a moment, and Jasper could sense the weight of his stare on his face. "I was worried about you, you know," Gideon offered, his voice soft. "Seeing you like that, and then... *not* seeing or hearing from you for weeks, I—I was worried about you."

Swallowing a lump in his throat, Jasper struggled to find the words to respond. Gods, he wanted to tell Gideon everything. He'd hated not being able to talk to him, and now more than ever Jasper was craving the comfort of his friends.

"Are you feeling better now, at least?" Gideon asked, drawing him from his reverie. When Jasper managed to nod, he dared a glance up at his friend. There was a sad sort of smile on Gideon's face, the corner of his eye strained as he regarded Jasper.

"That's all that matters, then," he affirmed, but that

conflicted expression remained. He hesitated to continue for so long that Jasper was startled when the man spoke again. "Jasper, I…"

Whatever Gideon had been about to say was interrupted by the sound of echoing shouts, a woman screaming in the distance. Jasper sprung into action immediately, sprinting towards the source of the sound. He knew instinctively that Gideon would follow as he jogged north, darting down an alleyway snaking towards his left. The curfew had fallen, and the first of the townsfolk were suffering the wrath of the king's men.

There were two women in the alleyway, one standing protectively in front of an elderly man as he recovered from being knocked to the floor. The forms of three knights of the city guard were looming over them, prepared to strike again. Overtaking Jasper, Gideon reached the offending city guards first, frighteningly quick as he shoved the nearest knight backwards. Jasper set to work helping the old man to his feet, gesturing for the women to move away from the guard.

"Can you make it to the crone statue in the graveyard?" Jasper asked them, searching the women's faces for recognition. The faded stone relief of the aged hag was one of the many entrances into the catacombs, and the nearest to their current location. The shorter of the two nodded quickly as she linked arms with the elderly man, and Jasper urged them to run as he drew his sword, joining Gideon as he fought off the guards.

Had he been alone, Jasper wasn't certain he would have stood a chance against the king's men. The knights of the city guard had more training than he did, more experience. It took all of his strength and his focus to parry their strikes, his only advantage being taller and heavier than they were.

On the other hand, Gideon fought like a demon. He had been holding back when he was sparring with Jasper – tonight, he unleashed the full fury of his abilities against his former comrades. He disarmed the tallest of the three with a sly feint, dancing around the guard before embedding his sword between the gap in his armour, deep beneath the other man's armpit. The guard made a strangled sound between a groan and a wheeze as Gideon removed his sword with a flourish, the knight's limp form dropping to the floor in a heap.

Screwing his courage, Jasper's grip on his sword tightened as he blocked the strikes of one of the two remaining guards. Something akin to fury blazed through his veins as his thoughts drifted to Charlotte, drifted to the truth that knights like this had allowed something so terrible to happen to her. He altered his tactics, mirroring the way in which Gideon sidestepped the enemy's attacks before exploiting their weaknesses. The guard's helmet was knocked from his head with a clang as Jasper flipped his sword, striking the man's jaw with a savage swing. There was an odd, sickening crack before the man's body fell to a heap on the cobblestones – and did not rise again.

Despite every instinct telling him to move, Jasper froze. For a moment, nothing existed outside of the guard's vacant eyes as he lay motionless on the ground, the unnatural angle of his neck as the bones jutted out. Jasper had never killed anyone in his life.

He was only distantly aware of the *thud* of a corpse, dropped to the ground in a heap as Gideon dispatched the last guard. The man was at Jasper's side in an instant. "Jas, look at me," he instructed, and there was no room for argument in his voice. Jasper managed to tear his eyes away from the dead guard to meet his friend's stare. "He would have killed you without a second thought. You did what you had to do, all right?"

His own heartbeat sounded distant. Jasper had known this was a possibility, known he couldn't avoid the finality of combat forever – but there was the idea of murder, and then there was the reality of the guard he had killed with what he had intended to be a stunning strike. Varus had attempted to brief them all on this before they had departed the manor, anticipating the casualties on both sides this night.

There is no room for disarming blows and stunning strikes. Do not fight as if surrender is an acceptable outcome. These men will not hesitate to kill you.

"Listen to me, Jasper," Gideon pleaded, and he reached out to grip Jasper's shoulder. He flinched at the physical contact, but Gideon wasn't finished. "We don't have the luxury of time to address how you're feeling right now, and I'm sorry. I will sit with you later and we'll drink as much as you need to forgive yourself for this, but you *need* to wake up and survive the rest of the night, you hear me?"

Drawing a deep breath, Jasper managed to nod. When it seemed Gideon was convinced that Jasper wasn't about to unravel in the middle of the street, he released his shoulder and took a step back. As Gideon had predicted, there was no time to analyze what had occurred; Caelfall resonated with the panicked shouts and cries of its citizens as the guards began to seize as many people as they could. His grip on his sword tightened as he forced himself to compress that complicated swarm of thoughts, shoving the guilt and shame to the back of his mind with all the other shadows he could not bear to stare into.

He would be forced to kill again. He could not afford to hesitate.

They were not the only ones fighting back against their oppressors on the streets that night. Some of the townsfolk were sellswords, employed in other districts for the strength and agility they now utilized against the guards as they attempted to apprehend them. Renegade mages were the first to resist arrest, and Jasper almost pitied the guard he witnessed set aflame by a familiar merchant. Jasper and Gideon pounded down the cobblestone streets, rescuing every stranded innocent they came across. Within an hour, Jasper's hands grew bloodied with the guards he struck as well as the civilians he could not save, and he wasn't sure whose demise would haunt him more.

Gideon had remained at his side until they came across a group of children who were unfamiliar with the crone statue. "Make sure they get there safely," Gideon instructed Jasper as he gestured for the children to follow him. "I can manage on my own for a bit."

His instincts warred against the instruction, demanding he remain at Gideon's side, but Jasper knew better than to argue. He waved at the five children, wide-eyed and frightened as they stared up at him. The walk to the graveyard was not a long one, but it was perilous with the current circumstances. Gratefully, what city guards they came across were already occupied with rebel townsfolk, oblivious as Jasper skulked past with the children in tow.

Cary was nowhere to be found, but Sasha was hunched behind the shape of another of the tombstones, keeping an eye out for any stray city guards. Jasper reached for the crone statue's left hand, the stone giving way to reveal a narrow entryway descending into the underground.

"Stay together, keep walking until you see the rest of the group," Jasper instructed, keeping the doorway open until each of the five children had made it safely through the passage. Stepping over the graves to where Sasha sat nearby, Jasper crouched down beside her.

"Where's Cary?" he asked.

From the silent sister, there came no reply – not that he had expected one, but Sasha had found non-verbal means of communicating with him before. He gently nudged her shoulder, thinking perhaps she hadn't heard him speak, and Sasha promptly slumped to the floor.

Jasper gazed at the girl's wide, flat stare, the blade in her neck. She had been carefully positioned against the gravestone, the emblem of a magpie visible along the hilt of the dagger wedged in her throat.

How long had she been dead?

He was on his feet in seconds, sprinting from the graveyard towards the city streets. Jasper didn't know what was going on, but he knew he needed to find Gideon. There was a hiss underfoot as he narrowly avoided stomping on a stray animal, the dark shape of a cat darting away from him as Jasper bolted. He lazily deflected a few stray blows from stragglers who had broken away from their group, wounded city guards and panic-stricken civilians. He shoved a guard to the side, his shoulder screaming in protest at the impact of the metal plate armour. Jasper didn't stop to process the sensation, the only feeling he was consciously aware of was the blood that pounded through his veins, roaring in his ears as he ran.

His heart thundered in his chest as he turned the corner to see Gideon fighting to the death – not against a knight of the city guard, but a familiar assassin of the Silent Sisterhood. The bodies of guards and townsfolk alike littered the ground as the two struck in rapid succession. Jasper couldn't run fast enough, as if time had unnaturally slowed, his sword gripped so tightly in his hand that his knuckles burned.

Gideon was a better warrior than Jasper, but everyone underestimated Cary.

Her hood had fallen from her face, her mask discarded as they fought. He had managed to bloody her nose, and she succeeded in cutting his face. They were a whirlwind of blades, and Gideon seemed to be holding his own... until a well-placed strike to his blind spot sent him stumbling backwards, his hand grasping the exposed ruby necklace around Cary's throat. Her next strike cleaved through Gideon's wrist, but not before the string of jewels came apart in his fingers.

"*Gideon!*" Jasper bellowed. Cary looked up at him then, her eyes dark as night as she grinned at him. Jasper raised his sword arm, prepared to strike—

There was a sharp pain in the back of his head. His knees buckled, and he knew no more.

ACT III
AUTUMN

AMENDMENT TO THE MAGE LAWS ACT (cont.)
As per His Majesty King Gustaf Edmund Davenport III:

Persons in contravention of the mage laws under this act shall be tried for wrongful use of magic.

Persons found to be willfully evading census registration and wristlet assignment shall be tried for non-conformance.

In the event of mortal peril or cataclysmic harm to Aethia and its people, His Majesty King Gustaf Edmund Davenport III reserves the authority to execute the mage protocol for registered mages within a region. Under this provision, all mages registered with county census and in possession of decreed wristlets will be subsequently nullified.

CHAPTER
SIXTEEN
DANTE

BENEATH THE LIGHT OF THE MOON, CAELFALL SAW AN unfair amount of carnage, the cobblestone streets bathed in blood. Donning a loaned set of armour from the Sisterhood, Dante had been assigned to the mouth of the bridge connecting Dornkeep to the southern district. His task was simple enough; allow fleeing and wounded civilians through, keep the city guards out.

The evening had started off according to plan. Varus had organized their allies strategically, coordinating individual and team strengths with the varying geography of Caelfall. Upon alerting the Silent Sisterhood, their figurehead Madame Rosaline had insisted on lending her forces to their cause, giving them just enough spread to cover the southern and eastern districts of Aethelind. Many of the assassins were hidden in pockets of shadow throughout the eastern district, defending the manor where their allies maintained a stronghold.

He hadn't initially wanted this assignment. Jasper had been assigned further towards the heart of the neighbourhood, closer to the town square. Dante's instinct had been to stay with his friend, but the groupings were capped at four to ensure they had enough people dispersed across Caelfall. Cary had beaten him to the punch, and so King Fenyang had found a use for Dante in protecting the most important component of their operation that night. At his side, Natalya of the Silent Sisterhood defended the bridge, daring any city guard seeking a quick demise to cross their paths. To Dante's surprise, Benkaei had volunteered to join him as well, the king's second-in-command electing to ignore Varus' suggestion that she remain with the rest of the council at the manor.

His childhood may have been spent suppressing his magic, but Dante had not been raised to be helpless. The first of the guards who attempted to apprehend them for being out after hours met a quick death at his hand, one of Jasper's daggers serving as a seamless extension of his arm. Benkaei had seemed to be pleasantly surprised at the evidence that Dante had been trained as a warrior, a smirk crossing her expression as she nodded approvingly. The Sisterhood assassin's tactics were frightfully similar to his own, the majority of her strikes aimed at the soft throats of the guards who wandered towards them.

He had lost track of how many injured townsfolk had been permitted to pass through, his focus trained on ensuring that none of the king's men had followed them across the bridge to Dornkeep. There was an echo against his mind, a recognizable brush of death magic. *"Dante."*

Tentative, measured footsteps behind them managed to draw Dante's attention away from Caelfall. Huda had left her post back at the manor, meeting them at the entrance to the southern district. A flexible cane in one hand, Huda used the device to navigate the uneven surface as she approached, her free hand guiding her along the barrier at the side of the bridge.

"What's wrong?" Benkaei asked immediately, her watchful stare still scanning the shadowed alleyways of Caelfall.

The necromancer's nostrils flared as she took in the scent of deceased guards and civilians, the stench filling the air as their blood pooled against the stone. "There are too many wounded for Eleni and Hasima to attend to," Huda explained. "We need Haeyin back at the manor."

Benkaei and Natalya exchanged glances with one another. "Go, Dante," the king's second-in-command instructed him immediately, as if sensing the conflict. "You're more familiar with these streets than I am. We can manage for now."

Noting the hole in their defenses that would result when Dante left his post, Huda stretched her hand towards the bodies on the floor. Her voice an ominous undercurrent to the rumble of thunder above them, she chanted a forbidden incantation in rushed Pharasathi that Dante could only partially understand. Fallen. Reform. *Rise*.

The forms of the guards began to twist and shift, melting into a mass of viscera and magic. A gargantuan form rose from the carcasses of the city guard, a golem of flesh and bone at Huda's command. The mighty fiend stood at Natalya's side, supplementing the absence of Dante.

Sensing his presence was no longer required here, Dante wasted no more time in sprinting towards Caelfall. It was a blessing that Haeyin used his magical talents for heal-ing, because the man was a terrifyingly powerful force. Anticipating the highest volume of guards at the town square, Haeyin had been assigned there alongside Rosaline and Eodan – rather, *Varus*. The change in identity still hadn't settled in his mind, and Dante had already misspoken multiple times that evening.

The night darkened into an inky blackness as the heavens opened, rain spattering Dante's face as he ducked through the alleyways he had grown accustomed to these past few months. There were ally casualties here as well as civilians, and he stared far too long into the vacant expres-sions of cadavers searching for Jasper's face. Dante knew he was getting closer to Haeyin as the bodies of the guards he encountered were less and less intact. Magical warfare rarely left a clean corpse.

He saw Haeyin's magic before he saw him, the golden glow of his power illuminating the square briefly with each strike. The market stalls had been set aflame, either inten-tionally by the king's men or accidentally by the mages who worked to defend the city. A crackle of scarlet electricity revealed Rosaline nearby, her fine overcoat illuminated by the magic that snaked across lampposts and along cobble-stones before dissipating. He couldn't see Varus in the dark-ness, but he must have been nearby.

Summoning a facet of his power, Dante sent a flare of his energy towards Haeyin in the distance as he closed the gap, jogging towards them. The doctor's gaze snapped towards Dante even as his grip remained taught on the guard in his hands. His open palm spread over the man's face glowed molten as the energy surged from Haeyin, burning the guard from the inside out.

It seemed a horrible way to die.

"What's the matter?" Haeyin called out to him, the golden light fading from his irises and the veins in his face as he dropped the smouldering form of the city guard.

The din of marching footsteps in the distance alerted them to the presence of a new wave of enemies, urging Dante to accelerate the exchange. "Eleni needs you," he replied quickly, his chest tightening with the exertion of bolting across the city. "There's too many injured at the manor, more than her and Hasima can handle."

Haeyin's emotions warred openly across his face, and Dante knew him well enough by now to know what troubled him. Following the loss of Verdis, they had weighed the consequences of leaving Haeyin at home as a doctor or bringing him to the field of battle, as both scenarios had differing advantages and disadvantages. They had eventually decided on having him on the streets, both as a warrior and a field medic... but they'd had no way of knowing this would be the outcome.

The sound of gunshots startled both of them, and instinctively Dante and Haeyin ducked down at the sound. A quick assessment of himself and the doctor assured Dante that they hadn't been hit – but who had fired the shots? None of the city guard they had encountered had been carrying firearms...

The storm overhead illuminated the square in a flash of light, and Dante saw a hundred soldiers as they marched towards them, previously concealed in shadow. The front of the group had fired into the square, one of them succeeding in striking Rosaline, the bloodstain that bloomed across her torso barely visible in the glow of her crimson lightning. As she staggered to her knees, her power sparked along the cobblestones to connect with a puddle of water—

"*Varus!*" Haeyin screamed over the calamity as crimson

lightning coursed through a dozen of the soldiers, connected by the puddle of water. There was a chilling, strangled chorus of agony from the men and women as they convulsed with the electricity, sustained until Rosaline collapsed into a heap on the floor of the square.

The soldiers that remained were readying their rifles, but faster than Dante could comprehend, their enemies had vanished behind a wall of fathomless darkness. Appearing seemingly from nowhere, Varus was already in the process of hauling Rosaline into his arms. "Take her, quickly," he instructed Dante and Haeyin as he assisted the woman into a seated position. His dark eyes locked on Dante before he continued. "I need you to shield the bodies of the soldiers she just felled."

Dante blinked, stunned by the request. "I—I don't know how," he admitted pitifully.

Despite the situation they found themselves in, Varus did not chastise his inexperience. "Picture it in your mind, the shape you want your magic to take," the kingpin instructed him, his voice astonishingly calm. "Focus on it, *do not* break your concentration."

The man turned away, leaving Haeyin to support Rosaline's weakened form. Dante did as he was told, struggling somewhat with the unfamiliar command on his magic. It was as if he were exercising a muscle he hadn't known to use, instructing it to follow his will instead of unleashing it in the form of an unrelenting storm. He recalled the shield that Huda had summoned at the palace, willing his power to adopt the same, protective form around the corpses. With some effort, silver light glimmered around them, a bubble of magic surrounding the bodies.

The wall of night that had blocked the advancing soldiers melted away with a lazy flick of Varus' wrist.

Collecting one of the fallen firearms from the ground, Varus fired into the sky as lightning snaked across the clouds. "Soldiers of Aethelind!" he roared as he stalked towards them, discarding the gun without a second thought. "This battle is over."

The shadows around the man grew long and dark, swallowing the firelight that glowed across the slick cobblestones. Dante felt very cold suddenly as he watched Varus disappear into that void, darkness consuming him and the soldiers that advanced towards him.

A hand reached up to grab Dante's wrist, and he was tugged forcefully to the ground beside Haeyin and Rosaline. The dark-haired woman had one hand pressed into the bloodied mess of the wound in her abdomen, the other in a death grip on Haeyin's wrist as he flooded his energy into a shield that encompassed the three of them. Through the golden dome of light, Dante could see and hear nothing beyond the inky blackness of the void that Varus had conjured. He could feel the dark presence of that power against the shield he had been commanded to summon, the cold nothingness that pressed against it.

The darkness dissipated at last, and beyond the golden dome Dante could see a lone figure illuminated by the firelight. Haeyin dissolved the shield as Dante stood, his hands trembling with the exertion of maintaining his own shield on the soldiers' corpses. What remained of their enemies was a bloodied mess of entrails and armour, not a single combatant left whole in the town square. Even the stray animals that had wandered the streets that night had been slaughtered, forever frozen in their panicked attempts to flee the violent death that had seized them. In the middle of the bloodbath, Varus stood alone, frighteningly still.

As he released his magic over the bodies he had been

commanded to protect, Dante was speechless. He understood now what he had sensed from the man standing before him, all those months ago in a carriage destined for the Valedian embassy. It was not merely magic, of that Dante could now be certain. This was something else, something older and darker and unfathomably dangerous.

Varus turned at last, seeming understandably exhausted. "I'll take Haeyin and Rosaline to the manor," he said, as if nothing had happened. Despite the knee brace visible on his leg, he seemed to limp more heavily as he crossed the square, assisting Haeyin as they lifted the woman to her feet. "Dante, use those soldiers to barricade the northern bridge to Aerindale. Find as many of our allies as you can and advise them to fall back."

He stared meaningfully at Dante, and with a jolt he realized the man was waiting for a response. The moment he nodded, the three people in front of him disappeared from sight, a cold wind caressing Dante's face. Varus had alluded to his mastery of teleportation in the briefing… but seeing it in action was another matter entirely.

Grounding himself in preparation for a long night, Dante set to work before more soldiers could arrive from Briardeen. His hands still trembled as he raised them towards the dozen cadavers he had preserved, embedding his power into each of them. They were relatively undamaged, marked only by vicious exit wounds from the electricity that had flooded their bodies. Dante kept two of them as his escorts, sending the remaining ten towards the mouth of the bridge to prevent any further unwanted visitors from the north.

He began his recon mission in the area where Jasper had been originally assigned. To his dismay, neither his friend nor the former knight Gideon were anywhere to be found. Dante rationalized it to the best of his ability, refusing to allow himself to panic. Jasper and Gideon had grown up in these streets; surely, they had utilized this knowledge to branch out and help others in the immediate vicinity.

Forcing himself to carry on, Dante alerted as many groups of their allies as he could. Some of them were still fighting stray city guards, and he was quick to lend his own blades to the combat if not the blades of his borrowed soldiers. It took some patience to convince the stranded civilians that the reanimated bodies were not threats, but eventually Dante had sufficient townsfolk already following him that he was deemed a friendly enough ally to allow for the strange company.

His final stop was the bakery, half a dozen stragglers following him as he knocked four times against the front door. The blinds parted briefly, a pair of blue eyes barely visible through the frosted glass before the door opened.

"We've not much room for more," Samuel warned even as he beckoned the newcomers into the bakery.

Dante gestured for them to follow the baker's instructions, waving the townsfolk into the shop. "The worst of it is over, I hope," he offered in reply. "Keep them here overnight, there may still be more of the king's men about. They called in the soldiers to assist."

Samuel's expression darkened as the last of the civilians scampered into the safety of the bakery, his eyes darting back and forth as he scanned the streets beyond. "Is Jasper still fighting?" he asked.

Not wanting to admit he had yet to find the blacksmith, Dante opted for a half-lie. "I haven't met up with him yet, I'll rendezvous with him soon."

The baker seemed to study his expression for a while,

and for half a moment Dante wondered if he had seen through the casual tone of his voice. "You be careful, all right?" he instructed in a gruff voice at last. Samuel shut the door firmly, leaving Dante and his two cadavers in the unnerving silence of Caelfall.

He made his way back towards Jasper and Gideon's zone, not wanting to dwell on any negative possibility. Dante's hopes that his worries would be assuaged by their presence were dashed the moment he arrived at that disturbingly empty area of the marketplace once more, though there was plenty of evidence of their passing. The guards that had been cut down by Jasper and Gideon were notable from those that Dante guessed were dispatched by Cary and Sasha, another of the Silent Sisterhood assassins.

As he neared the graveyard, he nearly collided with the form of Varus as the kingpin appeared from out of nowhere once more. "For the love of—must you keep doing that!?" Dante demanded as he all but crashed into the floor, his corpse soldiers steadying him dutifully before he could faceplant into graveyard dirt.

Varus tilted his head as he regarded him, a bemused expression on his face. It was strange to see the man look so human after Dante had witnessed the catastrophic damage he had unleashed upon the town square. "You should come and take a look at this," Varus said quietly, turning towards one of the graves at their feet.

Following his line of sight, Dante frowned at the still form of a woman in the dirt. He hadn't initially recognized her, but he saw now that she was not one of the guards, or even a soldier. Her night-black armour was that of the Silent Sisterhood, most her face concealed by dark fabric… and given their location was within Jasper and Gideon's domain, this must have been Sasha.

Her body was clean, with no visible injuries aside from the knife embedded in the base of her throat. The likeness to the way that Natalya had fought alongside him, the similar corpses of soldiers Dante had witnessed as he moved through the city... Frowning, Dante turned towards the kingpin – and the expression on the man's conflicted face suggested Varus' thoughts mirrored his own.

"That's a strange cause of death, to be killed in a way that copies your own tactics," Dante found himself murmuring.

The man remained motionless as he held Dante's gaze. "Perhaps it wasn't copying," Varus replied quietly, almost too quietly for Dante to hear.

Caelfall had taken on a sinister atmosphere in the aftermath of the battle, the eerie quiet of the night threatening to drive Dante insane as he considered Varus' words. There was no one left alive to question what had happened, no witness to whoever had killed Sasha.

Unless...

Kneeling in the dirt, Dante regarded the fallen form of the woman, the way she lay curled defensively in the soil. He had a solution for this dilemma, but he hated himself for even considering it. Tentatively, he reached for Sasha's fingers, finding them cold but not yet rigor-stiffened. He had hoped for a logical excuse for his terrible plan not to work, but it seemed Dante was out of luck.

"What's on your mind?" Varus asked, but Dante was far away. His heart hammered in his chest as he contemplated what he was about to do, the sacrilegious act he would commit for the sake of his friend.

Necromancy may have been a slight to the Keepers, but this was an affront to *Rhanigan*.

Dante scooted closer towards Sasha, mentally apologizing to whoever's grave he currently stepped upon. Taking a breath, he reached into the depths of his power for the ability he knew he needed in order to find Jasper, to discover the truth of how Sasha had died. He visualized the tendril of his magic as it snaked through his fingers into Sasha's chilled skin, threading through her body as silvery light pooled in her irises.

She gasped wetly, writhing on the ground as her fingers reached for her throat, the outline of her mouth gaping beneath the fabric of her mask. "Listen to me, listen to me," Dante hissed, pulling her hand away from the weapon. "If you can remember who attacked you, I need to know their name."

Sasha blinked up at him, wide-eyed and silent. His research was off to a rocky start. He had moments, seconds to get an answer; reanimating a cadaver to fight mindlessly was one thing, but reanimating a corpse for conversation took far more effort. As the magical tether wavered, Dante was forced to release one of his cadavers, the dead weight collapsing behind him as he stole back some of his own power.

"Even if she hadn't taken a vow of silence, Sasha has never spoken," Varus offered solemnly, and Dante could feel the man's eyes boring into the back of his head as Sasha stared up at him.

Resisting the urge to groan, Dante released his hold on Sasha as he buried his face in his hands. "Can you... can you write it in the dirt? Point me in the right direction? I'm begging you—something, *anything*, please!"

There was the softest breath of a pained gasp, and Dante's eyes flew open. With her hand freed from his grasp, Sasha had pulled the dagger from her own throat as half-coagulated blood spilled from her neck. His other reanimated cadaver fell behind Dante with the physical strain, his heart pounding in his chest as his magic was diverted. Sasha presented that knife to Dante, holding it out in front of her until he took it.

"Thank you, Sasha," Dante replied earnestly, his voice trembling as he spoke. With a wave of his hand, he cut the tether that bound them. "Return to the Soul Keeper."

The silver light vanished from her irises as she grew still once more. Dante reached forward to gently close the assassin's eyes before he stood, turning to face Varus. The man was silent as Dante presented him with the knife, staring at the little dagger for a long, long time. Dante hadn't thought it was possible for a man of his complexion to look so pale. For a moment, he wondered if Varus would ask him what had just occurred, what sin Dante had committed in the hopes of gaining answers.

Instead, it seemed the kingpin had other priorities. "You should... I found something, something you should see," Varus croaked after a moment's pause. Without meeting Dante's stare, he stalked towards one of the alleyways nearby, not waiting to see if Dante was following him. With the knife still clenched in his fist, he jogged to keep up with the man, weaving through the narrow streets.

Dante had seen this particular corridor. He had glanced down it, noted that it was empty, and pressed on. There were no bodies here, but as Dante followed Varus down the alleyway he saw how wrong he had been. There was a severed hand discarded at the foot of a residence, a collection of rubies strewn across the cobblestones, and a familiar sword.

Dante's blood ran cold. "That's... that's..."

Varus finished for him. "Jasper's sword, aye," he

confirmed, nudging the blade with his foot. "And if I had to guess... I think that was either his or Gideon's."

Dante refused to look at the severed hand, suddenly feeling quite nauseated between the dismembered limb and his magical exhaustion. "Keepers," breathed Dante, raking his free hand through his hair.

The man was silent for a moment. "That knife belongs to Cary," Varus said at last, and Dante lost all capability for rational thought. The rubies gleamed amidst drying blood in the moonlight, and his breathing quickened.

"You're certain? Keepers—it was in Sasha's *throat*, Varus," Dante protested, as if the man hadn't witnessed his interaction with the deceased assassin. "I... I'd volunteered to go with Jasper, but Cary beat me to it—was she planning this all along? Varus—"

The man grasped Dante's shoulder, shocking him out of his spiral. "Dante, this is neither the time nor the place for this discussion," he said sternly, his dark gaze and stony expression unreadable. "We need to get back to the estate. We will have time to speculate later, but it does not serve us to stand here debating betrayal. This will have to wait."

Betrayal. "Right, right," Dante agreed, swallowing his anxiety.

Varus stared at him for a few moments more, as if gauging whether or not Dante remained on the verge of a panic attack. Seemingly assured of his ability to remain calm for now, he released Dante's shoulder as he stooped to collect the hand from the cobblestones. Dante's stomach turned at the sight of mangled flesh and bones, and he focused instead on Varus.

Extending his arm, the kingpin searched his face with an empathetic expression. "Take a breath, lad," Varus instructed him sternly as Dante took the man's arm. "We'll help Haeyin and Eleni finish tending to the wounded, and then we can discuss this properly."

Before nightfall, Dante had been warned by Jasper to close his eyes, should he find himself travelling with Varus in this way. In the heat of the moment, however, he forgot this sage advice. The shadow world they had been sucked into stretched and warped around him, and he lost sight of where he ended and the void began. Willowy caricatures of humans watched Dante as he fell through the shadows, their eyes hollow and their faces drawn in a long, silent scream. A crude impression of his mother reached for him, paper thin flesh beginning to crack across the too wide, too sharp smile—

They landed against the cobblestones with a thud, and Dante stumbled backwards as his foot caught the stone at an odd angle. Varus still had a firm grip on his arm, catching him before he split his head open on the pavement. "Mind your head, lad," he chided. Dante turned away and promptly emptied the contents of his stomach, while Varus patted his back comfortingly.

After a few moments of dry heaving, Dante gulped for air as he scrubbed the back of his hand across his mouth. "What in the name of Celüne was that!?" he gasped raggedly.

Varus didn't respond immediately. When Dante finally managed to straighten up, he thought the man seemed conflicted. "Come on, we're not safe out here," the kingpin replied at last, reaching for the iron gate that surrounded the estate ahead of them. Varus retracted his hand quickly as if he'd been burned, leading Dante through the dense layer of magical wards that covered the perimeter of the manor property. Before they even reached the entrance to the grand manor, the door opened seemingly of its own accord. The manor butler, Derek, stepped into view with a wave towards his employer.

"Welcome back, sir," the elderly man greeted them with a bow. His grey eyes settled on Dante, and his expression grew sombre. "Where are the others?" Dante's heart sank at the simple, painful question.

"There are no others, Derek," Varus explained, groaning as he stepped into the house. He was hobbling now, and Dante wondered which part of the evening had most aggravated his wounded leg. "We'll discuss this in a minute, but first... how is Rosaline?"

Before Derek could answer the inquiry, a flurry of footsteps pulled Dante's attention away from the butler. Hands settled on his shoulders as the Valedian king drew Dante close, his golden eyes wide as he regarded him. "What happened?" King Fenyang spoke in an urgent tone, seeming panicked. His tunic was soiled with blood and dirt, and after a momentary once-over, Dante was assured it wasn't his own. "You didn't return with Benkaei and Huda, I..."

Blinking, Dante struggled to encapsulate the evening's events in as short a sentence as he could manage. "I left the bridge to find Haeyin, and then Varus told me to advise our allies to fall back," he stammered, distinctly aware of the pressure of the king's hands on his shoulders.

Shaking his head, King Fenyang lifted a hand from Dante's shoulder, only to pause midway towards his face. His fingers hovered inches from Dante's cheek, as if the king warred with himself over whether or not to touch him. "You're bleeding," he clarified eventually.

His heart hammered in his chest at the contact – at the *almost* contact. "It's nothing, Fenyang," Dante insisted quickly, sifting through his thoughts to find when an injury might have occurred. "It's probably just the scrapes from the embassy, they must have opened up again."

Something flashed in the Valedian king's expression, his eyes softening as his stare lingered on Dante. "You should head to the dining room, have them see to your wounds," Fenyang suggested. He released his grasp on Dante at last, and as the king's hands fell to his sides Dante found himself missing the sensation.

Clearing his throat, Varus leaned against the wall nearby. "Your Majesty, whenever you have a moment… you should probably be present for the conversation I need to have with Rosaline," their host explained, his expression serious.

Sensing an opportunity to escape before he embarrassed himself further, Dante ducked away towards the dining hall in the western wing of the manor. He had referred to the Valedian king by his name alone… he prayed King Fenyang would be sympathetic to the improper conduct, given Dante was not in his right mind.

The dining room had been converted into a makeshift hospital ward, with every spare table and collection of mismatched chairs that Varus owned dragged in to support the influx of guests. Some of the Valedian embassy staff had remained to help, with the civilians they had rescued suffering only minor injuries on their feet as well, carrying medical supplies and food back and forth. Mothers comforted frightened children while wounds were cleaned and bandaged, and Dante thought he recognized the back of Charlotte's head as she helped to stitch a man's arm shut.

"Dante, you're back!" a voice called out over the din, and a young woman in a wheelchair approached him. He had met her before, he was certain of it... for the life of him, Dante couldn't remember her name.

She tilted her head as she smiled up at him, her face dimpling around the scars that crept along her cheekbones. "Maya," she offered helpfully.

Shaking his head, Dante sighed. "I'm so sorry, I'm not thinking clearly right now," he apologized, bowing his head. He was struck by the sheer number of people they had squeezed into the manor in this room alone, the damage wrought by the king's men as they sought out Charlotte and the Valedian council.

"You're hurt," Maya pointed out. "You should have Eleni take a look at your face."

He shook his head again more fervently this time. "Not necessary," Dante insisted. "Her efforts are better spent on these people. How can I help?"

Glancing over her shoulder, Maya regarded one of the tables nearest them, the dwindling receptacle of opium powder and the emptied basket of fresh linens. "We're running low on material for bandages, and we could use more analgesic," she suggested. "Eodan, or rather Varus has been letting us tear up the bed sheets to use for dressings. Would you mind fetching some more?"

Dante nodded once, grateful for the distraction. A warrior had little purpose in a field hospital, and a necromancer had even less. He would busy himself in helping as many people as he could, even if that meant simply securing new bed linens for bandages. His heart had not ceased pounding in his chest since the discovery in the graveyard, since he had seen the dismembered hand and Jasper's sword abandoned in the alleyway. The discarded rubies of Cary's necklace still glittered in his mind, and Dante was not ready to confront the truth, not yet.

For what might have been an hour, maybe more, Dante went where he was needed. He was an errand boy, he was a medical assistant, he was an emotional support. For every dozen townsfolk who would live to see another day, there was one so horribly injured that there was nothing anyone could do. For them, Dante held their hand and relaxed the walls around his magic, allowing the frigid whisper of his power to curl around their temples as Charlotte sang soothing lullabies. The face of a little boy, barely twelve years old, would forever haunt Dante's dreams. He could see the calm wash over his face as he slipped away, his grip on Dante's hand growing slack.

Only once before in his life had Dante permitted his magic to probe the energy of someone on the brink of death. Tonight, he had comforted five strangers as they lay dying, and his soul shuddered with the magnitude of a grief he couldn't name.

He kept going for as long as he could, until his hands physically shook with the effort to keep himself standing. The reality of his own existence was a distant memory, his own thrumming heart a sound overheard from another room, another life. It wasn't until Charlotte threaded her fingers with his own that Dante became aware of something other than the death that lingered around him, the sensation against his frostbitten palms shocking him back to the present. He felt weightless, floating in the undertow of an ocean current as Charlotte led him out of the dining hall towards the sitting room.

It seemed a few people had congregated here, exhausted from the night's events. Charlotte led him to one of the plush sofas, seating him beside Eleni with a gentle but insistent push. Dante all but collapsed against the cushions, his body still trembling. He had come close to magical burnout before, but this was different. This emptiness, the gnawing ache within him… this was a burnout of the soul.

A mug was pressed into his wounded hands, the warmth soothing his frostbitten palms. "It will help you feel better," Eleni's soft voice advised him. Mo the cat was curled in her lap – no, her familiar, Dante realized. No wonder Eleni was still functional while he was a wreck, with Mo lending the woman some of her power while she worked tirelessly to heal the citizens they had rescued.

Before Dante had a moment to dwell on how insignificant he felt his assistance had been in comparison, Haeyin's sharp tone caught him by surprise. "I know that look," the doctor began sternly as he entered the room, taking a seat on the sofa opposite Dante. "Get those thoughts out of your head. You did well today."

"Not well enough," Dante insisted, his mouth dry. "Jasper…"

"Where is Jasper?" Charlotte asked, as if the question had been burning on the tip of her tongue all evening. She perched on the arm of the sofa beside Haeyin, searching the faces of the people around her. "Gideon? We haven't seen Cary either."

His heart sank. "Charlotte, I…"

A sudden commotion of slammed doors and hurried footsteps distracted him from the conversation he didn't want to have, raised voices from the hallway echoing towards them. "Don't you dare take that tone with me!" a woman's voice thundered. "How could you accuse one of my girls—"

"Rosaline, what other conclusion do you expect me to arrive at?" Varus rumbled. "We have indisputable proof, give me one good reason to believe it could be anything else."

The pair of them turned the corner with King Fenyang in tow, entering the sitting room looking rather a mess. Varus had retrieved his cane, the firelight illuminating the scarred surface of his armour. Rosaline's lavish overcoat had been discarded, her abdomen wrapped in bandages over her shirt as she clutched a bottle of wine in her bejewelled hand. Fenyang looked murderous, and it spoke to Dante's state of delirium that the sight of the king in such a state made his heart flutter in his chest.

"How many times do I have to tell you people," Haeyin wheezed, burying his face in his hands. "No alcohol when you're recovering." No one seemed to pay any attention to him.

The Valedian king surveyed the room, as if taking a headcount. "So much for having a place for a private conversation," he chuckled half-heartedly, elbowing Varus casually.

Shaking his head, their host barked a laugh in response. He looked considerably less composed than he had been on the battlefield, his hair escaping the knot at the back of his head. "Never thought I'd see the day that this blasted estate doesn't have enough rooms." Much to Dante's dismay, Varus addressed him. "Dante... You found this on Sasha's body, yes?"

He presented Dante with the dagger he had retrieved, still stained red with blood. Rosaline looked positively livid, which made answering truthfully very daunting. "Y—yes," Dante agreed, his eyes darting back and forth between Varus and the madame. "It was still in her neck when I found her."

"Not just in her neck," the Valedian king clarified, prompting Dante to continue. "Specifically, where was it?"

Varus had been purposefully vague, neglecting to mention how Dante had reanimated Sasha for his interrogation. He swallowed his nausea as he focused on the mug burning his hands. "It was—it was in her throat, the base of her throat," he stammered.

Her eyes narrowed as she regarded the conversation taking place, Charlotte spoke up. "Why does that matter?" she asked.

The colour had drained from the Madame's face as Dante delivered this piece of information. Varus turned to Rosaline once more, a sympathetic expression on his face. "The Silent Sisterhood isn't known simply for their members taking vows of silence," he elaborated for Charlotte. "Their tactics also focus on *silencing* their targets. That manner of death blow is a specialty of theirs."

Rosaline seemed distraught. "That's not possible," she breathed, shaking her head. "Not... not Cary, that's not possible."

"What other hypothesis do we have?" Varus asked slowly, his voice sounding exhausted. "Do we assume that someone obtained one of Cary's knives and killed *Sasha*, a skilled assassin, in the very manner they've been trained in?" For this, Rosaline had no immediate retort.

At that moment, Maya joined them in the sitting room, navigating around the three people standing in the middle of the space. "What's going on?" Maya asked tentatively, her eyes narrowing on the terse exchange. She came to a stop beside Charlotte, who had turned a rather disconcerting shade of grey.

Deflated, Rosaline sank into the sofa beside Haeyin, drinking deeply from the wine bottle. Varus and King

Fenyang remained standing as they exchanged grim looks. "Jasper and Gideon are missing," the Valedian king explained at last, the resignation in his voice devastating. "Sasha was killed, and we suspect Cary turned on them."

"And you know this from a knife?" Maya asked, squinting at the small weapon. "I thought all your assassins used that type of dagger."

Rosaline sighed, leaning against the arm of the sofa heavily, her head propped on her hand. "The blades are a gift upon completing Sisterhood initiation," the woman explained in a tone of deep contrition. "They have unique sigils engraved in them, specific to each assassin. Cary's were inscribed with a magpie."

The room fell quiet, the crackling of the fireplace the only sound permeating the shocked silence. "I don't believe it," said Charlotte, shaking her head. "We've known Cary for years. Why would she…?"

"Charlotte has a point," Haeyin agreed as Charlotte trailed off, his voice sounding hoarse. His expression stricken, he eyed their host. "It doesn't make any sense, why would Cary turn on us now? Is there any possibility she might have allied with Rasmussen, any of the underworld that turned on you at the meet?"

Before the kingpin could respond, Rosaline shut down the accusation. "Absolutely not," she insisted, even as doubt lingered in her eyes. "Cary fought with me *against* Rasmussen and his little coup."

"Then it seems more likely that Cary betrayed us for the king, not for any rival gang," Maya suggested softly.

The Valedian king turned towards their host, his expression remarkably unruffled. "Varus, are we safe here?" he asked, his tone measured and calm.

Leaning on his cane, Varus met the king's gaze. "My

house is heavily warded, and Dornkeep remains loyal to me. We will be safe here, for now," he explained slowly. Turning to survey his audience in the sitting room, Varus cleared his throat. "Trust me when I say that I am as gutted by this revelation as all of you are. Cary has been a part of our lives for a long time. No matter her reasoning, or how long she has been working against us, our primary concern is that Jasper and Gideon are gone."

Rosaline's gaze was transfixed by the fire, her grip on the wine bottle white-knuckled. "What are the chances they're still alive?" she asked softly, her voice barely above a whisper.

"The alleyway was empty when we got there," Dante spoke up, not wanting to mention the hand. "We found Sasha's body, but no one else." Only now did it strike him as odd that the alleyway had been empty, with no other indications of the struggle that must have taken place for Jasper and Gideon to have been taken.

"If Sasha's body is the only one we discovered, then there's a good chance they're still alive... albeit wounded," Varus agreed – a small comfort.

"That raises another issue, however," Fenyang pointed out, his eyes narrowing. "They've likely been detained."

Dante gripped the mug of tea tighter, taking a tentative sip before he spoke. The spiced tea was nearly scalding, but he was grateful for the warmth. "Varus, they know the truth about the Valedian embassy, Charlotte's whereabouts," he trailed off, chewing his lip. "If Cary hasn't already informed the king, if Gideon and Jasper are questioned..."

He didn't need to voice the rest of his thoughts for Varus to catch on, nodding solemnly. Dante didn't doubt for a second that if captured, Jasper and Gideon would take what they knew to the grave... but he wouldn't put it past the Aethian king to torture them for what information they knew.

Charlotte's eyes darkened with an untamed fury. Beside her, Maya seemed to be on the verge of tears, fiddling almost aggressively with her skirts. "If they've been detained, they won't just punish them," the girl murmured fearfully, her gaze fixed on the fireplace. "They'll hang for this."

CHAPTER
SEVENTEEN
JASPER

T̶HE WORLD RETURNED TO HIM SLOWLY, HIS ENTIRE BODY aching. It was the sort of pain that reminded Jasper he was alive when he probably shouldn't have been, another close call. His skull throbbing, his ears ringing in the silence, Jasper gingerly opened his eyes. It was dimly lit in here, but he was as unprepared for it nonetheless. Fighting the wave of nausea that threatened to overwhelm him, Jasper closed his eyes again. His face was sore, pressed against what appeared to be the rough surface of a plain bedroll, his shoulder numbed beneath his body weight.

Struggling to pull himself into a sitting position, Jasper became aware that his hands were bound, the sensation of the cold metal painful on his bare wrists. With some difficulty, he maneuvered around his restrained arms, propping himself up against a surface behind him. A stone wall, from the feel of it. Bracing himself for the light, Jasper opened his eyes once more; he was prepared this time, and the pain of it was bearable.

It was difficult for his vision to focus, and he felt as if he were underwater, his head churning in a riptide. He was in a small, cramped cell, with damp and mossy stone walls and floors. The only sources of light were a tiny window high above him and a torch outside in the hallway, beyond the set of iron bars ahead of him. Though he had never been inside them before, Jasper could only assume he was in the castle dungeons.

And he was alone.

The stone wall behind him was cool and damp, a welcome reprieve from the pain as Jasper leaned his head back against it. He struggled to recall the events that had transpired before he'd blacked out, the events that had led to him being imprisoned here. Distantly, he remembered Cary, and Gideon... but where was Gideon?

An ugly sensation twisted in his gut, dread and anger coursing through him. Cary... were it not for the fact that Jasper had awoken in the dungeons, he might have thought that his friend's betrayal was a nightmare. It *felt* like a nightmare, a horrid dream Jasper could not shake himself awake from, no matter how hard he tried. The memory of Gideon's severed hand flashed across his mind, Cary's dark eyes in the alleyway, and Jasper shuddered.

Dark eyes... that couldn't be right. He must have been concussed. It hurt to think, his head throbbing as he sifted through his memories, recollections of the night before sliding through his fingers like sand. When had their friend betrayed them? Where had it started, how had he missed it? The most he could recall was Sasha's fate, blood on his hands... but Jasper couldn't be certain he wasn't just imagining things, his imagination filling in the holes of his memory with things he thought made sense.

The harder he worked to recollect his thoughts, the sensation of nausea became overwhelming. The dungeon seemed to tilt sideways, the world spinning as Jasper fell hard onto his shoulder once more, stars sparking across his vision until all he could see was darkness.

Wake up, Jasper...

He awoke again to the icy sensation of water being dumped over his head, and Jasper gasped for air as he came to. He strained his shoulders attempting to stand up, his arms bound to the chair Jasper found himself seated in. Struggling fruitlessly against his bindings, Jasper blinked water from his eyes as he took in his surroundings.

To Jasper's chagrin, this room was brighter than the cell he had first woken up in, a rare display of electrical lighting illuminating stone walls and floors. The colder temperature was exacerbated by his soaking wet clothing, his feet bare against the stone tiles. His legs had been similarly secured to the chair, and as Jasper met the eyes of a masked man across the room, he had a fairly good idea what was about to transpire here. The man leaned casually against the wall behind him, and what Jasper could see of his face gave the impression he was smiling at the prospect of whatever torment would be inflicted upon his prisoner.

"Rise and shine, sweetheart." A voice from behind Jasper startled him as a second man stepped into view. His face was unobscured, but nothing about his sharp features was remarkable or familiar. "Kept us waiting long enough. Now we can begin."

Jasper squinted in a vain effort to limit the light that aggravated his throbbing headache. "Where am I?" he managed to ask in a voice hoarse with disuse, shivering in the too-thin fabric of his wet shirt.

The man closest to him gripped the chair as he leaned in, laughing cruelly as he prodded Jasper's temple. "Paradise, clearly," he scoffed. "We'll be asking the questions, here. What's your name?"

Clenching his teeth at the wave of nausea that roiled through him, Jasper managed not to vomit. "Jasper."

"Your full name, boy."

The finger at his temple prodded more forcefully, and Jasper squeezed his eyes shut. "Jasper *Gallagher*," he elaborated through gritted teeth.

Seemingly pleased by his cooperation, the man released his grip on Jasper's chair. "And how long have you lived in Caelfall?" the strange man asked him, his voice sounding distant as he stepped away. Jasper managed to open one eye as he turned his head, following the man's movements... but he'd stepped out of view, and all Jasper could see was the shape of a table nearby.

"All my life," Jasper answered reluctantly, relaxing his neck as he turned to face forwards once more. That masked man remained ever so slightly amused, his dark eyes fixed on Jasper's face. "Why am I here?"

The response he received was a blow to his face from the second man. Pain sparked across the bridge of his nose, momentarily blinding Jasper. "What did I say about asking questions?" he hissed. Not knowing his name, Jasper mentally referred to him as Asshole as he reeled from the strike, breathing through the motion sickness that rippled through him. "You're here because you killed city guards, you little shit."

Varus and Haeyin had sometimes referred to Jasper as a little shit, but it was usually an affectionate, chiding term of endearment. Blood ran freely from his nose, and Jasper struggled to breathe through his mouth. He remained silent as Asshole returned to whatever was on the table nearby, not trusting himself to speak again.

The other man sighed, adjusting his posture where he leaned against the wall. "He's concussed, Anderson... We gain nothing from his questioning if you kill him," the masked man reprimanded his colleague, his words difficult for Jasper to discern without seeing his mouth. "Try something other than smacking him in the head, if you wouldn't mind."

Despite learning his name, Jasper continued to refer to the man as Asshole. "I hear you're a blacksmith, Mr. Gallagher," Asshole pointed out as he rummaged for something on the table, the dull and heavy thud of multiple metal objects sending a jolt of panic through Jasper.

"That's right," Jasper agreed. He had no energy for conversation, his voice flat and monotone as he spoke.

"Am I correct in assuming your hands are quite important to your work?" The question was chilling in combination with the hammer in Asshole's hand, visible now that he stood in front of Jasper once more. No amount of questioning involving an instrument like that would end well for him.

What do you think? Jasper resisted the urge to bite back with a sarcastic remark. "Yes."

At the other end of the room, Mask crossed his arms over his chest. "This can go very badly for you if you lie to us," he reminded Jasper unhelpfully. "I'd say you have… ten chances to answer our questions truthfully."

Even with his addled consciousness, Jasper could understand a threat. None of it mattered; whatever bodily harm Mask and Asshole threatened him with, he was not so mentally injured that he could not remember why he was here. That didn't necessarily mean he couldn't fear for the future of his hands, however.

"Let's start off with something easy," Asshole mused, making a show of strolling back and forth in front of Jasper. The gleam of the metal hammer caught the light, painful for his vision to track. "Where is the Valedian council hiding?"

Despair flooded his gut, clogging his throat. He knew he wasn't any good at lying, knew he couldn't convince these men he was telling the truth if he didn't believe it himself. Even if they did believe his words, would they accept an undesirable response without retaliation? Jasper doubted it.

"I don't know," he replied anyway.

He had broken fingers before in his youth, smashing his thumbs instead of steel as he worked in the forge. Jasper should have known what the sensation of the hammer on his hand would feel like, and yet the shock of the impact as the instrument slammed into his index finger was beyond anything he could have prepared for. White hot pain lanced through him, and Jasper could not restrain the shout that ripped out of him.

"That's not good enough, Jasper," Asshole growled in response. "The Valedian council's bodies weren't recovered from the rubble of the embassy, we know they aren't dead. Where are they hiding?"

"I don't know," Jasper repeated, wheezing. He was ready this time, prepared for the strike before his middle finger was broken. The bindings over his right arm grew painfully tight as he struggled in vain to retract his hand, to move away from the source of the pain – but Jasper could handle this. For Charlotte and Dante's safety, he could handle this.

It was through sheer mental fortitude that Jasper did not lose consciousness as each of his fingers were shattered repeatedly by the hammer. Despite the fragmented pain that arced through his temples with each stuttering pulse of his heart, Jasper managed to retain the tidbits of information leaked by his captors. They knew of his friendship with Dante, knew of his connection to the embassy and the Valedian council through him. They knew of the affiliation with Eodan Melicus, but not Varus Emery.

After Asshole had started anew on his left hand, Mask stepped away from the wall. "Oh dear, that does look like it hurts," he mused thoughtfully, earning a gasping groan from Jasper as the masked man pressed down on one of his broken thumbs. "If you start being honest, we might still be able to get a healer down here to repair your hands."

In truth, Jasper hadn't pondered the possibility of surviving long enough for his bones to heal at all. Haeyin had repaired some of his gnarliest injuries, but... Jasper was avoiding looking down at the twisted mess of his fingers, lest he vomit at the sight. He kept his head up, leaning back against the chair so his hands were safely out of his peripheral vision. Every inch of his body was trembling in shock, his frayed nerves screaming for him to run.

Seemingly disappointed with Jasper's lack of response, Mask exchanged a pointed glance with his colleague. "Perhaps it's true that you don't know where the council is," he conceded as Asshole returned to the table, the heavy clunk of the hammer against the surface signalling a new torture device being selected. "Let's try something else, shall we? Who tried to kill the king?"

His heart sank, but Jasper's resolve solidified as his thoughts turned to Charlotte. "I don't know," he snarled, all but baring his teeth.

There was a surge of pain as Asshole grasped one of the broken fingers on his right hand, but it paled immediately in comparison to the sensation of a blade slicing through his little finger. Jasper roared as lightning blazed down his nerve endings, his body straining against the restraints as his vision faltered. He could feel the hot sting of his own blood as it dripped from his hand, spattering his feet as it fell to the floor.

"There's no reason for this to continue, Jasper," Mask spoke mournfully, as if he regretted what had transpired. "Just tell us where he is, and this will all be over."

Beneath the haze of pain, beneath the nausea and the dizziness, Jasper took a breath. *Tell us where he is.* Did they think a man had tried to kill the king? Or were they testing him to see if he would correct the assumption? If they didn't know about Charlotte... Jasper would willingly let them break every bone in his body, would let them amputate each of his fingers if it meant she would be safe.

He didn't dare respond, and his silence was perceived as an unsatisfactory answer all the same. His ring finger suffered the consequence of his defiance, and Jasper screamed in agony.

"Better be careful, blacksmith," Asshole teased cruelly as Jasper's entire body shook with distress. "You don't have many fingers left."

His veins were engulfed in fire, his head pounding as Jasper struggled not to empty the contents of his stomach. If there had been little hope of Haeyin saving his hands before, he knew there was no going back now; even a mage as gifted as Haeyin couldn't regrow limbs. His hand strained against the bindings of the chair, every muscle in his arm tensed as Jasper writhed in his seat – until the arm of the chair shattered with the force, the wood splintering as he yanked his arm back.

There was a heavy blow to the right side of his face as Asshole reacted instinctively, clubbing Jasper with the tool he had used to sever his fingers. Jasper could not hold back his nausea any longer, retching as stars flickered across his failing vision. He tasted blood pooling in his mouth, the sensation of dislodged teeth against his tongue testing the remnants of his sanity. He spat desperately in an attempt to remove them, his jaw and his face throbbing in time with his erratic pulse as broken teeth passed his lips.

"By the Lutaidhr, Anderson," Mask swore angrily. There was the sound of footsteps, the metallic thunk of an instrument dropping to the stone floor. "Are you trying to kill him?"

Distantly, Jasper was accosted by the worst smell he had ever encountered, as if he had wandered into a plague hospital. Another wave of nausea had him gagging, but his stomach was empty. His hand was growing colder and colder, his foot covered in his own blood. Someone grasped his face, but Jasper couldn't see who it was – all he knew was that the pressure against his wounded cheek was challenging his ability to remain conscious.

"Look… his eyes," one of the men murmured, and Jasper felt an uncharacteristically gentle hand brush his damp hair back from his face. He was too physically weakened to resist anymore, powerless as a finger swept against his cheekbone. "Tell Rilkor…"

His hand was as cold as ice, and Jasper could no longer

deny the call of the void. Each of his senses blinked out like stars in the night as Jasper slipped back into non-existence.

He was dreaming, swimming in oceans of inky darkness.

Jasper opened his eyes to the night sky, the stars above stretching beyond in ancient constellations he barely recognized. He floated on his back, an unfathomably vast sea surrounding him. There was a blurriness around the edges of his vision, a kaleidoscope that distorted the night into a myriad of colours he couldn't name. A voice spun through the clouds, whisper light and yet loud as thunder to his ears.

"You and I are as one."

Something writhed in the deep beneath him, a tentacle weaving through the fathomless depths. Jasper shuddered as it caressed his side, gauging his reaction as it drew closer. There was a low, ominous moan as the surface parted, a woman's face emerging from the deep to obscure the heavens above, stray droplets of water dripping from her face onto Jasper's chest. She wept from eyes of starlight, her tears threatening to drown him as she sobbed.

"You and I are as one." It was not the woman who spoke, but the monster in the deep. That curving appendage embraced him, cradling him – not a tentacle, but a scaled, reptilian tail. A great form shifted closer to him, clouds of hot steam surrounding Jasper as a beast breathed beside him.

"I am nothing like you," Jasper managed to say, his tongue slow and his mind addled.

The monster in the depths seemed amused by his response, a draconian snout nudging Jasper as its tail snaked around his chest. *"Cling to that falsehood while it still brings you comfort. Ignorance will not shield you for much longer."*

The water rushed over his chest as the beast tugged him beneath the surf. The woman's face crumpled as she wept over Jasper, her tears sending resonant waves crashing around him. "I don't understand," Jasper replied, his throat submerged.

A throaty chuckle resonated in the water around him as the beast tugged him closer. *"You will, in time. But you have slept too long, and the time has come to awaken."*

He was sinking, he was falling beneath the waves…

Wake up, Jasper…

Jasper gasped awake, his heart pounding in his chest as he struggled to sit up. Gratefully his injured hands had been bound in front of him, enabling him to use his elbows to some effect. He was back in the dungeon cell once more, the light even dimmer now that the sun had set. Closing his eyes, Jasper sucked in breath after shuddering breath as he pulled himself awkwardly into a sitting position, crossing his legs. Each of his maimed fingers – what remained of them – were bruised and purple, every minute movement of his hands leaving him in agony.

"You're finally awake," said a man's voice nearby, and Jasper startled in the darkness at the sound. His mind still wounded and disoriented, he squinted in the dim light until his vision focused on a face. "I was beginning to worry you might be comatose."

Jasper blinked repeatedly, multiple twisted forms of Gideon dancing in front of him. "Gideon," he replied at last, as if needing to be convinced of who he was speaking to. His tongue skirted across his raw gums, the absence of three of his molars disconcerting. "You weren't here when I woke up, where were you?"

The man appeared to be in rough shape, worse than Jasper had ever seen him. Gideon's right arm was bundled in a makeshift sling across his chest, the stump of his wrist hastily cauterized. Jasper still wasn't used to the man's blinded eye, but Gideon's appearance had been further marred by an assortment of bruises and lacerations. He hadn't seen his own reflection since he'd woken up in the cell, but Jasper imagined he was likely in similar shape, short a few teeth and unable to breathe through a likely broken nose.

Gideon shifted where he sat, as if he were trying to get comfortable on the filthy bedroll surrounded by raw hewn rock. "They didn't want us talking before they started questioning us," he explained in a low voice, glancing meaningfully towards the iron bars. "Didn't want to give us the chance to get our stories straight, you know."

"What stories?" Jasper asked, frowning at the turn of phrase. The expression aggravated his swollen face, and he winced back to a blank countenance.

The man closed his eyes. "I mean that they didn't want us conspiring before being questioned," Gideon elaborated, somehow managing patience in this state.

Jasper sighed, leaning his head back against the wall behind him. "They didn't like my answers," he offered in response, raising his bound hands.

There was a pained expression on Gideon's face as his eyes tracked the movement, his gaze resting momentarily on Jasper's similarly cauterized remnants of fingers. "There's... there's something I've been meaning to tell you," Gideon began, his voice cracking in a manner Jasper had never heard before. "I should have told you, I wanted to tell you, but…"

"What are you talking about?" Jasper asked wearily.

Gideon shifted where he sat, wincing as the stump of his arm was jostled with the movement. "Your Uncle Zeke, he… he made me swear not to tell a soul, not to endanger you. He was worried that if anyone knew the truth, if anyone found out, that you might be in danger of the noblemen of Briardeen. Not that any of that matters now."

"You're not making any sense," Jasper growled.

"The truth is…" the other man sighed, desperation cutting into his tone. "The truth is you're my brother, Jas."

He blinked, his pulse thundering in his temples. "You mean I'm… I'm *like* a brother to you, right?" he asked tentatively.

Gideon sighed, shaking his head. "No, you *are* my brother," Gideon insisted, his gaze settling on Jasper. His remaining blue eye was almost intensely bright in the dim light of the dungeon, and Jasper couldn't bring himself to hold his stare.

"What are you talking about?" Jasper demanded. "My —my parents… they died, Gideon."

"They did," Gideon agreed, his voice dropping to a whisper as he finally looked away from Jasper. Somehow, this confirmation was still painful, as if Jasper had been holding onto a fraction of hope that they were alive out there somewhere. "My mother… *our* mother met your father when I was young. I believe she planned for us to run away with him after finding out about you. My father's treatment of her was admittedly… well, it was despicable. He tormented her long before he started with me."

Our mother, but not *our* father. They had never discussed

Gideon's late mother before, never dared broach such a painful subject. "My father?" Jasper dared to ask.

Swallowing, Gideon hesitated before he continued, as if he still feared the repercussions of revealing the truth to Jasper. "Sir Piotr Gallagher," he confirmed softly. "He was assassinated, or so Zeke always used to say. Your uncle was afraid if anyone discovered your parentage... well, he feared they might try to kill you, as well. Knowing what I know now, of the king, of—of everything, I'm inclined to agree."

Jasper's hands were trembling. "Assassinated?" he repeated weakly. "Was... our mother, was she...?" All he had learned of his mother from Zeke was that she had died the day Jasper was born.

Shaking his head, the other man cleared his throat. "No, no, she wasn't," Gideon clarified, his voice uneven. "She was ill for some time, a sort of 'wasting illness,' my father called it. When he informed me that my mother had died, he claimed their babe had died with her, and I let him believe that. He didn't know that I knew the truth, that Zeke himself had delivered you in Caelfall, kept you hidden there."

The implication of Gideon's words was damning, a crushing weight settling on Jasper's chest. "So... she died because of me," he breathed, his voice failing him. "It's my fault." He had lived with the knowledge all his life, but the confirmation that Jasper had been the cause of his own mother's demise...

The man's face crumpled at Jasper's words. "No, Jas," Gideon insisted, his eyes glistening. "I think... regardless of her health, I think she *chose* to have you because of what you meant for her. What a future with your father meant for us."

The old ring box weighed heavily on his heart, forgotten in the pocket of his discarded clothing back at the Melicus manor. Jasper wasn't sure when the tears had started to fall, his eyes burning as the drops fell from his chin down his soiled shirt. "Why are you telling me all of this?" he asked finally, his voice trembling. He already knew the answer.

He could feel Gideon's gaze on him once more, feel the weight of that knowing stare. "They're going to hang us in the morning," said Gideon quietly. "You, me, and the rest of the people they caught that night. Thankfully only twelve of us, but... I'm having a hard time seeing the bright side of things right now, if I'm honest."

Such a gentle tone for such violent words, Jasper thought to himself. He buried his face in his trembling hands, pressing his palms into his eyes even as his broken fingers protested, pressed until he saw stars. The weight of everything sat heavily on his skin, and he fought to process the information Gideon had given him, the knowledge of his parents and the assurance that he would die tomorrow.

He thought of Gideon, of how it seemed he had always been up on a pedestal. It had been Jasper who had placed him there, bright-eyed and awe-struck by this boy he had grown up with, always ahead of him in every area of life. The notion that that two of them were related, with how different they were, was entirely nonsensical. Gideon was strong, and confident, and brave, and a *knight*. Jasper was awkward and clumsy and oblivious on a good day.

When Jasper was a boy, his uncle Zeke had raised him with stories of who his parents had been. Zeke's brother was handsome and brave, smart and capable. Jasper's mother had been wise and beautiful, compassionate towards even her worst enemies. To think that either of these wonderful people were no longer here because of him…

After several moments of silence, Jasper released his grip on his face, leaning back against the damp wall of the dungeon. "What was her name?" he asked finally, closing his eyes.

Gideon was silent a moment longer. "Clarissa," he responded finally, his voice uneven. "Lady Clarissa Reinhardt."

Piotr and Clarissa. Jasper whispered the name to himself, as if it were a secret he dared not repeat. His lips moved again and again, as if testing the shape and colour of the name on his tongue. Clarissa and Piotr. There was no familiarity, no spark of recognition as he uttered it under his breath. There was nothing that ignited within him at the mention of his parents' names, there was no missing piece of himself that after nineteen years finally clicked into place.

But he could imagine what might have been, had things worked out differently. He could imagine their mother, with Gideon's piercing blue eyes and his own rust-coloured hair, standing side by side with the faceless form of Jasper's father. Maybe they could have spirited Gideon away from his horrible sire, escaped Aethelind altogether to have a life somewhere far from here, somewhere they wouldn't have had to hide.

Jasper sighed, opening his eyes. "Well… it's nice to know, at least," Jasper managed to reply, meeting Gideon's stare once more. "I think I've always thought of you as my brother, though."

The man in the cell with him—his last living family member—smiled sadly, and it was a horrid, haunted thing to see. "But if I died without telling you that you're my little brother, I'd never forgive myself," Gideon said simply.

Wake up, Jasper…

The autumn wind rattled Jasper's bones where he stood, the threadbare fabric of his shirt doing little to keep out the harsh chill. The morning sun was too bright for his light-starved eyes, the daylight unforgiving for a man who had emerged from a cell.

Jasper had spent very little time in Aerindale other than his brief stint at the combat academy, but every citizen of Aethelind knew the gallows in the western city were reserved for more judicial executions. High profile court cases resulting in a verdict of capital punishment were open to the public. Jasper had never attended one, much less anticipated being put to death in Aerindale by summary execution. While he had witnessed the recent execution in Caelfall, it was practically unheard of elsewhere.

Their transport towards the gallows was about as comfortable as their stay in the dungeons had been. They were led into the vehicle roughly, shoved forwards with their hands and feet bound in irons. There were no benches or seating arrangements of any variety, merely a dark reinforced wooden crate with only the barest speck of light emanating from a tiny orifice on either side of the wagon. Jasper was shoved roughly into the back of the cart, grimacing as his chin caught most of the fall, his hands trying and failing to steady himself as he landed. His broken and cauterized fingers burned with agony as Gideon struggled to help him to his feet, his one arm still in a sling around his chest giving his manacled wrist marginally more give.

"Never thought I'd see you in here, git," one of the knights of the city guard sneered at Gideon as another gallows-bound prisoner was shoved into the wagon. "Hoped I would. Never thought I'd see the day."

A dull stare on his face, Gideon flexed his remaining hand into a rude gesture, but the guards were undeterred. Six men and four women were loaded into the cart with them before the doors were shut firmly, the dull thud of locks easing into place startling Jasper as the transport began to move.

The wagon smelled almost as bad as the dungeons, vaguely of sweat and piss and the crushed dreams of the people Jasper was sharing the space with. A boy a few years younger than Jasper sat sobbing across from him, his hand-me-down clothing hanging from his small frame. The oldest woman of the group was trying her best to comfort him, her worn face relaxed in an expression of resignation.

"I shouldn't be here…" a middle-aged man whimpered, rocking back and forth slightly where he sat on the floor of the wagon. "I'm not supposed to be here, this is a mistake…"

As their journey continued, Gideon nudged Jasper beside him with his elbow, turning to face him. "We're going the wrong way," he murmured in a low voice, so only Jasper would hear as he watched Gideon's mouth closely.

"What do you mean?" asked Jasper, his brow furrowed.

Gideon's icy gaze took in the faces of the prisoners around them, many lost in prayer or panicked confessions. "I've done this before, on the opposite side of the wagon," the former knight explained quietly. "I know the route. We're going the wrong way."

A thousand possibilities crossed Jasper's mind, but he schooled his expression before something as foolish as hope could appear on his face. "What does that mean for us?"

The other man shook his head, leaning back against the wall behind them. "I don't know," admitted Gideon. "Just an observation."

The reasoning for their detour became apparent as they were rushed to exit the vehicle, and they did not find themselves in the usual location for Aerindale executions. They were in the town square of the western district, a place not usually associated with death and despair, with the grand Aethelind hospital visible to the north. The gallows they saw there were hastily constructed, supervised by a dozen soldiers.

"What's all this?" one of the younger men in their group asked aloud, turning to face the knights who escorted them. "Too many of us to hang at the usual spot?"

The guard standing nearest to him gave him a harsh slap across the back of his head, causing the young man to stumble. "As if you lot didn't know," the man sneered. "Your freaky little friends set a light to it, so you all have the pleasure of a short drop this morning."

Gideon and Jasper exchanged glances as the guards led them towards the gallows, shoving them into single file with no real organization. Gideon pushed his way ahead of Jasper, turning his head slightly to the side as he spoke. "Wonder if that was our bunch," he muttered, the corner of his mouth twisting into a grin.

Jasper barely stifled his laughter. "Gods, I hope so." The young boy was behind him, still sniffling as he trudged along in his chains. He hoped it had been Varus and their allies, setting the gallows of Aerindale on fire as a further act of insurrection. He hoped that Dante and Charlotte were safe, and that they would join his former employer and set all the kingdom ablaze, if they could.

Pity he wouldn't live to see it.

It was unusually quiet today, the town square almost barren compared to the usual turnout an execution warranted. As the group of prisoners was led towards their demise, Jasper counted perhaps thirty people, a far cry from the hundred that would normally attend. Whether this was the aftermath of the night of the curfew riots, or simply the public becoming too jaded by death and despair to find entertainment in it, it was impossible to tell. Gideon's father was not in attendance to watch his only son be executed.

The sea of faces before him looked on in varying expressions of disgust, pity, and even a resigned sorrow. There were faces he almost recognized from Caelfall here, people he must have seen passing by in the marketplace. A woman with pale red hair and blanched green eyes stared up at him from the crowd, and Jasper averted his gaze when their eyes met.

The young man who had chided their location was first, and Jasper forced his gaze towards Gideon's shoulders as Nicholas Lancaster was led to the middle of the platform, his crimes announced to the crowd. Larceny and treason. He couldn't bear to look as the young man ascended a step ladder, one of the knights fastening a thick rope around his neck. His eyes were closed, his lips moving in a soundless murmur. Jasper recognized the name "Deltori" from his lips.

The step ladder was kicked out from beneath him with a vicious zeal, and Nicholas fell. There was a horrid sound as the man choked, his legs kicking out beneath him. The rope that strangled him quivered and shook, and after several terrible seconds at last stood still.

Jasper felt every inch of his body grow cold and numb as the line shuffled forward one person at a time. He jumped every time that ladder was kicked out from beneath the prisoners who went ahead of them, shuddered at the noise they made as the life was sucked out of them. The makeshift gallows began to swelter beneath the combined stench of fear and excrement. Some of them went quicker, a sickening crunch as their necks cracked the only noise before they were cut down from the gallows. One man dropped so violently his head was wrenched from his shoulders, rolling away as the rest of him thudded to the floor.

The old woman ahead of Gideon was beckoned forward, and a sickened dread settled in Jasper's stomach. His friend – his *brother* – seemed to feel it too, for he turned his head to the side to whisper behind him. "Don't be scared," said Gideon, a half-hearted smile on his face.

"I'm not scared," Jasper insisted quickly, his voice breaking.

Gideon might have laughed, his shoulders barely moving with the expression. "I hope you never become a good liar, Jas," he said softly.

They cleared the old woman's body from the gallows far too soon, and then Gideon was being led away from him, led towards the last spot he would ever walk to. He faced the crowd with all the dignity a former knight could have, standing tall and proud atop the step ladder as the rope was draped around his neck. Jasper's breath caught in his throat, and he thought he might vomit with despair.

This couldn't be real. This couldn't be happening.

Gideon turned his head towards Jasper and smiled.

"Gideon McClelland, by order of His Majesty, King Gustaf Edmund Davenport III, you are hereby sentenced to death for the heinous crime of murder and treason against the sovereign kingdom of Aethelind."

It was as if every nerve was on fire, hyper-focused on the nightmare unfolding in front of him as Jasper watched the knight step forward to kick the step ladder away once more. He wanted to scream, he wanted to burst forward to rescue him, he wanted to do anything he could to stop what was about to happen.

With a clatter the step ladder was knocked aside, and Gideon was falling—

He couldn't bear to look.

He couldn't bring himself to look away.

Jasper watched in muted horror as Gideon's body was cut down, horridly limp and flushed. Tears dripped down his chin as he was called forward, but his feet were rooted to the floor beneath them. Another of the guards grasped him roughly, practically dragging him towards the middle of the platform, towards that step ladder as they reset the stage for his downfall, his demise.

He'd thought about death before, about *his* death. As the rope circled his neck, the coarse texture unbearable against the sensitive skin of his throat, Jasper let out a shuddering breath. Death was a pale, formless god Jasper had danced with time and time again. He had always slipped away with the promise that death would come for him, soon – with the assurance that this was not the end of his story, but that one day his luck would run out.

He thought he'd have more time.

There was that woman amongst the crowd, marked by her familiar pale green eyes and light red hair. He had seen her so many times before now, hadn't he? Perhaps she was Death all along, come to usher him into the afterlife. Her form was so similar to the way Jasper had imagined his mother might look, her eyes rimmed with red as she stared up at him. As she held his gaze, the woman raised her hand slowly, palm facing Jasper with her fingers outstretched.

"Jasper Gallagher, by order of His Majesty, King Gustaf Edmund Davenport III, you are hereby sentenced to death for the heinous crime of murder and treason against the sovereign kingdom of Aethelind."

Jasper closed his eyes.

The ladder vanished beneath his feet, and now Jasper was falling, falling—

The rope around his neck snapped taut, and he gasped for air.

CHAPTER
EIGHTEEN
CHARLOTTE

IN THE CHAOS THAT FOLLOWED ONE OF THE BLOODIEST nights in Caelfall's history, Charlotte found herself in an uneasy breath between violent symphonies, unable to rest and unable to act. The following day, Varus held something of a war council in his sitting room, planning their next course of action. It was comforting that, amidst the insanity and bloodshed, they all agreed their most immediate concern was freeing Jasper and Gideon. While Charlotte knew their motivation was largely due to her friends' knowledge of the Valedian council's survival, of her own location, she was nonetheless reassured in their efforts.

Through a rather nauseating display of magic utilizing the severed hand Varus and Dante had recovered – which Charlotte had immediately recognized as Gideon's – the necromancer Huda had been able to track the former knight's location to a specific cell in the castle dungeons. Varus recalled a long-forgotten entrance through the catacombs, which Maya had been able to verify with the aid of her collection of pilfered maps and schematics. When it seemed a rescue mission was in the works, Charlotte had volunteered immediately.

Varus had given her a stern look, but it was Dante who had advised against it. "Charlotte… this might not be the most accessible mission for you," he offered tentatively, and she hated the sympathy in her friend's eyes. She had wanted to argue, wanted to protest. Gideon and Jasper were family, and she knew that they would have gone to rescue her in a heartbeat, were it Charlotte in those dungeons.

However, Charlotte also knew that Dante was right. She knew that there was a good chance she would freeze up in shock when she returned to that foul place, and Charlotte had no way of knowing with absolute certainty that she could handle it. Dante volunteered in Charlotte's stead to accompany Varus into the dungeons, and the pair of them left after sunset.

Within the refuge of Varus' study, the walls did not rattle with the nightly autumn winds the way Charlotte's loft would, or Jasper's flat. The outside world was entirely silent within the estate, as if the walls muffled the sound so completely it no longer existed at all. Charlotte sat curled up in the well-loved armchair, attempting to read a book she couldn't focus on. Eleni had brought Maya up through the elevator, and the pair of them were stationed at the cluttered workspace of Varus' desk. Though her adoptive mother had taken over Maya's studies, Eleni was consider-ably more lenient with the girl than her prior caregivers.

The woman seemed exhausted in a way Charlotte had never seen before, her blonde waves partially pulled back from her face with a spare writing utensil. "Darling, you may want to review this one," Eleni said around a yawn, leaning forward to point towards one of the papers in front of Maya. "This is a masculine noun, so you need to conjugate this verb appropriately."

Maya squinted down at her paperwork, silently mouthing the sentence she had written. Her frown deepened as she leaned forward and erased her work furiously, much to the chagrin of the cat resting in her lap. Maya's demeanour was different than it had been when she was sequestered in the cathedral, and her determination to work was borne of a desire to prove herself rather than to avoid punishment. Eleni seemed to notice this, and her face broke into a small smile as she leaned forward to gently touch the girl's forearm.

"It's all right, it's an easy thing to miss," she reassured her. "It's very similar to the word for 'table', which is feminine. Your sentence is correct otherwise."

Shaking her head, Maya smoothed the paper in front of her. "It's easier for me to start from scratch than to try and rework half a sentence," she explained simply.

Eleni nodded, smiling more genuinely. She turned her attention towards Charlotte, seemingly noticing she had fallen silent. "Are you all right, Charlotte?" she asked.

Charlotte, having given up on reading the book in her hands, jerked awake from her reverie. "I'm fine," she insisted quickly, closing the book as she set it aside. "I'm just tired."

The woman opened her mouth, about to respond, but she was interrupted by a knock at the door. Charlotte started, unused to being disturbed in this room. The butler called from the other side of the door, sounding very remorse at having to retrieve them.

"Excuse me, my deepest apologies," Derek began

solemnly from the hallway, his voice muffled. "Lady Eleni, Master... eh, *Varus* and young Dante have returned."

"Thank you, Derek," Eleni called back, but the butler wasn't finished.

"I hate to bother you, my lady, but if you could come quickly, please," the butler carried on, and he sounded rather distressed. "Master Varus is in quite a foul mood."

Eleni's eyes narrowed, smoothing her navy blue skirts as she stood. This did not bode well for them, considering the nature of the mission that had called Varus and Dante from the estate. "I'll be back in just a moment," she assured Maya and Charlotte as she swiftly exited the study, latching the door quietly behind her. There were distant footsteps and hushed voices as Eleni and Derek walked towards the staircase, and there was all of ten seconds of shared silence before Maya swivelled in her chair to face Charlotte, a meaningful expression on her face as Mo leapt down from her lap.

"Are we going to—"

"Absolutely," Charlotte agreed, already standing. She held the door open as Maya wheeled herself into the hallway towards the lift. Unlike the cathedral, this elevator operated on magic as well as the estate's illegal generator. The pair of them clambered in as Eleni's cat darted in behind them, hushing one another as Maya activated the lift, Charlotte pulling the gate shut behind them. The mechanical components of the estate elevator were in thankfully better condition than the cathedral's, and the girls glided downstairs in silence. Charlotte opened the gate carefully as she and Maya made their way down the hall towards the entrance, creeping as quietly as they could.

Charlotte hadn't been sure of what to expect, with Derek's explanation of "a foul mood" leaving much to interpretation. She saw now it was an understatement; the entryway was in a state of chaos, damaged pieces of armour littering the halls in a trail that led towards the kitchen. There was shouting echoing from within, multiple voices talking over one another. A finger pressed to her lips, Charlotte leaned her head around the wall leading towards the kitchen, cloaked in shadows as she watched.

The scene was obscured from her vantage point, but what she could see was unsettling. A blood-soaked Dante was led to one of the wooden kitchen chairs by Derek and Eleni, his arm contorted at a grotesque angle. The Valedian king was by his side moments later, examining Dante's injuries with a level of care that caught Charlotte by surprise.

"What on earth happened?" said King Fenyang, turning towards Varus – and by the goddesses, he was in a foul mood indeed.

There was a loud crash as Varus discarded a piece of his armour, the shuddering rattle of a liquor cabinet opening. "It was a fucking ambush," the irate kingpin growled, uncharacteristically shaken. His dark hair was loose and unkempt, his face equally bloodied as Dante's. As he crossed the room towards the kitchen sink, Charlotte watched as he took the retrieved bottle of vodka and proceeded to dump half the contents over his left forearm, multiple fragments of dark metal embedded in his skin. He let out a guttural snarl at the sensation before proceeding to drink a startling quantity of the remaining liquor, setting to work yanking the metal shards out of his skin.

Standing at Dante's side, Eleni was whispering hushed words that Charlotte couldn't overhear. She realized at about the same moment that Dante did that the king's presence was to distract him, and the man howled something awful as Eleni reset his shoulder with a sickening crunch. The woman was quick to flood the wounded area with soothing lavender light, shaking blonde hair out of her eyes as she addressed Varus.

"Slow down, love," Eleni said in her gentle cadence, the voice of reason. "What went wrong? How did you find her?"

In the darkness, Maya and Charlotte exchanged glances. *Her?* There was a faint, muffled voice from out of Charlotte's field of view, but she couldn't identify the speaker from that noise alone.

"It wasn't enough killing one of your own, was it?" Varus hissed, casting a dark look over his shoulder. "Landing Jasper and Gideon in the dungeons to be tortured, that wasn't enough either? You had to go and make sure there was no possible way we could rescue them, *damn you.*"

"Varus, what happened?" King Fenyang spoke as he stood, remaining at Dante's side even as he rose to his full height.

Turning slowly where he stood, the expression on Varus' face as he met the king's stare was nothing short of haunted. Beneath the fury, there was only hopelessness. It was Dante who replied at last, his voice strained in a way that tugged painfully on Charlotte's heart.

"It was as if every one of the guards on patrol knew exactly where we were coming from, as if they'd prepared for it," he explained weakly, seemingly struggling to remain conscious. "There was only one prisoner in the cell we'd tracked Gideon to, and it wasn't him or Jasper."

The Valedian king glanced towards the unseen person in the room, the aforementioned *Her.* "We may as well listen to what she has to say for herself," King Fenyang suggested, glancing towards Derek as he tilted his head in the direction of the sixth person in the room. The butler bowed his head before crossing towards the unnamed individual, and there was another muffled noise before the person spoke.

"*Varus*—I swear to you, it wasn't me! I had nothing to do with it!" a female voice protested, and Charlotte stiffened at the sound. She recognized that voice, hoarse and strained as it was. They had found Cary.

"Surely you understand why that might be difficult for us to believe," Eleni replied in a tone that Charlotte had never heard before, coldly logical and deeply hurt. "How much pain do you think the king's men will have inflicted, seeking to discover what information Jasper and Gideon have? Whatever information you yourself haven't already supplied them?"

His eyes burning with hatred, Dante's expression was uncharacteristically volatile. "We trusted you," he said slowly, as if every word took effort. "And you betrayed us."

Charlotte nearly jumped out of her skin at the sensation of fur against her ankles, but it was only Mo slinking past to skulk into the kitchens. Eleni's eyes tracked the movement, but she said nothing as Cary continued to plead her case.

"I had no part in it!" Cary insisted, and something about the ragged rasp of her voice made Charlotte's heart tighten painfully. "I swear — on my mother's soul, I would never betray you, I would never allow any harm to come to Jasper—"

Seemingly having heard enough, Varus crossed the room, a feral glint in his eye as he stalked out of view. Judging by the sound Cary made, Charlotte guessed he might have grasped her by the throat. "Give me one good reason why I shouldn't kill you, Cary," he urged in a low voice. "They'll hang for this, but you already knew that—didn't you?"

The strangled noise from Cary's compressed throat was more than Charlotte could bear. Risking Varus' ire, she stepped out from the shadows into the kitchen. "Wait!" she found herself interrupting. Every head turned to face her, and Charlotte felt her face heat under the intensity of the paused interrogation as she stole the attention of her companions.

"Charlotte? Maya?" Eleni asked gently, unsurprised by their presence. "When did you come downstairs?"

Without turning, Charlotte knew Maya had wheeled herself up beside her, not leaving her to face the prospect of punishment alone. "Wait." Clearing her throat, she half-considered coming up with an excuse for her presence but thought better of it. "We should at least hear what she has to say," Charlotte suggested.

It was Dante who questioned her decision, the first to break free of the stunned silence. "Charlotte, this woman is the reason Jasper and Gideon aren't here," he explained through gritted teeth. "She betrayed us."

"I know that," Charlotte insisted, her voice quivering. "I know, and I want... I *deserve* to know why." A smaller, quieter voice within her whispered another reason, one she wasn't able to voice; *I owe her this kindness.*

The Valedian king nodded approvingly, straightening up as he crossed his arms over his chest. "Very well," he agreed, nodding towards Cary. "By all means, enlighten us."

The Reinnarlei woman regarded her with pallid eyes as Varus slowly released her, the menacing way in which he stared at her strongly suggesting he was still keen on silencing her permanently. There was a heavy undercurrent of pain amongst Cary's audience, an ache caused by Jasper and Gideon's absence, by the number of wounded citizens still taking refuge in the manor with them. Many of their allies were still prepared to kill her at a moment's notice, and Cary seemed vividly aware of this. And what a state she would be in to fight back — she appeared barely conscious in the chair she was tied to, the ropes serving more to ensure Cary remained upright rather than to prevent any escape.

"After I dropped Charlotte off here, Gideon and I parted ways," Cary explained mournfully, her speech impeded by what appeared to be a wounded jaw. "I went back to Caelfall, I needed to check in with Madame Rosaline after I'd spent the evening with Fortia and the princess—"

"You were at the meet in the sepulchre that evening," Varus interjected, a dark gleam in his eyes as he gestured towards her with the bottle of liquor. "Try again."

"*No*, I wasn't," Cary emphasized through gritted teeth, managing a startling level of volume with her weakened form. "Princess Aurelia had arranged a last-minute meeting with Charlotte, she'd wanted to discuss the involvement of her father's advisor with the drought affecting Pharsat. I cancelled with Madame Rosaline at Fortia's request, I was patrolling the castle gardens with Gideon."

Her mind snagged on the detail, and Charlotte willed her voice not to break as she spoke. "Then why did the king find me?" she asked.

Charlotte found herself disappointed even before the woman spoke, shaking her head slowly. "I don't know," she admitted in a defeated tone. "My wards have never failed before, it must have been Aloysius' doing. By the time I realized the king and his men were in the gardens, it was too late."

Charlotte forced herself to look away, to address Varus before the memory of that night could overwhelm her. At her side, she could feel Maya's hand on her arm, supporting her silently. "As much as I want justice for what happened to Jasper and Gideon… Varus, it doesn't make sense," Charlotte offered in the woman's defense. "She was with me that night, she escorted me from the king's chambers to your door."

There was still a rather frightening expression on the kingpin's face, as if his wrath was only momentarily quelled. "Jasper and I saw you at the sepulchre with Madame Rosaline," he insisted.

"I haven't seen Jasper since the day of the summary execution in Caelfall," Cary retorted. "Varus, I've watched out for that boy for years after Zeke died, I would *never* let the king's men touch him."

The name jolted Charlotte's attention, unaware that Cary had been on a first name basis with Jasper's uncle. She opened her mouth to comment on it, but Dante beat her to it. "We all saw you at the clinic the day before the raid," he pointed out. "Charlotte and I were there, and so were Jasper and Gideon."

Her feet betraying her, Charlotte found herself walking towards the centre of the room. Cary watched her with trepidation as she approached, and as Charlotte drew nearer she saw the finer details that had initially evaded her notice. There were circles beneath the Reinnairlei woman's eyes, her face sharper and narrower than before. Her skin was a myriad of cuts and bruises, one of her eyes still slightly swollen. Her left ankle was oddly crooked where she sat awkwardly, and as Charlotte circled the chair she noted the remains of fingernails on Cary's mutilated hands.

"Varus, is there any way what she's saying is true?" Charlotte murmured, glancing towards their host. "These injuries aren't fresh."

Sniffing, Maya raised her hand with some trepidation. "Regardless of our feelings towards Cary… why would she have been held in the dungeons if she were working with our enemies?" Maya pointed out, lowering her hand. "Why would they torture her?"

The Valedian king chuckled darkly at Maya's remark, crossing his arms over his chest as he regarded their prisoner. "Perhaps after her betrayal, they had no further use for her," he offered as explanation. "Or perhaps we had an imposter among our ranks."

His words sent a shudder through the room. His wrath cooling, Varus seemed to deflate. The reality of their failure – and their dwindling time remaining to rescue Jasper and Gideon – seemed to have set in at that moment. Eleni crossed the room soundlessly, gently prying the bottle of liquor from Varus' hand.

"Search my mind, Varus—scry into my soul if you must, but I swear everything I've told you is the truth," Cary insisted in the kingpin's silence.

Dragging a hand down his face, Varus sighed. "We can shelve the matter of your innocence for now," he remarked. "We have a problem. Whoever their source was, the guards were prepared for an attempt to rescue Jasper and Gideon. Dante nearly lost his arm trying to get us in and it was about all we could manage to grab Cary and run."

His brow furrowed, King Fenyang seemed to be deep in thought. "Pardon the blunt inquiry, but… is hanging by the neck your usual method of execution?" he asked slowly.

Each of them blanched at the question. "It depends on the crime," Maya replied softly, fidgeting with her skirts in her lap. "We had a summary execution by firearm in Caelfall recently, but that was irregular. For treason, the king usually prefers something that sends a message – the gallows in Aerindale."

King Fenyang nodded at this information, turning towards Varus before he continued. "I have an idea, but it has a few variables I'm not comfortable with," he explained. "If we burn the gallows tonight, we might delay their execution, or we might force Gustaf's hand in the direction of something more unfavourable."

Shaking his head, Varus crossed his arms over his chest. The open wounds Charlotte had witnessed on his forearm had seemingly faded into nearly nothing, the barest hint of red marking brown skin. "It's the best chance we have," Varus admitted begrudgingly. "If we can't infiltrate the dungeons, our best bet is catching them in the transport or at the scene, and the Aerindale gallows don't give us much time or cover."

"How can I help?" Charlotte piped up, even as she immediately knew what the answer would be. Varus glanced back and forth between Eleni and the Valedian king, and even Dante seemed at a loss for a response.

It was Eleni who spoke, and somehow her dismissal was more painful than Dante's had been. "I don't think you'll be able to assist with this one," she replied solemnly. There was no further explanation, no justification for her decision, and Charlotte knew it was because none was warranted; she had no expertise or training that qualified her as an arsonist. The hurricane in her ribcage fluttered irritably, tension blossoming in her throat as she bit her tongue.

Cary was confined to Eleni's chambers while she healed

the woman, and Benkaei was nominated by the Valedian king to follow Varus to Aerindale. While the two of them ventured out to set a light to the gallows, Dante was forced to retire for the evening, his shoulder needing adequate time to heal after it had been so recently reset. Charlotte had questions as to how the injuries on Varus' arm had healed so quickly in comparison, but there was nothing further to prevent him from departing the manor immediately for another mission.

At a heinous hour of the morning, an admittedly exhausted Charlotte clambered into bed with Maya. Every nerve ending felt raw as she struggled to wind down for the night, her thoughts consumed with the absence of Jasper and Gideon and her own aggravating inability to help. Beside her, Maya watched her with a knowing stare.

"Talk to me," she coached gently, smiling.

Feeling as defeated as Varus had looked, Charlotte's shoulders sagged. "It's not fair," she muttered, scraping her hair into a hasty plait. "Those are my friends, I should be out there trying to save them, instead I'm just…"

"Stuck here?" Maya finished sympathetically.

With an exhausted sigh, Charlotte secured her braid with a spare bit of silk from the nightstand. "I'm preaching to the choir here, aren't I?" Charlotte asked, rubbing her eyes. "I'm sorry, Maya. I'm not being a very good friend at the moment."

Chuckling under her breath, Maya held her arms out, beckoning her into an embrace as Charlotte scooted towards her. It felt good to be held, to know that she wasn't alone. "That's not true at all," Maya assured her as she folded Charlotte into her arms. "You don't need to apologize. I just wish I knew how to help you."

Shaking her head, Charlotte exhaled a lungful of frustrations. "I don't know how to help me, either," she admitted softly, leaning into Maya's shoulder.

Her friend was quiet, as if deep in thought as she absentmindedly stroked Charlotte's hair. She couldn't be certain how long the pair of them sat there like that, holding one another in the silence of Maya's room. In the morning, she would face the reality of Jasper and Gideon's continued absence, her inability to save her friends. For tonight, Charlotte resigned herself to waiting.

The morning light that filtered through the sheer, gauzy curtains of Maya's bedroom shone gently on Charlotte's face, and though she would have liked to remain asleep she found it impossible to keep her eyes closed. Squinting in the daylight, she became aware of distant sound, voices from beyond the bedroom door. Slowly, the events of the night before crossed her memory, and Charlotte was suddenly wide awake.

She wriggled free of the covers, struggling not to wake Maya beside her. Her dressing gown was hanging from one of the wardrobe doors, left ajar with Maya's notebooks hanging out haphazardly from the shelves inside. Charlotte all but ran into the garment, arms outstretched to catch the sleeves as she opened the door as quietly as she could, bolting down the barren hallway. Her bare feet padded along the carpet as she followed the direction of the voices, hoping and praying to each of the three goddesses that she would see a familiar red-headed boy and a golden knight as she turned the corner…

The sitting room was tense in atmosphere, and to Charlotte's dismay it was only King Fenyang, Benkaei, and Varus in front of her. Their conversation ended abruptly as she entered the room, each set of eyes turning to stare at her as she approached.

"What happened?" she managed to ask between breaths, hating how small and broken her voice sounded to her own ears.

"The Aerindale gallows... someone beat us to the punch," Benkaei explained, amber-yellow eyes fixed on Charlotte. "We've sparked a full-scale rebellion in Caelfall, and they're as unhappy with the Aethian justice system as we are."

"What should have bought us time has hindered us," Varus continued for the warrior. "The king's men have assembled an interim short-drop in the western district town square."

Charlotte blinked. "Then what are we waiting for?" she demanded.

The Valedian king watched Varus with a careful gaze. "That location is... problematic," King Fenyang replied at last. "We would be completely exposed, with few places to hide and little opportunity to escape."

Her heart sinking, Charlotte felt her eyes burn, that hurricane within her threatening to burst forth once more. "What choice do we have?" she breathed. "We can't just let Jasper and Gideon die, we can't..."

"No," Varus agreed, shaking his head. "No, we can't."

Benkaei narrowed her eyes, crossing her arms over her chest. "Assuming that our imposter-Cary hasn't betrayed our location already... Clearly whatever torture those boys suffered wasn't enough to break them, or a hundred soldiers would have kicked down the door of this estate," she remarked coolly. "You just finished telling us how dangerous this would be, how we would be rodents running straight into a den of cats. What is it about Gideon and Jasper that is so vital we rescue them? What aren't you telling us?"

She should have protested at the callousness of Benkaei's words, insisted that her friends were worth fighting for, worth risking their lives to rescue… but something had tagged Charlotte's attention, a half-worded thought that bloomed in her sleep-muddled mind at Benkaei's comment. *Rodents.*

"The sewers," Charlotte found herself blurting out before Varus could respond. "The—the town square, there's a fountain there, and—the sewers, *Varus*—"

The man was already nodding in agreement, a spark in his eyes that Charlotte had not seen for a long time. "Yes," he agreed, nodding slowly. "Yes, we could… that could work."

"Varus, you've lost me," King Fenyang sighed, shaking his head. "Please, enlighten us."

Charlotte answered for him, too giddy in her excitement to stop herself. "The sewers in Aerindale run directly beneath the fountain in the town square," she explained, gesturing wildly with her hands as she spoke. "We could use that as a point of travel, lie in wait beneath the makeshift gallows."

Benkaei seemed impressed. "And then Varus can use his little shadow-stepping trick to whisk us out of the fray," she finished, nodding approvingly.

He shot her a dull stare at the remark on his abilities, but Varus was otherwise undeterred. "We should leave quickly," said the kingpin, already turning on his heel towards the hallway. "The sooner we get there, the more time we'll have to save them." Benkaei followed, and after a moment Charlotte was alone with the Valedian king in the sitting room. The brief shock she felt melted quickly before a wild fury that crackled in her chest, and soon Charlotte was running into the hallway after them.

"Varus!" Charlotte roared, moving quickly down the hallway. "*Varus!* Look at me, damn you."

The pair of them stopped ahead of Charlotte, perplexed by her outburst. Varus stared down at her, his expression blank. "Charlotte, there's no time—" he protested, but Charlotte wasn't finished.

"No. You are not leaving me here like—like some damsel in distress!" she protested, pointing a finger in his face. "I'm coming with you."

Something flickered across his expression, but the man was careful to keep his tone cool with her as she spoke. "Charlotte, this will be dangerous," Varus argued. "There will be soldiers, guards there."

"This plan of ours may very well go south," Benkaei agreed, something akin to concern in the warrior's voice as she regarded her, but Charlotte could not be deterred.

Taking a step closer, Charlotte allowed the full magnitude of her gaze to bore into Varus as she glared up at him. "These are my friends," she insisted, her voice low and even. The man towered over her, but she didn't dare falter, holding his stare with everything she had as she continued. "They are my *family*, and I am coming with you to rescue them. You can't stop me."

The silence that followed was deafening, Charlotte's chest heaving as her heart thudded in her throat. Varus stared at her for a long while, his eyes searching her face. After what might have been an eternity, the man finally conceded.

"Very well," he accepted with a slow nod. "Follow my lead."

Charlotte grew to regret her brilliant suggestion very quickly, as the sewers turned out to be the worst smelling environment she had ever found herself in.

Her surrogate guardians had attempted to prepare her as best they knew how, given she had made it quite clear she would not be dissuaded from the rescue mission. Haeyin had given her several yards of semi-rigid, supportive fabric, instructing her on how best to wrap her joints to prevent injury during the excursion. Varus had gifted her a dagger that Charlotte had strapped to her belt, fidgeting with it as she walked. Benkaei had lent her more appropriate clothing; an oversize coat, a plain shirt, and rugged trousers that felt secure and supportive, albeit strange. Charlotte had the excess fabric of her coat sleeve covering as much of her nose and mouth as she could as they trudged towards their goal.

They were travelling blind, having no visibility of the world above them. Their only indication of the direction they travelled was a half-remembered schematic Maya had stolen at some point from the cathedral, and Benkaei's approximate knowledge of where the makeshift gallows had been constructed. Varus walked beside her, and Charlotte could only guess what fueled the man. As far as she could tell, he'd been awake since the morning prior to the battle in Caelfall, and he was the only one among them who hadn't appeared to have slept since.

They trudged on through the sewers in silence until Charlotte dared to ask the question that had been on her mind since leaving the manor. "Why did you finally agree to let me come along?" she asked Varus, removing the fabric from around her face to speak. "What convinced you?"

The elevation changed slightly, and the tunnel widened to support a balcony on either side of the fetid water, enabling them to walk on dry ground once more. Varus grunted at the incline, stabilizing himself before he responded. "I must admit I've overheard a fair bit about the challenges you face from Haeyin," he explained. "I *am* your doctor's supplier, after all. At first, I confess I thought it better to protect you, to avoid placing you in situations that might cause further harm."

His admission was unexpected. Charlotte hadn't been aware that Varus knew so much, though it made sense if he lived with Haeyin. "And now?" she prompted him.

His eyes narrowed as he regarded her, his gaze shifting briefly towards her feet. "You're limping more often than not," Varus pointed out. "Which tells me you're well versed in dealing with pain, in overcoming it to get through the day."

Charlotte wasn't sure whether or not that was a compliment. "You limp everywhere," she protested as her face heated.

In response, Varus laughed as he shook his head. "And I know there is no force on this earth that would stop me," he assured her. To this, Charlotte had no response as they continued through the tunnel.

As they neared the town square, the sewers widened into a grand atrium of filth, several channels converging into one. The intake from the fountain area thundered into the canal ahead of them, the barest trickle of light leaking in from the sewer grates above them. As Benkaei and Charlotte slowed, she craned her neck around to better analyze her surroundings. There was ornamentation in the brickwork down here, careful thought and attention paid to the columns that supported the ancient walls.

"What is this place?" Charlotte wondered aloud. "Why such delicate architecture in a sanitation system?"

She hadn't really expected a response, but Benkaei snorted. "Perhaps Aethians need their waste pipes to be just as opulent as their toilets?" she suggested.

Comparatively, Varus seemed to have an actual answer, or at least a conspiracy theory. "There were rumours for years of an underground society meeting down here," he explained, kicking at a stray piece of broken brick in front of him. It skated across the slick tile, falling into the fetid water with a satisfying thunk. "Perhaps there is some truth in that."

As with many things Varus said to them, Charlotte wondered how much of it was true. Before she could respond, however, they were interrupted by a curious thud from above, a distant chorus of gasps. Charlotte felt the colour drain from her face as Benkaei spoke.

"This is it, this is as close as we'll get," she confirmed, nodding towards the ceiling. Benkaei was already scaling the nearest ladder to the surface, Charlotte and Varus close behind. "Varus, can you glamour our entrance at all? Obscure our arrival?" Benkaei called down as she climbed, strong hands and arms effortlessly in motion.

The man grunted in reply behind Charlotte as he assisted her on the first few steps, an equally endearing and annoying measure of care. "Aye, but only for a few moments," Varus agreed.

"A few moments is all we'll need," Benkaei assured him. Charlotte was less confident as she followed up the ladder, her hands squeezing each rung as tightly as she could. This would be a terrible moment to give in to a fear of heights.

Their ascent carried them out of the sewer atrium and into a narrow tunnel, nearing the surface.

As they approached the top of the ladder, Benkaei hooked her legs around the rungs to support herself as she reached for the sewer grate above them. She lifted it with ease, with no evidence of exertion or fatigue, carefully setting it aside out of view. Charlotte squinted in the sudden grey daylight, but she refused to falter. Feeling for the next rung as her eyes adjusted to the light, Charlotte followed as quickly as she could, Benkaei grasping her hand and assisting her out of the darkness as she reached the surface.

A horrid sight awaited Charlotte as she stood, turning to face the direction of the crowd that had gathered to spectate the executions. At first glance, she did not know the man that was hanging from the noose, his face flushed and bruised. But Charlotte had grown up with that face, and no amount of scarring could prevent her from recognizing her friend. *Gideon.*

They had been minutes too late.

Varus' hand was at her shoulder in an instant, forcing her to look away from the wretched scene. "Focus, Charlotte," he urged her, his voice hushed. "We can't save him, but we are going to save Jasper."

Her eyes burned, but Charlotte could not argue with the man's logic. She steeled herself as she looked towards the gallows again, as Gideon's corpse was dragged away to join the pile of bodies growing ever larger. She grasped the borrowed dagger at her side, the cool weight of it comforting in her hand. Varus and Benkaei flanked her as they slowly joined the crowd, blending in as they stalked towards their target.

Jasper was led to the stepladder, and Charlotte's heart clenched at the sight of him. He didn't see her in the crowd, but in that moment Charlotte wanted nothing more than to assure him of her presence, to promise it would all be better soon. The rope circled his neck, and his crimes were announced to the crowd.

"Jasper Gallagher, by order of His Majesty, King Gustaf Edmund Davenport III, you are hereby sentenced to death for the heinous crime of murder and treason against the sovereign kingdom of Aethelind."

Charlotte watched as her blacksmith closed his eyes, solemnly accepting his fate. She couldn't lose them both.

"On my signal," Varus warned, as if sensing Charlotte's urge to bolt. The kingpin was coiled and ready to strike, Benkaei aiming a dagger towards the gallows. The moment the stepladder was kicked out from under Jasper's feet, Varus bellowed, "*Now!*"

With terrifying precision, Benkaei launched the knife towards Jasper. The blade sliced through the rope, and before her blacksmith could be strangled, Jasper was falling to the stage in a heap. Charlotte bolted forward, using her elbows to shove her way through the remainder of the crowd. Nearby, Varus was blinking in and out of existence, appearing behind the supervising soldiers to slice their throats mercilessly. Withdrawing a folded metal contraption, Benkaei whipped her spear to its full length, the mechanisms locking into place with a snap. The reach of the weapon forced their opponents to give her and Charlotte a wide berth as they surged towards Jasper.

Charlotte only had one mission, the most important objective of them all. While Varus and Benkaei fought off the knights and the soldiers, her goal was Jasper. Her knees protested as she crashed to the floor beside him, her borrowed dagger making quick work of the remainder of the rope still deathly tight around his neck. The cord came away easily, and Charlotte pressed her fingers against the exposed spot on his throat, rope-burned but not broken. Against her touch, she felt that gentle thrum of blood in Jasper's veins, that defiant confirmation of life. Her strength renewed, Charlotte allowed herself a breathless giggle, relief flooding through her as she maneuvered to lift him from the platform.

Their actions had not gone unnoticed. Charlotte hadn't observed the growing tension in the crowd around them. With Varus and Benkaei in vicious combat with the king's men, their ferocity was the spark that ignited the kindling of a revolt. A woman's scream from within the crowd rallied the citizens, "*Do not serve a false king!*"

Mayhem erupted around them, the civilians drawing makeshift weapons from their coats to join the fray. While some rushed to support Varus and Benkaei, others ran for the remaining prisoners to free them. The line of convicts to be executed that had stood waiting behind Jasper stared at the chaos with wide eyes, too terrified to be hopeful. Charlotte locked eyes with a boy so young her heart tightened at the sight of him, his countenance reminding her of a younger Jasper. She waved him away as his fellow townsfolk freed the prisoners from their manacles, urging him to flee with the rebels.

Charlotte had only felt this way once before, this surge of adrenaline that seemed to lend her otherworldly strength, but it was different this time. Instead of fighting for her own life, she was fighting for *Jasper's* life. She lifted him as much as she could, every muscle in her body screaming in protest. In his unconscious state, Jasper was almost too much dead weight for her to carry. But Charlotte was built of something stronger now, her heart tougher and her bones tempered. Positioning herself behind him, she looped her arms beneath his, grasping Jasper's forearms as she tugged him closer. Charlotte heaved with all her might, dragging him from the makeshift platform towards Varus, towards the promise of safety.

"Varus!" she called to him as she approached. He appeared behind her almost instantaneously, giving a sharp whistle that popped Charlotte's ears. From within the calamity, Benkaei dropped one of the soldiers with a vicious strike of her spear, surging towards Charlotte's side in an instant. Varus' arm linked with Charlotte's as the warrior embraced them, and suddenly they were descending – through the cobblestones, through the underdark, through the void itself.

In the darkness, a figure in the distance caught Charlotte's eye. Paper-thin skin was stretched over a bony face, black eyes settled into deep sockets with a vacant expression. The chasm they travelled through stretched long and narrow ahead of her, that figure shrinking further and further into the distance.

She could not look away.

Noticing the creature, Varus tried to draw her attention. "Charlotte," he called to her, his voice distorted and distant. "Shut your eyes, Charlotte—now!"

No matter how hard she tried, Charlotte was too afraid. But no, it was not simply fear that gripped her, not some morbid curiosity, but a damning combination of both. At that moment, the creature shot forward at an alarming speed, the space between them shrinking into nothing. All Charlotte saw was an inhuman face, pale white with jaws stretched wide, a thousand rows of teeth—

Something snapped within her, a switch for a light she hadn't known existed, hadn't known how to operate. Her left arm tightened around Jasper's chest as she raised her right hand, fingers outstretched as Charlotte's eyes narrowed on the advancing monster. "*No,*" she whispered into that void, and from her palm a stream of light erupted into the darkness. There was an unholy screech emitted by the approaching figure as it was obliterated by that force, disintegrating in the wake of that mysterious light.

Before Charlotte could stop to ponder what had just happened, the four of them were colliding with the pavement outside of the Melicus estate. Instinctively, her arms tightened around Jasper once more, her body curling protectively around his unconscious form.

Groaning, Benkaei was the first to detangle herself from the mess of arms and legs. "Xiska…" she heaved a sigh as she stood up, leaning towards Charlotte to help lift Jasper's dead weight off of her. Sounding similarly affected, Varus assisted Charlotte to her feet, seeming to limp more heavily than before.

"What was that thing?" Charlotte demanded, not knowing what to make of what had just occurred, what she had just *done.* To her dismay, Varus only shook his head as he reached for the iron gate, the skin of his palm steaming as it made contact with the metal.

"We should get Jasper inside first," the kingpin instructed as he assisted Benkaei in lifting Jasper's limp form. "This isn't a safe topic of discussion for the streets."

While Varus supported Jasper under his arms, Benkaei braced the blacksmith's legs. "I have to hand it to you, Varus," the warrior grunted as the pair of them began to carry the young man towards the front entrance of the manor. "I still can't stand you, but you've got style."

Finding herself with nothing to do, Charlotte followed along slowly as the gate behind them shut of its own accord. Her body was trembling with overexertion, and she knew intuitively that she would suffer tomorrow for her overzealous excursion. The door opened ahead of them as Derek waved their group into the manor. She followed Varus and Benkaei into the manor as they carried Jasper towards the sitting room, with Derek shuffling off to summon Haeyin immediately upon their arrival.

As Charlotte crossed the threshold into the room, Eleni met her at the doorway still in her silken pyjamas, her blonde hair unusually dishevelled. "Charlotte, I was so worried!" the woman exclaimed, pulling her into a crushingly tight embrace. "Don't you ever scare me like that again, Maya and I had no idea where you were—"

"I'm sorry," Charlotte said immediately, too shocked to argue her case. Nearby, Varus and Benkaei deposited Jasper onto the nearest sofa, with the warrior leaning in to remove the manacles still binding his hands and feet. She had half a mind to ask her friend about what had transpired, the monster she had obliterated.

Eleni relaxed her hold on Charlotte, examining her at arm's length with an expression of deep concern. "What happened?" she asked, searching Charlotte's face for any signs of injury or exertion. "Where's Gideon?"

The mention of her fallen friend was more than Charlotte could take, and any other thought eddied away as the last of her composure crumpled. "It's my fault," Charlotte breathed around a lump in her throat. "If I hadn't… if I'd just let Varus and Benkaei leave without me, they would have reached Aerindale in time. It's all my fault."

She had known it the moment they'd emerged from the sewers, the moment Charlotte had turned towards the gallows and seen Gideon's body. There was a dull thud as the shackles fell from Jasper's wrists, and distantly Charlotte was aware of Benkaei leaving the room. She couldn't meet the warrior's eye, didn't dare look up to meet Benkaei's face in case the woman agreed with her.

Before Eleni could reply, there was another hand on Charlotte's shoulder, one she was unaccustomed to receiving comfort from. "The only person to blame for Gideon's death is King Gustaf," Varus assured her, his voice low and rough. "Remember that."

She wasn't sure she believed him. Had Charlotte wanted to argue her guilt further, she was distracted by Haeyin approaching. The doctor seemed as exhausted as he was when she'd last seen him, as if there were no amount of sleep that could restore him. He scanned each of their faces before his whisky-brown eyes settled on Jasper's wounded form draped over one of the sofas.

Sensing his work was cut out for him, Haeyin entered the room with a sigh, sneaking a kiss on Eleni's cheek as he passed by. "You should be resting, love," he chided her as he snapped his fingers in the direction of the fireplace, igniting the half-charred firewood. "Let me look after him, you exhausted yourself with Cary last night."

Visibly conflicted, Eleni glanced back and forth between Charlotte and Jasper. "Hae, it's too much for you to do on your own," she protested.

In a display of tenderness at odds with his kingpin persona, it was Varus who moved to gently coax Eleni out of the room. "Haeyin can manage for now," he assured her, pressing his lips to her forehead. "Come, let me make you a cup of tea."

As Eleni and Varus departed, the sitting room grew very quiet. Hastily wiping tears from her eyes, Charlotte startled at her own name whispered above the crackle of the fireplace. "Charlie?"

Her mind emptied at the sound of Jasper's voice. Stumbling towards the sofa, Charlotte managed to perch in the spare inches of space around his sprawled form. He was beginning to stir, his breathing growing more rapid as his bloodshot eyes fluttered open. As his gaze focused on her, he made to sit up, but Charlotte was quick to arrest his efforts.

"Don't move too fast," she said quietly, her hands splayed across his chest.

He obediently lay still beneath her touch. "Where am I?" he croaked.

She was reluctant to remove her hands, still grappling with how close she had come to losing him. "You're safe now, you're back at the manor," Charlotte assured him, struggling to smile. The sensation of the fabric of his shirt, the assurance of body heat beneath her fingers… she savoured each individual confirmation that Jasper was alive.

He exhaled a sigh, a lungful of tension and fear melting from his form. Even as he relaxed, Jasper's expression was sorrowful. "Gideon," he rasped, his voice cracking over the name of their friend.

Charlotte's heart fractured anew as her eyes welled with a fresh wave of tears. "I know, I'm sorry. It's my fault, I wasn't fast enough."

Wincing, Jasper seemed to struggle to reach for her, his wounds preventing him from doing so. "Not your fault, Charlie," he insisted immediately… but he didn't know.

"I thought, for a long while, that I might have lost both of you," Charlotte admitted in a low voice, the tears burning down her cheeks. She reached to brush his hair back from his face, her gaze falling on the scar along his brow.

Jasper blinked slowly, his gaze sliding back and forth as

he scanned her face. "I thought I'd never see you again," he agreed, his voice a ragged whisper. "I love you."

In gratuitous dreams and imagined fantasies, Charlotte had pictured how she might receive such a confession. She hadn't anticipated this, hadn't prepared for a response amidst the grief that clouded her heart. Despite the guilt she still felt over Gideon, the fleeting feeling of hope filled her chest at Jasper's words. His eyes flitted to her lips, and before Charlotte could spiral any further, she found herself leaning closer. He met her halfway, drawing on what remained of his strength to press his mouth to hers.

Tasting of rust and copper, his lips were chapped and worn as he kissed her, but Charlotte couldn't bring herself to care. She had dreamed of this, yearned for this – no mortal reminder of how close Jasper had come to oblivion could deter her. Leaning closer, Charlotte's fingers found their way into Jasper's hair, careful not to put any pressure on his wounded form as his arm loosely circled her waist.

For a moment, they were frozen in time, and nothing existed but Charlotte and Jasper. She had come so close to losing herself these past few days, so close to losing *him*, and the reality of their temporary safety felt almost too good to be true. She might have stayed there an eternity, but Charlotte couldn't bear to be selfish. She broke away as Jasper's head sank back against the cushions once more, gasping for air.

"My nose," he mumbled apologetically.

Charlotte swore under her breath. "I'm so sorry," she replied immediately.

He shook his head, mumbling something that might have been words, but his strength was waning. His eyes began to close even as he struggled to keep his gaze fixed on her.

"You should rest," she whispered, unable to stop herself from smiling. "I love you, too." She stole another kiss, pressing her lips to Jasper's brow before she sat upright.

Much to her chagrin, she had entirely forgotten Haeyin's presence in the room with them. Charlotte felt her face heat with embarrassment at what he must have witnessed, but thankfully the doctor seemed engrossed in organizing his medical kit. Her attempt to speak to him was interrupted by Eleni's cat, leaping onto the sofa gracefully with a soft mewl. As if oblivious to Charlotte's presence, Mo curled up on top of Jasper's chest, purring loudly as she did so. Haeyin looked up from his tools momentarily as he eyed the animal, as if debating the merits of leaving her there or shooing her off.

Now that they were no longer in immediate danger, Charlotte regarded the boy beside her – and clapped her hand over her mouth to prevent the cry of alarm that bubbled up her throat. She hadn't seen what harm had been inflicted upon Gideon, but Jasper's injuries gave her an idea of the hell her friends had endured. His face was bruised and inflamed, bloodied by an injury mostly obscured by his hair, his nose broken and twisted. But his hands…

"Can you heal him?" Charlotte found herself asking, hating the tremor in her voice. She had never doubted the good doctor's ability before, never had reason to question him. To Charlotte's despair, Jasper's hands were mangled almost beyond recognition, each of his fingers broken in multiple places. His right hand had suffered the worst of it, two of his fingers absent entirely.

The doctor turned to face her, his brow furrowed. In this light, there was more white in his hair than Charlotte had ever seen before, the creases around his eyes made more prominent by the shadows beneath them. As he looked at her now, however, Charlotte noted there was a hint of fire in those amber eyes.

"When I see this, the last thing I have on my mind is healing," Haeyin said slowly. "I see this, and I want vengeance for him, for Gideon. But I *can* heal Jasper, to the best of my ability."

He didn't need to elaborate for Charlotte to understand. Even a healer as gifted as Haeyin had limits, and this was not the first time he had been faced with something he couldn't fix. Her heart broke for Jasper, for the pain Charlotte had been unable to spare him from. Haeyin let her stay while he prepared his instruments and ointments, but eventually the doctor was forced to request solitude for him and his patient.

Exiting the room, Charlotte left Haeyin to his work and Mo to her favourite perch. To her surprise, Varus was waiting for her in the hallway, an unreadable emotion on his face. "Are you all right?" he asked her, studying her as he leaned on his cane.

Charlotte pursed her lips. "No, not at all," she scoffed half-heartedly. Seeking a distraction, her thoughts drifted back to the encounter with the monster. "What was that thing? How did I do that?"

He regarded her with a conflicted expression. "One of the demons that exists between realms, a creature that preys on fear," Varus explained in a low voice. He paused for a moment, his brow furrowed as he continued. "As for how you defeated it... I think you already know the answer to that."

Nodding slowly, Charlotte swallowed. "I've never done anything like that before," she admitted in a choked whisper.

There was something akin to empathy in Varus' gaze as he beheld her. "With everything that's going on… it might be more prudent to keep this to yourself for now," he suggested. "Given that you're already on the run for stabbing the king, I would hate for you to have another target on your back."

She scrubbed at her eyes with the back of her hand, errant tears dripping down her cheeks. "Probably not a bad idea," Charlotte agreed with a sniffle.

"I shouldn't have excluded you before, and for that I'm sorry," the kingpin continued quietly, his admission surprising Charlotte. "If I'd let you assist us, you wouldn't have had to fight tooth and nail just to take part. If you're condemning yourself for Gideon's death, I share a part in that blame."

To this, Charlotte had no response as she stared up at Varus. There were lines around his dark eyes she had never noticed before, hollow and haunted. She wondered briefly how many times Varus had lost someone.

"If you want to head up to the study and avoid everyone for a while, you have every right to do so," Varus offered, gesturing towards the stairs. "But if you'd like to be included, we're having a meeting in the kitchen. You're welcome to join us."

He didn't wait for her to follow him, turning down the hallway as he limped towards the kitchen, his cane tapping rhythmically on the wooden floor. The thought of hiding away for an indeterminate length of time was appealing… but Charlotte was done hiding away. She took a stabilizing breath as she followed Varus, mentally preparing herself for what would undoubtedly be an interesting discussion.

CHAPTER
NINETEEN
DANTE

As a consequence of having the crap kicked out of him the night before, Dante slept heavily. After wrapping his arm in a sling to support his wounded shoulder, Haeyin had given him something strong and foul-tasting that had effectively knocked Dante out for the night, and the result was a better night's sleep than he'd had in weeks.

When he awoke, Dante's initial reaction was one of brief panic, his heart thundering in his chest as he took in the unfamiliar surroundings. It took a moment to settle his anxiety, to recall the events of past few days. Just as Dante had started to grow accustomed to waking in the Valedian embassy, any sense of security and normality was torn away from him. It seemed his life was filled with these foreign awakenings, each place of shelter a stepping stone from one temporary safety to the next.

He explored the guest room he had no recollection of

falling asleep in, tentatively rifling through the luxurious wooden armoire at the far end of the room. He had been sent to bed wearing only the sling Haeyin had secured his wounded arm in, and Dante had no desire to leave the room wearing nothing. Struggling around the presence of the sling, he dressed as quickly as his body would allow. In the brief time he had spent in Aethelind, Dante's left shoulder had seen the bulk of his acquired injuries; despite Haeyin's handiwork, the now old bullet wound had never quite stopped hurting him. All but stumbling into a fresh pair of dark trousers, Dante settled for tugging one of his surviving sweaters over his head, sling and all. He looked comically round with the bulk of his arm concealed beneath the woollen jumper, but he didn't much care for appearances as he meandered into the hallway.

Dante oriented himself as he shut the door to the guest room behind him. He seemed to be at the far end of the east wing, his stomach growling in the silence as he caught the scent of food in the distance. Still half-asleep, Dante trudged towards the kitchens — abruptly coming to a halt as he passed the sitting room.

His first instinct was to go inside, to greet the familiar young man he eyed on the couch, the friend he had feared he might never see again. Dante's entire form seemed to be frozen, however, as he took in the details of the scene before him, the way Charlotte and Jasper were entangled. An odd feeling fluttered irritably in his chest, a sort of jealousy that Dante had experienced before. This intimacy, this display of affection... it was something he had never had before, something he could never have.

He was startled from his thoughts by the soft, nearly imperceptible creak of wood and steel as Maya wheeled herself down the hallway. She came to a stop beside Dante, beaming up at him. "Good morning," she said sweetly, giving him a quick once over. "It's good to see you up and about, how is your shoulder?"

He forced himself to look at her, to look away from the scene in the sitting room. "Better, thank you," Dante replied earnestly. "I was just heading back towards civilization."

Maya's gaze flitted from Dante and his ridiculous sweater towards their friends in the room beyond, and her smile faltered. For a moment, Dante was at a loss for words as he watched the girl struggle to compose herself. The jealousy he felt was directed at neither Jasper nor Charlotte, merely towards the freedom they found to be with one another. For Maya, however... Dante had a suspicion that her heart was breaking as she regarded the pair.

"Are you all right?" Dante hesitated to ask.

Whatever brief crack he had witnessed in Maya's visage seemed to vanish at his words, and she turned to address him once more. "Where is Gideon?" Maya asked softly. "I had a dream about him, about Jasper... is he all right?"

Dante didn't have to ask what the dream was about, given the fears they had all shared the night before. "I've only just left my room, maybe he's in the kitchens." He beckoned for her to follow him as he departed for the west wing, seeking the scent of food and caffeine that wafted down the hall as he and Maya approached.

Illuminated by the afternoon sun, Eleni and the Valedian king were sitting at the kitchen table in silence when Dante and Maya entered the room. Neither of them appeared to be very well rested, judging by the cup of tea clutched in Eleni's hands or the mug of coffee adhered to

Fenyang's. The king's eyes found Dante's instantly, and he immediately wished he were wearing something less laughable.

"Good afternoon," Fenyang greeted them, but the smile that crossed his face was strained. "There's more on the counter." He gestured towards the kitchen island, where a carafe of fresh coffee and the leftovers of a cooked breakfast remained. Maya wheeled herself towards the lowered countertop as Dante withdrew a clean pair of mugs from the cabinet for the pair of them. He offered her a plate as well, but the young woman declined as she carried the mug of coffee precariously between her thighs. Maya rolled towards the table in relative silence, her wheelchair squeaking on the pristine white tiles.

As Dante dispensed scrambled eggs and bacon onto his plate, he dared to ask the question that had been burning on the tip of his tongue. "Was the rescue mission a success, then?" he began, making his way towards the table, taking a seat beside Maya. The rich scent of coffee filled his nose as he carefully set his plate down with his good arm, the mug balanced around his serving of food.

Moments before Eleni replied, Dante was struck with a sinking feeling in his chest as he took note of how haggard she looked, the way her red-rimmed eyes and flushed nose indicated recent tears. *Oh, no.*

The woman cleared her throat as she rubbed her eyes. "Partially," Eleni managed to reply with a sniffle. "You may have seen Jasper in the sitting room with Haeyin."

"Partially?" he repeated, his voice faltering. In his heart, he knew the answer even before Fenyang spoke.

"Benkaei informed me that we were unsuccessful in saving Gideon," the king explained, taking a sip of his coffee. "Very nearly unsuccessful in saving Jasper, at that. But we should try to be glad of the small wins, as painful as it is to have lost one of our own."

Maya's face crumpled, her eyes brimming with tears. "Oh, that's awful…" she whispered. She shook her head as she clung to her mug of coffee, as if she might disappear within it.

Dante closed his eyes, cursing himself. His selfish feelings towards his friends felt all the more horrid now that he knew exactly what Jasper and Charlotte had endured. How could he deny them any small happiness together, knowing now how much they had lost? He took a large gulp of his coffee, feeling the heat burn down his esophagus, pushing the bitter feeling of envy down deep within him.

At that moment, Varus and Charlotte entered the room. The pair of them looked rather worse for wear, emotionally if not physically. Instinct took over, and Dante was on his feet in an instant, moving towards his friend. Charlotte had never felt so small to him as she did now, tucked into an awkward one-armed embrace. Her fingers tightened in the fabric of his sweater as Dante rubbed her back, rebuking every selfish thought that had crossed his mind.

"I heard about Gideon," Dante mumbled into her hair. "I'm… I'm sorry, Charlotte."

Charlotte sniffled against his chest as she returned the embrace. "Thank you, Dante," she murmured softly in reply. As Dante released her, he allowed Charlotte to take his seat beside Maya and Eleni, shifting his mug and his plate aside. Noting the movement, the Valedian king nudged his coffee aside to make room for Dante.

Varus assumed his place at the head of the table, his armour-clad form clunking against the wood. He looked exhausted in a way Dante could only partially understand, a despairing look in his eyes. If he had to guess, the man was running on fumes. No one spoke for a time, a solemn silence settling heavily over the five of them.

With some trepidation, Dante cleared his throat. "What do we do now?" he managed to ask, glancing back and forth between Varus and Fenyang.

"I think it's safe to say the curfew was a catastrophe," the Valedian king began. "I imagine we killed enough soldiers and city guards to send a very clear message to Gustaf, but… it came at great personal cost."

There was a small chorus of murmured agreement. Nodding solemnly, Eleni pursed her lips. "We've managed to release many of the citizens we took in that night," she offered reassuringly. "Most were only suffering from shock or minor injuries. Those that have passed have been collected by Haeyin's… contact." She said the word with some measure of distaste, and Dante recalled the conversation with the doctor and Cary about the morgue connection.

Cary…

Charlotte cleared her throat, wiping errant tears from her eyes with the back of her hand. "For better or for worse, our actions haven't gone unnoticed," she offered, her voice uneven. "It seems we've inspired a rebellion. Many of the people attending the executions were equally pissed with the king."

Maya sniffled, her eyes fixed on the wood grain of the table. "What purpose did any of this serve, why did the king do all of this?"

Beside her, Charlotte nodded in agreement. "And why did Cary – or rather, not-Cary – target Jasper and Gideon?" she continued, gesturing towards Fenyang. "Your

Majesty, if you and your council were the supposed targets, if *I* was a target... why didn't our imposter try and stay close to the manor?"

The Valedian king narrowed his eyes, nodding slowly in agreement as he sipped his coffee. His braided hair fell loose around his shoulders, tucked behind his ears. "Cary's innocence raises further questions," Fenyang pointed out. "Not only are we forced to question how long this imposter has been in our midst, but why they chose Cary as their persona to infiltrate our operation."

Dante frowned into his coffee, a thought tickling the back of his mind. "It makes sense though, doesn't it?" he wondered aloud. "Whoever decided to impersonate Cary must have put thought into it, must have known about how many social circles she was involved in."

As he glanced up from his beverage, Dante's face began to burn as he became aware of five sets of eyes fixed on him. "I mean, think about it," he continued, flustered. Dante set down his coffee, counting off his fingers as he spoke. "They must have known she worked at the castle in proximity to Gideon, at the clinic helping Haeyin. She's close with Jasper, with Eodan—*Varus*, rather, and she's a member of the Silent Sisterhood. Cary is the common denominator, but who knew this? Why and how did they know to exploit her?"

Turning towards Varus, the king eyed him carefully. "How long has Cary been in your employ?" he asked slowly.

"Longer than most," Varus replied evasively, idly twirling his cane at his side. After a moment's pause, he raked his fingers through his dark hair with a deep sigh. "Almost twenty years. She was a Silent Sisterhood assassin who was originally sent to kill me, but... I talked her out of it. I formed an alliance with Rosaline shortly after the failed attempt. Cary's worked for me on the side ever since."

Maya and Charlotte stared openly at Varus, wide-eyed at his casual confession. "Do you always invite your would-be murderers to your house, or was she a special case?" Charlotte murmured.

An unsettling thought crossed Dante's mind. "Can not-Cary still get into the estate?" he interjected, his gaze snapping up to Varus. "You said the gates were enchanted—can she get in?"

There was a flurry of nervous glances exchanged before the party's eyes settled on their host once more. Varus frowned. "I don't know," he replied, which was an equally upsetting and unhelpful answer. "The gates aren't enchanted per se, but... the iron can't be bewitched or tricked by magic, can't be fooled by glamours. It responds to blood, so whoever was impersonating Cary had to have been someone who was previously permitted entry."

"Or perhaps someone who merely followed a trusted person in," Fenyang offered, waving a hand. "I seem to recall Cary entering the estate with a group the last time we saw her before the battle, the day the curfew was raised."

"How did *you* of all people acquire a—a sentient iron fence?" Dante protested, waving at Varus with his good hand. He seen Varus' flesh burn back in the dungeons, when he reached through the iron bars to tug Dante's dislocated arm to safety.

The kingpin hesitated before responding. "Zeke," he replied eventually. "Jasper's uncle, rather."

That certainly asked more questions than it answered. "If you haven't already, it might be wise to reset, or recalibrate who is permitted entry," Dante suggested, poking at his untouched breakfast. "At least until we can determine who we can trust."

Their host nodded approvingly. "Haeyin and I worked on resetting the protections on the estate the night that Gideon and Jasper were taken," he explained.

Her voice sounding strained, Charlotte spoke up once more. "Varus, before we left this morning... Benkaei said something that hasn't been sitting well with me," she admitted, eyeing their host. "I thought it was callous at the time, but she raised a good point when she asked what was so 'special' about Jasper and Gideon."

Fenyang's expression softened at her words, suggesting he might have been present for this conversation. "Perhaps it could have been worded differently, but the point stands," the Valedian king agreed. "The imposter chose Cary for the social circles she existed in, and yet... our imposter made no effort to remain at the manor, which seems the more logical choice, going by the intel we received from Princess Aurelia and Gideon."

Appearing to be plagued by this very question, Varus exchanged a concerned glance with Charlotte and the king. "I had asked myself the same thing. I'm forced to consider that perhaps we don't understand Gustaf's motives after all."

Shifting in her seat, Maya idly picked at her fingernails as she spoke. "I do wish Gideon were here, so we could ask him questions about what transpired at the castle," she mumbled under her breath. Clearing her throat, Maya managed to speak up a little. "Perhaps Aurelia can give us more insight on the matter? She seems keen on betraying her father. Do we have a means of contacting her?"

Varus shook his head, pursing his lips. "Not securely, no," he replied. He paused for a moment before he continued, his tone hesitant. "Cary and Fortia are partners. Usually, being one of the castle servant staff, Cary was able to infiltrate to pass messages along as needed. However…"

"Varus, *no*," Eleni urged, reaching for the man's wrist. "I've only just set her ankle, the poor woman's been through enough."

"And we don't know who ordered not-Cary to betray us," Charlotte added, earning an approving nod from Eleni. "If they see the real Cary at the castle, we might be putting her in danger if she's caught."

His brow furrowed, Dante pondered as he took another sip of coffee. It was beginning to cool, and the flavour was less pleasant than it had been initially. "We may be able to use that to our advantage," he suggested tentatively. "If they don't know that *we* know about not-Cary…"

Charlotte and Eleni seemed vehemently opposed to the idea, while Varus and Fenyang appeared to agree with Dante. Maya seemed conflicted. "Maybe we should ask Cary what she wants to do," she suggested softly.

Varus seemed to consider her words, rubbing his chin as he leaned back in his chair. "Ultimately, it's up to Cary whether or not she's ready for the task," Varus agreed with a note of finality. "If she isn't, we'll have to find alternate means of contacting Princess Aurelia."

Their conversation was interrupted by a weary doctor entering the room, making a beeline for the kitchen sink. It seemed that every time Dante saw Haeyin, the renegade mage was always cleaning some substance or another off himself or his surroundings. He looked drawn as he turned to face them all, magical exhaustion prevalent in every aspect of the doctor's appearance as he dried his hands on a fresh towel.

"He'll be fine," Haeyin explained knowingly to the

curious eyes of his companions. "Not the worst injuries he's sustained, but… well, he'll live. They were undoubtedly tortured, as we feared."

Despite the healer's words, Dante and his companions picked up on the underlying meaning. "We definitely need to contact Princess Aurelia, if we can," Fenyang agreed with an air of determination. "If they were torturing Jasper and Gideon for information, we need to know what they were after."

A thought crossed Dante's mind, one that he immediately hated himself for. It seemed that Haeyin picked up on this, and the doctor exhaled a weary sigh. "If I may… if Jasper remembers this information, he may be willing to discuss this with us," Haeyin suggested, rubbing the back of his neck. "My expert medical opinion is that we at least give him some time for the anaesthesia to wear off beforehand."

"Is he awake now?" Charlotte asked, her eyes wide.

Haeyin hesitated before he responded. "He's coming around," he replied eventually. "He's not entirely lucid yet, but you can go and see him if you would like. He's in his room."

Across the table, Varus adjusted his armour as he stood up with the assistance of his cane. Haeyin narrowed his eyes. "And where do you think you're going?" the doctor asked accusingly, pointing at him with towel in hand.

"When was the last time you slept?" Eleni followed up, glaring at Varus. "You're a danger to yourself and others if you don't get some rest."

Varus gave his partners a blank look as he took in their betrayal. "I'm fine," he insisted, but neither of them were having it — and for good reason, given the startlingly grey pallor his skin had taken on.

"It seems you're outnumbered on this one, Varus,"

Fenyang chuckled, shaking his head. "Go, take some time to yourself. We can handle things for a bit."

As if sensing the time for a group discussion was over, Charlotte darted out of the room, waving for Maya and Dante to follow. His breakfast cold and forgotten, Dante abandoned what remained of his coffee as he and Maya followed a limping Charlotte down the hallway towards Jasper's room.

The door had been left ajar, and the scene that greeted them within was almost serene — almost. The red-headed blacksmith was propped up on multiple pillows, his chest bare beneath the form of the black and white cat currently nestled on his abdomen. Dante's eyes tracked the faded bruises across the side of Jasper's face, the faint pink line along the bridge of his nose that hadn't been there before. Most unsettling were his hands, splinted and bandaged and notably lacking two fingers.

He was already stirring as they approached, his eyes barely opening as his head turned. "Good to see you," he mumbled as Charlotte curled up beside him on the bed. Maya wheeled herself near the bedside table as Dante sat on the edge of the mattress, careful not to disturb his heavily bandaged hand.

Any semblance of coherent thought had left his mind the moment Dante had seen just how partially successful the rescue mission had been. He could smell the tang of magic in the air, the wounds Haeyin had been forced to leave unmended for the sake of his dwindling magical energy. There was a reddened collar of rope-burned skin around Jasper's neck, and Dante swallowed a lump that formed in his throat.

"How are you holding up?" he asked tentatively, not knowing what more to say.

Despite his injuries, despite what he had endured, Jasper laughed hoarsely, much to Mo's chagrin as his chest jostled with the movement. "I've had better days," Jasper wheezed, and Dante noted a few of his teeth missing from the right side of his jaw. The man lifted his left hand, the least damaged of the two, and petted the cat on his chest apologetically. Dante opened his mouth to speak, but all he could focus on was the raw and red lines on Jasper's wrists, the evidence that remained of recently removed manacles.

As if noting his turmoil, Maya came to the rescue. "We're glad you're safe," she replied warmly in her soft, gentle voice. "And… we're so sorry about Gideon."

The measured movement of his hand as Jasper petted Mo faltered, his expression falling. "I'd hoped I dreamt that part," he murmured in reply. "But I know I didn't. Hasn't… hasn't really set in, yet."

There was a moment of silence shared between them, at a loss for what to do or say in the wake of such tragedy. Just as Charlotte seemed to be about to say something, Jasper spoke up once more. "In the dungeons, Gideon told me he's my brother," Jasper explained. With a wince, he added, "Was my brother."

Nothing could have prepared Dante for this information, and nothing could have prepared him for how vastly different each of their reactions were. Charlotte only momentarily surprised before her eyes widened, as if she had replayed every memory shared with the two of them and understood the clues she had missed. Maya, in comparison, seemed unsurprised.

Even as Dante watched the pain and grief in his friend's eyes, Jasper managed another soft huff of laughter. "Said he was keeping it a secret, in case his father found out," he elaborated, his words somewhat slurred. "Said my father was killed, and my... our mother died having me. Gideon and Zeke were the only ones who knew."

The silence that followed the admission was heavy with sorrow, the confirmation that no living member of Jasper's family remained with them. After a moment, Maya nudged Dante. "Dead parents club?" she asked tentatively, glancing back and forth as she raised a hand. Jasper's shoulders shook with barely restrained laughter at the remark.

"Dead parents club," Dante agreed solemnly, struggling not to smirk at the dark humour of it all. The three of them glanced towards Charlotte, who shook her head in response.

"Abandoned, more like," she replied mournfully. "Though she *could* be dead, I'd have no way of knowing."

"You can be an honorary member," Maya replied, earning a nod of agreement from Dante and Jasper. For a few seconds, there was only silence. Jasper was the first to laugh, sounding as if he was trying desperately not to and emitting a strangled snort as a result. He groaned in pain, clutching his nose with one of his bandaged hands even as he continued to laugh at Maya's remark. After that, the rest of them dissolved with infectious giggles, shocked and sad and giddy with relief that despite the kingdom's best efforts, their friend was still alive. It was a small victory amidst an ocean of tragedy, but it was a victory nonetheless.

The shared joy soured for Dante once more as their laughter died down and Jasper turned to face Charlotte, her fingers tentatively brushing his hair back from his face. He struggled to suppress the envy that bubbled up within his chest, determined not to ruin what happiness the two of them would find in one another. As his gaze fell to the floor, Dante panicked as he tried to come up with something to say that wouldn't be cruel, some reason to leave the room that wouldn't ruin this reunion.

At that moment, there was a gentle knock against the door frame of Jasper's room, and the four of them turned in unison to face the newcomer. Fenyang was stooped casually beneath the threshold, smiling at Jasper. "I'm pleased to see you back at the manor, Jasper. Might I borrow Dante for a moment?"

Dante tried and failed not to appear eager to leave as he rose from the bed, navigating around Maya's wheelchair as he made to exit the room. "I'll come and visit you later," he promised Jasper before leaving, closing the door over behind him as he joined Fenyang in the hallway.

As he turned to face the man, Dante was reminded for the millionth time just how much the Valedian king towered over him. "What did you need?" Dante asked when the man did not immediately supply an explanation for summoning him.

The king's eyes darkened as he searched Dante's face. "Come with me," he instructed. Dante followed obediently, shuddering as Fenyang brushed past him in a corridor wide enough for the both of them. They traversed the hallway in silence, the estate oddly quiet at this time of day. With so many of the manor's occupants resting at odd times, having worked all night or recovering from recent injuries, the activity levels varied widely throughout the day. Fenyang led them to an empty guest room, a rarity amidst the new population in the estate, peering inside to ensure no one was resting within.

The choice in meeting location was confusing, to say

the least. "What can I do for you?" Dante asked the king as he closed the door behind them.

Fenyang glanced at Dante with a knowing stare, an eyebrow raised. "You seem troubled, *d'viin*," he replied simply. "I suspected it in the kitchen and confirmed it when I walked past Jasper's room and you were dissociating."

There was that term again, that Pharasathi word that Dante hadn't yet learned. Finding himself without an immediate response, Dante was unable to come up with a convincing answer. "I—I'm just tired," he lied feebly, cringing internally as he watched the king's eyes narrow.

"Why don't I believe you?"

Dante scoffed defensively, gearing up to retort... but something stopped him, some mental wall he'd placed around himself faltered at the prospect of lashing out against Fenyang in particular. "Why don't you?" he managed to reply instead, his voice sounding weary to his own ears.

The king watched him knowingly, and Dante's heart fluttered at that stare in an especially damning way. "Are you envious of your friend?" he suggested.

This was easier to deflect, and Dante's response was immediate – and clumsy. "Why would I be envious of Charlotte?" he replied, waving dismissively with his good hand. The back of his neck prickled at his words, at the confirmation to a question that Fenyang had not asked.

"I'm... I'm not envious of either of them," he insisted, even as his face heated. He began pacing the room in what he hoped was a casual excuse to break eye contact.

Fenyang was not easily shaken off. "Then what is it that troubles you?" he asked, his tone sincere. He would not allow Dante to distance himself, following him slowly as he wandered the room.

The instinct to shut down and barricade himself behind his mental walls was unbearably strong — but Dante was tired, and against his instincts he trusted Fenyang. "It's not that I envy them," he clarified as he paced, flapping his uninjured arm as he sounded out his thoughts. "I don't… I don't feel that way about Charlotte, or Jasper. I mean, they *are* my friends, and I care about them, but not in that regard. It's just that… they're both free to be their own people, to be together. I envy that more than anything."

It was the most honest he had been in a long time, and it felt strange to speak so freely. He could practically feel those golden eyes boring into the back of his skull, stripping him bare. "And why don't you have that freedom, Dante?" the king asked him.

Dante refused to answer, refused to incriminate himself further. He shook his head, biting his lip. "I can't say," he replied. He was determined not to look at him, not to meet that stare, knowing his resolve would crumble against the man. But Fenyang would not back down easily.

"*Why* can't you say?" Fenyang demanded.

Raking his fingers through his hair, Dante laughed manically as he turned to face Fenyang, his back to the wall. "You're the king of Valedia!" he protested. "This is hardly the sort of subject I'd bring up with a monarch!"

"No," Fenyang said firmly, closing the distance between them. "No, do not censor your words as if they may offend me. You no longer use honorifics to refer to me in private, nor do I want you to."

Dante flinched at his words, at the truth in them. He had been slipping, coaxed into a sense of safety and security with Fenyang he should never have allowed himself to fall into. It was a mistake, and he hadn't even been fully aware of it; only now as he heard the truth confirmed for him,

Dante could count the strikes against propriety in a deadly tally that raised alarm bells in his mind.

"Don't do that," Fenyang protested, grasping Dante's undamaged shoulder. His grip was surprisingly gentle, as if he sensed Dante's despair and feared frightening him further. "Don't hide from me. In this room, I am not a king and you are not my subject. In this room, I am a friend — I am a friend who is concerned and wants to help. Please, don't shut me out. I will ask you again; *why* don't you have that freedom?"

Tension rippled through him, his hand curled into a fist at his side as Dante met the king's stare—met *Fenyang's* stare. Was he no longer a king in his presence? Then Dante would speak openly, he would not censor his words for Fenyang's benefit. The truth burned within him, a tangle of secrets so deep and dark and terrible he had buried them within the shadows of his soul. He could feel the acidic texture of it burning within him, threatening to emerge. It needed no further encouragement as the floodgates opened.

"Because my name isn't really 'Dante'," he growled, his words tumbling through his teeth. "Because it wasn't enough that I've never loved a woman, it wasn't enough that I was a better scholar than a warrior, I just happened to be fucking *cursed* as well — had to be born with the one brand of magic that no one in Fraecath can be allowed to practice, had to be born *good* at it.

"That day we went to the castle, the day General Byron had the templars attack us," he continued, desperation in his voice. "Do you remember when Huda said that was my first use of my powers? It wasn't — not even one of the first. I was a child when it manifested, raising dead rabbits and reanimating mice caught in traps set in the kitchens. When my mother died, I touched her face and accidentally resurrected her. I didn't know how to retract my power, and my father locked me in that church with her until I figured it out.

"I have *no* freedom, do you understand?" Dante asked breathlessly, tears welling in his eyes. "As long as I breathe, I can never live up to my birthright so long as I remain who I am, who I was born. I can never live with my mind unguarded, with my magic loose in my veins. I can never share a throne with someone I truly love, and having a secret affair beneath a false marriage is *not* a solution to that. I was shackled in that life, and so I ran away — but I will never be free. Does that answer your question?"

The silence that followed was deafening, Dante's ears ringing as he stared at Fenyang, waiting for a response. The man watched him with those amber eyes, and his expression was carefully guarded. After a few moments, he slowly extended his hand towards Dante. "My name is Fenyang," he spoke at last. "What's yours?"

Dante stared openly at the man, at the Valedian king. "Did you listen to any of what I just said?" he asked weakly.

"I did, I assure you," replied Fenyang, his hand still extended. "And it seems that even after all this time, after all that we have been through, you and I have been living with a wall between us. I would like to get to know you properly this time."

He stood in stunned silence, desperately searching for any hint in Fenyang's expression that would give some indication of what he was truly thinking, of what he really felt towards him. But there were none, for if there was one thing Dante had learned about the Valedian king, he was honest above all else. His fingers were trembling as he took Fenyang's hand, fighting every instinct within him that told him to run, told him to lie. He took a deep breath as he met Fenyang's golden gaze.

"My name… my name is Vincenzo Dante Cacciatore di Anima," said Dante in a low voice.

Fenyang's darkened gaze searched Dante's expression for a moment longer. "The lost prince of Fraecath," he mused quietly, his deep voice a low rumble in his chest. "Not so lost after all."

He laughed bitterly at the title, at the destiny he had abandoned. He closed his eyes as the face of the Valedian king became too bright to behold, the tears spilling freely as Dante tried in vain to hold onto some shred of his mask. Releasing his hand, Fenyang cupped his face tenderly as his thumbs brushed those errant tears carefully from Dante's cheeks.

"It is truly an honour to meet you, and to know you," he added in a low voice. There was truth in each word, too heavy and too pure for Dante to bear. A shiver ran down Dante's spine as he struggled to resist the urge to lean into that touch, to lean into the strength of such a gentle gesture.

"You deserve to be yourself, you know," Fenyang continued, and his voice seemed rough. "You deserve to be with whomever you fall in love with, with magic in your veins and hope in your heart."

When Dante opened his eyes, the man that stared back at him was a version of the Valedian king he had never met before. There was a mask that had been lifted, a wall of his own that had been brought down brick by brick, and it was breathtaking to behold. Honey-gold eyes stared back at him, scanning Dante's expression as if waiting for a clue or a signal to proceed.

"And what if I fall for someone I can never hope to be

with?" Dante dared to ask. His heart hammered in his chest, his every instinct screaming at him to fall into silence once more, but there was no turning back now. "What then?"

There were mere inches between them now. "Never?" Fenyang breathed. "What makes you so certain of this?"

Swallowing around a lump in his throat, Dante struggled to hold the king's intense stare. "He is... otherwise occupied," Dante explained, struggling to keep his voice even. "With a woman, no less."

The space between them grew smaller still, even as Dante became aware of the fact that neither he nor Fenyang had moved. The king seemed conflicted, and the realization that he was as nervous as Dante was... it was invigorating. "In the foolish hope that you're referring to me, I will speak plainly," Fenyang began, taking a breath. "You should know that what you'd said, your sentiment about a secret affair beneath a false marriage... Huda and I have had a similar arrangement for the past year or so, that I might ward off unwanted proposals from women I can never hope to commit myself to."

At the man's confession, Dante could only stare in amazement. To think that Fenyang might be *nervous* because of him... "It's a very convincing arrangement," Dante offered in reply, managing a smile.

Fenyang's hands had not moved, still cradling Dante's face as they stood there. At the sight of Dante smiling, the king's eyes tracked down towards his mouth. "Please, put me out of my misery," Fenyang pleaded teasingly. "If I've misread this, please let me know. My arrangement with Huda need not continue if you would walk in the light with me."

With no small measure of trepidation, Dante covered

Fenyang's hand with his own, as if he might physically prevent the king from releasing his hold on him. "Just because I've abandoned my kingdom, I could never ask you to do the same," he whispered, even as his actions betrayed his desires. "Would that not hurt your reputation, to be seen with a man?"

Shaking his head, Fenyang brushed a thumb across Dante's cheekbone. "Pharsat is different from Fraecath, *d'viin*," he assured him, smiling in return. "There is no obligation for me to sire an heir, no expectation for me to wed a woman."

His thoughts snagged on the unfamiliar word, the term he had heard applied to no one but him. "You've called me that a few times now... what does it mean?"

For a moment, Fenyang was silent as he regarded him. The distance between them was so small that Dante could see the minute scars on the king's cheek he had never noticed before, the way his eyes were flecked with green and copper. He leaned towards Fenyang instinctively, stretching up on his toes as the king moved closer towards him. The warmth of his lips against Dante's mouth sent another shiver travelling down his spine as they connected.

In his twenty-four years, Dante had never felt the way he did now. His experience with intimacy had been limited to rushed, practical encounters of physical need, detached from emotion or sentiment. This was different in every aspect.

With a renewed vigor, Dante found himself releasing his hold on the king's hand, winding his fingers through Fenyang's hair as if he might pull him closer still. He cursed his still healing shoulder, for there was nothing Dante wanted more than to embrace Fenyang fully as he deepened the kiss. His lips were soft and warm, and Dante could feel the strength in Fenyang's large hands, kept at bay for his benefit. The distance between them was all but nonexistent, the blood in Dante's veins electric and volatile as his tongue parted the king's lips.

In response, Fenyang groaned against Dante's mouth, and it was the most delicious sound he could have imagined. Fenyang's touch traced down from his face, his fingers leaving trails of fire in his skin that ignited the blood in Dante's veins. The turmoil from earlier had been burned away, and all he could focus on was Fenyang – the scent of sandalwood, the warmth of his hands through Dante's sweater, and the taste of coffee as his tongue graced his lower lip.

And yet, Fenyang pulled away all too soon, breathless with a hunger that thrilled Dante. Those golden eyes were blown wide, the thinnest ring of amber circling a void that threatened to swallow him whole. "I should slow down," Fenyang murmured, his voice low and rough.

He restrained the despair that bubbled within him. "I don't want you to," Dante breathed. They remained frozen where they stood, with Dante's back against the wall behind them, Fenyang's hands still on his body.

The man looked mournfully at the sling over Dante's shoulder, carefully adjusting the fabric where it was visible above the collar of his sweater. "You're still injured," replied Fenyang, ever the voice of reason. "And if I were to aggravate that, I'm sure our mutual friends would kill me, royalty or not."

Dante felt his cheeks flush. "I'm fine," he insisted, his fingers leaving Fenyang's hair to brush along the man's jaw tentatively. He didn't want to leave this room, he didn't want Fenyang to let go of him.

Fenyang laughed low in his throat, his lips curling into a

smile. "Of course you are," he murmured, tucking Dante's hair behind his ear. "Don't tempt me, Dante. I'm struggling to be sensible as it is."

It was difficult not to tempt the man when Dante could still taste the remnants of him on his tongue. "I can't even feel my shoulder at this point."

Chuckling, Fenyang leaned forward to press his lips to Dante's forehead, and the tenderness in that gesture left him weak in the knees. "I am not so desperate that I would jeopardize your healing for my satisfaction," the king insisted, much to Dante's despair. "Besides... I brought you something."

Taking a step back, Fenyang proceeded to rummage through one of the pockets of his trousers. Dante watched in mixed fascination and selfish impatience as the king retrieved what appeared to be a small container.

"What is this?" Dante asked.

"Something for the pain," Fenyang offered, gesturing with the container. "May I?"

At the realization that the Valedian king was asking him to remove his shirt, Dante's face heated... but he did not refuse. With some difficulty, he lifted the sweater over his head, grateful for the reprieve from the sweltering environment it had created for him. Struggling not to be self-conscious wearing so little clothing before the Valedian king, Dante settled onto the edge of the unmade mattress of the guest room. The bed creaked as Fenyang sat beside him, opening the jar of ointment.

"You undoubtedly know this already, well-educated man that you are," Fenyang began to explain, the scent of herbal salve filling the air. "What few mages Pharsat produces tend not to be healers, with Verdis... my grandmother being a rare exception. She taught me to make a great many non-magical remedies, should I ever find myself in need of them."

As the king massaged the substance into Dante's skin, into the ring of bruises around his shoulder blade that had come up overnight, his heart grew heavy with sorrow. "I'm... I'm sorry about your grandmother, Fenyang," he managed to reply.

The man was silent for a moment, his fingers gently easing the salve into Dante's wounded shoulder. "Varus is formulating plans to bring myself and my council back to Valedia," he continued. "When we return... we must conduct funeral rites for my grandmother. Would you come with me?"

Turning his head, Dante glanced towards the king over his shoulder. To his astonishment, the ointment had served its purpose; he could already feel a pleasantly numb warmth where the ache in his shoulder had once lived. "I... is that allowed?" Dante asked tentatively. Funeral rites for the royal family were a secretive affair for Fraecath, limited only to the nobility and the immediate family.

The king looked up at him with a wry smile on his face. "I've just invited you," teased Fenyang, the rumble of his voice causing Dante's heart to flutter. His skin was saturated, yet still the king's fingers stroked Dante's injured shoulder soothingly. "You aren't required to attend, but—"

"I would love to," Dante agreed earnestly.

The smile on Fenyang's face widened, and it was a strange, thrilling thing – to be able to witness this, to have caused this, and to experience it so freely. His fingers slowed on Dante's back, his hand travelling down Dante's spine in a way that gave him goosebumps. "How does that feel?" he asked softly.

"Better, much better," Dante stammered insistently,

glancing at the king over his shoulder. He leaned into that touch, leaned into the vast space between him and Fenyang.

A dark mischief crossed the king's face, his smile a promise of more to come. "Good," he said simply, his hand circling Dante's waist as the king pulled him closer, the salve still present on his fingertips tingling against bare skin. Dante reached for Fenyang with his uninjured arm, his fingers cradling the king's face as he closed the space between them once more.

TWENTY

JASPER

The guttural breath of the beast teased at Jasper's hair, alerting him to its arrival before the creature spoke, the resonant voice echoing in his mind. *"You have rested too long. You must awaken."*

He opened his eyes to find himself in unfamiliar surroundings, naked and forlorn on the shoreline of what he could only assume was the Aethian Sea. Morning light temporarily blinded him as Jasper pulled himself upright, his body startlingly pain-free. Frowning, he struggled to remember what had transpired prior to his arrival here, wherever here was.

The sensation of the sand beneath his palms irritated him, and instinctively he made an effort to rub his hands together to wipe away the offending texture – but something about the movement felt wrong. Jasper raised his hands, regarding their unblemished appearance and the presence of ten fingers.

"This is a dream, then?" he said aloud.

The monster chortled, the crunch of the sand beneath its clawed feet signalling its approach. *"Dreams need not be disregarded so readily,"* the creature spoke. *"Some say dreams are missives from beyond."*

Despite the knowledge that he was dreaming, Jasper's mind felt painfully clear. "So... that was all real," he confirmed, his heart sinking. "Gideon is gone." In the distance, a great form rose into the sky, a warrior molded from the fabric of the universe. The entity raised her arms, and the ground beneath Jasper began to shake.

In a startling display of affection, the monster behind Jasper seemed to be... nuzzling him, the scaled form of its head brushing against his shoulder with an empathetic whine. *"We cannot change the things that have come to pass,"* the beast responded mournfully. *"Nor can we change that which has been predetermined by fate."*

Clenching his fists, Jasper regarded the way the muscles and sinews in his fingers shifted with the movement. If this was a dream, it was remarkably convincing. "Are you saying that he was destined to die?" Jasper questioned, his temper rising. "No, I refuse to believe that." The ground trembled beneath him, the sand shifting in his peripheral vision as aged bones broke through the surface.

"Believe what you want, Jasper," the creature replied patiently. That smouldering breath all but burned the back of his neck as the monster huffed. *"It cannot change the truth – the time has come for you to awaken."*

Humanoid skeletons emerged fully formed from the shoreline, their chattering teeth ringing in his ears. A frigid hand circled his neck, and Jasper gasped as boney fingers clamped down on his throat.

His chest heaving, Jasper awoke with a start, blindly clawing for his throat as he shot up. The impact of his amputated fingers against his own skin sent a jolt of pain through his arm, and Jasper groaned with the effort it took not to cry out. He sucked in breath after breath of blissfully cool air, his sweat-soaked skin clinging to the bed sheets unpleasantly.

Following his most recent run-in with death, Jasper had been plagued with ghosts. Though his dreams had always been vivid, he never considered them terrifying enough to qualify as nightmares. No, the nightmare in comparison was awakening from the terror of imagined monsters to find that the waking world was worse in every way. No matter what grim tale his unconscious mind could weave, he had surfaced from a world where Gideon had not died, where Jasper had not met Death herself with her similarly red hair and pale green eyes.

As the fire within his veins calmed and his heart no longer thundered in his chest, a cloying loneliness settled into his skin. It was a wound no healer could mend, a homesickness that could not be eased by simply returning to his flat above the forge. Jasper wondered how he had managed to spend so much time apart from Gideon, how he had purposefully stunted one of the few connections he had left. How had he gone so long without knowing his only remaining family was right beside him all along, only to lose him so painfully?

Despite the way his hands ached with the movement, Jasper pressed his palms into his eyes as his breathing settled. Selfishly, a part of him wanted to look for Charlotte, the one person he knew could understand the depth of his grief. Haeyin had strongly urged he sleep alone while his hands recovered, and Charlotte had taken to sharing a room with Maya ever since she'd started staying at the estate. It would be so easy to cross the hallway to look for her, and he knew instinctively she would understand… but no, he didn't want to burden her with his emotions. She was the one bit of sunshine in his life, a single god ray in a clouded sky that kept Jasper going. He knew Charlotte was struggling with Gideon in her own way; there was no need for her to shoulder Jasper's emotions as well.

His stomach growled in the silence, giving Jasper the motivation to venture out of his room for another source of comfort. How many days had passed since his arrival? It was dark enough outside to be early morning or late at night, and the medication that Haeyin gave him made Jasper sleepy and confused. Despite what must have been several rounds of magically assisted healing, every inch of Jasper's body ached as he struggled out of the bed, rummaging in his forgotten satchel for the clothes he had brought with him to the estate. Each benign sensation against the knuckles of his right hand brought a disproportionate level of pain, and Jasper quickly learned to rely on his left hand as he dressed. Donning his favourite, threadbare old sweater and a rumpled pair of trousers, Jasper made for the corridor towards the kitchen.

Despite the many occupants of the manor and the unusual schedule they kept, the place was quiet. Even the oft-used sitting room, ever the multi-purpose setting, was abandoned. As a result, it caught Jasper by surprise when he walked into the kitchen and found he was not alone.

Looking up from the pantry, a housecoat-clad Eleni seemed equally startled at his presence. "Jasper? What are you doing awake?" she asked. "Do you need more medication?"

Shaking his head, Jasper swallowed around a lump in his throat. "No, thank you," he insisted immediately. At Eleni's inquisitive stare, he cleared his throat. "They make me feel... odd."

She smiled sympathetically. "The side effects can be unpleasant," Eleni agreed. Her eyes skimmed over him, as if she were searching for the right thing to say, and Jasper all but cringed beneath her watchful gaze.

"What are you doing up so early?" Jasper asked, hoping to divert the conversation away from him. It was difficult to tell, but judging by the direction of the faint light coming from the kitchen windows... if Jasper had to guess, it was very early indeed.

"I could ask you the same thing," Eleni teased, a wry smile on her face. She retrieved a satchel of rice from the pantry, raising an eyebrow towards Jasper. "I seem to have regained my appetite. You must be hungry, why don't you give me a hand?"

It took a moment for Jasper's addled mind to understand the instruction within Eleni's words, and he clumsily made to assist her with food preparation. Though Haeyin had healed his fractured fingers, he had not yet regained the strength in his hands completely; he grew frustrated as he attempted to grasp kitchen utensils, finding the grip strength of his right hand crippled. Eleni seemed to have prepared for this, giving him tasks that required fewer fine motor skills.

As Jasper washed the batch of rice for a second time, the rhythmic sound of Eleni chopping vegetables paused momentarily. He dared a glance over at what appeared to be onions, peppers, and… mushrooms. Seemingly noticing his chagrin, Eleni jumped to assuage his worries.

"You don't have to eat these if you don't want them," she assured him, separating the chopped vegetables from the excess stalks and seeds. "I'm just adding them for the flavour. They'll be large enough to pick them out."

He relaxed a bit as he drained the rice a final time, the clouded water swirling around the sink basin. "Zeke used to make rice that way," Jasper found himself mumbling as he ignited the stove top, filling the now clean rice with a fresh helping of water. "I never bothered with it so much after he died."

At the mention of Zeke, Jasper thought Eleni might ask for clarification. Instead, she seemed to pause before continuing the conversation, as if debating how best to respond. "This has always been one of the few things I can get Varus to eat," Eleni explained, setting aside a skillet nearby for later on. "I tend to prefer something with a bit more excitement, but… nowadays, I find my palette more temperamental."

Jasper blinked, astonished. "I'm sorry, you mean to tell me Varus *eats*?" he asked incredulously.

Covering her mouth with her hand, Eleni struggled to suppress her laughter. "Hard to believe, isn't it?" she agreed conspiratorially, winking at Jasper. Her expression sobered after a moment as Eleni brought the rice to a boil, a twist of her hand raising the temperature of the water faster than the stove could manage. "Don't repeat this, but… it's an ongoing struggle for him. Haeyin and I try not to nag, but if we don't remind Varus to eat, he won't."

To this, Jasper had no immediate response, no reaction to Eleni's information that seemed appropriate. It was true enough that he'd never seen Varus eat, but what was previously an amusing quirk had become a solemn concern. He fell into a neutral silence beside Eleni, stirring the rice into the skillet to join the now seared vegetables. Intermittently, she would verify additional ingredients with him to ensure he would still consume them, much to Jasper's relief. Despite never having met his uncle, he thought Eleni had unintentionally followed Zeke's recipe rather well.

The kitchen smelled delightful by the time they were done, with Eleni assisting Jasper in picking out all the mushrooms from his portion of rice. As he took a seat at the wooden kitchen table, he could feel her insistent gaze on the side of his face, but Jasper had no intention of reliving his recent capture just yet. As it was, it was taking most of his concentration to focus on chewing with the left side of his mouth. The silence engulfed him as he mindlessly consumed the bowl of rice, his use of a fork one of the many things affected by his missing fingers.

"Jasper…" Eleni began hesitantly, gingerly picking at her own food as she propped up her chin on her free hand. "We don't need to talk about it right now, but at some point Varus and the Valedian king will want to speak to you about what happened in the dungeons."

A strange emotion overcame him at the mention of the dungeons, something Jasper could only describe as the sudden and distinct sensation of imminent danger. He forced himself to swallow a mouthful of rice before he choked it back up, setting his fork aside with little grace.

"I don't know if I can," Jasper admitted.

The woman regarded him with ageless blue eyes, as if she saw far more than merely his physical form. "Would it be easier to talk to me about it? Or someone else, just one on one?" Eleni offered.

He pondered the thought, if a more intimate discussion

would be less impactful on his anxiety. "I'm not sure how helpful it would be, if I'm honest," Jasper elaborated, leaning back in his chair. The absence of movement seemed to exacerbate his aching muscles, as any amount of rest caused them to seize up painfully. "I don't remember much, but they asked me about the council, about the king's assassin. I didn't tell them anything, if that's what Varus is worried about."

As he raised his right hand for emphasis, Eleni's brow furrowed as her gaze tracked the movement, the absence of his fingers. She opened her mouth to speak, but another voice interrupted from the threshold of the hallway.

"Why did they stop?"

Jasper's scalp prickled at that cadence, a voice he had not heard in a while – one he had hoped not to come across again. He knew as he rose to his feet, even before he turned to face the doorway, that he would come face to face with Cary. She looked almost exactly as he remembered her, though Jasper's mind was quick to note the differences; she was thinner, seeming wan and drained with newly short hair scraped back from her drawn face.

"This isn't a good time," Eleni cut in sternly, and a note of warning laced her tone as she stood.

Something dark and venomous curdled his blood as Jasper took in the sight of the woman who had betrayed them, the reason that Gideon was dead. As if sensing the imminent promise of danger, Cary raised her hands in a gesture of surrender, tilting her head as she regarded him.

"You have every right to want to kill me, but I owe it to you to explain what happened," Cary began, her rose-hued eyes wide as she pleaded her case.

Jasper blinked. A circle of blood-red rubies falling to the floor. Dark eyes, malicious laughter. His memories of that wretched night flooded back to Jasper at a speed that was physically painful. Instinctively, his left hand flew to his head as if he might stem the flow of his recollection.

"Jasper?" came Eleni's voice beside him. She hesitated inches away from him, torn between touching him and giving him space. He recalled the way Cary had been so uncomfortably close to him at the clinic the day he had been captured, the way he had inched away from that unpleasant contact.

"Was it really you?" Jasper managed to ask the woman, opening his eyes as his head throbbed. "Or was it someone else?" He willed his vision to focus on Cary's face, searching for a glamour he could scrub from her visage to reveal an intruder beneath... but there was nothing.

Shaking her head, Cary lowered her hands. "It wasn't me, but perhaps you already had your suspicions," she explained, her voice trembling. "I was rescued from the dungeons when Varus and Dante ventured out looking for you and... and Gideon."

Remaining a measured distance away, Eleni hovered beside Jasper protectively as he regained his composure. "We don't have to have this discussion now," she emphasized in a low voice, glancing from Cary to Jasper.

He appreciated how thoughtful the woman was, but... no, his resolve had solidified. Inhaling slowly, Jasper steadied himself. "No, maybe... maybe we should," he insisted as he straightened up. "There's not much I remember from the dungeons, but maybe we can compare notes. You asked me why they'd stopped."

Narrowing her eyes, Cary's stare darted briefly towards Jasper's hands before focusing on his face once more. "Don't misunderstand me, I'm grateful you still possess most of your fingers," she elaborated, crossing her arms over her chest as she leaned against the threshold. "But if you gave nothing away, what caused them to stop?"

Jasper stilled at her words, struggling to recall what transpired in the painfully bright room he had been tortured in. The memory of the altercation, the vivid sensation of his bones breaking... his stomach turned as Jasper relived the moment his fingers had been severed. Absentmindedly, he thumbed at the bandage still present on his hand, protecting his wounded knuckles. The feeling pained him, but the discomfort served to ground his thoughts.

"I... I think I broke free of my restraints," he explained slowly, searching his mind for the series of events. "I don't remember much, I think they might have knocked me out after that."

Tilting her head, Cary seemed to be deep in thought. Sensing an opening in the discussion, Eleni cleared her throat. "Cary, I cannot stress enough how much I would rather we shelve this conversation for another day," she pleaded, her voice sounding weary.

Cary's expression was guarded as she replied. "I know Varus wants me to try and contact the princess," she insisted, gesturing idly.

"To hell with what Varus wants!" Eleni snapped in response, achieving a level of volume that startled Jasper. "We have lost too much already, and I will not sacrifice you simply because you want to prove your loyalty to him."

"We don't know what the king's motives are, and I have a means to provide intel," insisted Cary, jabbing a finger into her chest. Her throat seemed empty without the presence of her mother's necklace. "I am not a child, Eleni – I am more than capable of sneaking to Briardeen without raising suspicion."

"You shouldn't go alone," Jasper pointed out, but Eleni interjected before he could continue.

"And that is *not* an invitation for you to risk your neck, either," Eleni implored him, her eyes glittering.

The words came out before he could stop them, before Jasper was even consciously aware he had spoken. "We already lost the best chance we had when Gideon died," he retorted, his voice breaking on his brother's name. "He knew all the inner workings of the castle, he was trained to fight longer than I was. He was the one who told me about the curfew, and now he's gone — anything else Gideon knew about Gustaf's motives died with him. I need to know the truth."

It seemed for a moment that Eleni would argue further, and for half a second Jasper thought he had overstepped. He thought he ought to apologize for lashing out, for the bluntness of his response when Eleni was only trying to help. She heaved a sigh that seemed to drain the last of her energy, wiping flyaway blonde hair back from her face with a trembling hand.

"I am not keen on throwing either of you into danger so soon after you've been rescued," Eleni emphasized in a low voice. "Especially not when we know someone was impersonating you, Cary. We still don't know who our imposter was."

"We will *all* be in danger until Gustaf is stopped," Cary insisted, her rosy gaze molten in the dim light. "And until we know what he's planning, we can't prepare ourselves."

He wasn't sure what swayed Eleni at last, whether it was their words or the naked expression of desperation on Cary's face. Jasper recognized that raw emotion, knew it as well as he knew his own turmoil; he needed this, to be in motion and to be at work, or his thoughts would drown him.

"All right," Eleni sighed at last, but there was a worried gleam in her eyes. "You want to do this? Convince me. Tell me what the plan is."

For the first time in all the years Jasper had known her, Charlotte did not protest when he explained what he was about to partake in. Perhaps it was because she knew she could not volunteer in his stead, still aching so horribly after dragging him from the gallows. Perhaps it was because she had accepted that safety was an ephemeral state, and there was nothing any of them could do to stay out of danger forever. Standing on her toes, a sleepy Charlotte kissed him gently before he departed, wishing him luck and warning him to be careful.

He enjoyed this, the effortless intimacy with her. He would fight tooth and nail to make it back to her, to make it back to the warmth of her presence.

They sought out the estate armoury first, given that both Cary and Jasper had lost their primary sets of armour. After Jasper had squeezed into an ill-fitting ensemble that was the most similar to the armour Varus had given him, Cary wove a quick glamour into their outerwear. Gratefully, the poor weather had given them an overcast morning for their venture outdoors, aiding their cover. Jasper tucked his now black hair beneath the hood of his coat as they left the estate grounds, heading to the northern bridge towards Briardeen.

They hadn't been out long when Jasper stopped abruptly before a community notice board in Briardeen, caught off guard by the damning signage that had been nailed over an autumn equinox party flyer. He scarcely believed his eyes as he took in the bold font of a wanted poster, a grainy depiction of his own face staring back at him.

WANTED: DEAD OR ALIVE
JASPER GALLAGHER — £5,000

He wasn't sure whether he wanted to swipe the poster down immediately or bolt at his likeness plastered across a public space. Was it recognizable enough that he should tread more carefully?

"You're not the only one," Cary noted, rapping her knuckles against the notice board. There were more, one for each of their allies it seemed – there was a notice for a Dante Styvacino for violations of the mage laws and grievous bodily harm; for a Haeyin Valkae for unlicensed physicians' practices and mage law contraventions; even one for an Eleni MacKay for owning and selling banned books.

The worst of them all by far was the one posted in the middle, and the familiar face staring back at Jasper made his blood run cold.

WANTED: DEAD OR ALIVE
~~VARUS EMERY~~ — £10,000
EODAN MELICUS

"Is this new?" he asked weakly.

Cary hummed as she regarded the posters, her keen gaze scanning each of the names on the board. "Varus has always had a target on his back. Now, it's just more visible."

Jasper joined her in scanning the notice board a second time, cataloguing each of the names and faces he recognized. "She's not on here," he pointed out in a low voice. "Charlie."

"Nor am I... a small comfort," Cary agreed, nodding slowly. "It seems the resistance is growing bolder, for better or for worse." She lifted one of the wanted posters, a poor rendition of Dante's face that obscured a defaced advert for the Aethian military. Someone had smeared Gustaf's face with what appeared to be blood, adding their own campaign.

~~*HAVE FAITH IN YOUR KING,*~~
~~*HAVE FAITH IN YOUR COUNTRY*~~
DO NOT SERVE A FALSE KING

Nudging Jasper gently with her elbow, Cary gestured for him to follow. "Come on, it's best we don't linger," she urged, leading him towards the palace. They shuffled along with the sparse crowd as they headed north, a light drizzle allowing their cloaked forms to blend in as numerous civilians shuddered along in similar protective garb. The glamour on Jasper's appearance worked well enough that the city guard patrolling Briardeen didn't so much as blink at his passing, and they ventured on.

Cary's passage towards the castle gardens turned out to be more involved than Jasper had initially thought. The way she had described it, they would enter through a side entrance rather than the main gates. By the looks of it, Cary was leading Jasper through the bushes and over a wall.

"We'll have to time this carefully, because we'll only get one chance," Cary warned him, her rosy eyes assessing their surroundings as she led him to the westernmost wall surrounding the vast castle gardens. The closer they approached, the taller it became, and Jasper stared incredulously back at her.

"How are we getting over that?" he despaired, gesturing towards the obstacle. He had no confidence in his ability to scale a stone wall before his injuries, and Jasper was doubtful he could support his weight with eight fingers.

Shaking her head, Cary smiled wistfully. "Ye of little faith," she chided him. Walking ahead of Jasper as they approached, she scanned the unremarkable brick as she peered through the dense foliage. After some time, just as Jasper was about to point out that they were sitting ducks, something glimmered at the edge of his vision. He narrowed his eyes, willing himself to see through the glamour before him - there was a gap in the wall, sheltered by the foliage that surrounded it. It was one of the best glamours he'd come across, undetectable from a distance.

"How was this concealed so well?" he asked.

Biting her lip, Cary regarded him mournfully. "I've always been a dab hand at glamours," she began, her fingers fidgeting at the base of her throat where her necklace used to rest. "I know how incriminating that is, given my defense that someone was impersonating me."

Shaking his head, Jasper crossed his arms loosely over his chest. "I'm not accusing you of anything right now," Jasper insisted. "We both ended up in the dungeons. If you *were* out to get me, you're shit at it."

She blinked once in shock at his words before convulsing with breathless laughter, her hand pressed against her mouth before she gave away their cover. "We'll shelve that for another time then," Cary agreed.

"In the meantime, I hate to put a damper on your

plans, but... I am not certain I'll fit through that," Jasper pointed out, frowning at the hole in the wall.

Cary, who was slender enough to have danced through it, seemed to reassess the hole. "If you can squeeze through the catacombs, you should be fine," she insisted, pulling back some of the brush to climb through.

"That is *not* the same," Jasper hissed, but Cary was already disappearing through the wall, positioning herself with care as she eased herself through the gap. Finding himself with no alternative option, Jasper groaned as he ignored every instinct in his mind that told him he would be trapped in the wall. Mimicking Cary's movements, he guided himself through the narrow space, his bandaged hands gingerly grasping at the bricks.

Despite Jasper's apprehension, it seemed Cary's assessment of the situation had been correct. Though a few stray pieces of broken stone jabbed into his sides and his stomach as he ventured through, Jasper did not get stuck. The too-tight armour seemed to aid him through the ordeal, and Jasper was grateful to climb out the other side relatively unscathed. Nevertheless, Cary seemed to have been poised as she waited, prepared to tug him out of the wall if he had gotten stuck.

"I should have warned you it would be a tight squeeze," admitted Cary apologetically, leaning in to brush brick dust off his armoured shoulder. "I promise you, I wouldn't have suggested this route if I thought you wouldn't fit."

He shot her an exasperated look as he adjusted his cloak. "Did you forget I'm twice your size?" Jasper asked. "Why is this gap here, anyhow?"

Something clouded Cary's expression as she looked up at him, but it was gone a moment later. "I can't exactly stroll into the palace gardens dressed as an assassin now, can I?" she teased. She patted his arm reassuringly before setting off again, leading him through the garden. "Let's hurry, I want to be out of here as soon as possible."

Exploring the castle gardens was a harrowing experience, even though Jasper trusted Cary's knowledge of the layout and the guards' rotation. He had been to the castle on numerous occasions with Charlotte for the church's food drive, but he had never ventured through here. They were simultaneously dense enough for Jasper to feel lost but also dangerously exposed in the open space. Cary led him down a winding path, often through hedges and trees in lieu of following the stonework completely.

They came to a stop beneath a large weeping willow near the epicentre of the gardens. Cary withdrew a small mirror from her pocket, angling it back and forth repeatedly in the direction of the castle. A small beam of light ricocheted across a western-facing window on one of the higher levels, back and forth three times. As Cary pocketed the mirror once more, Jasper pondered how strange it was to be here, when only a few days ago he had been rotting in the dungeons below their feet.

"What do we do now?" he asked.

Cary's eyes narrowed as she regarded the window, and Jasper was momentarily blinded by a similar beam of light appearing from behind the glass. "The signal was seen," Cary explained while Jasper blinked the ghost of the light out of his eyes. "Now, we wait."

Somehow, the waiting part proved to be the most anxiety-inducing intermission of their journey. When he was on the move, Jasper would already fret internally. He had the unfortunate gift of appearing unruffled even as he was falling apart on the inside, and now especially his heart pounded in his chest while they waited. Beside him, Cary also appeared deceptively relaxed – but Jasper had known her long enough to recognize the stress in her posture, the way her jaw was clenched as she rubbed at her bare throat. He wondered what had become of her mother's necklace, if those rubies still lay scattered in the alleyway where Gideon had yanked them from the false Cary's neck.

As his thoughts drifted towards his brother, Jasper swallowed the threat of a meltdown as it bubbled up his throat. He could not afford to be distracted now.

The gardens were eerily silent, absent entirely of any wildlife Jasper was accustomed to seeing and hearing on the outskirts of Caelfall. The sudden sound of crunching gravel had both Jasper and Cary on high alert, preparing to bolt at a moment's notice. To their immense relief, it was not the royal guard who emerged from the hedges, but Fortia. Her steel-grey hair was pulled back from her face in a tight plait, that bold line of ink across the bridge of her nose made her gaze all the more intimidating as she glared at Jasper.

As her eyes slid towards Cary, however, there was a crack in Fortia's façade. The woman dissolved as she drew nearer to Cary, her strong demeanour vanishing as her eyes glistened. A rapid string of Reinnairlei words preceded a fervent embrace, too fast and too foreign for Jasper to comprehend.

"Shadows—never scare me like that again," Fortia breathed, clutching Cary to her as if she thought the woman might vanish once more. Fortia released her only to shift her grasp, turning Cary's face in her hands as she examined the healed wounds on her face and her shorn hair. "Oh, my love… what happened to you?"

Shaking her head, Cary gently removed Fortia's hands from her face. "There isn't time, dear," she insisted apologetically. "I should be glad to catch up with you, but it's quite urgent we speak with Aurelia."

The mask of the princess' guardian slipped back into place as Fortia regarded Cary and Jasper closely. "I'm afraid that won't be possible, she's being fitted for her masquerade costume as we speak," Fortia explained stiffly, nodding towards the castle. "I doubt I could whisk her away for a discussion, and the longer I keep you out here waiting, the more danger I place you in. Patrols have been difficult to work around following the attack on the king."

"Dramatic bastard," muttered Cary, rolling her eyes.

"What's this about a masquerade?" Jasper interrupted.

Fortia cleared her throat. "The castle will be hosting a masquerade ball in honour of the princess' birthday on the night of Samhain," she announced sarcastically, idly brushing a few loose strands of hair out of her eyes. "That's the official reasoning, anyhow."

"And… the unofficial reasoning?" Cary prompted, batting her eyelashes.

It was Fortia's turn to roll her eyes. "You'll be the death of me. The king had hoped to use the ball to announce the royal engagement, but with Prince Vincenzo still missing… he's obviously hoping to host a ball for one reason or another, and Aurelia's birthday happens to be an acceptable back-up occasion."

Jasper frowned as he mentally framed the recent turn of events, searching for a pattern or a trend he could map out amongst the information he had collected. Seemingly doing the same, Cary pondered aloud. "What is he up to now?" she said. "None of this makes any sense."

"Indeed, it's all rather strange," Fortia agreed, her vermillion gaze sliding over to Jasper. "What I would like to know is this… why were the executions scheduled so urgently? What intel was acquired through torturing citizens like yourself that warranted such drastic measures?"

He was unprepared for such a pointed question, and he didn't much care for the way Fortia was looking at him. "Nothing," he blurted in response, his face heating with the interrogation. "I don't—I don't know why."

Cary cleared her throat primly, but Fortia's piercing stare lingered on Jasper. "What is it then?" the warrior barked. "Nothing, or you don't know? Whatever it was, the decision to advance your pending execution was made so quickly that even the princess and I were too late to intervene."

Jasper bristled at the woman's pointed words, his hands trembling. Beside him, he noted how Cary stepped protectively before him, as if she sought to physically separate him and Fortia. "My love, how long ago was Aurelia betrothed to the prince of Fraecath?" Cary interjected sweetly, pulling Fortia's attention away from Jasper.

The grey-haired woman frowned, momentarily caught off guard by the question. "About... six or seven months ago, now," Fortia replied, staring off into the distance. "It was shortly after the beginning of the new year, of that I'm certain. Prince Vincenzo went missing shortly after it was determined, and so it was never announced."

At the information, Cary's frown deepened. Her gaze flitted back and forth without ever really focusing on anything, as if she were mapping out a mental wall of notes and hypotheses.

"Gustaf is many things, but he is not impulsive. This sort of decision wouldn't happen overnight, and it wouldn't be something Aloysius would suggest," Cary pointed out, with a roll of her eyes at the mention of the king's advisor. "Was there anyone who joined the king's inner circle around that time? Some new advisor that was appointed? Violating the accords, the attack on the Valedian council… Gustaf is making risky decisions, and for what? For whose benefit?"

Fortia began shaking her head, but there was an uneasy air to her voice as she replied. "Not to my knowledge, but…" the warrior trailed off, regarding Jasper warily. "Since he was injured, Gustaf has been largely confined to his chambers. On more than one occasion, myself and the other staff members have heard voices from within."

"So… he's meeting with someone in his chambers?" Jasper prompted, grimacing. "That's not unheard of for the king, from what I've heard."

Cary cleared her throat, though she didn't immediately disagree with Jasper. "True enough, though his usual 'meetings' typically don't contain much dialogue, I can assure you."

Though Fortia appeared distressed at the mention of the king's predatory habits, she did not refute their words. "My suspicion is that someone he was meeting with privately before is now forced to work around Gustaf's inability to travel very far," Fortia elaborated. "Oftentimes, he would be away from the castle for unspecified reasons. Now the king remains at home, but in seclusion… with audible meetings taking place in his chambers while he recovers."

This information appeared to exasperate Cary. "A mysterious benefactor asks more questions than it answers," she complained, raking her fingers through her hair. "We could speculate all day about who it might be and get nowhere."

"There is another thing," Fortia admitted with some trepidation, glancing around once more to ensure they were alone. "The allegiances within the castle give me pause. There are knights I do not recognize, staff members I am certain are here with ulterior motives."

Shifting where he stood, Jasper was beginning to tire. "Does the castle not normally have a high turnover?" he asked. He and Charlotte had never been further than the courtyard for the food drive, but the servant who assisted with the royal family's donations seemed to be a new person every single time.

The warrior shook her head fervently. "Absolutely not," Fortia clarified. "To work here, there is a strict hiring process with a thorough background check. Staff do not merely appear overnight. My allegiances have always been to the princess and to Cary, and I do not speak freely with the others – but I have heard stories of cooks sent to hang after their words were overheard by the wrong person, maids never to be seen again."

"Anything about staff members being impersonated?" Cary remarked dryly. At Fortia's apparent confusion, the woman heaved a long-suffering sigh as she smoothed her hair back from her face. "After I left here, after... after the king hurt Charlotte, someone attacked me and stole my identity. The reason Jasper found himself nearly being hanged for treason was my fault—rather, the fault of the bastard impersonating me."

Fortia stared in stunned silence, her face ashen. "How would I know if such a thing occurred here?" she breathed, her eyes wide. "What traces would that kind of trickery leave?"

"Nothing, unfortunately," Jasper clarified grimly. His mind weary, he struggled to articulate the wrongness he had felt about the false Cary, the red flags in his memory. "The only clues I had were subtle, things I only picked up on in hindsight. Whoever was impersonating Cary was good, but they made mistakes."

Fortia's expression was pained as she took in the healing marks on Cary's face with a renewed interest. "If I find the demon who did such a thing, I will kill them myself," she swore, a dangerous glint in her eye. "I will remain vigilant here, pay more attention to these new members of staff."

Her hands rubbing at her bare throat, Cary was deep in thought once more. "The secret meetings, the strange new staff, this imposter…" she murmured, her brow furrowed. "It has to be related, somehow."

Glancing at their surroundings, Fortia seemed ill at ease. "You have lingered too long, my love," she warned, a pained sadness in her expression. "Though it pains me, the sooner you depart, the better. They will be patrolling these gardens shortly."

Jasper looked away as the warrior shared a quick, chaste kiss with Cary. "Be safe, dear heart," whispered Cary, lingering a moment longer. "I'll come back when I can."

∽ ⚬ ∽

To say that Varus was furious was an understatement. His was not an explosive anger, visible rage and destruction in his wake. Instead, he regarded Jasper with a careful calm that was terrifying, those hellfire eyes staring into his very soul.

He had met with Cary and Jasper in the sitting room, half-dressed as if this exchange were too important for such idle delays as clothing himself. He wore dark patterned trousers that might have passed as pyjamas, foregoing a shirt and looking all the more intimidating with the ink that was on display beneath his open housecoat. At this distance,

Jasper could make out the words "Rhey'lu" and "Nouseva" on Varus' sternum, and he desperately wished not to be so close to the man's wrath.

"I sleep for a night, and I wake up to Eleni telling me that both of you scampered off to the castle, of all places," Varus sighed as he pinched the bridge of his nose. He balanced a pipe between his teeth as he exhaled a lungful of smoke that made Jasper's nose itch. As he leaned back against the sofa, Jasper noted that Varus' abdomen was suspiciously unblemished, and he wondered what limits existed on his employer's ability to heal.

Cary sighed, crossing her legs casually as she stretched her arms across the back of the sofa. "You wanted me to talk to Aurelia, so we went to the castle," she said sweetly, deceptively casual even as Jasper watched the way her jaw tightened under Varus' hawkish stare. "We didn't get to speak with the princess, but Fortia gave us some interesting information."

Turning towards Jasper, Varus' gaze shuttered. "And as always, I see your near-death experience has done little to instil any sense of self-preservation in you," said Varus in a low voice. "Do you have any idea how dangerous this was?"

His employer's tone vexed Jasper, his patience throttled by his fatigue. "I do, actually," he huffed in response, his face heating beneath the weight of the kingpin's judgment. "Varus, your name and your face are plastered all over wanted posters in Briardeen—*both* of your names."

The atmosphere of the conversation shifted, and to Jasper's surprise, Varus did not retort. As the man dragged a hand down his face in weary forfeiture, something shifted in Jasper's vision, a trick of the light that changed what he saw for half a second. There were lines in the man's face that he didn't recognize... but the moment Jasper blinked he saw only Varus' unmarked face, exactly as he remembered it.

"I can't refute that argument," Varus admitted with a sigh. "Very well. What information did Fortia provide?"

As the smoke curled from Varus' pipe into the air of the sitting room, Cary relayed the details of their conversation with Fortia. The mention of secret meetings with an unknown party gave Varus pause, and his dark eyes narrowed at the guardian's suspicions of the staff members within the castle. He leaned back against the sofa as he digested the information with several deep breaths of smoke, the firelight casting shadows on his face that aged him ten years.

"If he's meeting in secret with his newest advisor, I figure it can mean one of two things," Varus decided, his gaze far away. "They're a known party whose alliance would be divisive if the public learned of it, or perhaps their presence would be alarming for some other reason. Either way, a mysterious alliance doesn't bode well for anyone."

"What are you thinking?" Cary asked.

The man rubbed his chin as he pondered. "Though I had hoped to avoid further danger, it seems we have little choice if we're to discover the truth about our enemies," he decided. "It seems we have a masquerade to attend."

Blinking in shock, Jasper reeled from what felt like emotional whiplash. "After you berate us for sneaking away to the castle, you want us to attend a ball?" he replied.

"If it's all the same to you, Varus… I'd rather sit this one out," Cary returned casually. She regarded her nails idly, but Jasper noted her hands trembled in a way he had never witnessed before.

Something in his employer's expression softened as he

regarded Jasper and Cary sitting before him. "You have no obligation to partake, but if you won't be joining me I would ask you to assist in something else," Varus offered. "While the masquerade is under way, I'll need people at the docks to prepare our ship for an escape."

While Cary nodded gratefully in response to the assignment, Jasper's stomach dropped at the thought of leaving Aethelind. "Escape?" he repeated.

Varus nodded solemnly. "King Fenyang has been away from his people for far too long, and I intend to see him safely out of Aethelind," his employer elaborated, retrieving his cane from the arm of the sofa and rising to his feet with a groan. His bad leg seemed to be bothering him more than usual, and Varus favoured his right knee as he limped towards the hallway. "You are welcome to join me, of course."

The kingpin exited the room before Jasper could respond, leaving him to ponder the mass upheaval such a decision would cause. Leaving Aethelind... he had never left the kingdom, never been to the mainland below, let alone Pharsat. It was a terrifying thought, and it was the mere thought alone that had Jasper's palms sweating.

Cary interrupted his thoughts with a rare touch to his shoulder, accomplishing what she had likely sought to do; halt Jasper's train of thought with a jolt of physical contact. "Darling, don't think too much about that right now," she said soothingly, retracting her hand once Cary saw she had his attention. "You don't need to make a decision about that just yet."

Jasper took a deep breath. "It's... it's a lot to think about," he managed to reply.

Cary smiled sympathetically. "I know," she agreed, standing up from the couch herself. "Let's focus on one thing at a time, and you can let Varus know what you want to do when you're ready."

As Cary left the sitting room, Jasper mumbled a thank you as he rubbed his palms against his knees, focusing on the rough fabric of his trousers. Despite how much he had slept since being rescued from the gallows, Jasper could no longer ignore the weariness that had crept up on him. Seeking the comfort of a bed and a locked door, Jasper exited the sitting room and wandered down the hallway towards his borrowed bedroom. As he unlatched the door, he was comforted by the sound of Charlotte's voice.

"I heard you were back, I was just about to come looking for you," she said. "How are you feeling?"

He turned to face her, and Charlotte looked more alive than he'd seen her in some time. "I should be asking *you* that, after you had to drag me from the gallows," Jasper joked half-heartedly. "Are you feeling better?"

She held her medicated tea in one of Varus' antique porcelain cups, her dark hair freshly washed and braided. "It'll take some time. I haven't exerted myself like that in a while." She tilted her head, as if warring with herself over whether or not to continue, what to say next. When Charlotte eventually responded, he had the impression that it wasn't the first thought that had been on her mind. "Are you all right?"

With a sigh, Jasper shook his head. He didn't have the energy to even attempt a lie, certainly not with Charlotte. "No," he admitted softly. "Not even a little bit."

She studied his face with keen hazel eyes, and in that way Charlotte always knew him better than he knew himself, she seemed to sense what Jasper needed. She nodded towards his room, following him inside as he shut the door behind them. Setting her tea down on the nightstand, Charlotte set to work helping Jasper out of his armour.

"How did it go?" she asked as she undid the fastenings on the boiled leather breastplate. Jasper all but sighed with relief as the constricting sensation across his chest and his abdomen subsided. His old set of armour had been tight, but comfortingly so; this set was far too small in comparison, and he was grateful to be free of it.

"We didn't end up getting to see Aurelia, but we spoke with Fortia instead," Jasper began.

"What did you learn?" Charlotte prompted as he trailed off, peeling away each layer of armour until Jasper was back in his threadbare old sweater and his trousers.

Feeling like he could breathe again, Jasper sank into the mattress as he took a seat on the edge of the bed. Retrieving her tea from the nightstand, Charlotte curled up beside him, listening intently as Jasper relayed the days' events to her, counting the subsequent debrief with their host. He included every detail, right up until Varus' plan to attend the masquerade and depart from Aethelind afterwards.

When he was finished speaking, Jasper was lying down in the heap of unmade bedsheets, exhausted and wired all at once. Charlotte had drained her tea, setting her empty cup aside as she scooted closer towards him. Without thinking, Jasper's arm circled her as she drew nearer, tucking her against his chest.

"Maybe it's not such a bad idea," Charlotte offered, getting comfortable as she nestled beside him. "I agree, a masquerade with our current notoriety is dangerous, but… knowing who that ally is could mean everything."

"Does knowing outweigh the risk?" Jasper asked.

Charlotte was silent for a moment before she

responded, and her words caused Jasper's hold on her to tighten. "What would Gideon do, if he were still here?" she asked softly.

Despite the distance that had spanned him and Gideon in the last year, Jasper knew the answer immediately. "He would have sought the truth, no matter what," Jasper replied, his voice fracturing. "He was so… *tormented* by what the king was doing, by what he'd learned was going on under his nose. He would have done anything he could to right that."

Murmuring in agreement, Charlotte sniffled beside him. After a moment's pause, she pulled away from him slightly to look up at Jasper, and her hazel eyes were sparkling with defiance. "I want to go," Charlotte insisted. "To the masquerade."

Jasper blinked. "You're sure? Charlie, you don't have to do this. We could go to Pharsat with Varus, we could bring your father with us."

Drawing in a shaky breath, Charlotte's expression was filled with determination. "I was thinking I *would* go to Pharsat, once I work up the courage to ask my father about it," she explained. "But I want to do this as well. I… I need to prove to myself that I can do this, that I can be brave enough."

Even as his chest tightened at her words, Jasper understood. He and Charlotte were alike in many ways, and he could empathize with that need to carry on, to survive after tragedy. He understood, and he knew as much as he wanted to protect Charlotte and to keep her safe, there was nothing Jasper could say to dissuade her.

"You're the bravest person I know," Jasper stated immediately. "I love you."

At his words, Charlotte smiled. "I love you too, Jazzy-boy," she whispered in response. She wriggled closer once more, and as she tucked her head against the hollow of Jasper's throat, he realized something strange and wonderful.

For as long as he could remember, Jasper had hated being touched. Casual affection and greetings from other people, whether a simple handshake or a loving embrace, made him feel ill. With Charlotte, it was as if everything around him finally stabilized, as if Jasper had found the peace at the eye of the storm. Jasper didn't feel homesick here, because she was the home that had always been waiting for him.

In all the years he had known Charlotte, he had loved her as deeply and as truly as he knew how, more than Jasper had ever loved anything or anyone. It was a fact written into his very skin, as if his body had been privy to some secret truth that his mind had rebuked. It was a truth he had been denying all his life, and only now did he see it for what it was — the single greatest truth he had ever known.

TWENTY-ONE

DANTE

THE COMING DAYS AT THE ESTATE WERE EXTREMELY chaotic as their rebellion made preparations for the masquerade – and ultimately, planned their escape from Aethelind. The news that many of them had found their way onto a wanted list was unsettling, and the information obtained from Fortia on the nature of a secret alliance with an unknown party was more ominous still.

The sitting room seemed to have reached its maximum capacity as Varus and Fenyang called upon their allies for a mandatory meeting. The remaining embassy staff who had relocated here joined them, seeming nervous but ultimately curious by the meeting agenda. The butler Derek seemed uninterested in the topic at hand, instead busying himself with finding as much seating as possible for the influx of people in the sitting room.

Waiting for the meeting to begin, Dante opted to stand against the wall, leaning against the wooden frame of one of the many bookshelves. A tendril of familiar magic brushed against his unguarded mind as Fenyang assisted Huda towards one of the plush sofas. She tilted her head, a gentle smile on her face as Dante responded with a flicker of his own energy. Though he knew Fenyang hadn't yet broken the news to the rest of the council, Dante had insisted that Huda be filled in on what had transpired between him and the Valedian king.

In front of the fireplace, their host regarded his audience with a conflicted expression on his face. "Thank you all for joining us here," Varus began, his stern countenance and formal attire setting the stage for a serious discussion.

"As some of you are already aware, my council and I will be leaving for Valedia soon," Fenyang continued for Varus, taking his place at the kingpin's side. His amber eyes flitted back and forth as he scanned the faces surrounding them, taking in their attention. "We will be evacuating this manor on the day of Samhain, and we will depart for Pharsat that night."

Nodding approvingly, Varus crossed his arms over his chest. "For those of you wishing to vacate Aethelind, you are welcome to join us," he offered. "I will have my own vessel departing from Dornkeep for evacuees. I would ask that if you do choose to leave with us, you wait for us in the shipyards – we may need a quick escape, and your assistance will be vital."

Pausing for a moment, Varus surveyed the crowd. "That said, you are welcome to remain in Aethelind," their host suggested. "I have contacts in Caelfall and Dornkeep who will work to secure safehouses for those in need of a place to lie low. There will be no ill will towards any of you who choose to do so, but I would ask that you leave the sitting room before anything further can be discussed."

A murmur of hushed conversation travelled through their audience as each of the estate's occupants weighed their options. From across the room, Jasper and Charlotte exchanged glances with one another before meeting Dante's gaze. After a few moments, Varus called for a show of hands to count who would choose to remain in Aethelind, and not a single hand was raised.

A slow, sad smile appeared on the kingpin's face, the slightest crack in his demeanour. "All right," he said approvingly. "Let's get started."

There was a sense of pride in Dante's chest as Varus and Fenyang explained what needed to be done, what preparations were required at the docks. There would be two ships departing for Pharsat, the Valedian vessel *The Veiled Siren* and Varus' personal craft *The Laughing Crow*. Those assigned to preparing the ships for their escape were tasked with discretely gathering supplies for the voyage, loading the cargo holds with as much as they could carry. As the discussion concluded, much of the room exited with their assignments, including most of the Valedian council. Those who remained were tasked with a much more sensitive mission, one that couldn't be discussed outside of Varus' trusted inner circle.

As the sitting room quieted, Dante was amongst those that remained. Seated around him were Charlotte, Maya, and Eleni, while Jasper and Haeyin stood leaning against the bookshelves in a similar fashion. Even when a seat became available, Benkaei claimed the arm of one of the sofas, perching on the edge as if she feared she might have to vacate the room quickly herself.

"Right," Varus began, raking his fingers through his hair as he exchanged a glance with Fenyang. "With the knowledge of the recent imposter... this cannot be discussed with anyone outside of this room, other than the Valedian council."

With a lazy twist of his hand, Haeyin summoned a ward without so much as blinking, his stare fixed on Varus as the man spoke. The magic devoured any sound within it, the crackle of the fireplace briefly muted before Dante too was enveloped in that protective magic, shuddering at the sensation. With the ward settling in at the corners of the room, Haeyin gave an approving nod towards the Valedian king and their host, confirming it would be safe to continue as he took a seat beside Eleni.

"As some of you are already aware, the castle is hosting a masquerade ball to celebrate the princess' birthday, apparently," the kingpin continued dryly. "The plan is to crash the party in order to determine the identity of the Aethian king's mysterious new ally."

At Varus' side, the Valedian king smiled grimly. "This plan is not without its faults," Fenyang continued exasperatedly, as if he were the one who had pointed out to Varus the flaws in the plan. "There will be precautions, costume masks glamoured to conceal your identity, and Varus' armoury will be at your disposal."

Eleni raised a hand, clearing her throat primly. "Assuming this plan is as bad as Varus' usually are, am I to assume those are the *only* precautions that have been thought out?" she asked sweetly.

At her side, Haeyin seemed greatly concerned by Eleni's involvement, drawing her attention with a hand against her knee. "I cannot express how much I would rather you didn't attend," he began, his touch against her leg gentle but imploring. It seemed there was more and more white in his hair every time Dante saw the doctor, all but glowing in the light of the fireplace.

Eleni pursed her lips, unimpressed. "Not in front of the children, darling," chided Eleni with a sigh, even as she threaded her fingers with Haeyin's own. Dante became aware of the fact that he was included amongst "the children" at the same time as Jasper, Charlotte, and Maya did, each of them growing equally discomforted. Varus watched on in silence.

The healer's golden eyes flashed, his face flushing. "You can't just volunteer for a mission at the castle and expect me to say nothing!" Haeyin protested.

Her determination unrelenting, Eleni sat up straighter. "Listen to me, Hae," she replied slowly, and her tone made it quite clear there would be no dissuading her. "You know as well as I do that you will be at a disadvantage if I am not there. What would you rather I do, sit in safety on the ship and wait for you all to return? How am I to live with myself if some of you *do not* return, when I could have helped?"

The doctor spluttered, torn between immediately responding with *yes* and knowing Eleni had a point. The expression on his face indicated he had come to the same conclusion that Varus had the moment Eleni had raised her hand, the reason their partner had not intervened. Their host had stepped forward, a hand on Eleni's shoulder before he spoke.

"You won't convince her not to join us, Hae," Varus addressed the doctor, a knowing look in his eye. "No more than I can convince any of our party to stay behind, even if I don't agree with the decision. We let everyone choose for themselves, and this is where we stand."

Clearing her throat, Maya raised a hand. "Almost all of you have a price on your heads," she pointed out, her small voice tentative. "And even if Charlotte doesn't, she's still in danger returning to the castle."

Sensing a gap in the conversation, Benkaei cleared her throat. "None of us are without risk, but we all volunteered anyway," she pointed out shrewdly as she cleaned one of her knives, seeming rather amused by Haeyin's failed attempts to dissuade Eleni.

Despite their support of her decision, Dante couldn't help but empathize with Haeyin's concerns. A cursory glance at Jasper and Charlotte confirmed for him that they shared his worries as well. None of them were keen on losing Eleni or her unborn child.

Her expression softening, Eleni cradled Haeyin's hand in her own as she addressed him. "I know you're worried about the baby, but you can't shelter me from everything," Eleni told the doctor, her voice wavering as she reached to brush his mostly auburn hair back from his face.

Haeyin shook his head, a tormented expression on his face. "I'm worried about *you*," he insisted. To this, Eleni had no immediate response. Her partner sighed, lifting their joined hands to kiss her knuckles. "Just promise me you'll be careful."

Clearing his throat, Dante sought to bring the conversation back to its original purpose. "Do we have a plan, beyond storming the castle during the ball?" he inquired, stepping away from the bookshelf to stand beside Maya. "Does it factor in the strengths of our allies?"

"I had the *beginnings* of a plan, but… I admit I am hoping for input from anyone who has ideas," the man admitted. His gaze flicked back and forth between each of the faces that watched him, as if assessing their expressions.

"All of us will enter the masquerade as guests," Fenyang continued for Varus, and his inclusion of himself in the statement took Dante by surprise. "At some point, as many of our party as we can spare will be tasked with sneaking away from the main event to investigate the castle, namely searching the king's quarters for evidence."

Jasper made a noise in his throat, a sort of amused grunt. "That sounds like an excellent way to be charged with treason a second time. Can I be sentenced to hang twice?" he asked, earning a barking cackle from Benkaei and a withering stare from Charlotte, even as she covered her mouth to conceal a smirk.

"At that point, you may be burned at the stake for illegal use of magic," Eleni remarked dryly, managing a strained laugh. "Considering you escaped your first death sentence."

Haeyin pinched the bridge of his nose, sighing in exasperation. "Going back to *the plan*," he groaned, waving his hand as if to hurry the conversation along. "Varus, please tell me you aren't planning some drastic diversion again."

Blinking rapidly, Varus had an expression of feigned innocence. "Define 'drastic', Haeyin," replied the kingpin, which earned another exasperated groan from his weary partner. Across from him, Maya and Charlotte exchanged confused looks, while Dante mouthed *Again?* towards Jasper. He only shrugged in response.

"A diversion might work, but we need to be careful about it," Benkaei pointed out, raising an eyebrow. "Security at a masquerade in honour of the dear little princess will likely be increased."

Maya made a small noise at the warrior's words, resulting in every pair of eyes swivelling towards her. Turning quite pink, she cleared her throat once more. "Do you think... would it be at all similar to that night in Caelfall, with soldiers employed as extra guard detail?" she suggested.

Snapping his fingers, Varus pointed towards Maya, who appeared as alarmed by the attention as everyone else was by the sound. "Security *will* be increased," he agreed, a manic gleam in his eye. "So will the response to any perceived threats – but the calibre of personnel will very likely have deteriorated with the casualties from the night of the curfew. We may be able to use that to our advantage."

Haeyin seemed to be beside himself. "That sounds like a drastic diversion," he murmured. They continued to deliberate long into the night, roleplaying amongst themselves as they assessed every angle, every weakness, every potential for a trap. After several hours spent in intense discussion, it seemed at last they had a plan – now, the work could truly begin.

The days that followed passed by in the blink of an eye, with every inhabitant of the manor occupied with preparing for their escape. Everyone who had elected to attend the masquerade was given a crash-course in typical Aethian dances they would be expected to know, some with more success than others. From Maya's collection of stolen blueprints and maps, they plotted their course of action.

On the morning of Samhain, their inhabitants dwindled significantly. Those assigned to the shipyards were set to work taking as much as they could carry towards the Valedian council's vessel and Varus' airships. For anyone unable or unwilling to depart Aethelind, Rosaline had offered to take those seeking refuge under her wing, tasking the Silent Sisterhood with locating safe houses within Caelfall. Convincing Samuel to depart for Pharsat with them had been no small feat, but it was determined the baker would accompany Jasper and Charlotte as they fled Aethelind with the Valedian council.

Obtaining costumes ended up being the easiest undertaking, with Varus revealing multiple walk-in closets filled with an obscene amount of regalia, suits, and gowns. When Dante had questioned the acquisition of so many clothes, Varus merely shrugged his shoulders. "For my varying moods and expressions," he had answered, as if this were a perfectly reasonable explanation.

Even more mystifying was the range of selection available, and everyone in need of masquerade-worthy attire found there were multiple options in their size, albeit needing an adjustment or two here and there. Maya proved to be proficient with a needle and thread, expertly stitching invisible modifications into gowns and suits to custom fit their costumes to each of them – and more importantly, to sneak weapons into the ballroom.

Dante still wasn't at the size he had been when he had departed Fraecath all those months ago, but he had managed to regain enough body mass that he didn't feel perturbed by his reflection in the mirror. He stood in Eleni's chambers before a floor length mirror they had retrieved from an unused storage room, unaccustomed to wearing clothing that fit him so well. Varus had procured a costume of deep emerald for him, the fabric intricately woven with a pattern of embroidered serpents.

In a gown of pale blue and gold trimmings, Charlotte twirled past him as she tested her modified costume. Her dark curls had been pinned back with care, a few stray ringlets caressing the back of her neck. Jasper had been dressed in a navy blue suit to match, which Maya had purposefully made larger for him to wear a leather armour set comfortably beneath it. Dante had watched with curiosity as Jasper hurriedly stuffed a small box into his jacket pocket before proceeding to dodge Eleni's attempts to comb his hair.

"You can't go to a royal ball looking like you were dragged through a hedge backwards," insisted Eleni, all but brandishing a comb as she paced after the blacksmith in her housecoat. His hair had grown out a fair bit in the time Dante had known him, looking more and more unruly as the weeks went by. He couldn't help but laugh as Jasper ducked behind Charlotte to avoid the comb.

"I can't—my ears!" Jasper protested, trying and failing to hide behind Charlotte's voluminous skirts.

Maya giggled at the amusing display, Fenyang's dress jacket in her lap as she took out the seams. Eleni's desk was filled with similar pursuits, piled high with the girl's sewing projects for their evening affairs. "Your mask will be glamoured, silly," Maya pointed out. "No one will even see your ears except us."

Judging by the way Jasper's face coloured a shade of red to rival his hair, he was not comforted by this knowledge. Charlotte spun around to face him, beaming as she took his arm. "It's all right, we already know what they look like," she said softly, gesturing for Eleni to hand her the comb. Sensing this was a battle he couldn't win, Jasper obliged with a heavy sigh as Charlotte gently brushed his hair back from his face.

Admittedly, Dante had never really seen Jasper's ears entirely. Incorrectly, he had assumed his friend was merely self-conscious of the size of them, or the fact that they turned as red as his face when he was flustered. Instead, Dante saw now that they were delicately pointed, a distinctly uncommon trait. It gave him pause as he watched Charlotte tame the man's rust-coloured hair, causing Dante to reassess his evaluation of his friend's origins. Dante forced himself to look away, not wanting to cause Jasper any further discomfort.

As he turned his head, Fenyang strolled into the room to join them, adjusting the cuff links on a black shirt that fit him superbly well. There had been no dissuading him from joining them tonight, as the Valedian king insisted that if he were to accuse Aethia of crimes against his people, he himself required indisputable proof.

Meeting Dante's eye, Fenyang grinned. "Well, don't you look handsome," he noted approvingly, which was high praise coming from a man as beautiful as Fenyang. He turned away only to address Maya, who was holding up his costume jacket with a grin on her face.

"All finished," she exclaimed proudly, a thimble on her finger catching the light as Fenyang took the garment from her. "I added an extra pocket for a knife sheath as well."

"Maya, you are an angel," the king returned, bowing his head. "Thank you."

The girl smiled widely in reply, but there was a sort of sadness that lingered in her gaze that Dante was painfully aware of. He hated that the decision for Maya to bow out of the masquerade had been made for her, that there wasn't some way they could make the mission accessible for her, but their options were limited. Besides, Maya had proved herself as their most effective tactician, with her almost photographic memory and encyclopedia of knowledge. They couldn't risk anything happening to her.

Eleni seemed to notice that expression on her adopted daughter's face as well, taking a moment to squeeze Maya's shoulders. "One day, we'll take you to a ball," she promised, pressing a kiss to the top of Maya's head. The girl seemed to smile a bit brighter in response.

At that moment, Varus entered the room bearing a large wooden crate, Haeyin in tow as they made the last adjustments to their costumes. Rather than walk the shortest distance to Maya and her nearby table of sewing projects, Varus skirted around Dante as he ducked around the commotion in the room, as if he were trying to stay as far away as possible from the looking glass. Dante knew there was no credence to the rumours of vampires lacking reflections, but it was strange behaviour from an already unusual man nevertheless.

"Are you afraid of mirrors?" Maya piped up, seemingly sharing Dante's observations.

Having finished taming Jasper's hair into something resembling a polished nobleman, Charlotte looked up at last. Her expression seemed oddly stricken, but she offered no input. Setting the wooden box down on an empty corner of the desk, the kingpin looked up with an unreadable expression on his face before he smiled crookedly.

Whatever response he had been about to supply, Haeyin interjected with a sigh and a roll of his eyes. "He remains the most singularly vain person I have ever met," he noted with a tone of amusement, casually adjusting the collar of his deep indigo jacket. "If he catches sight of his reflection, we'll arrive an hour late to the masquerade while he insists upon fiddling with things that don't require fixing."

Scoffing, Varus delicately placed a hand to his chest in mock hurt. Eleni had changed from her housecoat to her ballgown, an empire waist dress of shifting lavender and turquoise hues, a waterfall of silks flowing from a golden filagree collar. Maya had adjusted the fastenings on the dress to accommodate Eleni's growing abdomen, the dancing flow of the fabric managing to conceal her silhouette as she glided towards Varus' side.

"It's true," she confirmed with a wink in Dante's direction, pressing a kiss to Varus' cheek. "We would miss the ball entirely, I fear."

"Your betrayal stings," Varus teased as he regarded his partners with no small measure of affection. As Eleni threaded her fingers with his own, the kingpin reached with his free hand to brush Haeyin's hair back from his face. He paused for a moment, regarding the pair of them as though he hadn't seen them in years. "We should get going as soon as we can. The ships are almost loaded, so all that remains is..."

"Treason and espionage?" Fenyang remarked dryly, pulling on his suit jacket with a flourish. Keepers, Maya had done some beautiful work tailoring each of their costumes, but what she had managed to accomplish with the king's was superb. The scarlet embroidery in the lapels of his costume was reminiscent of a phoenix, a fitting emblem for Fenyang.

"That about sums it up," Varus agreed. "We don't have the luxury of carriages, given our notoriety, so I'm afraid we'll be 'shadow-stepping', as it were."

There was a knock at the open door of Eleni's room, where an armour-clad Cary regarded the scene within. "My, don't you all look marvellous," she noted with an amused expression. Her cropped hair was slicked back from her face, leaving the sharp angles of her cheekbones on display. She looked less hollow than she had these past few days, donning fresh leather armour from the Silent Sisterhood. "I fear I may be underdressed."

"I didn't think you were joining us," Jasper pointed out, his cheeks still a perpetual red. Dante hadn't seen much of

Gideon before his passing, unfamiliar with the man's countenance. With Jasper's hair off his face, the lamplight illuminating the scars normally hidden beneath it, Dante at
last saw the resemblance. Had Gideon's ears also been
pointed?

Cary shook her head in response, leaning casually
against the doorframe. "I'm here to escort the princess to
the docks," she explained teasingly, her gaze settling on
Maya. "If she's done with her seamstress duties."

As each set of eyes settled on Maya, her golden skin
took on a pink hue. "It's an inside joke," she insisted, chuckling nervously. "We learned the princess and I have the
same birthday."

Charlotte looked slighted. "You told me your birthday
was the same day as Jasper's…" she spluttered.

Clearing her throat, Maya became very focused on the
finishing touches of her last project. "In my defense, we
only found out when my birth records were 'magically'
found after Eleni adopted me," she admitted, rolling her
eyes. "Prior to that, I'd always thought it was the spring
equinox – that's what I'd been told, in any case."

With a soft huff of laughter, Varus crossed the room to
kneel before Maya, maneuvering around his bad leg. From
his trouser pocket, the kingpin withdrew a beautifully
crafted dagger with a mother of pearl sheath, presenting it
to Maya. "Happy birthday, *princess*," he offered warmly, a
crooked smile on his face. "You be careful out there, aye?
Straight to the docks, wait for us there."

Nodding in agreement, Maya beamed as she exchanged
the dagger for her last sewing project, Varus' finished dress
jacket. "You have hidden weapon sheaths as well, but I also
sewed some of your armour into the fabric," said Maya
proudly.

Varus' smile widened as he stood up, pulling the jacket on with a flourish. The almost-black fabric shifted with a deep red effervescence as it caught the light. "It's perfect," he enthused.

Beaming, Eleni withdrew a colourful patterned scarf from her vanity, draping it around Maya's neck before planting a kiss on her brow. "Happy birthday, darling," she enthused in a soft whisper. "We'll see you soon."

Crossing her arms over her chest, Cary regarded the room's occupants. "This is goodbye, I suppose," she offered in a small voice. "I'll be staying with the Silent Sisterhood in the hopes of securing Caelfall as a safe haven."

"Until our paths cross again, then," the Valedian king replied, bowing his head in Cary's direction. Maya wheeled herself out of the room to follow Cary to the elevator, a chorus of goodbyes accompanying their departure. Shortly afterward, with everyone's costumes composed and their weapons concealed in the hidden compartments Maya had provided, it was time for them to depart as well.

"We will be able to recognize one another as long as we're all wearing these," Haeyin instructed their group as they each took one of the enchanted costume masks. Dante felt the cold mist of the glamour settle over him as he secured his mask to his face, the rest of his companions following suit.

As they descended the staircase, Benkaei was already waiting for them in the foyer of the estate, her attendance as non-negotiable as Fenyang's. She had chosen one of Varus' least ostentatious suits for the masquerade, her hair slicked back from her face in a neat chignon. She gave Dante an approving nod as she accepted the mask he placed in her hand, similarly plain black as her attire. At the entryway, the butler Derek held the door open for them to depart, the last occupant to remain in the manor.

The weathered old man bowed his head as they passed, waving them off one by one. "Do be safe, and I shall hope to see you all back here at some point in the near future," said Derek as he bid them farewell.

"The manor is yours, Derek," Varus replied, dipping his head. "Take good care of her."

The merchant district was almost entirely deserted at this hour; luckily for their group, many of the shops had closed hours ago, and Dornkeep did not entertain bars and brothels the way Caelfall did. The moonlight cast eerie shadows across the beautiful manor gardens as their group ventured beyond the safety of that ethereal wrought iron fence. As the gates closed behind them, Dante turned to wave at the butler, still standing at the doorway to watch them depart.

There was an almighty bang, a thunderous crash as a shockwave pulsated from the Melicus estate. From behind the magical veil of the wards woven into the fence, Dante watched on in horror as the manor was consumed by fire and gunpowder. Every window in the building shattered at once, flames billowing from each entryway. The magic of the wards spluttered in a pulsating wave of light as they struggled to contain the inferno, the fires raging within the shell of the barrier.

"What in Xiska's name..." Fenyang breathed. He had been standing nearest to Dante, but seemed to have instinctively moved closer in response to the blast. "What was that?"

"What just happened!?" Charlotte stammered, secured in the loop of Jasper's arms as if he had sought to physically shield her from the flames.

Benkaei whirled on Dante, her gaze flitting between him and her king. "Who did this? How did they get through the wards?" she demanded, as if either one of them might know the answer. Dante hadn't a clue; he thought they'd assessed every weakness, analyzed every hole in their security after the imposter – but they had a destroyed manor to prove otherwise.

Eleni and Haeyin were silent as they stared in the direction of where the manor had been. Dante's heart sank as he regarded the chaos within the warded fence, where the Melicus estate lay in ruins. The flames licked the walls of the place he had considered home not so long ago, the most recent in a series of lodgings he had felt safe in. The fire roared within, and from the blackened walls and broken glass, Dante knew there was no one alive inside.

From the way the kingpin stood deathly still ahead of them, Varus knew it too. The man stared into that blaze, stared into the roaring fire ahead of him.

Dante could no longer ignore the question at the front of his mind. "Was Cary working against us all along?" he wondered aloud. "Is Maya safe?"

Shaking her head, Eleni assuaged his worries. "We confirmed Cary's innocence, it couldn't have been her," the woman insisted, the flames reflected in her blue eyes. "The rest of the council is already at the ships, Maya will be safe with them."

"Was this... was this Rasmussen?" Jasper dared to ask. "The Dominion, or one of their allies?"

Varus laughed, a harsh and deadly sound. "What does it matter?" he murmured in reply, almost too quiet for Dante to hear. "Our enemies are numerous. Whether it was our underworld adversaries, the imposter... my home is in ruins. Where is Derek?"

A pained silence followed, the fire roaring and crackling beyond the safety of the wards. It was Haeyin who dared to venture forward, reaching for Varus' shoulder where he stood motionless. "Varus... if he's still in there, he's gone. We have to go."

There was a shuddering sigh before their leader turned around, and there was something in his expression that Dante recognized, something he didn't like. It was a desolate sadness, a hopeless anger. Dante knew then that their enemies had finally pushed too far. They had pushed Varus Emery beyond his breaking point, and he would respond in kind.

"This changes nothing," Varus decided hoarsely. He closed his eyes, affixing his chosen mask to his face, the twisted visage of a demon. When he opened his eyes once more, his countenance was filled with a savage determination. "Let's raise hell."

※

There was little said between them as they made their way towards the castle in silence. Varus "shadow-stepped" the group as far as the graveyard by the church, wordlessly leading them towards the illuminated palace. There were several other late guests that joined them, and their arrival was further deemed non-threatening by a persuasive wave of Varus' hand, the strange application of his power unsettling Dante. The entrance guards seemed unharmed albeit dazed as their group passed by, agreeing that invitations weren't required.

But no – these were not the usual castle guards, these were merely soldiers stationed as guards, betrayed by their uniforms. Perhaps their plan had a chance of success after all.

The castle was as grand as ever, beautifully decorated in the spirit of the Samhain season. They were corralled towards the eastern wing, numerous stern-eyed soldiers barring the corridors leading deeper into the palace. The ballroom was illuminated by an ornate chandelier, strings of gold and silver adorning faceted glass shards. Where the light scattered across the partygoers and their lavish costumes, Dante saw many were engaged in a dance, a lilting ensemble of strings seated on the dais ahead of them. They were surrounded by walls adorned with dark silver décor in the likeness of ghouls and demons, swirling shapes that caught the light as the guests danced. Dining tables had been filled with pumpkin tarts and spiced wine, a hundred candles flickering as people passed by to collect hors d'oeuvres.

In a sea of skirts and suits, the princess stood apart in a gown of scarlet and silver, her hair coiled in an elaborate tangle of braids. She beamed beneath an ivory mask as she twirled and spun through the complicated dance, hungry-eyed noblemen watching her like birds of prey. It was the closest Dante had ever been to his would-be fiancée.

Their plan was simple, but with deadly consequences should any of them misstep. They dispersed as they entered the ballroom, some of them mingling at the buffet while others joined the dance. Haeyin smiled half-heartedly as he led Eleni towards the swirling costumes, the pair of them having attempted to teach their group all the steps in the dances they were seemingly experts in. Benkaei gestured for Varus to follow her while she strolled over towards the spread of hors d'oeuvres and wine. Meanwhile, Charlotte and Jasper assumed their positions in the dance, ready to play their parts.

There was a gentle touch against the back of Dante's hand as the Valedian king brushed against him. "May I have this dance, Your Highness?" he asked in a low voice, quiet enough that only Dante could hear him.

A shudder travelled down his spine, the sound of Fenyang's voice enough to have Dante flushing. "Is that... wise?" he forced himself to ask, his self-preservation still managing to override his desires. A cursory glance towards the dancing party guests revealed few similar couplings, and standing out amongst the crowd could be risky.

Stepping closer, Fenyang chuckled sadly. "I am not a king, and you are not my subject," he reminded Dante. "We're nobody here. Let's enjoy that while we still can."

He felt his face heat beneath his mask as Fenyang took his hand, leading Dante effortlessly into the dance. Beneath his own mask, Fenyang's golden eyes regarded him with a singular admiration, as if Dante were the only thing worth watching in the entire ballroom. His pulse quickened beneath his skin at the hand pressed against his waist as they moved gracefully through the crowds of people, and for a moment the sounds of the masquerade faded into the background.

"How does it feel to attend your engagement party?" Fenyang mused, his mouth twitching into a smile.

Despite their circumstances, Dante managed to smile in return. "More enjoyable than I thought possible," he admitted coyly.

Spinning him effortlessly, the Valedian king was surprisingly graceful, his mastery of Aethian dances startling. He moved and weaved through the steps fluidly, and for a moment everything seemed perfect. For the briefest of seconds, amid the swell of the music, Dante permitted himself to pretend that *this* was his life. The destruction of the Melicus estate, the true reason they were here... all of it was cast aside for one perfect dance.

The king's gaze left his own briefly to track some movement behind Dante, and his heart sank at the way Fenyang's face tightened. "That's our cue," he murmured, and something in his voice sounded mournful at the reminder of their purpose here.

There was no sense in arguing a moot point. The pair fell into silence as they slipped through the dense crowd, easing their way casually towards the exit. From the opposite side of the ballroom, Varus skulked towards the doorway as well, following Jasper and Charlotte as they scampered past. The guests were permitted to leave the ballroom to refresh themselves as needed, but Dante knew beyond a certain point the soldiers would impede their progress.

While Varus had disappeared immediately from his vision, Dante sighted his blacksmith friend ahead of them as they rounded the corner. Charlotte was leading him by the hand down a corridor deeper into the castle, towards an area off limits to civilians. She was seemingly oblivious to the group of soldiers calling after her, hot on her heels as they chased the errant party guests. Fenyang and Dante followed quietly behind, ensuring no other soldiers followed them. A cursory glance towards a wall-mounted mirror revealed the third soldier's identity, a glamoured Varus stalking his un-witting prey.

Their preparations for the masquerade had included carefully plotting this route through the castle, towards an abandoned corner of the palace. Charlotte and Jasper were leading the guards towards a dead end, and the soldiers followed without a moment's consideration for their own safety. Playing her part perfectly, Charlotte tittered as she dragged a stumbling Jasper into a room on the left side of the empty corridor, one that Maya had mapped out and suggested. As the soldiers pursued the wayward lovers, Dante and Fenyang slipped into the room to close the door behind them.

"You shouldn't be here," one of the soldiers admonished as Dante approached silently. Charlotte looked up innocently at the king's men, her hands still on Jasper's face while her skirts were balled up in his hands, cleverly concealing the damning appearance of his maimed fingers.

Before any action could be taken against them, Fenyang had the soldier in a headlock. The third soldier's glamour vanished, revealing Varus Emery as he followed suit, snapping the smaller soldier's neck with a fluid motion of his hands.

Fenyang eyed him warily. "Is that what we're doing?" he asked with a bemused expression on his face, adjusting his grip on the guard to break the man's neck. It should have been alarming, watching him kill a man so casually – but then, Dante would be a fool to think that Fenyang had never killed anyone before.

Varus only shrugged as he eased his soldier to the floor slowly, as if he might still protest being dropped. "Better they don't regain consciousness and warn the rest of their little friends," he explained. His gaze shot towards Charlotte and Jasper, nodding approvingly. "Good work, you two. Best get back to the ball for now, we'll reconvene with you later."

"Good luck," Jasper replied with a nod of his head, Charlotte taking his arm as he led them back to the ballroom.

Glancing after their allies, Fenyang assessed the bodies of the soldiers. "Would it be better if I didn't tag along?" he asked. "Surely they'll question the absence of the door guards."

Shaking his head, Varus' glamour slipped back into place as one of the king's soldiers. "Leave that to me," the man offered in response. From the taller guard's belongings, Varus retrieved a handgun from the man's personal effects. Handing it to the Valedian king, he added, "I assume you will make better use of this than I will."

Fenyang accepted the weapon, regarding the condition of the revolver. His eyes met Dante's curious stare, having never seen the king wield a firearm before. "I was a hunter before I was a monarch," Fenyang offered in response, a wry smile on his face.

Assuming the post of one of the two soldiers they'd killed, Varus left Dante and Fenyang to dress themselves in their acquired disguises. Swapping enchanted masks for armoured helmets, the dark metal obscuring their faces entirely, they made their way through the palace towards the upper floor. From Maya's stolen blueprints, she had plotted a path towards Gustaf's chambers. They encountered numerous guards along the way, but none of them questioned the presence of two soldiers; as Varus had predicted, the increased security personnel meant their passage through the castle was viewed as yet another patrol, nothing to cause alarm. Dante was sweating buckets under his borrowed armour nevertheless, his body heat becoming sweltering within the costume crumpled beneath the plain military-issue cuirass.

When they finally arrived at the corridor leading towards the king's quarters, there were two guards stationed at either side of the grand wooden door – true castle guards, not military conscripts. They eyed Dante and Fenyang with an icy glare, recognizing they were somewhere they weren't supposed to be. Before either of them could object, Dante dove forward with a well-aimed knife launched at the guard immediately in front of him, landing it in his eye. He surged ahead to catch the man before his corpse fell to the floor with a crash, and in the corner of his eye Dante could see Fenyang making quick work of the other guard.

"Well done," said Fenyang approvingly, his hand over the guard's mouth as he buried his own dagger deep within the man's throat. "Best we tuck these two out of the way for now."

Nodding in agreement, Dante raised his palms, focusing on the two recently deceased guards. As their eyes glowed with his magic, he directed them to stand within the alcoves on either side of the threshold of the king's chambers. They waited obediently against the wall, hidden from sight should anyone walk past. As Dante assumed what he hoped was an intimidating stance in front of the royal chambers, his king checked to ensure no other patrols were on their way before shoving the wide wooden doors open. A few moments of silence passed as Fenyang ventured into the king's chambers alone, and when he returned far too soon, there was a grim expression on his face.

"What's the matter?" asked Dante.

Swallowing, Fenyang shook his head. "There's... there's no one in here," he explained, gesturing for Dante to follow him inside.

To their shared alarm, the king's chambers were silent and still, abandoned in the darkness. Tentatively, Fenyang approached the nearest lamp, leaving Dante momentarily blind as his eyes adjusted to the sudden light. The grand room was lavishly furnished, the large bed frame adorned with lush fabrics and furs – and a thin layer of dust. Most notably, the room was devoid of a supposedly bed-ridden monarch.

"This doesn't make any sense," Dante said aloud. "Fortia said the king hadn't left his chambers, but… it doesn't look like anyone's been here for a while."

His eyes narrowed, Fenyang turned towards Dante. "What reason would Fortia have to lie?" he asked. "Would she betray us?"

The thought was unsettling, after so much that evening had already gone wrong. Dante scanned the room, searching for something that might shed a light on the king's whereabouts, his gaze settling on the study nearby. Here was the only sign of recent passing, an assortment of documents scattered across the workspace the only evidence of life.

"According to Varus, Fortia is loyal to the princess, not to Gustaf," Dante explained even as his thoughts betrayed him, his eyes scanning the papers strewn across the desk. "It's possible she's as in the dark as we are, but…"

Dante trailed off as he glanced at the miscellaneous documents, maps of Aethia and her surrounding nations, letters from unknown parties, ignored missives from Pharsat… Fenyang eyed a particular sheet of paper, plucking it from the desk as he regarded the looping penmanship.

"This wasn't written by Gustaf," the Valedian king noted.

Dante leaned closer, seeking to scrutinize the paper. "Does it say anything noteworthy?"

Fenyang shook his head. "Nothing that stands out to me," he admitted, though he paused a moment before continuing. "It mentions a term I'm unfamiliar with – do you know what 'Rilkor' is?"

The word garnered no familiarity for Dante either, his mind struggling to parse it as a word in any language he could think of. Something was horribly wrong, and he could no longer ignore the current of fear in his skin, the instinct in his blood commanding him to run.

"We need to get back to the masquerade," he urged. "Something is going on here, and I'm worried about our allies. Between the estate blowing up, and Fortia giving us bad intel – or betraying us – the fact of the matter is that Gustaf isn't here. This could be a trap."

A grim expression on his face, Fenyang nodded. "I fear you may be right," he agreed. "Let's go, we need to get out of this damned country as soon as we can." As they exited the barren chambers without another word, Dante prayed they weren't already too late.

CHAPTER

TWENTY-TWO

CHARLOTTE

The rush of elation following their staged act of indecency had Charlotte flushing darker than Jasper for once, giggling as they rejoined the ball. A glamoured Varus had made a show of chastising them as he caught up to them, appearing to corral them back towards the masquerade as he winked at them. As they returned, Jasper tugged her away from the throngs of partygoers glancing down their noses at the lovebirds causing the disturbance.

"It's all right, it worked," Jasper reassured her as they made their way towards a quieter corner of the ballroom. "Take a breath, Charlie." His hands on her shoulders grounded her, secured her in this moment.

She hadn't realized how badly her hands were trembling, her chest an anxious flutter as her heart thundered in her ribs. "I can't believe that worked," Charlotte breathed, housed in the fortress of Jasper's arms as she curled her fingers in the dense, embroidered fabric of his navy dress jacket.

When Jasper fell silent, she knew it was for the same reason her momentary euphoria had settled; they weren't out of the woods yet, far from it. Charlotte took a sobering breath, releasing a lungful of anxieties with her exhale. "I'm all right," she assured Jasper, and it was mostly the truth. The lingering fear that she would see the king still weighed on her mind, but the glamoured mask on her face was helping; she was not Charlotte here, and only Charlotte had cause to fear that wretched man.

"I'm all right," she repeated, for herself or for Jasper's benefit. "I can do this."

Jasper beamed down at her. The way his smile lit up his face, dimpling his chin, gave Charlotte no small amount of joy. "I know you can," Jasper agreed. "I'm so proud of you."

As the flicker of interest at their re-entry had faded, Charlotte glanced about at their surroundings, assessing the curated perfection of Aurelia's birthday party. It seemed a pity that under the circumstances, she could not go over to the princess – to her friend – and wish her well… but she knew that Aurelia would understand, that the princess would rather she be safe at a distance. The masquerade was a veneer of perfection lacquered over a festering wound. There were wolves hidden amongst the crowd, monsters in the forms of men who would turn them all in at a moment's notice.

"I was saddened at the prospect of leaving, at first," Charlotte remarked with a sigh, frowning beneath her mask as she regarded the twirling forms of the guests engaged in the dance. "Now, it's all I can think about – getting away from here, starting anew somewhere else."

He was quiet, analyzing her words before he verbalized a response. "I know the feeling," Jasper replied finally, his voice rough.

Turning her gaze away from the twinkling swirl of lights and sound behind them, Charlotte smiled up at Jasper. "What do you want to be?" she prompted him. "In this new life of ours, who do you want to be?"

Jasper stared at her in silence for a moment. "There is one thing," he admitted with a wry smile. She waited patiently while Jasper rummaged through his costume jacket with a level of care warranted by his injuries. As his movements revealed a small, wooden box, Charlotte felt her chest constrict.

"I meant what I said, Charlie," Jasper murmured, his hands shaking as he pried open the box. "One day, when we're finally safe and we aren't running for our lives… I will marry you, if you'll have me. Until then—"

"Yes," Charlotte said immediately, her throat tightening as she regarded the rings revealed within that little box. They were a wedding set, from the looks of things, both welded silver expertly woven into an intricate braid. An amethyst lay nestled in the heart of the smaller of the two rings, and Charlotte knew instinctively that this was the work of Jasper's late uncle – his parents' rings.

There was a breathy noise that escaped Jasper's lips, an incredulous chuckle blended with what might have been a relieved sob. The boyish grin that spread across his face was the most beautiful thing Charlotte had ever seen. There were tears in her eyes as she waited in silence, as Jasper competed with the tremor in his fingers to place his mother's ring on her hand. The cool metal seemed to mold to fit her perfectly, the amethyst catching the light as Charlotte retrieved his father's ring, carefully easing it over Jasper's trembling, scarred finger.

"Our first dance was cut short," Jasper began, his voice uneven as he regarded the crowd of guests moving in time with the orchestra. "Shall we have another go?"

She would have said yes in a heartbeat, eager to be close to him, giddy at this shared moment of bliss amidst an ocean of horrors their life had been bombarded with. At that moment, however, Haeyin and Eleni had left the throng of dancing guests to rejoin them, having located familiar faces – or rather, familiar masks in the crowd. Noticing their adorned hands, a breathless Eleni made to ask a question before she was interrupted by Benkaei, the warrior surging towards them.

"We need to leave here, now," she urged, glancing around as if she expected danger to emerge at a moment's notice. "Where's Varus? These ballroom decorations – they're *iron*. Something's wrong."

"Ladies and gentlemen – your attention, please!"

A chill ran down Charlotte's spine in tandem with the jolt that Jasper suffered at the sudden volume. The music from the orchestra ground to a painful halt, every face in the ballroom turning towards the dais. She had feared she might recognize the speaker, feared the Aethian king had finally made an appearance... but it was only General Byron, set apart by his distinctive armour and war medals pinned to his chest. The royal guard stood on either side of him and the king's withered old advisor Aloysius, and it pained Charlotte to see armour and dressings she had come to associate with Gideon.

"We are grateful to all of you for attending tonight," the general began, his speech addled by the thick scars carving through his cheek. He regarded the audience he had accrued with a cruel stare as he spoke. "However, it is with deepest regrets that I inform you my royal guard has discovered enemies of the crown within our numbers."

Haeyin's eyes widened as Dante returned with King Fenyang, with Varus still notably missing from their party. "What did you do?" the doctor hissed.

"Until these fiends have been apprehended, I am afraid we cannot permit these festivities to continue," Byron continued mournfully, a hand over his heart at odds with his stern countenance.

His eyes narrowed on the general, Dante's hand itched towards the daggers concealed in his dress jacket. "I ought to wreck the other side of his face," he murmured darkly. Turning to their allies, Dante's expression was grim. "King Gustaf isn't in his chambers, it's a trap."

It seemed there were multiple "fiends" within the audience who took issue with General Byron's manifesto. Amongst the crowd, several guests raised their fists in defiance. "Do not serve a false king!" one of them roared. There were a few shocked gasps, but their alarm was quickly overpowered by the clamour of a riot in the making as several others joined in with the chant, their hands raised high.

Do not serve a false king, do not serve a false king…

There were mages amongst the audience, revealed as they launched projectiles of elemental magic towards the nearest royal guards. Their efforts succeeded in destroying a few in such a gruesome manner that Charlotte nearly averted her eyes. One of the party guests launched a fireball at the sparkling chandelier overhead, sending it toppling with an almighty crash as partygoers and soldiers alike scattered in alarm. In the distance, she could see Princess Aurelia seized from the crowd by an irate Fortia, ushered by the remaining royal guard to safety as the crowd grew increasingly hostile towards the crown.

With a dismissive wave of his hand, General Byron turned towards Aloysius. From this distance, Charlotte could barely discern his hushed words, but it sounded as if the general had said, "Execute the mage protocol."

As the weathered old man on the dais began to chant something unintelligible to Charlotte's ears, Haeyin seemed quite panicked. They watched in puzzled horror as Aloysius wove what appeared to be an intricate spell, his likeness distorting in Charlotte's vision as the exertion drained his energy.

Dante was gesturing animatedly towards the Valedian king, a similarly distressed expression on his face. "Now— do it *now*, Fenyang," he urged as the man armed a revolver.

The Valedian king paused only momentarily before pulling the trigger. With a sound like a crack of thunder, the bullet struck true. There was a scattering of horrified gasps and screams as the Aethian king's mage recoiled, Aloysius' form jerking unnaturally as his skull was dismantled with the impact – but not before his spell was complete. As the old man collapsed in a heap, his magic was unleashed upon the ballroom.

There was a chorus of screaming as the mages scattered throughout the ballroom found their cuffs constricting their wrists painfully, the metal twisting around their darkening hands. Charlotte flinched as one of the masquerade guests in front of her was quickly relieved of her extremities, shrieking in pain and shock. She and Jasper turned to Eleni instinctively, fearing for the fate of her friend's hands – but it seemed Haeyin was already working to prevent this outcome. As their resident doctor appeared to be using a barrier spell between Eleni's skin and the traitorous metal on her wrists, Varus surged through the crowd to try and pry them off of her.

To her credit, Eleni seemed to be taking this quite well. "I must admit, I had heard of… specialized jewelry manufactured for such a purpose," she jested, a bead of sweat dripping down her temple as she regarded her reddened hands. "This isn't quite what I'd imagined."

While maintaining the spell that was saving her limbs, Haeyin shot her an incredulous stare through his dishevelled hair. "Are you joking about this? Really?" Haeyin wheezed.

Managing to yank one of the cuffs free, Varus cast the warped silver aside as he set on the second one, the twisted metal cuff immediately curling in on itself. "Have you met Eleni?" he asked teasingly, his hair falling away from its neat plait as he labored with the second cuff. Jasper was struggling to assist, managing a startling level of strength with his maimed hands. They removed the second cuff not a moment too soon, Eleni's wrists weeping as Haeyin shifted into a physician's stance, analyzing her injuries as he took her hands in his own.

"I'm fine, Haeyin," Eleni assured him, even as her hands trembled in the doctor's grasp. "The others weren't so lucky, we should help them…"

She trailed off as her eyes widened in alarm, and as Charlotte followed her gaze she felt a similar fear grip her heart. While the rebels aligned with their cause had grouped together protectively, the remainder of the masquerade guests had shifted to block the ballroom exit, barring their escape. Charlotte watched in mute horror as a hundred strangers removed their masks in unison, staring vacantly ahead. There was no commonality between them, no similar characteristics of their attire or their appearance… and yet each of them sported the same vacant expression, the same flat, dead eyes in their gaunt countenance.

Beside her, Jasper nudged her gently, and she instinctively took his arm as Charlotte stepped closer to him.

"That woman… that's the woman they executed in Caelfall last summer, I'm sure of it."

Charlotte stared at the sea of faces slowly advancing towards them, searching for anyone she might recognize. She hadn't witnessed the execution, but there were a few people who looked frighteningly familiar. A man with silver hair at his temples stared through her, a scar through his brow. These were strangers she might have seen at the bakery, at Haeyin's clinic, passing by in the streets of Caelfall… Her heart hammered in her chest as the crowd took slow, measured strides towards them, advancing on them and the rebels.

"What is this?" Jasper questioned. "Necromancy?"

"Varus…" Haeyin urged their leader, all but shoving him. "What do we do now?"

"We can't shadow-step our way out of here," Benkaei warned, as if sensing Varus' first suggestion. "Unless you want to splice yourself through the iron décor."

The kingpin was silent a moment longer, scanning the crowd. Charlotte could almost see the thoughts turning in his mind. "We meet back at Dornkeep, at the ships," he said slowly, carefully. "We have no choice but to run. Focus on getting out of here alive, but we'll have to fight our way through… whatever these are."

"Damn it, Varus, that's a shit plan," King Fenyang growled as he armed his revolver, retrieving one of the swords sewn into his costume for good measure.

"I hadn't *planned* for a corpse mob," Varus all but snarled in response through gritted teeth.

At her side, Jasper was scanning the crowd, assessing their chances of escape. "If we can just get out of the ballroom, we might make it," he murmured.

They stared at the mob that advanced towards them – slowly, unhurriedly, as if they somehow knew the rebels had nowhere to run. Across the ballroom, General Byron smiled cruelly, and for a moment it seemed all was lost.

Varus cracked his knuckles, his shadowy magic swirling across his palms as he prepared to strike. "Run," was all he said before launching that dark energy at their surroundings, the shadow stealing the light and plunging them into near darkness.

There was an infernal shriek as the ballroom exploded into chaos. The rebel mages struck with all they had, their collective survival hinging on their ability to destroy whatever manner of creatures faced them now. Haeyin summoned that golden fire from his veins, planting his feet as a plume of flame burst from his palms to lash at the oncoming mob, melting the front line.

If they had needed any confirmation that their opponents were no longer mortal humans, their proof lay in the remains of their attackers. Haeyin's power had melted the human faces off the creatures, and a pile of twisted metal and clockwork remained. Charlotte could see what appeared to be a human heart beneath the rubble of the nearest one, twitching as it struggled to compensate for the damage the doctor had wrought. A blackened hand still reached for Eleni, petrified into stillness.

Benkaei withdrew her spear from her suit jacket, the weapon snapping from its compacted form into its full length. Whipping the spear in a wide arc, she cleared a path towards the door. "Come on, let's move!" she roared, ushering them towards the exit.

Clinging to Jasper's arm as he led her in a run, Charlotte gathered her skirts in her free hand as she leapt over the deformed bodies. They followed Varus and King Fenyang as they navigated the chaos within the ballroom, leading their party through the onslaught. Plumes of magic burnt and boiled the creatures as Haeyin and Eleni fired what magical energy they possessed towards their opponents, buying them time to escape.

"Dante, can you build us some reinforcements?" Varus called behind him.

Beside her, Dante struggled to keep up with them between his failed attempts at casting. "There's nothing for me to reanimate," he shouted back in response. "There's just—there's nothing!" He extended his hand repeatedly, but the silver light in his veins sputtered and died, finding nothing to attach itself to.

The castle entrance was in sight, and for a moment Charlotte had a flicker of hope they might make it out of this hellish party yet. A foolish flicker of hope, as a panicked shout nearby was her only warning before an elbow was driven into her ribcage. One of the wounded mages knocked into her, the pair of them losing their balance in the struggle. Charlotte rolled on her ankle, her face striking the marble as she collapsed, her mask lost in the onslaught. She gasped for air as she was buried beneath the weight of two, maybe three people, her bones aching in protest. She tasted blood in her mouth as she struggled to curl up, to shield her head with her arms.

The weight crushing her vanished after a few terrifying moments of agony, and there was a trembling pair of hands lifting her from the floor. "I've got you, Charlie," a soft voice said, a familiar head of red hair appearing in her vision as Charlotte was hoisted to her feet. Jasper's arm around her waist steadied her as he shouldered her weight, leading them to the exit.

Charlotte's body was reaching its limit, her steps faltering on her wounded ankle as her bruised joints struggled to keep up. She could already see that they had fallen behind, the heavy footfalls of the undead creatures drawing closer. Their allies were nowhere to be seen, and they were dangerously far away from the safety of the herd of rebels...

Another group of the monsters cut in front of them, blocking their escape – they were trapped.

Jasper's grip on her tightened as he assessed the crowd, his left hand brandishing his smuggled sword as the mob drew closer. Charlotte's heart sank at the tremor visible in that blade, at the vacant eyes staring back at them.

"Jasper..." Charlotte whispered, fear catching in her throat. "Go, you can still make it out of here." There were too many of them, and they did not fear pain, dismemberment, or death. Still, he held her tighter still, determined to save them somehow.

She loved him with everything she had.

The corpse mob's hands reached blindly for their targets, reached for whatever they could grasp – clothing, skin, hair. One of the undead knotted its cold fingers in Charlotte's curls, yanking her back with startling force, far more than Jasper's right hand could contend with. She screamed as she was dragged into the swarm, the delicate fabric of her ballgown ripping at the seams.

Jasper spun around, eyes wide with horror as he struggled to reach her. "Charlotte!" he yelled, his mask knocked from his face as he too was pulled by the mass of creatures. *"Charlie!"*

"Jasper!" He reached for her, his left hand a distant lifeline in the chaos. She strained against the hands that pulled at her, her eyes watering as the pins were tugged out of her hair. Charlotte called for him again, her fingers just barely brushing his... until he was swallowed by the mob, any sound muffled by the swarm of bodies between him and Charlotte.

Dread seized her heart, lightning surging through her veins as desperation took hold of her. Charlotte shrieked as those blank faces pressed in on her, hands reaching to grasp every available inch of her. Their assault was the spark that ignited the kindling of that foreign power that slumbered deep within her, that unspeakable force she had only wielded once before. It was the most basic instinct of her blood, that desire for survival above all else – for herself, and for Jasper.

Summoning that power within her, Charlotte inhaled as much as she could, drawing the magic from her heart into every vein in her body. She let it burst from the palms of her hands, ooze from every pore in her skin. The mob of creatures screeched in protest as that blinding white light made contact with them, arcing bolts of lightning searing their cold skin as an acrid smell filled the air. Charlotte screamed as the energy threatened to consume her, scorching through her skin as it vaporized their enemies.

A distant memory of a forgotten friend resurfaced in her mind, a conversation from another era warning about magical overuse. *It's rare, and every single mage is taught to avoid it at all costs, but with some varieties of magic — and some* quantities *of magic — it's inevitable.*

Was this her fate, to burn out in one brilliant and

singular use of the power she had never known existed? Charlotte felt like it was, felt the very fabric of her existence dissolve as the exertion drained her resolve, until there was nothing left.

"*Charlotte!*"

She gasped, uncertain if she had heard Jasper calling her name or if she'd simply imagined it. Charlotte squeezed her eyes shut, focusing all of her strength on reining in that unstoppable force, that raw magic she had yet to master. Goddesses, it hurt – it hurt more to contain that obliterating force than it did to unleash it, as if she were trying to contain a waterfall at the source… but she had to try. Her throat raw as she cried out, Charlotte shut off her power at the source, her heart thundering in her ribs as the blinding light vanished.

As she gasped for air, the silence that fell around her was deadly. Charlotte opened her eyes, her palms blistered and bloodied up to her forearms, surrounded by the ashes of her enemies. Goddesses, she prayed it was only her enemies… she looked up in alarm, searching for her blacksmith – but Jasper was lying unharmed a few feet away, unconscious but alive. She could see the rise and fall of his chest, and Charlotte breathed a sigh of relief.

The last of her strength failing her, Charlotte's eyes grew heavy as she swayed. A pain began to bloom in her temple, blood running freely from her nose as she collapsed against the ashen stone tiles in complete exhaustion, her vision fading to black.

"Please, Charlie… Please, wake up, just open your eyes…"

When Charlotte came to, she found herself face down

on a cold, stone floor. Her recollection of what had transpired before she'd blacked out was hazy, and with the throbbing pain in her temples it took effort simply to remember. Her bones ached, her mouth felt dry...

"Wake up, dear one," an unfamiliar voice spoke nearby, his strange cadence startling her into full consciousness. "We have much to discuss."

"Don't touch her, don't—" Jasper's voice was cut off in a strangled grunt as a blow landed, and Charlotte's heart clenched at the sound of it. She obeyed for fear of more harm being inflicted upon Jasper, wincing as she pulled herself to her knees with burnt hands.

She was in the cathedral... when had she been brought here? Why? The statue of the three goddesses loomed over her, Deltori's tear-stained face staring down at Charlotte. The stone structure was all but desecrated, the pews set aflame and the stained-glass depictions shattered. A few yards away from her, a bloodied Jasper knelt with his hands bound behind him, iron chains scraping against the stone with each minute movement. He had been stripped of his costume and his armour, left only in his dirtied undershirt as he bled from his brow and his lip.

There were a dozen people she didn't recognize surrounding them, still dressed in similar masquerade costumes. They seemed to be responsible for the destruction at the cathedral, laughing gleefully as they smashed the pews. One of them wore a mask over the lower half of his face, his cold eyes visible over the brim of the dark fabric.

"Kind of you to join us, Charlotte," the masked stranger said pleasantly. "I must say, I consider myself a patient fellow, but you have... tested that patience, truly."

"I'll be sure to wake up sooner the next time I lose consciousness," Charlotte responded dryly. She expected a blow, some manner of retaliation, but none came. Hesitating, she struggled to her feet, favouring her injured ankle as she assessed their chances of escape.

There were fewer adversaries here than there were at the masquerade, but with Jasper in chains… The strangers wielded firearms and deadly-looking swords and war hammers. Even if Charlotte could summon her fledgling magic once more, she didn't think she could win against all of them. Having narrowly dodged magical burnout once already, Charlotte knew instinctively it would be unwise to attempt to wield it again so soon, her hands and arms already wounded by the energy she had used.

"Speaking of waking up… there is something I need from you," the masked man drawled, pacing in front of her. From the way the others regarded him, waiting for a signal, Charlotte assumed he was their leader. "You see, our little friend here needs to wake up as well. Specifically, he needs to *Awaken*."

Charlotte scoffed. "What are you talking about? He's clearly conscious."

The masked stranger laughed cruelly, his lackeys chuckling in unison as if Charlotte had said something preposterous. "Foolish girl, don't you know what he is?"

She bristled at the question, at the way they referred to someone so dear to her. "*He* is my husband," Charlotte spat back at them. She thumbed the ring on her finger, the cool weight of the metal soothing against her skin. She didn't need a ceremony, didn't need a goddess as witness to prove the validity of her devotion. Jasper was the only person for her, and Charlotte knew he loved her equally.

Another of the strangers spoke then, his harsh features incredibly intimidating in the dim light. "You would sully yourself with his kind?" the other man barked in an accent

Charlotte couldn't place. "This is the reincarnation of Deltori's spawn – this is the prophesied downfall of the Lutaidhr!"

She stared at them, horror dawning on her slowly. They were… cultists? They must have been, to follow the god of the void, to assume Jasper was the reincarnation of a demigod. "You're insane," breathed Charlotte. "All of you, you're… do you even hear yourselves?"

The man with the accent reached for Jasper, grasping him roughly by the collar as he raked his rust-coloured hair back from his face. "The Oracle foretold this!" he exclaimed, gesturing to Jasper's pointed ears. "'Descendants of the cursed prince,' he has the same damned knife ears!"

"That doesn't mean anything!" Charlotte protested.

"Enough," the masked man silenced his colleague with a gesture of his hand. With a sigh, their leader turned to face Jasper, a displeased expression on his face. "Very well, Jasper. If you need some help in gathering your bearings, perhaps a little motivation will encourage you." He gestured towards two of his henchmen, and Charlotte was seized roughly by her arms. She immediately moved to resist, to kick or headbutt or do *something*—but the sharp edge of a dagger pressed into her throat, halting her efforts.

Jasper's reaction was instantaneous, surging to his feet. "Let her go!" he roared, straining against the iron shackles binding him. "Let her go, she hasn't done anything to you! What do you want from us?"

"Jasper, just—calm down, it's going to be all right," Charlotte lied against the blade at her throat, swallowing her fear. Tears welled in her eyes despite her brave words, more terrified than she had been in her entire life.

The masked stranger paced back and forth, unhurried in his movements. "Now, now, Jasper… Those shackles are iron. You'll have a hard time escaping that." He paused beside Jasper, standing just out of range as he regarded Charlotte. "We didn't want it to come to this, but it seems we have no choice."

"Don't hurt her," Jasper pleaded, and hearing that raw desperation in his voice nearly broke her. "Let her go—I'm the one you want, right? Leave her out of this, just let her go."

The masked man's eyes narrowed as he turned to face Jasper, searching his countenance for something he seemingly never found. With a sigh, he snapped his fingers towards his men. "You can dispose of that one," he commanded nonchalantly, as if Charlotte's life were of no significance to him. "Perhaps that will be sufficient motivation to Awaken him."

That was it then – her life cast aside in an instant at the snap of someone's fingers. Charlotte had never given it much thought, never dwelled on her death other than hoping that she might live to see a modestly old age, perhaps with a certain blacksmith at her side. Faced with her death sentence, Charlotte had the brief thought to attempt to summon her magic anyway, burnout be damned. If she was to die, she would drag the lot of them to the hells with her.

But she couldn't risk hurting Jasper, couldn't guarantee the explosion of magic wouldn't kill him too… and Jasper deserved to live, even if Charlotte was destined to die. Her thoughts drifted towards her father, waiting on that ship destined for Pharsat, waiting for her to return.

After a lifetime of pain, Charlotte barely felt the knife in her flesh as her throat was cut, was only distantly aware of the hot gush of fluid that soaked the front of her dress as it sprayed out in front of her. The pain was secondary to the sudden wave of ice through Charlotte's body, frost forming in her fingers and toes as it crept up through her arms and legs. As her arms were released, her grip instinctively sought her throat, clamping down on the open wound in an attempt to stem the flow as Haeyin had once taught her.

She was cold, so cold...

There was a ringing in her ears as Charlotte's eyes locked on the boy in front of her, those green eyes wide with horror as Jasper screamed her name. Squeezing harder on her throat, Charlotte felt her knees shake as her wounded ankle gave out beneath her, a strange gasping sound escaping her mouth as she collided with the stone floor. Somewhere in the distance, Jasper was calling out for her, the chains that bound him rattling with his futile efforts to reach her.

She knew then – Charlotte knew in that moment that she was about to die, and she mourned all the time together that they had been robbed of. What wouldn't Charlotte give for just a little more time in this realm?

Struggling against the wound on her neck, the blistered hand that strained to stopper her lifeblood, Charlotte craned her neck around to meet his eyes once more, and she

CHAPTER

TWENTY-THREE

JASPER

In his short life, Jasper had lost three people for whom his entire worldview had shifted with their passing.

The first had been his uncle, always caught between the desire to raise Jasper with love and the need to keep his heart shuttered for his own survival. He couldn't recall ever being hugged by the man, and Jasper no longer remembered if that was due to his own aversion to touch or his uncle's aversion to admitting he cared for anyone. Jasper was only twelve years old when Zeke had fallen ill, the house reeking of opium as his uncle lay in his death bed. After a year spent choking on his own breath, Zeke succumbed. He had looked so much smaller than Jasper had known him to be as he was lowered into the frozen ground of the Caelfall cemetery, coins placed delicately over his eyes and a sword clasped in his rigor-firm grip.

The second had been Gideon, a loss still so recent it hurt Jasper to dwell on it for too long, fresh and raw in his heart. Each memory of his childhood spent running through the city streets with Gideon at his side had been highlighted in vivid, painful detail. Despite every black eye he earned from his father's fist, Gideon would risk Lord McClelland's wrath to sneak into Caelfall to be with Jasper. There was never a time that he and Gideon had been apart until the older man had joined the combat academy, and Jasper had eagerly followed suit… up until the fateful day of his breakdown and the months of silence that followed. He sorely regretted shutting out his friend – his *brother* – and Jasper would give anything for a second chance.

And now, Jasper was powerless as he watched the light leave Charlotte's eyes, her gaze forever frozen on his face. Less than an hour before, she had been alive and alight with arcing magical lightning as she fought to save them both from the clockwork creatures – and now she was gone.

Time lost all meaning. His sense of self grew blurry as his mind fractured, and his vision swam as he stared at Charlotte's hazel eyes as they grew flat and lifeless. There was a horrid, hollow feeling in his chest, a sinking despair that threatened to swallow Jasper whole. He strained against the iron that bound him, his shoulders shrieking in protest as he reached for her with all his might. He was screaming, shouting her name until his voice was hoarse, as if by will alone he would bring her back to this mortal plane.

After a few moments, Asshole the henchman glanced towards his leader, awaiting further instruction. "Perhaps we were wrong," he conceded.

The masked man sighed wearily, as if the most devastating moment of Jasper's life was little more than another disappointment. "Perhaps we were," Mask agreed with a dismissive gesture of his hand, his muffled words barely coherent for Jasper. "He is useless to us now. Get rid of them."

The confirmation of his death sentence was of little importance to Jasper – he had already died, his soul crumbling to ash as he stared blankly at Charlotte's body, at the amethyst on her finger glinting in the dim light. Fingers knotted in his hair as he was grasped roughly by another assailant, his head yanked backwards to expose his throat. Jasper barely made a sound as the blade slid across his skin, the pain hardly registering as a sensation in his splintered mind. In that moment, he wanted nothing more than to die, to follow Charlotte into the void she had tumbled into. Jasper closed his eyes as the blood bubbled and spewed from his throat, soaking the front of his shirt.

Wake up, Jasper...

He opened his eyes to find he was no longer in the cathedral. He blinked as his surroundings came into focus, unable to recognize this location. Jasper was kneeling in the snow at the foot of a great mountain, aurora borealis shimmering overhead. His blood still spread down his shirt, drops of scarlet falling into the snow beneath him. Ahead of him, a woman stood alone in the cold night, a woman he did not immediately recognize. Her eyes were blindfolded, her feet bare as she tread on the undisturbed snow. Raising her hand towards Jasper, she revealed fingers tipped with a harpy's talons.

"This is the first death," the woman spoke in a voice of rolling thunder, a voice he had known all this time. *Deltori.* "You will not be the same when you awake."

The snow around them shifted, a great beast taking shape as a reptilian face emerged from the frost, a creature

Jasper knew only from myth. A gargantuan shape followed, a great pair of wings folded behind it as the dragon skulked forward, moving fluidly as if it snaked through water. Its silver scales glittered in the light as they scattered stray snowflakes, the rumble of its breath shaking the earth beneath them.

Jasper sucked in a gasp as the dragon approached, feeling the heat of that fiery air on his skin. Despite his apprehension, it seemed the creature was wary of his fear. It regarded him with green eyes, as sharp and as bright as emeralds. Speaking in thoughts rather than words, the beast probed Jasper's mind with a gentle touch.

"*I am not here to hurt you,*" the dragon assured him in a man's voice, and Jasper recognized that cadence. This was the monster of his dreams, the presence he had felt for months lurking within him. "*You and I are as one. It is time.*"

The words echoed in his mind as Jasper stared up at the creature, in awe of his majesty and utterly terrified all at once. From deep within his soul, something shifted – a power great and terrible had been unearthed by his sorrow, a connection to something ancient and unimaginably powerful. The goddess Deltori raised her arms as they shifted seamlessly into feathered wings, taking flight with one beat. The dragon snaked around him, nudging his great head beneath Jasper's weary form as he collapsed against the scaly mass.

When Jasper opened his eyes once more, it was the most devastating thing that could have happened to him. His vision focused on the scene at the cathedral, and he knew he had lived despite his singular wish to have departed this world. His vocal cords shredded, Jasper was soundless as his gaze fell on Charlotte's still form. His heart cleaved anew at the sight of her broken body, at the way her eyes had grown flat and lifeless.

"*There is nothing we can do for her now,*" the dragon advised, his voice caressing Jasper's mind. He startled at the presence of the beast, the confirmation that his meeting with Deltori had not been merely a dream. "*But we can avenge her. Show these fools how grave a mistake they have made.*"

As he nudged Jasper's focus back towards the villains that surrounded them, the balance within the cathedral shifted. Jasper was no longer a prisoner, powerless as a lamb for the slaughter. His captors became aware of this truth as they regarded him, each of them stumbling backwards at the sight they beheld. A guttural growl reverberated from his chest as his flesh heated beneath his clothes, magic stitching the skin of his throat together as it pulsed through his veins.

No, not magic – this was a goddess' unrelenting strength, his *birthright*.

In his desperation, Jasper had no desire to resist. No, he gladly welcomed that power, welcomed that fierce beast that had been slumbering deep within himself. His teeth elongated as his body began to shift, vicious fangs pricking his lips as his vision blurred. Every vein in his body throbbed with liquid fire, the razor-sharp angles of his spine threatening to pierce through his skin. The manacles binding him snapped like string as Jasper strained against them, the muscles in his arms burning as he struggled to stand. There was unimaginable might surging through his bones, but Jasper was no more in control of it than he was the weather, or the setting sun, or the passage of time. It commanded him; Jasper wanted justice, wanted to avenge Charlotte, but the beast wanted vengeance in the most archaic sense. It wanted blood.

"*Trust me,*" the monstrous soul within him beckoned. "*Let me in.*"

He staggered forward as his joints crunched, brought to his knees as the strange power within him commanded Jasper to take his mark, to prepare for the next phase of the battle. Where his palms had been splayed flat against the stone floor of the church, useless human nails fell from bloodied nail beds as his remaining fingers lengthened, his father's wedding ring slipping from his grasp as his arms became wings. The fabric of his shirt fell away in chunks as the bones of his spine protruded from his skin, shredding what remained of his masquerade costume. Talons pushed through the leather of his boots as his feet scrambled for purchase in the stone beneath him, slipping on the remains of his trousers.

The men around him were panicking, tripping over debris as they struggled to place distance between themselves and the horror unfolding before them. "It's him, it's him!" one of them screamed, pointing animatedly in Jasper's direction. "Kill him!"

"*What's happening to me?*" Jasper breathed, caught between the wonder and horror of the transformation, his life as he knew it torn apart at the seams. "*What did you do to me?*" The words emanated in his mind but did not leave his ruined throat, a snarling growl replacing any semblance of words.

"*This is what you were born to do.*"

A shudder rippled through him as pinpricks of agony ignited along Jasper's skin, bloodied silver plates bursting forth from human flesh. There was a splitting pain in his head as his skull elongated, vicious horns erupting from his scalp, along his jaw, above his brow. He stumbled as his limbs shifted to accommodate his size, assuming a stance that could hold his mass as the counterweight of a tail became available to him.

At last, it seemed the pain had subsided as Jasper leaned on his wing joints, his vision focusing on the sight of his own blood muddying the stone floor, a viscera of red hair and ruined flesh beneath him. When he lifted his head once more, he towered over the humans that had sought to destroy him.

"This is who you are."

He leaned back on his legs, the stone cracking beneath his talons as he spread his newly formed wings wide. With a snap of his wingspan, his enemies were knocked aside with the force of a mighty gale, screaming as they lost their footing. As the resulting wind teased over Charlotte's hair, the scent of vanilla and soap gave pause to the fury in Jasper's blood, his heart shuddering at the memory of her. As he turned his head to look down at her, he saw a few of the braver humans were attempting to drag her body away. A terrible rage flooded through him, a guttural roar escaping his snout as he turned on the cultists.

Leaning forward on his wing joints, he lumbered forward as he snapped his jaws at the nearest person, colliding with the goddess statue with a crash. He recognized the masked man as his teeth closed around flesh and bone, severing his arm just above his elbow. A foul taste coated his tongue as Jasper spat out the limb, turning to the remaining two assailants still attempting to drag Charlotte by her feet. One of them was wise enough to give up on his mission and flee, but the other was caught between Jasper's jaws.

"Subdue the beast!" the masked man bellowed as reinforcements thundered through the corridors towards the main hall. Clutching what remained of his arm, the man retreated beyond one of the hallways, too narrow for Jasper's snout to reach him.

"Put that one down," the voice of the dragon admonished as the wave of humans entered the cathedral, wielding spears and lances. *"Take a deep breath, pull courage from within."*

He jerked his head to the side, sending the corpse between his jaws flying towards the wall to his left. As he inhaled dutifully, there was the odd sensation of a reflex Jasper wasn't familiar with, a sort of clicking of cartilage in his throat as his lungs filled. Instead of exhaling air, Jasper spat flames towards the reinforcements that flooded the cathedral, incinerating each of them. The force rekindled the fire of the burning pews around them, flames blazing higher and higher. His human form would have melted in the inferno, but Jasper had been hewn and forged into something stronger now. He lowered his weight to the ground, shielding Charlotte's body with the impenetrable fortress of his scales.

"Jasper?"

The sound of his own name gave him pause, for he knew he was unrecognizable in his current form. He turned his head towards the source, careful to keep Charlotte concealed beneath him as he eyed the shape of a girl in a chair. Maya's hair fluttered around her face where it escaped her braided crown, her dark eyes wide as she wheeled herself towards him from the entrance of the cathedral.

"Maya," he breathed, coming back to himself for a moment. With his sharpened vision, Jasper could see every tiny scar on her face, could smell the adrenaline in her veins – but not an ounce of fear. *"How did you get here?"*

She shook her head as she approached, examining their surroundings before she responded. "I... I've dreamt this before," Maya explained in a far-away voice, as if the flames and the corpses were second to the revelation she was experiencing. "I knew you would be here, and that I needed to find you."

Her words were not nearly as startling as the fact that she had responded to him, despite the fact that Jasper was distinctly aware he was no longer capable of human speech. "*You can understand me? How?*" he asked as he shifted, struggling to turn his body to face her in the narrow space.

Maya blinked as she nodded slowly, the molten wind teasing her hair as the fire flickered in her eyes. "I don't know," she admitted. "It's as if you're in my mind, some-how, you and... whoever that other voice is." Her face fell as her eyes shifted to the crumpled form beneath Jasper, revealed by his movements.

Jasper's beastly heart contorted as he followed Maya's gaze, the emotion his adrenaline had struggled to bury surging anew. A sad, keening noise escaped his snout against his will. He couldn't save Charlotte, and even vengeance was a pitiful consolation prize to losing the love of his life, the only home he had ever known. Charlotte was gone, and Jasper was gone with her.

The dragon's soul within him seemed to understand his distress, soothing his mind once more. "*We need to flee this place,*" he urged him. "*You are not easily burned, but you can still be crushed in the rubble if this place is destroyed. Let Maya onto your back, it will be faster to fly.*"

Jasper had never experienced an affliction such as a fear of heights, but the thought of flying made his stomach turn. He felt the scaled frill around his ears flatten against his skull as a growl echoed in his throat, his uncertainty plain in his body language as Maya drew nearer, startlingly at ease with the scene before her. He glanced down towards the body of the girl he still sheltered beneath him, Charlotte's skin a ghostly grey that Jasper had never seen before, never wanted to imagine. He had half a mind to bring her with him, to carry her in his arms – his legs? – and bury her somewhere far away from here.

"*No,*" the voice of the dragon insisted, though he could sense the empathy in the beast's tone. "*Your right wing is incomplete, you will not survive the flight to the mainland encumbered. I am sorry.*"

Tentatively, Maya reached for his metallic snout, her fingers brushing his nose soothingly. "Whoever that is… he's right, Jasper," she confirmed, her voice breaking as slow tears dripped down her face. "We need to get out of here. There's nothing we can do for her now."

Despite his other senses being heightened, Jasper was startled to discover the touch of the girl's hand was not unpleasant against his skin… but then, Maya's hand danced over a layer of impenetrable scales, a natural coat of armour that covered every inch of him. Jasper leaned into that touch a moment longer, leaned into the closest physical comfort he could accept when it felt his heart was breaking a thousand times over. He knew that she was right. He hated that she was right.

A glimmer of light caught his eye as the fire danced around them, and Jasper spotted his ring amidst the viscera of what had been his human body. Maya followed his line of sight, wheeling herself closer to reach the blood-stained metal. Noting the matching band on Charlotte's finger, she looked up at Jasper, as if waiting for permission to collect her ring as well.

"*Leave it,*" Jasper instructed, grateful his mental voice would not break with the tears that his human eyes would have shed. "*It belongs to her.*"

Awkward in his new body, still unfamiliar with the musculature and bone structure he now found himself with, Jasper stumbled into something of a bow as he lowered himself closer to the ground. If the beast soul thought it odd that Maya could not scale Jasper's back unaided, he declined to comment. As she pocketed his ring, the girl maneuvered herself as close as she could before hoisting herself up by her arms onto Jasper's lowered spine, seating herself at the base of his neck just before his wings. Sensing the need for additional support, she removed the scarf that had been coiled at her throat, tossing it around Jasper's neck to give herself makeshift reins.

A noise of approval echoed in his mind before the beast spoke once more. *"These are undesirable conditions for a first flight lesson, but we have little choice. When you leave this cathedral, spread your wings and keep your limbs tucked in."*

Maya gave him a reassuring nudge, as if to confirm she was securely boarded. Jasper stalked forward towards the cathedral entrance, balancing his weight on his wing joints and with the length of his tail. He struggled to keep his wings tucked in as tightly as he could, certain he lost a few scales as he squeezed his immense form through what remained of the stone archway. The sharp pinpricks along his shoulders were the first sensations of pain he had experienced in this form, and Jasper noted the weakness.

The night air on his reptilian skin felt no different to the heat of the blaze within the cathedral, but his human passenger shuddered with what must have been a drop in temperature. Maya clung tightly to the scarf wrapped around his neck as he leaned back on his legs, spreading his wings wide. He gave a few tentative flaps, feeling the way his weight shifted with the movement, but he didn't immediately shoot skyward as he had hoped. It seemed his missing human fingers had translated into a dragon's wing ill-suited for take-off.

"Perhaps you should give it a bit of a run," the beast suggested hopefully. *"Lauch yourself over a bridge, or something. You* do *live in a floating kingdom."*

Though the suggestion made him uneasy, Jasper did not have the luxury of time to compose himself. Maya flapped at his shoulder with particular urgency, and as he turned his head he saw their presence had not gone unnoticed. The remnants of the fleeing masquerade guests were screaming in terror, and Aethian soldiers were advancing on him and Maya. Many of them looked positively terrified by the creature they witnessed, their breeches soiled as they stared on in horror. Others were less startled, their rifles raised and pointed at Jasper.

"Run, please – run *now!*" Maya commanded, and Jasper bolted forward. He stumbled once with the awkward combination of limbs he was still so unused to, but pressure demanded he become acclimated to the rhythm of this new body as he ran. Civilians ducked and dove to escape the enormous creature that barrelled through the streets, narrowly avoiding being trampled. The crackle of gunfire irritated his oversensitive ears, the bullets ricocheting off his scales harmlessly as he galloped down the streets of Briardeen. Even if Jasper was invulnerable, however, it did not mean his passenger was.

A hand reached for his neck, giving him a reassuring pat. "I'm fine," Maya called over the noise, evidently sensing his concern. Had he given voice to his thoughts through whatever psychic link they shared? "Just keep going!"

The edge of the county drew nearer, a brick wall separating civilians from a sheer drop to the Aethian Sea far below. Jasper planted his feet, talons chipping the cobblestone beneath him as he pushed off his wing joints, aching as he lunged forwards. He flailed his wings in an ungainly sprawl as he leapt into the empty air beyond the wall, plummeting to the depths below. Maya screamed behind him, clutching his neck as they descended in horrific free-fall.

"*Spread your wings!*" the monster roared.

Something clicked within him then, another instinct Jasper was learning. He tucked his enormous legs beneath him, angling his tail as his great wingspan stretched wide. It hurt to use his right wing, smaller than the left on account of his missing fingers, but Jasper pushed through the sensation, adjusting the spread of his left wing to compensate. His form caught the wind with a sharp tug as his muscles strained against the pressure of that unseen force, and Maya clung on for dear life as they gracelessly stopped falling and began to glide.

The beast within him seemed to purr in approval. "*Good work. We can improve on your form later, but… for now, it seems we may yet live another day.*"

Maya had stopped screaming, though her arms were still wrapped in a death grip as far as they could reach around Jasper's neck. He chanced a look back at her as his wings steadied them, catching sight of her hair as the wind teased it loose from the plaits Eleni had woven. The tear tracks through her soot-covered face had dried, and she managed a breathless laugh as Jasper struggled to regain his gliding form.

"That was … incredible," she said at last, her voice barely audible over the roar of the wind. Jasper was inclined to agree; he had never flown before, never even stepped foot on an airship, but it must have been as magical an experience for him as it was for the girl on his back.

As Jasper led them in a slow descent towards the mainland, the distant flicker of lights barely visible in the murky night, the adrenaline in his veins quieted. None of this felt real, and yet Jasper knew with painful clarity that it was. Charlotte's eyes still haunted him, and he knew without words that Maya was hurting as well. Neither of them would ever be the same.

Shifting where she sat on his back, Maya cleared her throat. "Now that we're no longer in immediate danger, I believe an explanation is in order," Maya called over the wind. She relaxed her grip on his neck, adjusting her makeshift reins.

Jasper leaned gently to the right, guiding them west. He flapped his wings once for good measure, taking note of the way his body utilized the air currents as they descended. *"Maybe we can start with who you are,"* he addressed the soul of the beast within him.

To his credit, the dragon's spirit was not offended by their words. If anything, he seemed pleased by their curiosity. *"Indeed, it is time,"* the beast agreed, sounding almost sorrowful. *"My name is Daes. Listen well, for if the three of us are to survive, we will have to work together from now on…"*

CHAPTER
TWENTY-FOUR
DANTE

HE GASPED FOR AIR AS THEY CLEARED THE CASTLE PREMISES, the cool night wind a blissful reprieve from the stench of burning undead. Dante didn't have time to process whatever abominations pursued them, but he had never been so horrified as he was to discover a cadaver he couldn't command. All of his life, he had feared the innate power of necromancy he had struggled to bury within himself. Dante had never known how much more terrifying the lack of connection with the dead could be, that unnerving silence he felt as that army of corpses advanced.

Their party regrouped momentarily at the bridge towards Dornkeep, the chaos from the castle leaking into the streets as the flickering lamplight illuminated their escape. They all seemed to be unharmed, albeit winded. Eleni's hands were gratefully intact, and for a moment it seemed they had escaped the disastrous masquerade unscathed.

576

As the seconds ticked on, Dante did a quick mental headcount. "Where are Jasper and Charlotte?"

The silence stretched on, a horrified realization dawning on each of them. "They must have fallen behind," Fenyang spoke at last, announcing the truth no one else dared voice.

Varus cursed under his breath before turning to face Eleni, pressing a kiss to her forehead. "I'm going back for them," he decided. "Continue on to the docks, I'll meet up with you there."

The woman's confusion at the sudden affection hardened into anger at Varus' words, but Eleni was interrupted before she could oppose him. "I'm going with you," Haeyin announced, earning a glare from his partner as she bristled.

"Count me in," Dante agreed. Jasper and Charlotte were his friends, and he wouldn't lose them — not this close to the end, to their chance at escape. His king regarded him with a wary countenance, as if he too wanted to protest, to insist that Dante stayed with him or that Fenyang assisted with the rescue in his stead... but the Valedian king was too important an ally to lose. The way he looked at Dante now, it was as if he were warring between this knowledge and the potential to reveal that Dante was just as important as he was.

Whatever thoughts warred in Fenyang's mind, the man said nothing of them. "Come back to me," was all he urged with a quick squeeze of Dante's hand. A shared glance with Eleni seemed to settle the woman, but the expressions of worry remained on their faces as they turned in the direction of Dornkeep.

"This way, Your Majesty," Benkaei directed, her spear at the ready. She turned her hawkish stare towards Varus, a conflicted emotion in the set of her mouth. "If we reach the docks and you still aren't there…"

"Leave without us," Varus instructed immediately. "Do not jeopardize your safety, we will find our own way to you."

The warrior looked almost wounded at the order, but she nodded in response as she turned to shepherd Fenyang and Eleni to safety. Varus gestured for Haeyin and Dante to follow him as they sprinted towards the castle at full speed, dodging fleeing rebels. Any solitary corpses that had shuffled this far were quickly obliterated by Haeyin or Varus, the latter molding darkness into blades of shadow, lacerating the clockwork cadavers. As they reached the grand entrance gates to the castle, it was immediately obvious that something had gone horribly wrong, the foul stench of burnt flesh filling the air. Dante felt his chest tighten with fear as they crossed the threshold into the entrance hall and saw the carnage.

From a singular space on the soot-stained floor, a lightning storm had erupted—brief and devastating. Scorch marks stretched from that sole spot outwards to where Dante and his allies stood now, and in between sprawled the incinerated remains of a hundred of the undead. There was one peculiar aberration in the carnage, one place that almost appeared to have been shielded from the blast.

Varus exchanged a look with Haeyin. When neither of them deigned to share their thoughts immediately, Dante prodded. "What is it?"

Raking a hand through his white-streaked hair, Haeyin regarded the calamity. "This… this is a magical outburst," he concluded. "And it appears our dear Charlotte had the makings of a mage, so it's possible this was her doing."

At Dante's apparent shock, Varus cut in. "When we

rescued Jasper, there was a moment when... while we were shadow-stepping, Charlotte saw something. When it attacked, she obliterated it — with *magic*."

"What do you mean, 'had the makings of a mage'? I'd never sensed any sort of magic from her," Dante protested, bewildered by this information.

"It was new, barely manifested," Varus explained, shaking his head. "I doubt you would've sensed a thing from her, so early on."

Dante was at a loss for words, the unscathed spot on the floor becoming the most terrifying sight in the room. "Burnout?" he whispered weakly.

The doctor shook his head. "I don't think so," Haeyin disagreed. "Charlotte's magic is in its infancy, and the mind has countermeasures to prevent such an outcome when the ability is so newly harnessed. She more than likely passed out from the exertion." Dante shuddered at the memory of his first use of his deadly power in years, the way he had lost consciousness immediately afterwards from the resulting exhaustion.

"And what of Jasper?" asked Varus, gesturing towards the second spot on the floor. "What are the chances he was incinerated?" There was a note of desperation in his voice, as if despite his blunt wording the kingpin prayed this was not the case.

Haeyin shook his head. "In all fairness... if she had truly lost control, there wouldn't be a space here. There would be another body."

His stomach turning at the notion, Dante looked away from the sea of ash and viscera, deciding to cling to the possibility that they were both alive somewhere. The train of thought gave him pause. "If Charlotte had passed out..." he began, trailing off.

"Then where is she?" Varus finished, nodding in agreement.

There was a distant guttural moan as another army of corpses announced their presence nearby, somewhere deeper within the castle. "We should go," Haeyin decided, rubbing his palms. "I am not keen on fighting any more of those creatures."

"What about Charlotte and Jasper?" Dante protested, even as his feet began to move towards the exit of their own volition.

Gesturing for them to depart, Varus all but shoved Dante towards Briardeen. "If they're still alive, they would have gone to Dornkeep," he insisted, and Dante couldn't fault the logic. Their party in agreement, Haeyin and Dante followed the kingpin as they jogged back through the castle gardens, praying to every god that would listen that their friends were safe. Ahead of him, Varus' footsteps were uneven, his gait suffering with the influx of physical activity. Dante was struggling himself, his lungs burning with exertion as they sprinted through Briardeen, heading towards the bridge for Dornkeep.

They were halfway through the eastern district when Dante nearly lost his footing, the ground shaking with a thunderous roar in the distance. "What in the name of the Keepers was that?" he breathed. It was close, it had come from Briardeen, surely.

Haeyin appeared similarly shaken, Varus stabilizing him as he turned in the direction of the sound. "Keep running to the ships, I'm going to investigate," the kingpin instructed.

Something in his gut was ill at ease with Varus' words. "Why?" Dante demanded, coming to a complete stop. They had lost precious time already, what could possibly be more important than getting to the docks? "What aren't you saying, Varus?"

The doctor elbowed his partner, seemingly echoing Dante's thoughts. Varus appeared conflicted, glancing between the pair of them. "I think that sound came from the cathedral," he explained, a response that didn't answer Dante's question.

"*Why*, Varus?" Dante growled.

The kingpin raked a hand through his hair, all but loose from the wind. "I think Charlotte and Jasper are in there," he admitted at last, seeming exasperated. "I can't explain right now, please just – just trust me."

A frigid dread settled in his heart at Varus' words, at the prospect of his friends; if Varus insisted upon running back, he must have thought they couldn't reach the docks without assistance. "Fine, *we* go to the cathedral," Dante insisted, leaving no room for argument. Varus conceded, sensing their dwindling time allowed no room for argument.

They backtracked through Dornkeep towards the bridge leading to Briardeen. The military still patrolled, likely for them, searching the faces of everyone who passed by. Terrified citizens were still seen throughout, many packing their bags or retreating into boarded houses. Their terror multiplied tenfold when the ground began to shake, a great reptilian animal surging forth from the entrance to the cathedral. Stray stone clattered to the ground in its wake, the dark form of a rider clinging to the monster's back.

For a brief moment, Dante was motionless. An icy terror spread through his veins as he stared at a mythical beast. The creature was hurtling towards them, a monstrous silver form of claws, teeth, and—

His instincts snapped into place, forcing Dante to react. "Get back!" he bellowed, tackling Varus and Haeyin aside as the beast surged past in a streak of silver. They hit the ground with a thud, largely landing on top of Varus as they collapsed into a heap on the rubble littering the streets. The Aethian soldiers advanced, a cacophony of gunfire unloaded towards the creature before their movements were arrested by a rebel mage, casting a plume of fire in their wake with only one hand.

"What was that?" Haeyin grumbled irritably as he helped Varus and Dante up from the ground.

Without responding, Varus dusted off his jacket before hobbling the remaining distance to the cathedral. The great stone structure was damaged at the entrance where the massive creature had forced its gigantic form through the too-narrow archway, smoke and fire curling around the remnants of shattered stained-glass windows. Dante had no choice but to follow as he and Haeyin sprinted to catch up with the kingpin, lungs aching with the exertion and the smoke-filled air.

Whatever Dante had anticipated finding in the great cathedral could not compare to the chaos that awaited him, running over bodies and debris. There was no sign of Jasper or Charlotte at first glance, but by the state of the cathedral, Dante prayed they had not been here. Broken glass and stone were strewn every which way, and there was blood—*Keepers*, there was blood, spattered and pooled beneath mangled, partially-charred corpses. One such corpse lay beneath the remnants of a statue on the far side of the cathedral, a dress of blue and gold shielded from the destruction of the fire—

Wait. No, no, *no*…

The air took on a frigid chill as Varus and Haeyin seemed to notice the same details, reached the same conclusion that Dante had. The doctor ran faster still, faster than

Dante had ever seen him run, sprinting at full speed to the body of the young woman who lay crumpled on the floor ahead of them. Haeyin crashed to his knees, pulling her broken form into his lap as he searched for vital signs he would never find.

"Charlotte, can you hear me?" he asked, his voice breaking. "Charlotte, please wake up… Charlie…"

As Varus and Dante caught up to their companion, they stared in breathless silence at the tragedy in front of them. Her throat torn asunder, there was a glassy look to Charlotte's once bright hazel eyes, a grey tinge to her lips. Dante knew intuitively that his friend was far beyond their reach now, even for a healer as gifted as Haeyin.

"Haeyin… she's gone," Dante said softly, his throat raw as he spoke.

"No," Haeyin ground out through his teeth as he choked out a sob, clutching Charlotte's limp form against him. He summoned that golden light anyway, the magic illuminating the grisly wound in her throat. "No, I can fix this, I can… I can save her…"

It was a fruitless and dangerous pursuit, to attempt to heal someone so obviously deceased. Dante cast a warning look at Varus, knowing Haeyin had already exhausted much of his power in an effort to save Eleni's hands, to defend them all from the empty corpse army.

Varus placed a hand on the doctor's shoulder, his grief as palpable as his partner's as he spoke. "Hae, don't do this," he pleaded with the man.

"You can't bring her back," Dante added in agreement.

"*Yes*, I can!" Haeyin protested with a shout, his hand trembling as the magic wavered, his control over his power faltering. Varus sprang back as if he'd been burnt, golden light sparking from every inch of Haeyin's body. Dante's heart hammered in his chest as Verdis' face flashed in his memory, her eyes aglow with the unbound magic that ran freely through her decaying form.

Instinctively, he pulled Varus back, fearing the imminent explosion that was about to take place. "Haeyin, let her go!" he yelled. "You'll burn out, *let her go!*"

His veins glowed with that deadly golden light, and Haeyin's head fell back as his power began to consume him. The power to mend was never meant to take souls back from Rhanigan's grasp, and to do so was one of the cardinal sins of healing. Even Dante's power couldn't truly resurrect anyone; necromancy was an act of borrowing, not taking, and his own energy was traded for that temporary bargain. What Haeyin was attempting…

Something shifted in the air as the ground began to shake, and that brilliant light dimmed to obsidian. Haeyin's golden eyes darkened to an unearthly crimson as a shriek emanated from his throat, a sound unlike anything Dante had heard before. The skin of his face cracked, fissures emerging as his power leaked from every orifice, a dark gloom pooling around him. Varus and Dante staggered backwards as the cloud of darkness circled the doctor, obscuring Charlotte's body from view entirely. It stretched across the cathedral, swallowing the lingering flames as it spread across the stone floor.

Instinctively, Dante attempted to build a shield from his own power, protectively willing his energy into a wall around himself and Varus. He could taste the magical signature of that dark resonance against the roof of his mouth, something beyond his understanding.

A humanoid shape yawned into existence, a cruel laugh echoing across the ruined cathedral as Rhanigan stepped into the realm, dark robes trailing behind as the god stepped barefoot onto the ruined stone. The Soul Keeper might have passed for a human, the details of their physical appearance as fluid as water, as malleable as their magic. Rhanigan's form was constantly in flux, and in scripture Dante had seen many creative interpretations — and now he understood why. It was as if the deity in front of him shifted constantly, at once appearing as both masculine and feminine, strong and delicate, welcoming and intimidating. A fiend disguised as an ally.

The god tilted their head, regarding Haeyin with an almost fond expression. The doctor's motionless form was lifted into the air effortlessly as the Soul Keeper addressed him. "Rhey'lu," purred Rhanigan, their voice reminding Dante of a whispered curse. "Do we never learn? How bold of you, practically kicking down my door to seize a soul…"

Rhey'lu. The name of the demigod seized Dante's soul in a vice of iron, and his grip on reality began to fracture. It was impossible… but then again, Dante was staring the Soul Keeper in the face – what did he know of possibility at this point? Rhanigan's face was a beatific smile as they regarded the fractured mage before them, the son of their sister goddess, the Tide Keeper. Dante could barely maintain the perimeter of his shield as his entire body trembled with shock.

"Let him go, Rhanigan," Varus spoke suddenly, his voice an ominous rumble in the near-silence of the Soul Keeper's quiet deluge.

The god assessed Varus, curiosity in their eyes. "I remember you," they noted, their gaze narrowing. "Always meddling."

That familiarly deadly energy was swirling around Varus' fingers, and Dante realized with a jolt that it was not his own magic that was keeping Rhanigan's death mist at bay. As he retracted his power, he saw a ring of darkness swirling around him and Varus, a shield that dared to defy the god of chaos.

"*Let him go!*" Varus roared, flexing his fingers. That circle of magic spread wider still as the kingpin fought against the Soul Keeper's influence, his power pushing against the force of the god with everything he had to spare. Dante watched as Rhanigan's expression faltered, that unfazed confidence slipping as the deity regarded Varus in a new light.

Heaving a sigh, Rhanigan withdrew the aura of death. "Very well, have it your way," the Soul Keeper conceded. "You may as well enjoy what *limited* time you have together."

Those last words were added with a fiendish grin as they waved a hand dismissively, sending Haeyin flying across the cathedral. As the god of chaos faded into the darkness with a final cackle, a weakened Varus was already hobbling towards where Haeyin had landed. He was at the doctor's side in an instant, kneeling beside his partner as he assessed the damage.

"Haeyin... Haeyin, it's me," he spoke quietly, tentatively as he cradled his face. "Can you hear me?" Varus swept the man's hair back from his face, and the doctor looked so much older than Dante knew him to be. The front of his hair was nearly entirely white where the kingpin brushed his fingers through it.

At his partner's touch, Haeyin's freckled skin seemed to seal up, the jagged fissures fading until they disappeared entirely. Black ichor dripped from his eyes as they fluttered open, amber once more, the last of the Soul Keeper's presence draining from him as the tears fell.

"Azrael?" he breathed, searching Varus' face. Dante's

eyes narrowed. He could practically feel the way Varus tensed up at the name.

"You'll be all right, Hae," he affirmed in a whisper, brushing tears from Haeyin's cheek with his thumb.

The doctor's form was wracked with sobs as he sagged against Varus, weeping against the man's chest. It was an alarming sight, for Dante had witnessed Haeyin exhausted, infuriated... but never so distraught. "I tried to save her, I tried," he sobbed. "Charlotte, I—what have I done?"

"I know," Varus assured him, pressing his lips to the top of Haeyin's head. Turning to address Dante, the kingpin looked nearly as tortured as his partner did. "We need to get out of here. Grab Charlotte, we can take her body with us."

Accepting he would receive no answers immediately, Dante begrudgingly nodded in agreement. As he went to retrieve Charlotte, however, he was panic-stricken to discover she no longer rested near the foot of the goddess statue. Dante's heart raced as his gaze searched the ruined cathedral around them, but none of the corpses that littered the stone floor belonged to his departed friend. There were broken pews, the remains of what might have been a wheelchair, and so many bodies... but no sign of Charlotte.

He turned to face Varus, the doctor's limp form still cradled in the kingpin's arms. "She's gone," Dante breathed.

Varus frowned at the information, a question even he did not have the answer for. He paused for a moment, his mind calculating the next course of action. Outside, explosions erupted beyond the walls of the cathedral, the chaos and violence of the evening continuing without their notice.

"We have no choice," Varus confessed, sighing. "I'm sorry, Dante. We have to go."

Whatever Dante might have wanted to retort with, he knew there was no use in arguing. As much as he wanted answers, wanted to find Charlotte, to find Jasper… they were out of time. He nodded briskly, accepting Varus' hand as they shadow-stepped away, leaving the bloodied cathedral ruins behind them.

Despite the chaos that had upended Briardeen, the docks were seemingly unaffected by the disorder. The workers were evidently accustomed to operating in their own form of bedlam on a daily basis, merely pausing briefly to frown at the arrival of Varus, Dante, and Haeyin as they appeared from thin air.

"As you were," Varus barked at them, earning a respectful nod from his employees as they went about their business. He and Dante struggled to carry the near-unresponsive doctor towards *The Veiled Siren*, thankfully still awaiting their arrival. Aboard the airship, a slender young woman in dark, form-fitting armour spotted them, her dark eyes widening as she ran to assist them.

"Nadine, you had orders to leave without us," the kingpin reprimanded the woman as she took Haeyin in her arms, relieving them of the doctor as they climbed aboard the ship.

Her gaze snapped up towards her employer, her expression darkening. "It's not so simple as that, Varus," Nadine remarked grimly. "We have a situation—"

There were rapid footsteps as Eleni met them on the deck of the airship, all but launching herself at Varus. Her eyes were a mess of tears and smeared ink, her golden hair in disarray. "Is Maya with you?" Eleni demanded, her blue eyes wide with alarm. Hasima followed at a laboured pace behind her, a look of concern on her face as she leaned on her cane.

Varus went very still in Eleni's grasp. "She was supposed to be here," he emphasized slowly, his eyes searching Eleni's face. "Cary was supposed to escort her here, what do you mean?"

Her face crumpled as Eleni took in his words, as if her last hope had been dashed by his response. As she burst into tears in Varus' arms, Hasima stroked the woman's back soothingly. "She was here, but..." the queen mother began with a sigh, shaking her head. "Maya said something about Jasper before she left, I didn't catch what it was. When she departed, we had hoped she had met up with you."

Dante's heart sank. He recalled the destroyed wheel-chair in the cathedral, a seemingly meaningless detail at the time. He had half a mind to mention it, but a shout from the docks drew their group's attention away from Maya.

"Sir, the soldiers have crossed the bridge," one of the workers called up to the airship, waving at Varus. "We can't delay your departure any longer."

The kingpin seemed genuinely tormented, glancing between the dock worker and Nadine where she still supported Haeyin. Dante knew the man was running on fumes, leaning on his left leg as he turned to Nadine once more.

"Leave without me," he determined grimly as his companion signalled to the first officer to push back, the rumble of the engines nearly drowning out his voice. "I'll go back and find Maya—"

"You will *not*," Eleni all but growled, tears streaming

down her face as she pulled away to stare up at her partner. "I will not lose you as well." Her grip tightened on Varus' arms, as if she might physically keep him on the ship with her.

"Eleni…" Varus began to protest, but the airship was already in motion, a gentle shudder emanating through the hull of the craft as they began to depart Aethelind once and for all. Evidently too drained to even teleport, the kingpin sagged in Eleni's grasp, his face lined with crushing acceptance. As the distance between the ship and the Dornkeep docks grew more and more, a hollow sensation began to fester in Dante's chest, a chasm stretching between his ribs.

Charlotte was gone, Jasper was gone, and now Maya as well.

Readjusting her grip on Haeyin's waist, Nadine glanced between the sullen expressions on the people surrounding her. "We should get him inside," the woman called over the roar of the engine. "We're not out of the woods yet, and I wouldn't put it past the king's men to fire at us now that we're airborne."

Supporting Varus with a surprising level of strength, Eleni and the kingpin led their party towards the captain's quarters of *The Veiled Siren*. Dante followed along in an uneasy silence, a numbness spreading through his veins, frost crystallizing around his lungs as he was ushered by Hasima through a narrow galley towards the far end of the airship. Varus opened the door for Nadine as the woman carried Haeyin into the room, setting him down on the cabin bed with ease.

"Dante," a familiar voice spoke, the sound of his own name giving Dante pause as he turned to face the speaker. He was immediately bundled into the arms of the Valedian king, and suddenly the ice in his chest began to melt as quickly as it had formed.

"I'm all right, Fen," he reassured his king, his arms tentatively rising to return the embrace. Part of him wanted to protest at the impropriety of such close contact, but part of him didn't care. Being in this stillness now, after running for his life less than an hour ago, felt fundamentally wrong. His heart ached for his friends, as if Dante felt he should still be running through those ruined streets searching for Jasper... but with the king's arms around him, it pained him a little bit less.

"I feared for a moment that I'd lost you as well," Fenyang admitted in a low voice, quiet enough that only Dante would hear him. He lingered for a moment before pulling away, his eyes searching Dante before he addressed the group gathered in the cabin. "What happened? Did you find Jasper and Charlotte? Maya?"

At the sound of his friends' names, Dante's chest felt cold all over again. "No," he breathed, barely wanting to confirm the truth.

Wincing as he eased himself into a chair, Varus rubbed at his right knee irritably, dismissing Nadine with a wave of his hand. The woman nodded once before exiting the cabin, closing the door behind her. The kingpin heaved a weary sigh, raking his fingers through his hair as Varus addressed his audience.

"We should start with what we know," he began solemnly, his gaze fixed on the floor as the airship gently rocked. "So far, Charlotte is... Charlotte is dead. Jasper and Maya are missing."

The words settled painfully around them as Varus spoke, and Eleni sobbed anew at the confirmation of her friend's passing. Hasima gently guided her towards the edge of the bed, sitting down beside her as she rubbed the woman's back soothingly, murmuring quietly in her ear. Dante resisted the urge to join her, his eyes burning as he forced himself to breathe through the sensation of his throat sealing up.

"I am… saddened to hear of Charlotte, truly," Fenyang responded, his voice uneven. "Do we have any idea of where Jasper and Maya are? Are we certain they aren't also…"

He trailed off, as if the thought of losing anyone else was too terrible to speak of. Varus glanced up from the floor to meet the king's gaze, a haunted look in his eyes. "I may have some idea where they are," he admitted in a low voice.

At Varus' words, something cracked in Dante's chest, the ice forming over his heart giving way to a searing rage. He turned towards their host, unable to stop the words that left his mouth. "By all means, share the joy," Dante inter-jected, startled by the venom in his own voice. "Because after what I just saw, I need more than a few good reasons to trust either of you after that stunt in the cathedral."

Varus stood frozen in front of him, deathly still at Dante's words. It was the queen mother who dared to speak, narrowing her eyes at the kingpin. "What stunt in the cathedral?" Hasima repeated, a grim curiosity in her tone.

"We found Charlotte's body there," Dante continued, gesturing towards the unconscious Haeyin as he spoke. The walls seemed tight around him, cramped in the hull of the ship. "And 'Haeyin', who may or may not be a demigod, summoned *Rhanigan* in his efforts to resurrect Charlie, and 'Varus' here didn't seem too bloody surprised by that."

"Dante…" Varus began, his hands raised in a gesture

of surrender. "I understand you will have questions, and I'll answer everything I can, but—"

"Oh, I've got questions, *Azrael*," Dante spat, taking a step back for good measure. The kingpin seemed to flinch at the name, but Dante ignored him. "But we don't have time for all of them. Let's start with why you're so at ease with the fact that we didn't find Jasper's body? Maya's?"

At the edge of the bed, Eleni hiccupped as she pressed a wounded hand to her mouth, fresh tears spilling down her face at Dante's words. He almost felt some regret at speaking so callously, but his ire towards Varus' secrecy, the loss of his friends, was overwhelming every other sensation. Each of them watched and waited for Varus to respond. The man in question still stared back at Dante, his dark eyes ominously flat.

"Because they're still alive."

A silence fell over them as Varus' words settled. Eleni's sobbing had subsided, still sniffling softly as Hasima brushed the woman's golden hair back from her face. Against his better nature, a sliver of hope grew between Dante's ribs at what he hoped was the first ounce of good news that evening.

Crossing his arms over his chest, Fenyang raised an eyebrow. "Please, elaborate," he urged the man to continue. "I think we could all benefit from a bit of clarity right now."

"We saw something, a creature bolted from the cathedral prior to our arrival," explained Varus. "A dragon — a wyvern, specifically, with someone clinging onto its neck. When we arrived at the church, we found Charlotte's body there, but no trace of Jasper or Maya. Given the circumstances, and the beast we saw… I fear it's possible that our enemies attempted to provoke Jasper's Awakening with Charlotte's death."

Dante stared in abject horror at Varus' words. "What are you talking about?"

Varus pursed his lips. "Dante, you may not be aware of this, but your attempts to reanimate the corpses at the masquerade this evening confirmed something for us," he explained slowly. "They were not merely cadavers, but automatons built from clockwork and void magic."

"It seems we've finally determined the identity of our enemy," Fenyang agreed with a slow, deliberate nod. "Gustaf has allied with the Children of the Lutaidhr, the cultists who follow the god of the void."

"What does this have to do with Jasper?" Dante asked flatly.

There was a conflicted expression on Varus' face, one that Dante now recognized as the man warring with himself on what to say. "The Children of the Lutaidhr believe in a prophecy that foretells the destruction of their god," he continued in a low voice. "It specifies that Deltori's champion will be reborn, and that hero will be the demise of the Lutaidhr. They believe Jasper is that prophesied hero."

In the aftermath of the masquerade, Dante's scattered mind struggled to piece together Varus' words, to gather his own knowledge of dark prophecies. His heart pounded in his chest at the chilling words, at the coldness in Varus' delivery. "You said they wanted to provoke his Awakening," Dante repeated, realization dawning. "So... you believe this prophecy as well?"

"I have a *wyvern* sprinting through Briardeen to confirm it," Varus insisted, pointing towards the window of the cabin.

"You expected this to happen," Dante continued, blistering realization spreading through his chest. "All this time, you've just been... watching him? Waiting for something like this?"

His revelation yielded no immediate response from his allies, as if he hadn't spoken at all. Varus' gaze never once left him as the silence stretched on, the wind howling outside of the ship. It was Fenyang who at last broke the silence after an eternity, and his words sank like stones in the bed of a tumultuous river.

"You owe him an explanation, I think," the king pointed out, eyeing Varus warily. "No more secrets, no more lies. Just the truth."

"I never lied," Varus said immediately, his tone defensive.

"But you do conceal so much, especially when you believe it is information best kept secret," Hasima noted matter-of-factly. "Keeping him in the dark will do you no favours."

Something ugly settled in Dante's gut at their words, an acrid sensation coiling in his stomach. *You owe him an explanation* — not "us", but solely Dante. "You... you knew?" he asked Fenyang.

The Valedian king turned to face him, a pained expression on his face. "I told him to tell you sooner rather than later," was all he offered in response, the only defense he supplied. But then again, what defense was a king compelled to supply?

The floor had shifted beneath Dante, and his legs felt numb and weak. He leaned against the wall behind him, seeking support while it felt like a rug had been torn out from underneath him. He was on an airship for the second time this year, heading to a country he had never been to before, and everyone in this room had been lying to him.

"Dante..." Fenyang began, but whatever he had been about to say was interrupted by a figure bursting into the room, the door slamming open as Samuel appeared in the threshold.

"Where is she?" the baker demanded, his eyes scanning each face in the room. His gaze settled on Dante, the ghost of hope in his expression. "Where is my daughter?"

His eyes burned as he met Samuel's stare, his heart breaking anew. Rage burned through his veins as he addressed the kingpin once more, fists clenched at his sides. "This is on you," Dante growled at the man, crossing the room. "*Charlotte* is on you. You alone should have the honour of breaking the news to her father."

He shoved past the man as he sprinted for the galley, for the stairs leading to the deck. The wood and iron hull of the ship seemed to press in on him, his chest constricting as he bolted through the airship. In the distance, he heard the haunting cries of the baker, the despair of a man who had lost everything. Dante was suffocating, his lungs screaming for air as he stumbled gracelessly up the stairs leading to the deck.

He tore across the airship, colliding with the bulwark on the starboard side as his chest heaved with sobs, retching over the ledge of the ship. He hadn't eaten in hours, and there was nothing in his stomach to eject, but Dante couldn't stop the visceral reaction of his grief. The damned heavens had opened up once more, and rain quickly soaked through to his skin as he leaned over the ledge of the ship, his tears disappearing down his dampened face.

A pair of hands gently brushed his hair back from his face, and even in his heartbroken state Dante was grateful for the warm presence of Fenyang. When at last his convulsions had dissipated, Dante sank against the deck of the ship, his clothes thoroughly saturated by the rain. His hair plastered against his temple, he leaned against the bulwark as he closed his eyes, praying that somehow this would all be a bad dream, a nightmare he would awaken from.

With a sigh, the Valedian king took a seat on the deck beside him, the warmth of his arm spreading through Dante's shoulder. "I am sorry, Dante," he began. "I don't expect you to forgive me, or even to trust me. I should have told you about all of this sooner."

The words settled low in his sensitive stomach, as if his body threatened to convulse once more. "Please, don't... just don't," Dante protested. The rain was beginning to chill his skin, his masquerade costume ill-adapted for inclement weather.

"Varus has every intention of searching for Maya and Jasper," Fenyang continued despite Dante's words. "After we land in Valedia, he plans to—"

"I don't give a shit about what Varus plans to do," Dante interrupted, opening his eyes. The Valedian king stared down at him mournfully, his golden eyes dark. "And even if he does find Jasper and Maya, it doesn't change the fact that Charlotte is *dead*. He knew that Jasper was being targeted, but he didn't tell us — and Charlotte paid the price."

Fenyang hesitated before he responded, as if weighing the consequences of speaking to Dante in this state of heightened emotions. "I'm sorry," he repeated softly.

A chill ran down his spine as Dante leaned his head back against the bulwark, his tears blending with the rain as his eyes burned. The crew of *The Veiled Siren* worked around them in silence, paying no mind to the two figures crouched on the deck in the rain. Beside him, Fenyang made to touch his hand, hesitating so near his skin that Dante could feel the warmth radiating from him.

"Please come inside," Fenyang pleaded, dragging Dante from his reverie. "You have every right to be upset, but that doesn't mean you can sit out here and freeze to death. Please, come back inside."

He shivered against his will, his body betraying him. The king beside him stood, his knees popping as Fenyang pulled himself to his feet before offering Dante a hand. He stared at that hand far longer than necessary, his gaze lingering on the water dripping down Fenyang's palm. He stood unassisted, ignoring the king's eyes on him as he turned to glance at the distant lights behind them, all that was visible of the frigid kingdom in the sky.

Mother Moon, guide her to an easy slumber...

Wherever Charlotte was now, Dante could not follow her. He prayed she had been lovingly carried by the Soul Keeper to paradise, to be blessed with a painless afterlife. As for Jasper and Maya... Dante would see them again. Somehow, despite everything, he was certain of this, *needed* to be certain — for his own survival as well as theirs.

Tearing his eyes away from the distant lights of Aethelind, Dante took a deep breath as the rain fell harder still. Without a second glance back at the kingdom in the sky, he ventured back below deck, the Valedian king following him in silence.

Acknowledgments

To say that the completion of this book is a dream come true would be an understatement. If you've made it this far, allow me a sappy moment to thank all the wonderful people who've made it possible for this book to be completed and subsequently shared with the world.

First and foremost, thank you to Bel for Eleni and to Caiden for Haeyin, without whom there would never be "The Trifecta" – for where would "Varus" be without his librarian and his doctor? Bel, in many ways you are my Eleni, from our origins as shy internet friends bonding over our love of LOTR and the Elder Scrolls, to our conversations lasting long into the night about all manner of hopes, dreams, and fears. Caiden, you have always been privy to the entirety of my unfiltered thoughts and ideas for this series, and somehow you continue to put up with my nonsense – thank you for being *A Clockwork Melody*'s first ever reader.

Brittany; my darling, my dream, my boat. Thank you for always supporting me, for being a steadfast friend for twenty-four years, for cheering me on through my creative endeavours. Thank you for reading this draft when it was raw and unpolished, and thank you for loving me when I have been raw and unpolished myself.

Justin; for always supplying me with chaotic whimsy when I need it most. You have raised the standard for how

I expect to be treated by others, showing me that I am not as difficult to love as I sometimes feel I am. I am so incredibly lucky to have met someone like you, and I'm truly blessed to call you my friend.

Grandpa, where would I be without you? Between our conversations on life, the afterlife, and the love that transcends both, you have been an invaluable part of this story. Thank you for your suggestions on how to complete chapters that I was stuck on, your feedback on the cover artwork letting me know I was on the right track, and for listening to me as I went through some of the most difficult years of my life.

To my little brother, my twin... even when we fight, you're the other half of my soul. So much of Jasper is inspired by you, Eli — even if you can't turn into a dragon, you're still a hero to me.

For my mum and dad, thank you for everything you've done for me. I'm sorry I never let you read this book while I was working on it. I promise it's not because I didn't want you to read it, it's just because I'm shy.

Rebe, wherever this story would be without your sage wisdom and advice, I certainly wouldn't read it. Your input has always been appreciated, your thoughts and commentary on my ideas for the future have been invaluable. Even if you never read this, know that it could never have come to fruition without you. I hope that we continue to write stories together for many years to come.

To Jenny, my ride or die — thanks for sticking with me through my self-titled "crazy bitch theories" during one of the most difficult break-ups I've ever gone through. I don't know if I would have handled it half as well as I did without your support.

Danny, even if we're not coworkers anymore, I'll always

remember "philosophy Danny hour" fondly… closely followed by "loopy Danny hour". Thank you for being one of my beta readers; I hope one day to read a story of your creation, as well.

Jen, you gave me the kick in the arse I needed to finally start writing again. The years we spent apart were painful, but I plan to spend the rest of my life making up for lost time. Thank you for inspiring me to follow my dreams.

And to you, dear reader – it is no small thing to pick up a book you're unfamiliar with and dive headfirst into it, and I am so grateful you chose to read this novel. Throughout the course of writing, editing, writing, and editing again, there were several times where I asked myself if anyone would want to read this story. The creation of *A Clockwork Melody* has been cathartic for many reasons, a healing journey for myself as much as it is for the characters in it. I hope that it can provide you with some catharsis on your journey as well, wherever you may be.

And for those of you who are rightfully upset with me for the ending… trust me, I'm upset with myself, too. All I can ask is for your patience and your forgiveness. I promise you; this is not the end.

All my love,

J.P.

PRONUNCIATIONS

(Any words and names not included here can be assumed to be pronounced phonetically.)

Aethia EE-thee-ah

Aerindale AIR-in-dayle

Aethelind EE-th-lind

Briardeen br-EYE-r-dean

Caelfall KALE-fall

Castavar KASS-ta-var

Daes DESS

Damhn DAH-vin

Deltori DELL-tor-ee

Dornkeep DOORN-keep

Eirodys AIR-ah-diss

Eodan AY-din

Fraecath FRAY-cath

Fraeling FRAY-ling

Gwynti VIN-tee

Lutaidhr LOO-tay-r

Miagne me-AW-nah

Pharsat FAR-sat

Pharasathi FAR-a-SAW-thee

Rhanigan RAW-na-gen

Reinnairlei rain-AIR-lee

Rhey'lu RAY-loo

Siatch sai-ATCH

Siatha sai-ATH-ah

Styvacino STIV-ah-CHEE-no

Theian THEE-an

Thelind THEY-lind

Tyiadai Daru TEE-a-die DAH-roo

Valedia val-AY-dee-ah

Vol Ciacci vahl CHA-chee

Xiska SHISS-ka